BATTLESTORM

BATTLESTORM

S U S A N   K R I N A R D

TOR

A Tom Doherty Associates Book
New York

BATTLESTORM

A Tor Book
Published by Tom Doherty Associates, LLC
175 Fifth Avenue
New York, NY 10010

www.tor-forge.com

Tor® is a registered trademark of Tom Doherty Associates, LLC.

The Library of Congress Cataloging-in-Publication Data is available upon request.

ISBN 978-0-7653-3210-3 (trade paperback)
ISBN 978-1-4299-5339-9 (e-book)

Our books may be purchased in bulk for promotional, educational, or business use. Please contact your local bookseller or the Macmillan Corporate and Premium Sales Department at 1-800-221-7945, extension 5442, or by e-mail at MacmillanSpecial Markets@macmillan.com.

First Edition: March 2016

Printed in the United States of America

0 9 8 7 6 5 4 3 2 1

With thanks to my excellent editor, Melissa Frain,
and, as always, to Serge

BATTLESTORM

1

TRILLEMARKA-ROLLAGSFJELL
BUSKERUD COUNTY, NORWAY

Rebekka struggled through the snow, aware that the Nazis were not far behind them. Uncle Geir was helping to break the trail, but Mist had gone off to find the enemies and stop them before they got too close.

Uncle Aaron put his heavily padded arm around her. "Hurry, little one. We must move fast."

She sighed. Her legs were tired and sore. She wished she were still perched high on Mist's shoulders, above everyone else, imagining that she was riding on an elephant far away where it was warm and there were no bad men.

But Uncle Aaron was too tired to carry her, and he wasn't very strong. He kept hurrying her along, his breath making clouds that covered his face and the scared look he tried not to let her see.

The sound of gunfire stopped everyone. Rebekka's heart jumped in her chest. That had to be Mist, killing Nazis. She'd learned all about killing a long time ago, and it didn't make her sick the way it used to. She knew the bad men had to be stopped.

"Move on," Uncle Geir said, though he really wasn't her uncle. She just liked to pretend. He skied alongside the others, waving his hand. "Let's keep going."

Slowly everyone started forward again, huddled against the wind. She heard the noise first, though she didn't know what it was until it was too late. Someone rushed out of the saplings to either side of the trail and raised a gun. Mrs. Dworsky fell, her chest blossoming with red, and then Mr. Becker and Miss Hammerschlag staggered and dropped beside her. Another German soldier emerged from the trees and knocked everyone else down with a spray of bullets.

Uncle Aaron dragged Rebekka to the ground, covering her body with his. She didn't see anything else, just heard—the bullets, the screams, the silence afterward. Then Uncle Aaron collapsed on top of her, and she couldn't move, couldn't breathe until someone pulled her out and carried her away.

Uncle Geir pushed her underneath a pine heavy with snow and aimed his own gun at the soldier running toward them, his boots kicking up red-stained snow. She caught a glimpse of someone fighting, not with a gun, but with a long staff. Horja, who always carried the long stick but had never done anything with it until now. She knocked a Nazi down while Geir fired at another German soldier.

Then the staff broke, just like it was a branch snapping under too much snow. Horja fell, one half of the staff still clutched in her hand. Her arm was bleeding, but Rebekka could see that she wasn't going to die.

Neither was Uncle Geir, because suddenly the Nazis were gone. Dead, like all of Uncle Aaron's friends. Like Mama and Papa, though no one else seemed to know that she'd already figured that out.

Rebekka sniffled, but she didn't cry. And when she finally saw Mist . . .

"No!" she screamed. "Orn!"

◑◐

Anna opened her eyes. Tilted elven eyes gazed down into hers—Hrolf's, dusk-blue framed with unusually pale lashes. It was those eyes that drew her back out of the memories. Memories that were not and had never been her own.

"Are you well?" Hrolf asked. Anna almost thought she detected anxiety in his voice.

But elves, she had learned, were remarkably even-tempered, dispassionate by human standards. She wasn't going to let him see how disturbed she really was.

"Fine," she said, sitting up. The lean-to Hrolf had constructed was still standing firm, though the snow was falling steadily. Rota and the elves were on watch, armed with bows and daggers that never seemed as if they'd be much good against automatic rifles.

Fortunately, unlike the Nazis, the enemies who pursued them were confined to pre-industrial weapons themselves. That "rule" had never been fully explained to Anna, but Freya and Loki had agreed to it when they had begun their "game" for possession of Midgard. The "game" wasn't a game anymore, but apparently there were lines even the trickster god, Loki, wouldn't cross.

"Jotunar?" Anna asked, brushing her gloved hand across her face.

"We seem to have evaded them again," Hrolf said, rocking back on his heels. "But the weather grows worse. We must find the Treasures soon."

"I know." Anna stared out at the white world, so like the one she had just left behind in her dreams. "I thought Horja's memories would have come to me by now."

"Then your dreams were of the other. Your kinswoman."

Anna closed her eyes. She hated it when Rebekka took over. The blood, the screams, the darkness . . .

"You should go back to sleep," Hrolf said, offering her his blanket. "Perhaps the right memories will come to you if you aren't so cold."

"You sound like Dainn," she murmured.

Instantly Hrolf stiffened, and Anna ducked her head. "I'm sorry," she said. "I never got to know him really well. But I still can't believe he's a traitor."

"Let us not speak of it," Hrolf said.

Anna sighed and closed her eyes, too exhausted to argue. Five minutes later—or what seemed like five minutes—the same slender hand shook her awake again.

"Frost giants," Hrolf said.

"Where?" Anna asked, grabbing her own pathetic little knife.

"Too close." He picked up his bow and ran outside. He and Rota consulted in low voices, and Hrolf dashed off. Rota, her bright red hair escaping her cap, crawled inside the lean-to.

"They know our tricks now," she said. "Hrolf has gone to warn the other Alfar. You'll run while we hold them off."

"Run where?"

"We'll know in a few minutes."

Feeling a little sick, Anna let Rota help her put on her pack. They were always ready to travel at the drop of a hat—or a Jotunn's nearly silent footfall—so she had all the provisions she needed. Rota strapped on her snowshoes and herded her outside. Hrolf reappeared, his breath raising a white cloud that wreathed his fair head in a veil of elvish mystery.

"North," he said. "There's a narrow gorge perhaps half a kilometer from here. Find a place close to the brook that flows between the mountains. There, you will find cover enough to hide until we come for you."

Hrolf took her arm, but Anna shook him off. "Rota said they know our tricks now," she said. "It's different this time, isn't it?"

The elf exchanged glances with Rota, who made a helpless gesture with outspread hands. Hrolf sighed.

"We have been fortunate in throwing them off our scent for so long. But they have not yet prevailed in any of our skirmishes."

Tell that to Eilif, Anna thought, remembering the slight elf-woman who had been killed only a week ago.

Killed defending me.

"And what if none of you comes back?" she asked, wondering why she was no longer astonished to hear such cold, blunt words coming out of her own mouth.

"It is possible that we must lead the Jotunar on a false trail well away from here," Hrolf said, "but one of us will return for you." He hesitated. "You may be alone some little while, but—"

"What's 'some little while'?" Anna interrupted. "Do you think I can survive out there for longer than a day?"

"You have learned quickly," Hrolf said, his dark eyes earnest in a way that made her feel like she was five hundred times his age rather than the reverse. "You know what is most important."

"If worse comes to worst," Rota said, "find a way to call on Horja's memories. *She* knew how to survive."

"And if I can't?" Anna shook her head. "No. I'd rather take my chances with you."

"You don't have a choice," Rota said, pulling Anna away from the lean-to with all her irresistible Valkyrie strength.

Anna had learned a lot more over the past few weeks than just basic survival skills, or how to be detached—even cold-blooded—when she needed to be. She'd also learned to recognize when she was beaten.

"Don't let them kill you, okay?" she called to Hrolf over her shoulder as Rota plowed ahead of her through the snow.

"I will do my utmost to prevent it," he said.

Once she and Anna had put a good quarter mile of snowbound forest between themselves and the temporary camp, Rota slowed and began to look for the gorge Hrolf had mentioned. The ground began to rise, growing steeper with every step, and soon Anna spotted a high, rocky outcrop thrusting up out of the hillside.

"There," she said.

Rota nodded, and they kept going until they found the gorge, thick with trees and cradling a white, fast-moving stream at the foot of a narrow falls.

"Be careful going down there. And don't worry about us." She held up her hand. "*And* don't argue. Now, vamoose."

"Vamoose? Really?"

"Go," Rota said, giving Anna a gentle push.

Anna began to scramble down the rocky side of the gorge, resisting the urge to look back. She had just reached the bottom of the slope and was walking into the cover of the pines when she saw the Jotunn.

He grinned at her, all teeth, and strode toward her. Anna shoved her pack off and fumbled for her knife. Hrolf had tried to teach her, but there hadn't been enough time. And she wasn't nearly good enough.

Especially not for—

Vidarr? Anna blinked twice to make sure she was seeing correctly in the snow-glare. But it *was* Vidarr, in his SS captain's uniform, a Walther pistol trained on her chest. Anna stepped back and nearly fell over a dead branch. Vidarr Odin's-son had gone missing after he and his brother Vali had set Dainn up in Asbrew. But this could all be part of the past.

It *had* to be, because Vidarr shouldn't have a gun. Not in *this* war. But if she was wrong . . .

"Where are they?" he asked, continuing to advance.

"You've already lost them," she said, feeling her way.

"Don't lie to me," Vidarr snarled.

"Where have you been, Vid?"

He tightened his grip on the pistol. "You tricked me."

"It's not *me* who's been playing tricks," she said. "How did you find me?"

Vidarr's heavy brow wrinkled. "I . . . I don't—"

"I'm surprised you're still in one piece after the beating you took from Loki."

"Loki." Vidarr blinked several times, as if the name were strange to him, or hadn't been spoken in his hearing for a very long time. His shape seemed to waver, one moment decked out in the SS uniform, the next in the kind of clothes any cold-hardy Jotunn might wear in the winter forests of Norway.

"I don't even know if you're real," Anna said with a sudden laugh.

The uniform returned, perfect in every detail. Vidarr snapped out of his confusion and aimed at Anna's head.

"*This* is real," he said, his deep voice taking on the distinctive, biting cadence of a classic film Nazi villain. "I will give you one last chance. Surrender them to me, and I may show mercy."

"I don't have them, and you'd kill me anyway," she said.

Vidarr grinned. "You're right," he said, and pressed down on the trigger.

Time stretched, a single second spun out to minutes as Anna realized that she was going to die. She saw Vidarr's finger move millimeter by millimeter as the trigger strained to fulfill its deadly purpose, felt her muscles contract to carry her out of the bullet's path.

She was far too slow. But an endless instant before the hammer hit the bullet, a heavy clump of snow broke free from a branch over Vidarr's head and splattered over him, driving him to his knees. His shot went wild, but in another moment he was on his feet again, shaking the snow from his clothing and taking aim.

Anna didn't wait. She didn't even think. She felt the pistol cold against her palm and shot him full in the heart. And then she shot him again, and again, until she had no bullets left.

With a look of utter shock, Vidarr sank to his knees, clutched at his chest, and slowly fell into the snow facedown as if he'd been practicing his death scene for months. Anna began to tremble, and the world turned sharp and bright and immediate, as clear as the fast-running stream a few feet away.

The man she had shot wasn't wearing a uniform, and there was no gun in his hand.

Or in *hers*.

Turning sideways, Anna vomited into the snow. Suddenly Hrolf was at her side, guiding her to a boulder and sweeping the snow away with a gloved hand so that she could sit.

"I . . . killed him," Anna whispered.

"Who?" Hrolf asked, looking back toward Vidarr's body.

It was gone. None of it had been real, after all.

Except that there was still a single black spot of blood in the undisturbed snow.

"There," she whispered, pointing at the spot.

Hrolf followed her gaze, rose, and crouched again near the place where Vidarr had fallen. He removed his glove and touched the dark spot with the tip of his finger.

"Animal," he said. "I am not yet familiar enough with Midgard's beasts to be certain, but perhaps it is a—"

"It isn't human?" Anna asked. "Or . . . god?"

"Another of your dreams?" Hrolf asked, getting to his feet.

"It must have been . . . Horja's memories," Anna said. "But this wasn't like the others. I felt like—" She shivered violently. "Like myself the whole time."

"Whom did you see?"

"Vidarr."

"What did he say?"

"He wanted 'them.' "

"The Treasures?"

"That's what I assumed."

Hrolf frowned. "If he were real, we might assume that he was still aiding Loki. It would explain his disappearance, if the Slanderer had been hiding him."

Anna remembered mocking "Vidarr" about the beating Loki had given him after he'd defied the trickster god. He would have hated Loki for that, even though Loki had left him alive. Why would he help Loki now?

Anna touched her neck, feeling for a familiar weight on her skin. Like Vidarr, the pendant—along with her very special "parrot," Orn— had vanished before Freya had come to Midgard in an elf-woman's body. Anna still didn't fully understand the purpose of the pendant, though she knew it was somehow responsible for blending her soul and memories with those of its previous carriers, the Valkyrie Horja and her own grandmother, Rebekka. She had tried to make herself believe that Orn would return to her, or at least to Mist. He'd wanted so badly to convey some message to the Valkyrie.

And he'd made Anna believe she had some purpose in helping him complete a vital task, some divine objective he'd dragged her all the way across the country to achieve. He'd made her believe she was safe.

She'd made the mistake of trusting him.

"The Jotunar are gone," Hrolf said, pulling her back to the present. "We must return to the others."

"Was anyone hurt?" she asked, berating herself for not having thought about it earlier.

"Minor injuries," Hrolf said. He helped her to her feet. "If you can walk . . ."

Anna nodded, and they climbed out of the gorge. When she and Hrolf returned to the lean-to, she didn't even notice the raven until it spoke.

"Anna," Orn said. "Go now."

Her mind filled with whirling black feathers, crowding out every other thought. When she came to, she found herself sitting in the snow, the elves looking down at her with the grave expressions that passed for alarm among their kind. Rota was crouched beside her, peering into her eyes.

She knew *they* hadn't seen Orn. But it didn't matter now.

Taking Rota's offered hand, Anna scrambled to her feet. "It's okay," she said. "Horja knows where to go."

∞

Orn flew in wide, sweeping circles over the Alfar as they began to dig. He knew that the cache was under four feet of snow—not deep, but deep enough to conceal it from the eyes of the casual passerby, as if any such could be found in this vast track of wilderness. In fact, the magic that warded the chest—powerful Rune-staves etched into the steel lid—would be very difficult for even a former resident of the Eight Homeworlds to counter.

Horja had learned those Runes from him. The memory was vague. When he'd been with Anna, all he'd known was that he must find Mist, and that he was carrying a vital message. But his brief contact with Odin's Spear, Gungnir—as well as with the seeds of the Apples of Idunn—had begun to change him. He had *remembered* how important it was to find the other Treasures and make physical contact with them.

And he knew that a little more of himself would return with each Treasure. He had not been able to stop Vidarr from kidnapping him and Anna during Mist's battle with the World Serpent, Jormungandr, but they had escaped. Even Vidarr's act of treachery had aided him. He had grown stronger. He had brought Odin's sons to heel and made them serve his purpose.

He had also realized that he must hide, especially from the enemy who had tried to take him and Anna before. Hide himself with spells of concealment until he was strong and wise enough to face that enemy and fulfill his destiny.

That meant that not even Odin's chief Valkyrie, Mist, could know where he was. He had sent Vidarr to follow Anna when she left the city where the battle would begin and end. He had taken the pendant from Vidarr and kept it safe.

The pendant was important. Orn knew he was very close to making sense of all the fragments of thoughts and memories buzzing around in his head, and the stone with the raven's-head etching was where all the fragments would come together.

The fragments, *and* the Treasures. The three that Mist held—the Chain, the Glove, and the Steed—were too well warded for him to touch unless he exposed himself before he was ready. But once he had *these* . . .

"The ground's too hard," the Valkyrie Rota said, her voice carrying up to Orn as he flew above her, her red hair a blaze against the backdrop of white snow and blue shadow. "You boys have any spells that can break it up a little?"

One of the Alfar stepped forward and began to sing. Orn circled lower, watching intently. The earth heaved and trembled as the ice trapped within it began to thaw, and trickles of water welled up from a dozen tiny fissures in the ground.

"Let's try again," Rota said, setting to work with her spade. It was not long before the Valkyrie gave a low hoot of triumph as her spade touched the lid of the coffer. The Alfar knelt to brush the mud away and lifted the coffer from the cache. Anna stood by, hovering like a female raven defending her chick.

As if the Treasures were as important to her as they were to Orn. As if she, like Horja, had in truth been Odin's Valkyrie. And would be again.

Once the coffer had been placed on the cleared earth beside the hole, the fair elf, Hrolf, crouched over it and laid his hand on the lid. He snatched it back with a very unelvish oath.

He, Rota, Anna, and the other Alfar huddled together in soft conversation, though Orn could easily hear their words. After a moment, Anna knelt beside the coffer, closed her eyes and began to chant the Rune-spell, pronouncing the words as perfectly as if she had been born among the ancient Norse. The lid opened with a faint moan of protest.

Orn descended swiftly and landed on Anna's shoulder. She started, stumbling back from the coffer. Rota cursed and reached out to steady the mortal, while Orn flapped his wings to keep his balance.

Anna froze. "You're *real,*" she stammered, tentatively reaching up to touch Orn's breast feathers. "I thought I was dreaming."

"You *saw* him?" Rota asked.

Anna ignored the Valkyrie. Her eyes glittered with moisture, drops suspended on the fringe of tiny feathers surrounding her eyes. "I didn't think you were coming back, Orn," she whispered. "No one could find you. Where did you go?"

"Here *now,*" Orn said, deliberately keeping his speech simple.

"Did you follow us? Why didn't you let me know?"

Orn cocked his head, peering at each of her companions in turn. "Dangerous," he said.

"Why? Was Loki . . . was someone watching you?"

Loki. Orn's crest rose.

"I saw Vidarr," Anna said. "*He* wasn't real, was he?"

Pretending not to understand, Orn glided down from her shoulder to land at the edge of the hole. He pecked at one of the half-frozen clods of earth cast aside by the spade and the magic the elves had used to soften the ice-locked soil.

"He doesn't seem to have much more to say now than he did when he was with you and Mist," Rota said. "I'm sorry, Anna, but this whole 'Odin's messenger' business . . ."

"Orn didn't exactly get a chance to deliver any message," Anna said, her voice rising. "Vali—"

"The raven could have returned to Mist any time once the battle was over. He'd have been safe with both Mist *and* Freya to protect him."

Ignoring mortal and Valkyrie, Orn hopped up to the rim of the coffer and examined the contents. The soft leather pouch and broken staff lay cradled in nests of padded velvet. He dipped his head inside the coffer and lightly pecked the pouch and each half of the staff. Painfully bright light burst inside his head. There were pictures there, too, but he couldn't quite make them out. He hopped down into the snow, drawing patterns with his feet as he moved this way and that.

"What is he doing?" Rota asked. "Those almost look like Runes."

Hrolf crouched to examine the tracks as Orn fluttered out of the away. "They are," he said, "but they make no sense. If the raven knows what the symbols represent, he has no understanding of how to give them meaning."

Orn laughed. Of course they did not understand. The power contained in these Treasures had altered him yet again; he could feel the strength growing inside him, pushing outward as if it would burst through skin and feathers. He had laid the spell as easily as he might pluck a sparrow out of the air.

"What if it's a message from Odin?" Anna asked. She looked at Hrolf. "Do you think you might figure it out if you studied them for a while?"

The fair-feathered elf shook his head. "We must not linger. The Jotunar may have found our trail again."

"He's right," Rota said. "We've been lucky so far. Luckier than we've had any right to be."

Smearing the Runes with his beak, Orn shook out his feathers. The fools didn't know that *he* had been protecting them almost since they had arrived in this familiar country—leading the pursuing giants astray, giving subtle warning to the elves and Valkyrie that they had been too blind to recognize.

He flew back to Anna's shoulder. "You," he said, staring into the eyes of the Valkyrie. "Say nothing." He looked at each of the elves in turn. "You did not see me."

One by one they looked away, as if he had become invisible.

"Orn?" Anna murmured, reaching up to touch him.

Such was the nature of their long association that she had unconsciously resisted the spell. But Orn was not displeased. He leaned his head very close.

"I go," he said in his softest croak. "You did not see me. Danger. Understand?"

"Yes," she said slowly. "I understand, but . . ." Her throat bobbed. "You're not the same, Orn. You've changed again. Why? Why did you leave me without saying any—"

Orn didn't wait for her to finish. He spread his wings and launched himself skyward, leaving her and the cold earth far behind.

Soon he would have no need of these wings, this puny body. He would have another far more powerful.

Many as one. The second prophecy was the answer, the prediction he had built his strategy upon, the part his enemies, even Freya, did not know.

When he was whole they would all bow to him, and he would have both revenge and victory. Traitors would fall, and a new world would rise.

His world.

2

It hadn't yet begun to snow in the San Francisco Bay Area, but Ryan Starling could feel the cold seeping through his jacket—the kind of cold no one in their right mind would have believed possible just a few years ago. September, he thought, and already plants that had once thrived in this moderate climate were beginning to wither, the birds flying south in greater and greater numbers.

And a storm hung over the city, swirling clouds that seemed to spin around and around in a crazy dance. Sometimes lightning flashed horizontally from one edge of the constantly spinning circle to the other, making the clouds glow from within.

From here, you couldn't tell that there was a battle raging in San Francisco. It wasn't on the news. No one blogged about it . . . well, almost no one, except the people everyone thought were crazy, the kind who believed there were signs and portents hidden behind the bizarre weather and the shadows that crept through the streets, slowly stealing what light remained.

Of course most of those crazy people weren't crazy at all. And Ryan had seen Loki in videos, pictures of him in places he didn't have any right to be.

"What do you see?" Mother Skye asked.

"Nothing," he said. *Thank God.* "Nothing but the bridge and the city and the storm."

The old woman touched his arm. "You can control your gift now. You'll know when a true vision comes."

At a price, Ryan thought. There was always a price, and he wouldn't necessarily be the one to pay it.

Zipping his jacket up to his chin, he imagined Dogpatch as he had last seen it, the neighborhood swathed in snow and ice and dangerous magic. He was dreading this reunion, knowing what it would dredge up: emotions he didn't want, unrequited feelings for the elf who could never return them, memories of a foolish boy who had been too stupid to recognize the part he was to play.

At least Gabi was okay. Mother Skye had made sure he was up to date on the basics. She just couldn't tell him what the future would hold, even though that had once been her job.

Now it was *his.*

"If you're ready . . ." Mother Skye said.

With a sigh, Ryan returned to the car. It was as beat-up looking as Mother Skye. Both had earned their dents the hard way.

He pulled onto the Golden Gate Bridge, wondering if he'd feel the changes before he saw them. He didn't know how many mortals Mist had recruited for the fight for their world, how many allies she'd brought over from the Void, or if Loki had managed to summon his three monstrous children to join in the battle.

He didn't even know who was winning.

"You sure you won't come all the way?" he asked Mother Skye, though she'd answered the question about six times already. "It's not like you'd be unwelcome. If you just explained—"

"They would demand the very things I can no longer give," she said in her soft, aged voice, staring out the window at the tollbooth. "And you cannot tell them what you have become, lest you change Fate before the time comes."

"But I'll *have* to give them some proof if I'm to stay with them," he said, "or they'll just try to send me away again."

"Only something small. Never let them guess the magnitude of your abilities. Not until it is unquestionably necessary."

"And I'll know when that is," Ryan muttered.

"You will." The words held a note of sadness, and Ryan knew why.

Before the war was over, a lot of people were going to die. He would have to be very careful about sharing his gift, because every time he intervened he could set the future on a path even he could not predict.

Except for the sacrifice. He knew that would come in any possible turning of Fate. A terrible sacrifice that he couldn't see.

And never wanted to.

"Be strong," Mother Skye said. "You are the only one who can complete this duty. You are the last Norn."

◑◐

No one saw the skirmish. Like all the rest, it was warded from mortal sight. That was one of the few "rules" of engagement, such as they were—like the prohibition against firearms—and so far the enemy had stuck to them. More or less.

Mist swallowed a battle cry as she hacked at a frost giant, slicing a ragged piece of flesh from his half-armored shoulder. He yelped in pain, but the wound hardly slowed him. He swung his arm, adorned with a hundred razor-sharp icicles, at her head.

Konur, lord of the elven allies, caught the blow on his own sword, staggering a little under the weight of the blow. He recovered quickly, elf-swift, and danced aside. Mist slipped into his place and stabbed at the Jotunn's belly.

Fortunately, this particular giant was more bulky than fast, and he failed to get out of the way in time. He moaned and fell like an ancient redwood cut down by elements even its formidable strength couldn't withstand.

Mist pulled Kettlingr free and wiped the blade on the Jotunn's clothing. She caught her breath and brushed her hand across her forehead, sweeping up a damp strand of hair that had come loose from her braid, and watched the dark-haired elf-lord take on another frost giant.

For a moment she imagined Dainn fighting there, just as swift and sure, concealing a savage beast behind his dispassionate face. She was barely prepared when another Jotunn came at her from behind.

Fury beset her whenever she thought of Dainn, and this time was no different. She spun wildly to catch the Jotunn's ice-sword on hers, and felt the frost giant's weapon cut through her sleeve.

Chanting the Galdr as she built the Rune-staves in her mind, she added the smallest touch of forge-magic, as if her blade had just been pulled from the fire. The Jotunn was briefly confused by the glint of flame and attacked empty air. Mist cut off his head.

Two of the surviving Jotunar fled for the mouth of the alley and the relative safety of Grant Avenue. Mist knew better than to pursue them; true dawn was still a good half-hour away, but on a Tuesday morning there would be people already headed to work, drivers and pedestrians not quite groggy enough to ignore a sword-and-ax fight in the middle of the street.

She turned back, ready for the next opponent. But there was no one left to fight. The asphalt was slick with melting ice, the buildings on either side splashed with blood both red and blue. One mortal lay dead. Two mortals and one elf were wounded, but Mist's warriors had accounted for three Jotunar.

Mist sheathed her sword and knelt beside the human warrior, sketched Runes of peace and protection on his brow and gently closed his eyes. She knew his name, but little of his life or what had drawn him into this fight.

It wasn't easy keeping track of the two hundred or so mortal recruits who'd trickled in over the past spring and summer, especially since they were spread out all over the city countering Jotunar assaults and tracking the giants' increasing encroachment into the city's underworld.

Hel, Loki practically ran all of it now. And more.

A lot more.

"He died well," Konur said, coming up beside her. "Do not grieve for one who willingly gave his life to save his world."

Mist wiped the sweat from her forehead with the back of her hand.

"He wouldn't have died at all, if we hadn't brought this war down on mortalkind."

"*We* did not bring it," Konur said, cleaning his own sword before sheathing it and reducing it to the size of a small dagger. "He was as like to have died in one of the mortal's own wars, and for a far lesser purpose."

Biting back a sharp retort, Mist got to her feet. "What about your people?"

"Only the one is injured, and not severely. Our healer sees to the mortals." He concealed the dagger in his jacket—the Lord of the Alfar still looked bizarre to Mist in his very ordinary human clothes—and glanced up at the lightening sky. "We must go as soon as they are able to travel."

Mist followed his gaze, clenching her fingers around Kettlingr's hilt. Konur touched her shoulder.

"You are hurt," he said.

She glanced at her bloodied sleeve. "I can't even feel it."

"You will."

Yeah, she thought. *It's always afterward, isn't it?* Pain, grief, guilt. Regular as clockwork.

"Why don't you ever sweat?" she asked Konur, pretending she hadn't heard him. "Too good for such distasteful bodily functions?"

"We try to avoid them as strenuously as possible," he said, mockingly grave. Like Dainn had been.

Fighting the pull of memory, Mist went to check on the two injured mortals. The man was only half-conscious, but the young woman managed to smile at her with something disturbingly like hero-worship in her eyes. It was an embarrassing cult of personality Mist knew was fed by the unwanted glamour she had inherited from her goddess-mother Freya.

But without the magic of attraction, love and lust, she might not have mortal allies at all. Gods knew that Freya hadn't done anything to pull in ground troops.

And neither have you, Mist thought, wielding guilt against revulsion as she had done so many times in the past. Revulsion kept on winning, but she knew it was only a matter of time before—

"Mist!"

She jerked out of her thoughts to find the young woman pointing toward the mouth of the alley. A lone Jotunn stood there, ax in hand, as if he were about to challenge her to single combat. She drew Kettlingr and jumped to her feet, rage warring with sense.

Sense was winning when she finally noticed the Jotunn's face.

He looked like Svardkell. Svardkell, the Jotunn father she had never had the chance to know. The one she'd killed, believing he was Loki's spy.

Before she could think, she was running toward the street. The Jotunn waited until she was almost within reach, and then spun and ran north toward Bush Street. Mist had nearly caught up with him when she heard the squeal of tires and the whooping of a siren.

A moment later the sleek black-and-white Interceptor was nearly on top of her, and someone was shouting at her to put the weapon down. She lowered Kettlingr and turned to face the cops. Both had their pistols trained on her, and one was already calling for backup.

Mist weighed her options. If these were Loki's men, they wouldn't be able to shoot her. But there was a loophole in the "no modern weapons" rule Freya and Loki had agreed to in their original "game," and still abided by; "unaffiliated" mortals weren't bound by it, and there were still a few good cops who hadn't been caught in the web Loki had been industriously spinning around the city.

Those good cops were fighting an uphill battle against a system that used their honesty against them, turning them into unsuspecting weapons, and Mist didn't want innocent blood on her hands. A passing car had slowed down to rubberneck, and a couple of teenagers had stopped to stare, seemingly unconcerned that they might be drawn into a violent confrontation.

This could get bad very fast.

"Put down the weapon!" one of the cops yelled. "Hands behind your head!"

Slowly and carefully, Mist laid Kettlingr on the sidewalk and raised her hands. "It's all right," she said. "I won't—"

A gun went off. Mist felt strong fingers grip her arm and yank her aside as the bullet whizzed past her ear.

"Go back," Konur hissed, pushing her in the direction of the alley. "I will—"

"How many times must I tell you not to put yourself at risk?" a new voice interrupted, honeyed and dulcet as always in spite of the scolding words.

Freya waved Konur away and insinuated herself between Mist and the cops, who stared at Freya in utter confusion. Even in a borrowed elven shape—dark-haired, indigo-eyed, a body far more slender than Freya's own—the goddess projected a sensual allure that required no glamour to work its magic.

But she *did* use the glamour, and the cop who'd prematurely ejaculated lowered his gun and carefully laid it on the ground. The other remained frozen except for his mouth, which dropped open almost comically.

Smoothing the silk of her ruby-red gown over her hips, Freya smiled. "We really don't want any trouble, do we?" she purred. "Why don't you boys forget this ever happened, and go about your business."

The cop with the dropped jaw closed his mouth and turned his head to look at his partner. The other cop bent to pick up his gun, holstered it, and turned back for the Interceptor. They drove away at a snail's pace, craning their necks to keep Freya in view until they were in danger of breaking them. The bystanders drifted away, encouraged by Freya's judicious use of what Mist called the "anti-glamour."

When the Interceptor had turned the corner onto Bush Street, Freya lifted her skirt and walked back to the alley, gracefully poised on four-inch spike heels. Her face burning, Mist cast a rueful glance at Konur.

"I guess they weren't Loki's" she said.

The elf-lord frowned. "This is no time for levity," he said. "You were exceedingly foolish to fall for such a trick."

"You saw the Jotunn's face?"

"You well know that some Jotunar are capable of assuming other features," Konur said. "This one knew how to draw you out."

Because, Mist thought, she went into every battle wondering if the Jotunn she fought could be direct kin, like Svardkell. A cousin, an uncle, a brother . . .

"It won't happen again," she said.

She was still furious with herself when she and Konur reached the alley. Freya stood in the middle, wrinkling her pretty nose with distaste at the smell of blood and sweat. Mortal eyes followed her every move, as they had previously followed Mist's. Only the elves seemed indifferent. Or pretended to be.

Dainn had been anything *but* indifferent, in another time and place. Freya had used his weakness to control him. If he had betrayed Freya, she had betrayed him first.

Unfortunately, he'd also betrayed Mist.

Curse it, Mist thought. *Get out of my head.*

"Take the wounded," she said to Konur, resuming control of herself and her fighters. "I'll be along soon."

The elf-lord nodded to his fellow Alfar, who jointly worked another concealing spell and carried the wounded toward the other end of the alley. Konur lingered, observing Freya from under his dark, slender brows. She gazed back at him, smiling slightly, as if they shared some vaguely unpleasant secret.

"You have my leave to go, Lord Elf," she said.

Konur glanced at Mist. "Do you wish me to remain?" he asked.

"What do you fear will happen?" Freya asked with a musical laugh. "That I might spank her?"

"Stay out of it, Konur," Mist growled.

"Wise advice," Freya said to the elf-lord. "You did, after all, agree to serve *me* for a very generous reward."

"What reward?" Mist asked.

"I have not forgotten," Konur said, ignoring Mist's question. He turned to go, and Mist just kept herself from calling him back. She'd decode the mysterious conversation when she could speak privately with Konur, because she knew she cursed well wouldn't learn anything more from Freya.

Pretending her mother wasn't there to comment on her distinctly inelegant magical technique, Mist worked a fairly simple Rune-spell to clean the alley of most of the mess left by the battle, brushed her hands briskly against each other, and realized that her arm was bleeding again. Konur was right: it was beginning to hurt.

But it would heal more quickly than her pride.

"We must talk," Freya said when she was finished. "I believe there is a coffee bar not far from here."

Mist didn't bother arguing about the wisdom of discussing divine business in a very public place. Freya had a way of taking care of those little problems.

Together they walked around the corner to Bush and north two blocks to the coffee shop, where sleepy work-bound mortals congregated in search of early morning restoratives. Not one of the men and women within or passing by on the sidewalk had any idea of what had just happened such a short distance away.

Mist wondered again just how much longer that ignorance could last, especially when so many things had changed in the city over the past nine months. Things like the growing political corruption, housing shortages as people of modest income were driven from their homes by the most unscrupulous methods, rising unemployment, and a correspondingly steep decline in social services. The rich were getting richer and the poor were sinking at a much faster rate than anywhere else in the country.

And then there was crime. Far too few people seemed willing to acknowledge the increases in sexual assault, robbery, human trafficking, and other felonies. Loki's police, encouraged by the chief himself, allowed major gang fights in the streets, but harassed minor lawbreakers, filling the jails with petty offenders who faced the choice of trumped-up charges or a certain kind of "cooperation" with those in positions of influence. Drug pushers operated openly in schoolyards and on corners in every part of town, selling new, highly addictive designer drugs. Some had become especially popular with the disenfranchised people who could least afford them.

Even as Mist watched, a dealer appeared across the street. He was Jotunn, like so many of them, but he'd done such a good job of disguising his true nature that no mere mortal would ever have recognized him as anything but human.

The giant pricked up his ears as a rowdy group of tourists, bearing paper lanterns and wreathed in colorful streamers, performed a parody of a Lion Dance as they made their drunken way back to their hotel from Chinatown. They came to a sudden stop as the Jotunn stepped in front of them, and in minutes the transaction was complete.

As the tourists staggered away, a thin girl in torn jeans and a threadbare hoodie crept out of an alley and approached the Jotunn. She spoke to him in a weak voice, and he answered with a laugh and a shove that sent her sprawling on the sidewalk. A siren hooted nearby; another Interceptor squealed up to the curb, lights flashing, and the cop in the passenger's seat shouted at the girl though the open window.

These, Mist thought, were definitely *not* the good cops. She stepped into the street, fists clenched.

"Daughter," Freya said.

Mist glanced back at her mother. A small crowd of pedestrians had gathered around Freya, staring at her with rapt attention. When Mist looked across the street again, there was no sign of Jotunn or girl, and the Interceptor was pulling away.

She strode back to the sidewalk and took Freya's elbow. "I thought we were going to keep a low profile," she muttered.

"Was that what *you* were doing?" Freya asked. "When will you learn that you cannot protect every mortal in this city?"

With a negligent flick of her fingers, Freya worked the "anti-glamour." The observers scattered, and Freya glided to the door of the coffee shop. She waited for Mist to hold the door open and sailed in, sweeping the room with a half-lidded glance. Everyone left, including the men and women waiting in line to pay for or collect their hot beverages. The two baristas disappeared through a door to the back room.

Choosing one of tables at the back of the café, Freya twitched her gown aside and took her seat as if it were a thickly cushioned throne. Mist took the opposite chair.

"What reward did you offer Konur in exchange for his service?" Mist asked, heading off Freya's inevitable reprimand.

For a moment the Lady stared at Mist, playing with the gold-and-diamond necklace resting on the smooth white skin at the base of her elegant throat. Mist remembered that it had been the gift of an influential businessman who had become enamored of her. A man who might not be on *their* side yet, but wouldn't be going over to Loki anytime soon.

"That is between me and Lord Konur," Freya said.

"Are you sleeping together?" Mist asked.

Freya laughed. "Not every male in Midgard is my lover." She passed her hand over the table, clearing it of coffee rings and crumbs. The perfume of primroses wafted from her body, quickly replacing the earthy aroma of ground coffee beans with cloying sweetness. "Do not try to distract me, child. You cannot continue on this path, risking your life like any common warrior. If you are killed, there will be no one to lead our allies and hold this city until the Aesir arrive."

Mist grimaced. If Freya had actually been anything like a real mother, her impersonal words might have stung. For a while, the Lady had tried to convince Mist of her good faith, apologizing for ignoring her daughter in Asgard, promising to atone for her failures as a parent. She hadn't expressed any regret for what she'd done to Dainn, the broken promises that might have driven him to the other side. Or for spying on Mist when she was at her most vulnerable.

Over time Mist had come to realize that Freya was, in her way, as superb a liar as Loki. She simply used the glamour and her seductive beauty to make people believe her, not the subtle persuasion, open threats, and deft illusions the Slanderer might employ.

Yet in spite of all that, a small, weak part of Mist had refused to let go of a treacherous hope that Freya actually cared for her. Not as a warrior, not as a useful tool, but as her daughter.

That hope was long gone.

"Do you know why I went after that Jotunn?" Mist asked. "He looked almost exactly like Svardkell."

As always, Freya showed little reaction to the name. And, as always, Mist knew she wasn't going to get any new answers. She'd been careful to relay only part of what Svardkell had told Dainn, and Freya had never questioned Mist's story that the Jotunn had been a spy for Loki.

But she'd never admit that Svardkell had been her lover. *And* Mist's father.

Unless, of course, Dainn had been lying.

"We have had this discussion before," Freya said, examining her nails for any flaw in their glossy red surfaces. "Since he is dead, whatever you believe you may have seen today was clearly an illusion."

Mist folded her arms across her chest. "Since you obviously think I'm screwing this up," she said, "remember that you're always welcome to take my place. Or you might try to help out the way you did this morning."

"I am no leader of crude warriors."

"But you could still take a little time off from your parties and fund-raisers to save a few lives."

"I am saving *many* lives with my 'parties and fund-raisers,'" Freya said. "I divert the attention of important mortals who might otherwise join Loki's ranks." She looked Mist up and down. "Given your preferred mode of dress and your coarse manners, you could certainly not manage my part in this war."

"It's a good thing I don't want it, then," Mist said. She stared pointedly at the ring that almost overwhelmed Freya's fine-boned hand. "It isn't exactly unpleasant work for you, is it?"

Freya shook her head, very slightly disarranging her artfully arranged coils of glossy black hair. "You do not understand," she said. "The glamour is a great drain on my magic and my strength, and even I must pay the price."

Her admission of weakness caught Mist's attention. There *was* always a price for magic, even in the hands of the gods, but Mist had never seen evidence that Freya suffered from overuse of her talents.

Now, studying her mother's face, she noted the small flaws in the Lady's matchless beauty, flaws she'd never noticed before. There were very faint lines around her mouth, and her lips didn't seem quite as firm and plump. Pale shadows painted the delicate skin under her vivid eyes.

The glamour would prevent most mortals from registering such details, but the changes were real. And suddenly Mist remembered what Freya had said about her borrowed body: *"It cannot contain my magic indefinitely."*

"Freya—" Mist began.

But suddenly the Lady was on her feet and standing over her daughter, as if she had realized just how vulnerable she had made herself and was eager to undo the damage.

"You must believe that I fear for more than myself," she said, taking Mist's face between her hands. "I fear for you, and for your recklessness. But you waste your abilities, and unless you permit yourself to recognize and accept the extent of your magical potential, we may lose everything."

3

Mist stiffened. This was another conversation they'd had before. Freya had witnessed Mist's "magical potential" when the Lady had descended to Midgard in her elven body and fought by Mist's side against Loki's forces.

Faced with a small army of frost giants and desperate to protect mortal followers who had yet to take part in a real battle, Mist had fallen back on what she and Dainn had dubbed the "ancient magic." Neither Galdr nor Seidr, elven nor Jotunn, it was elemental and feral, blending the forces of fire and water, wind and earth.

More than once, Dainn had suggested that those elemental powers were derived from the Vanir, the elder race of gods defeated in cosmic battle by the "younger" upstarts, the Aesir.

Freya was Vanir. It had always seemed odd to Mist that she had never revealed similar abilities.

Perhaps she was afraid. Mist knew all too well that each time *she* used it, she felt as if she were losing herself. As if she might fall into the "fugue state" Dainn had always warned her about, and turn into someone else completely. Someone she didn't want to be.

"You must see how essential it is that you make use of every resource you possess," Freya said, dropping her hands before Mist could jerk away. "Your magic has unique qualities even I cannot match, and I have never seen the likes of it before. Not even in the All-father."

Mist stared into her mother's eyes, hardly able to believe what she was hearing. Freya never admitted inferiority. In anything.

This is just another game, Mist thought, glancing toward the door and almost wishing a Jotunn would barge in to start a fight. "I can't explain it, either," she said.

"The traitor did not teach it to you."

"No. Dainn had nothing to do with it." She rose and walked to the counter. Two hot beverages had been abandoned when their buyers had left the premises at Freya's behest; Mist chose the strong black coffee, returned to the table, and sat down again. "What about your Seidr?" she asked, determined to divert Freya from the subject of Dainn Faith-breaker. "You still haven't shown me how it works."

"Soul-travel requires even more effort than the glamour, and takes many years to master," Freya said, taking her seat again. "My brief use of it here in Midgard has delayed my plans to create true bodies for myself and the other Aesir, so that we might live again as we once did."

Mist didn't remark that the first time Freya had taken her on a "soul-journey"—to prove that Dainn had gone over to Loki—she hadn't seemed particularly drained. "You were able to get here in this elven body," she said.

"As I was able to help the other Alfar generate physical forms and cross the bridge from the Shadow-Realms of Ginnungagap," Freya said. "But the bodies of the Aesir are another matter entirely. I must continue to build my strength."

Mist knew she had no choice but to accept Freya's word for that, but she still wasn't satisfied. "What about the Falcon Cloak? It belongs to you. Getting a bird's-eye view of what's going on in the city could be very useful."

"Do you think that requires any less effort?" Freya asked irritably. "What of your search for the remaining Treasures and their guardians?"

"We have four of the other eleven Valkyrie on our side—Eir, Hild, Bryn, and Rota—along with their Treasures," Mist said, as if she needed to remind herself of what they'd actually accomplished. "Horja's dead, but Anna used her memories to recover the Cloak and Horja's Staff. Sigrun stayed in Italy with the nuns, but we have the unbreakable Chain she guarded in the convent."

"That means that five Valkyrie and their Treasures remain unaccounted for," Freya said, counting off on her bejeweled fingers. "Ol-run with Freyr's magic Sword; Regin and Thor's Hammer; Skuld and Megingjord, the Belt of Power; Hrist with Bragi's Harp; and Kara with the Gjallarhorn. Unless, of course, Loki already has them in his possession."

Mist knew that was a very real possibility, though Loki had shown no sign of having achieved that particular advantage. "I have people working on it night and day," she said. "We'll find them." She stared at a particularly recalcitrant coffee ring on the table, imagining that it was the evil serpent Jormungandr biting its own tail. "It would help if we knew what we were going to use the Treasures for."

"Odin never saw fit to tell me," Freya said with a curl of red lips.

She had some reason to be pissed, Mist thought. Odin had sent the Treasures to Midgard just before the Dispersal, the event that had blasted all the inhabitants of the other Eight Homeworlds into the Void. Freya had speculated that he hadn't believed the prophecy that foretold Ragnarok, the final battle between Loki and the gods that would herald the end of the universe as the Aesir knew it.

But Odin had left Freya largely ignorant of his ultimate plans, in spite of her important role as ambassador to Midgard after so many centuries of silence from the gods. Through Dainn, she'd approached Mist with orders to find the Treasures scattered over the Earth, though Mist hadn't seen or spoken to their guardians for decades.

The coffee turned bitter in Mist's mouth. Odin was her sworn lord, but sometimes—

Swift as a striking serpent, Freya reached across the table, pushing Mist's coffee cup aside with a minor spell. She grabbed Mist's arm, twisting it to display the black-and-bloodred tattoo of interlocking wolves and ravens encircling her wrist. Odin's symbols.

"Does it still give you trouble?" she asked.

"Not often," Mist said, carefully prying her wrist from Freya's grasp. "I've had it for centuries, but it never acted up until Hrimgri-mir arrived to threaten me, just before I found Dainn. You know, in the park where the bridge to Ginnungagap suddenly *vanished* while we were chasing Loki and Gungnir."

Freya withdrew her hand, her expression turning cold. "Do not presume to lay that at *my* feet. I have told you that I was unable to reach Midgard earlier because I was attempting to prevent the bridges from disappearing entirely."

"I remember when you claimed that you'd closed them again just to get back at Loki."

"I only meant to befuddle him," Freya said. "Clearly, the bridges have never been entirely stable, and that is why I have been unable to reach the Aesir. But I *have* succeeded in bringing more Alfar to Midgard since my return. And Loki has done no better than I."

And apparently, Mist thought, he hadn't managed to convince his son to open another portal. Danny, uncanny child that he was, had created a magical passage between San Francisco and the Russian steppes, where his half-brother—the eight-legged Steed Sleipnir, one of the Treasures—had been hidden away from Odin's enemies.

Mist hadn't discussed the portal with Freya after it had closed. Dainn's last communication with Mist had come in the form of a terse note: *Danny is safe. Say nothing of him. Do not trust Freya.* And since Mist had presumed that Freya hadn't seen Danny on the other side of the portal, she simply hadn't mentioned the boy or his remarkable abilities.

"Have you heard anything more of the raven?" Freya asked, unerringly turning to another very touchy subject. When she'd finally arrived in Midgard, Freya hadn't been aware that Odin had sent another messenger to Mist, and she'd been less than pleased to learn that the All-father had hidden that from her, as well.

"Nothing," Mist said, relieved that she could be honest. "Not a sign." She pushed her chair back from the table. "Look, we've both got work to do," she said. "Unless there's something else . . ."

"You are stubborn, my child," Freya said, reassuming that air of serenity that concealed so many contradictions. "But I ask you to remember what I said before about your peculiar magic. If you fear wielding it so much, perhaps we might work on it together."

Immediately Mist was on her guard. "How would we do that?" she asked, already fearing the answer.

"By joining our minds," Freya said, "as I once did with the Faith-breaker."

Mist suppressed a shiver. She never wanted that again. Not with Dainn, whose mental touch had left a scar that had never healed, and certainly not with her mother, whom she couldn't trust.

"We can begin slowly," Freya said. "I know you hesitate to use your glamour to call mortal warriors to swell your pitiful ranks; I will help you overcome that hesitation. It is even possible that your magic might provide the raw power that will enable me to stabilize the bridges." Freya's eyes shone with rare excitement. "We might counter the advantages Loki has won in these past months and turn the tide of this battle, even before the Aesir arrive." She moved away from the table. "I urge you to think on it. But remember that every day you hesitate, Loki gains ground, and more of your mortals die."

Before Mist could say another word, Freya was gone. Mist swallowed half a cup of cold coffee and headed for the door.

A knot of confused and aimless mortals clustered around the entrance to the shop. They didn't notice Mist as she left, but soon after they seemed to remember why they had been there in the first place and filed back inside. Mist almost felt guilty about the coffee she'd stolen.

Don't you deserve a little reward for saving mortal hides?

She laughed at her own hubris and started back to the loft. It wasn't a short walk, and she was tired and sore, but she needed to clear her head and prepare herself to meet her people again.

When she reached what was now the allies' headquarters and base of operations, she slowed to examine the area. It looked much the same as it had nine months ago, though the loft had been repaired since the earthquake, and the factories had been converted into more appropriate living quarters. Only those with magic could detect the glimmer of the powerful wards that not only protected the people inside but also repulsed the residents of the apartments and condos around the loft, who generally found themselves avoiding this particular part of the neighborhood.

Or noticing what went on inside it.

She forced her feet to move again, though she would have been very glad of the chance to go somewhere quiet and think over the morning's events. But Bryn, Rota, Hild, the Alfar leaders, and several of the Einherjar—Bryn's biker club, named after Asgard's eternal warriors—would be waiting to give reports on their own recent skirmishes, list the casualties, count the costs.

She had just enough time to visit the injured mortals at the infirmary before the scheduled debriefing. Eir was already there, showing Gabi how to treat a fractured wrist with a combination of healing magic and medical skill.

It had been months since Gabi had paid for her own *curandera* magic with burnt and swollen hands. Though Mist glimpsed occasional signs that the young woman hadn't overcome the psychological shock of the Serpent Jormungandr's attack—and nearly being eaten alive—it was clear to her that Gabi was becoming adept at calling on her own unique magical heritage under Eir's gentle guidance.

"We could do a lot more if you'd let me go get *mi abuela* in Mexico," Gabi was saying to Eir as Mist walked into the room.

"We can't afford to lose you," Mist said, joining girl and Valkyrie. "And your grandmother may very well choose not to get involved."

Gabi scooted around to face Mist, a characteristically stubborn expression on her face. "If I tell her what's happening, she will. And there are others who'd come, too."

"Perhaps if they were meant to join us, they would have arrived by now," Eir pointed out.

"But more fighters keep coming," Gabi said. She searched Mist's eyes with that hard-won trust that still cut Mist to the heart. "The medics we got now ain't real doctors. We can barely keep up, and it's gonna get a lot worse."

Mist glanced at Eir. The healer's face was much more deeply lined that it had been when Mist had gone to get her in New Mexico, her body far too thin and fragile for a healthy Valkyrie. She moved as if her joints were riddled with arthritis, and her breath often came short and harsh.

When her gaze met Mist's, it conveyed a question that shamed Mist as deeply as the bitterest remonstrance. Freya had said it herself: Mist was afraid to call the people they so desperately needed. Just not for the reason the Lady supposed.

Dainn had made very clear that she could summon mortal allies with a focused and deliberate use of the glamour she'd inherited from her mother. And she'd been putting it off again and again, simply allowing the mortal descendants of gods, elves, and ancient Scandinavian heroes to turn up on their own, driven by some primal instinct to join in the fight against an enemy who would bring chaos to their world.

But those relative few would never be enough. If Freya couldn't bring the Aesir and their Einherjar warriors across from the Void before Loki took complete control of the city, the allies would fall.

The man Gabi had been treating groaned, and Mist bit down hard on her lower lip. She'd run out of excuses. It had to be taken care of, even if she had to turn herself into the thing she loathed most.

"You're right, Gabi," she said, getting to her feet. "Something has to be done."

She turned to leave, but Eir called after her.

"You've been with Freya?" the healer asked as Mist returned.

"Yes," Mist said. "And I'd rather not talk about it."

Eir rose awkwardly and glanced at Gabi, who was completely absorbed in her work. "May we speak in private?"

"You shouldn't be on your feet," Mist said, more sharply than she'd intended. "You're exhausted."

"And you're hurt, and discouraged. When will you learn that you can't do this alone?"

"Funny," Mist said. "Freya said almost the same thing. She wants to combine our magic to—"

"You didn't agree?"

Mist frowned and took Eir's arm, leading her to the walled-off area where the injured were triaged. Mist eased Eir down into one of the mismatched chairs.

"What's eating you?" Mist asked, sitting beside her.

"What isn't?" Eir said with a faint smile. "I know that you've been putting a brave face on our current conditions to keep morale as high as possible. But you and I both know the Aesir should have been here by now."

"Freya says she's working on it."

"Of course." The healer closed her eyes. "That is her claim. But she also claimed that she and Odin were working together closely, and yet she knew nothing of Orn. Why would Odin keep her in the dark about his messenger?"

"He's obviously not in touch with Orn now."

"Yet I've often wondered why Orn showed up when Freya was absent from Midgard, and disappeared again when Freya returned."

"Loki kidnapped him and Anna just before Freya arrived."

"Still, Orn has proven to be something of a paradox. Odd that Freya should still be unaware of him."

"Even I can't be sure of Orn's role in all this."

"But you think that Orn is connected with the pendant Odin gave you before we came to Midgard with the Treasures centuries ago," Eir said. "You don't know if he intended to give you a message before you gave the pendant to Anna's grandmother during the Second World War."

"If he did, he waited a cursed long time to bring the pendant, and himself, back to me," Mist said. "And then he had nothing to say." Eir ran her thin hand over her face, and Mist realized how much strength the conversation was costing her.

"We can talk about this later," Mist said, "after you've—"

"What if Orn is hiding?" Eir said.

"From Loki?"

"Not only from Loki. Maybe he's smarter than we gave him credit for."

Mist shifted uneasily. "What are you getting at?"

Abruptly Eir slumped in the chair, her head lolling on her chest. Mist scrambled to her side and gathered the healer in her arms. Eir weighed no more than a scarecrow stuffed with feathers.

"You're going to bed," Mist said. "And you're not to do any more work until you can stand on your own two feet without listing to one side or the other like a sinking ship in a storm."

"But that is what I am," Eir said, her voice a hoarse whisper. "A sinking ship."

"You're not sunk yet." Mist carried her to the area set aside for the medical staff and laid her down on her cot. "Leave Freya to me. Gods know I wouldn't wish her on anyone else."

"Not even Loki?" Eir said with a short laugh.

"Sleep," Mist said. She covered Eir with the wool blanket, kissed her forehead, and turned away. The healer grabbed at her hand and hung on with surprising strength.

"Promise me," she said. "Listen to your instincts. Sometimes you give people more credit than they deserve, and too little to yourself." She let go of Mist's hand and covered her mouth, muffling a dry cough. "I think I'll rest now."

Mist hesitated, her eyes filling with tears. She'd told herself again and again that she should never have let Eir help her fight Loki in the desert, or against Jormungandr so soon after she and Mist had returned to San Francisco. A healer wasn't meant to use her talents to bring harm, and Eir had paid the price with her health. Possibly with her life.

But the healer hadn't lost her quiet wisdom, and her words continued to echo in Mist's mind. They so closely mirrored the doubts *she'd* tried to push aside, because refusing to accept Freya's help wasn't an option.

Even now she didn't really want to think about it. But Eir didn't have to remind her to listen to her instincts. Gut feeling had very clearly told her not to tell Freya everything about Orn's involvement, just as it had nagged her to heed Dainn's last communication.

Do not trust Freya. Not all is what it seems.

◑◐

Exhausted by the latest council meeting, Mist trudged back to the loft. She still half-expected a certain elf to be waiting for her at the kitchen table.

Instead, someone from Anna's small computer team had left a whole stack of printouts with information on the possible locations of two of the missing Valkyrie. Mist picked up the top page and stared blankly at the report. Anna had been trying to match Vali's expertise since he'd betrayed them and gone over to Loki, and working herself nearly to death seemed to be her way of trying to forget that Orn had abandoned her.

Returning the paper to the stack, Mist took a bottle of beer out of the fridge. She set it on the table and sat down, too exhausted to twist off the cap.

"Need some help?"

Koji sauntered into the kitchen, smiling at Mist with his usual warmth. The young lawyer was wearing sweatpants and a loose T-shirt, still perspiring from training in the gym. Even a five-dan practitioner of Japanese martial arts needed to keep in condition, and he was one of the handful of men and women who could teach the newest mortal recruits how to fight with bladed weapons . . . not to mention taking on the legal problems Mist and her allies ran into with increasing frequency.

The one thing Koji never did, in spite of his considerable skill with a katana, was actually join in the fighting. He'd said something about his religion and how taking a life was against his principles, but Mist had never forgotten how ferocious he'd been when he'd faced Dainn during the battle in the gym last winter.

She returned Koji's smile. He wrapped his arm around her shoulders and kissed her—gently, because he knew she wasn't in any mood for passion. Their sex life had been sporadic over the past couple of months, but Koji didn't seem particularly upset about it, or bothered by her frequent bouts of preoccupation.

That was what made him such a good companion and lover. He didn't demand things Mist couldn't give. And when she'd finally told him the truth about what was really going on, he'd been remarkably quick to accept the fact that the world as he knew it was a false front for the kind of reality most mortals had never dreamed existed.

"Hey, you're hurt," he said, gently pulling Mist's slashed sleeve away from the gash across her arm. "Anything I can do?"

Mist carefully extracted her arm from his grip. "It'll heal in a few hours," she said. "You know you don't need to worry about me."

A slight frown crossed Koji's usually affable face. "You can still suffer pain."

She grabbed the half-forgotten bottle and sagged over the table. "I'm tired, Koji."

"I know," he said, taking the chair nearest hers. "I'm not sure if you really want to hear this, but the mayor's holding a press conference just about"—he glanced at his watch—"now."

"The groundbreaking for the new monument," Mist said bitingly, "thanks to Lukas Landvik's generous financial support for our fair city's most recent frivolous embellishment."

"And for the mayor and his supporters," Koji added. At Mist's nod, he turned on the small, ancient TV sitting on the kitchen counter.

Ostensibly, the mayor was the focus of the coverage. The cameras were trained on him as he gesticulated and grandstanded about the improvements he had made to the city's infrastructure; the many employment opportunities offered by various construction projects and the refurbishment of the more public parts of the city; the booming tourist industry; and, of course, the new private hospital, which was being built where it could best cater to the most wealthy and privileged.

What he failed to mention was how he and the Board of Supervisors were encouraging the "relocation" of numerous small businesses in favor of big-box chains offering minimum-wage jobs and poor benefits, or the fact that scores of projects favored by local politicians and business interests—replete with kickbacks and every kind of corruption—had been given priority over essential improvements and programs that actually enhanced the welfare of the citizens.

She was pretty sure the smiling politician on her screen was still ignorant of the tremendous price he'd have to pay for all the "positive" changes in the city, the ones that so successfully lined his pockets. He obviously didn't realize that the man standing just behind his left shoulder—the charismatic "philanthropist" Lukas Landvik—was the very person who would demand that price.

Again and again, the cameras slid toward Loki in his handmade Italian suit and A. Testoni Norvegese shoes. His midlength red hair was artfully tumbled around his fox-like, handsome face. Green eyes caught the light in a way no ordinary eyes would. Loki smiled, and the reporters, male and female, virtually swooned.

"I've seen enough," Mist said. She was about to switch the TV off when she glimpsed the man directly behind Loki. Her hand froze on the remote.

"Don't torture yourself, Mist," Koji said, laying his hand on her shoulder. "He made his choice."

"Don't you think I know that?" she snapped, punching the power button. The images went black.

But she couldn't get the last one out of her mind. Dainn, every bit as handsome as Loki, his long black hair nearly swept back in such a way that it just covered his ears. He wore a suit hardly less expensive than Loki's—the Slanderer, after all, had to have the best of everything, even for his servants—and he had garnered nearly as much attention as Loki.

But Dainn's face had been utterly blank. That, in itself, was no surprise. It had taken many weeks of Mist's working with him closely and intimately before she had begun to realize that his seeming indifference concealed strong emotions he didn't want anyone to see.

But he wasn't trying to conceal anything now; he was simply empty, as if everything that had made him what he was had been drained out of him and left him no more than a walking ghost.

"Sit down," Koji urged, guiding her back to her chair. "You need that beer."

Mist let him coax her, and worked her way through three beers without feeling so much as a buzz. Koji played with his own bottle but never seemed to drink.

"Listen," Koji said after a very long silence. "You can't stop believing in yourself. And I'm not talking about the fact that everyone is rely-ing on you. I mean what's in here." He tapped his temple with one forefinger. "You have more strength than you know."

How many times had Dainn said nearly the same thing? "I can't tell anymore if my judgment is sound," she said. "In anything."

"Doubts are natural. You'll pull through this."

"Thanks for the vote of confidence," she said, hoping she sounded sincere. She glanced at her watch. "And now I've got to get moving. I have a meeting in an hour, and a few new recruits came in yesterday. I have to give them the usual warnings and pep talk. Then there's the—"

"It can wait," Koji said. He stroked her face with the back of his hand. "Let me take care of *you* for a little while."

Mist closed her eyes and let him pull her to her feet. He was right . . . an hour wouldn't make much difference.

◑◐

Ryan crouched beside Eir, trying very hard not to vomit.

In only a few days' time, she had become nearly unrecognizable. Her eyes were sunken deep into her skull, and her lips were dry as brittle leaves. It was as if her skin had been stretched over her bones so tightly that he could see right through it.

Before, when he'd been helpless to control his visions, only *he* had suffered. But now, seeing Eir like this, he finally understood Mother Skye's warnings.

He laid his hand on Eir's shoulder as gently as if he were touching the disintegrating paper of some ancient, precious book. "Eir?" he whis-pered. "Can you hear me?"

Her eyelids fluttered, but she didn't show any sign of waking. Maybe, Ryan thought, she was in a coma.

Maybe there was still a chance to save her.

I'm not ready, he told himself. *I can't do this.*

The sound of footsteps outside the door pulled him to his feet.

Guilt and shame were like angry dogs, doing their best to chase him into hiding.

He stood his ground, and the intruder entered the infirmary.

Gabi.

4

She stopped as she saw him, brown eyes widening in shock.

"Ry?" she said.

"Gabi," he said, his voice cracking, "Eir needs help."

Her gaze fell from his face to the woman on the cot. She crossed the room and bent over Eir, quickly checking the Valkyrie's pulse.

"Shit," she breathed. She looked up at Ryan. "How long you been here?"

"Not long." Ryan swallowed. "I found her like this. Can you help her?"

"I don't know." Gabi looked around the room as if she were seeking help from someone Ryan couldn't see. "Mist is still away. There's no one else who can—" She broke off. "Get more blankets. They're over on those shelves."

Ryan did as she'd told him, grateful to get away if only for a moment. As he gathered the blankets, he watched Gabi kneel beside the cot, speaking softly in English and Spanish, touching Eir's arm, her forehead, her chest. She reached inside her shirt and pulled out the cross she always wore, enfolding it in her hand. After a moment she let the cross fall back inside her shirt, crossed herself, and laid her palms on Eir's chest just below her collarbones.

Her hands were suffused with a red glow, and some of that glow seemed to trickle down from her fingers to bathe Eir's chest. But it died as soon as it touched the Valkyrie, like coals doused in ice water.

"No," Gabi moaned. "Eir! You have to fight!"

Eir's eyes opened a crack, and her rigid mouth relaxed in a half smile. "Gabi," she whispered. "It's all right."

Gabi set her jaw. "You have to try harder!" she said. "I can—"

"No." With obvious effort, Eir lifted her hand and laid it on Gabi's wrist. "You're burning. If you keep up, you . . ." She coughed, turning her face into her shoulder. "They need you."

"*I* need you!" Gabi cried.

Eir patted Gabi's wrist and turned her head to look at Ryan. "Don't feel badly, Ryan. I wasn't afraid then, and I'm not now."

"What is she talking about?" Gabi demanded, meeting Ryan's gaze. "Eir, what do you mean?"

"Don't blame your friend," Eir said, her smile fading. "It was necessary, even if I—" She gasped, as if she couldn't catch her breath, and settled again. "It will be difficult, for both of you. But never forget to hold on to each other."

Tears spilled over Gabi's cheeks. "I don't understand," she said.

"It will come." She smiled again and relaxed into the mattress.

"No!" Gabi jumped up, her muscles rigid. "You *fight*!"

"I've done far too much of that already, child."

Without another word, Gabi dashed out of the infirmary. Eir closed her eyes and shuddered, gripping the sheets with her fragile fingers.

"Are you in pain?" Ryan asked, fussing with the blankets just so he could have something to do with his hands.

"No," Eir said. "I'm weak. But it doesn't hurt." She sighed, her breath rattling. "I don't know if I succeeded in warning Mist. I was careful, as you suggested . . . perhaps too careful. But she isn't stupid, Ryan. She already has doubts. Maybe . . . that's enough."

"I'm sorry I asked you to do this," Ryan said, barely able to speak. "I only made you worse."

"Don't be. I've . . . spent a lot of time listening to the voices of other peoples, other spirits, and I think . . . I *know* this is not the end of all things." With an obvious effort, she reached up to touch Ryan's wet face. "This was meant to be."

Her arm fell back to the mattress, and her eyes began to glaze over.

"Wait!" Ryan said. "You have to say good-bye to Gabi!"

"*You* tell her," Eir said, closing her eyes. "Tell her she's ready."

And then the life went out of her, a gentle force Ryan could feel like a breeze brushing past his face, free of fear and sadness. When she was gone, he cradled Eir's hand between his and imagined her flying off to whatever might be waiting for her. A good place, where she could get the peace she deserved.

"*Farvel*, Eir," he said, kissing her withered cheek. "Good luck."

He covered the Valkyrie with one of the blankets and rose stiffly. He felt old, even though he was only eighteen. He felt as if he'd lived a hundred lifetimes.

"Eir!"

Gabi rushed into the room, a small suede pouch cupped in one palm. She fell to her knees beside the cot and pulled the pouch open with trembling fingers. She dug out a single hard, black seed and tried to wedge it between Eir's lips.

The Apples of Idunn, Ryan remembered. The fruit that was supposed to help keep the Aesir virtually immortal.

The cure had come too late.

"Gabi," he said softly.

"Eat it!" Gabi said, ignoring him. "Chew on it, Eir!"

"She's gone," Ryan said, reaching across Eir's body to touch Gabi's arm.

She jerked away, staring at the seed still resting on the Valkyrie's lower lip.

"What did you do to her, Ry?" she whispered, silent tears tracking over her cheeks. "Why did she tell me not to blame you?"

Ryan got up and backed away. "I'm sorry, Gab," he said. "I didn't want this."

She sprang to her feet again, fists clenched. "How long were you with her? Why didn't you get help?"

Unable to meet her accusing eyes, Ryan looked away. He'd wanted to see Gabi so much, and it was ruined. *He'd* ruined it.

"Will you listen to me, Gab?" he asked. "Because if you won't, I'll go."

"You mean like you did before?" Gabi brushed hard at her face. "When all you did was leave me a fucking note?"

"I'm sorry," Ryan said. "There was something I needed to do, and I had to do it alone."

"Do *what*? Where the hell you been?"

"If you'll let me explain—"

"Shut up! Just shut up!" She returned to Eir's bedside, sank down, and rested her cheek on Eir's chest. Her expression relaxed into grief.

"She was good," Gabi said. "Real good. One of the best people I ever knew."

"I know," Ryan said. "She told me to . . . tell you that you were ready."

Gabi laughed brokenly. "She's wrong."

"I'm just as scared as you are, Gab." He swallowed. "I need your help."

For a long time she didn't say anything, just sat beside Eir, looking at her face and crying silently. After a while she gently took the seed from Eir's lips and put it back in the pouch.

"No one was supposed to touch the Treasures," she said in a flat voice. "But Mist told me how to get the Apples if Eir started to—" She swiped at her face again. "You know, they're supposed to be what keeps the gods alive and young. Mist said there were always consequences if anyone besides the gods tried to use them."

"I know about consequences," he said. "I didn't mean to hurt Eir, but it *is* my fault that she—"

"You better tell me what you did," Gabi said, something almost like hatred in her eyes, "or I might hurt *you*."

It was the first time she'd ever threatened him and meant it, and it felt to Ryan as if she'd taken a knife, slashed his chest open and pulled out his heart.

"I *want* to tell you," he said thickly, "but you have to promise not to tell anyone else. Not even Mist."

"Why should I promise you anything?"

"Because it all has to do with what's happening and what's going to happen to the Earth, and the people we care about. It could all go to hell if anyone finds out before the . . . the right time."

"Your visions," Gabi said slowly.

"Yes." Ryan took a deep breath. "You may hate me when I tell you, but someone else has to know. Will you listen?"

In the end, she did. He told her almost everything but the part he still had to figure out himself, the part he couldn't predict. He told her about Mother Skye, and how she'd taught him to control his visions so he wouldn't have seizures or be helpless when they came. He told Gabi how, when he'd returned, he'd spent several days just watching and moving quietly around the compound, trying to decide if he could get someone to help him before he came out into the open.

"Why didn't you come straight to me?" Gabi demanded. "Why did you have to hide at all?"

"It's different than it used to be," he said. "I'm not the same, Gab. I wish we could go back, but—"

"We can't. I know."

The way she spoke gave him hope that maybe she would understand. So he kept talking, explaining how he'd found Eir and realized what was happening to her.

"You knew she was dying?" Gabi asked, pacing around the room as if she was looking for something to punch.

"Yes," Ryan said. "I knew she was going to die no matter what anyone did. She knew it, too. When I asked her to help me, she understood that it would make it . . . happen faster."

"Why? Why would helping you hurt *her*?"

"Because . . ." Ryan met her gaze, though he was scared half to death. "I can see things more clearly now. Things that might or might not happen depending on what someone decides to do. I can see turning points, when the future might change. And right now . . . *now* is really important. This week, this month. I don't know exactly, but even though I can see stuff, I can't say anything about it. Because if I do, terrible things could happen."

"But you told Eir?"

"Some of it, yes. I asked her to do something I couldn't, hoping the consequences wouldn't be so bad."

"But she died!" Gabi started to cry again, though she didn't make a sound. "What did you ask her to do?" She dropped down beside him. "Ry, *what did she do?*"

All at once he understood that he couldn't tell her after all. Not because he didn't trust her, but because Gabi would probably decide that *she* had to warn Mist about Freya, regardless of the risk.

"I'm sorry, Gabi," he whispered. "It isn't safe to tell you any more than I already have."

"So you aren't going to trust me?"

"For your sake, Gab. I don't want you to get hurt, too."

"Maybe you should let *me* decide. Eir was willing to die—"

"And I won't let it happen to you!" Ryan shouted.

She looked at him for a long time, her face full of anger and fear and confusion and grief.

"You *are* different, Ry," she said at last. "I used to always try to protect you, but now you're trying to protect *me*."

"That's why I left without telling you," he said, pleading with his eyes and his voice. "If I make one mistake, everything could go wrong. Everything could *end*, Gab."

"So you're more important than Mist, or Freya, or anyone else? Is that what you're saying?"

"Not more important. But if I interfere, I have to be completely sure. And I may only have one or two chances. They have to be the *right* ones. And there's still so much I can't see."

"This Mother Skye didn't train you too well, did she?"

"She did her best," Ryan said, trying not to sound defensive.

"And she found you through a vision?"

Ryan couldn't bring himself to tell Gabi how Koji Tashiro had been involved. The lawyer had deceived him, and Gabi. He wasn't what he'd seemed to be. But if he'd been dangerous to any of them, Mother Skye would have warned Ryan.

"She can't act on her visions of the future anymore, even in small ways," he said. "That's why she needed me to help fight Loki, and for Midgard."

"But who *is* she?"

"I'm sorry, Gab. She asked me not to tell. I can say that she's old. Old as the gods. Someday, I promise you'll understand."

"Sure," Gabi said bitterly. "Just like everything else."

"Gab . . ." He took a risk and reached out to touch her. She started to move away, but stopped and let him put his hand on her shoulder.

"I didn't want this," he whispered. "I never did. If I hadn't seen Mist in that dream . . . if I'd listened to you, and we'd just gone away instead of—"

"*Maldito,*" Gabi said, the word filled with anguish. "It ain't your fault. You said certain things happen depending on what someone decides to do. I could have made you leave, but I didn't." She grabbed his hand and held on to it with so much strength that Ryan thought she might crush his bones. "Why did I have to lose Eir and get you back at the same time?"

"I don't know," he said. "If I could trade my life for hers—"

She leaned over and grabbed him, locking her arms around his shoulders and hugging him hard. "*Idioto. Estupido.*" Her tears dribbled on his shirt, and he found himself crying like a baby. The knot in his heart began to unwind.

"I need you, Gabi," he said when he could talk again. "Will you help me?"

Gabi let him go and looked into his eyes. "Eir said to hold on to each other. I'll do whatever I can." She turned back to the cot and uncovered Eir's face gently. "I don't know what we're going to do without—"

She gasped, and Ryan stared at Eir's face. She looked . . . normal. Not shrunken, not old, but young and beautiful and strong.

"*Madre de Dios,*" Gabi murmured. She crossed herself and bowed her head. "*Está en paz.*"

Ryan had never really been sure that there was a God with a capital *G*. At least not one that would hear a person's prayers. But he was grateful that, somehow, Eir's death had turned into something so peaceful. As if she really had been ready to go.

"I need to get the Apples back to the vault," Gabi said, rising again.

"The vault?" Ryan asked.

"It's protected by hundreds of spells. Freya, Mist, the Alfar, all of them put their magic into it."

"And you know how to get in?"

"Mist trusts me," Gabi said, pride lighting her face.

"Will you let me come with you?"

After a moment's hesitation, she nodded. "I trust *you*," she said.

Gabi led him though the warehouse, out into the cold, windy afternoon, and across an expanse of concrete parking lot to another decrepit factory. Though he couldn't see them, Ryan could feel many watching eyes, not all of them mortal. No one was going to get into this place unnoticed.

Apparently Mist really *did* trust Gabi, because she'd given her a series of spells that counteracted the others. "The opening spells change every day," Gabi said by way of explanation. "Only three other people know them."

As she entered the vault to replace the pouch in its nest of velvet, her hand brushed a piece of what looked to Ryan like some kind of staff, snapped raggedly in unequal halves. She gasped and snatched her hand back.

"What is it?" Ryan asked, touching her shoulder.

"Something . . . I don't know." She stared at the broken staff and slowly reached for it again. Her hands began to radiate warmth, and when she touched the polished wood she made a little sound of surprise.

Ryan looked on in astonishment as the two pieces of the staff slid toward each other. They came together with a click like a key fitting into a lock, and a moment later there was one flawless object extending well beyond the edge of the case, a beautiful weapon inscribed with Runes and all kinds of intricate Norse designs.

"*Mierda!*" Gabi said, awe in her voice. "I didn't know I could do that."

"You . . . healed it?" Ryan asked.

"I don't know." She ran her fingertips along the length of the staff, murmuring to herself. "*Esto es de locos,*" she said. "It's alive."

"What?"

"I mean, it *was* alive. There's a place where . . ." She muttered again. "Where a soul used to be."

"A *soul*?"

"That's what I said," she snapped. "I don't get it any more than you do. I'm just telling you what I feel."

Ryan wondered if the idea was as crazy as it sounded. The Treasures were special. No one—not even Mother Skye—knew what their ultimate purpose was, but from the very beginning Mist had been instructed to find them before Loki did. Everyone assumed they were weapons, but until Gabi had told him that Mist had given her permission to try using the Apple seeds on Eir, he'd thought no one but the gods could do anything with them.

In a way, he thought, the Treasures might symbolically carry the "souls" of the Aesir in terms of what they had been in Asgard, and what they hoped to be in the future.

Or maybe that was bullshit. Whatever it was, Mist obviously hadn't known about it. Or about how to fix the staff.

"I'm gonna have to tell Mist what I did," Gabi said, staring down at the staff. "How can I explain what happened? I shouldn't even have been touching it." She lifted her head. "Shit, how am I gonna tell Mist about *Eir*?"

Ryan felt sick all over again. He didn't want to face them. He'd always known it would be hard to meet Mist again, but Dainn would be the worst. Knowing what Dainn was, how it could go wrong, but not being able to see that moment when the elf would have to make his most terrible choice, or exactly what that choice would be . . .

Just like with Mist. *She'd* have the biggest choice of all.

"It's okay, Ry," Gabi said, reading him as easily as always. "I won't tell her anything you don't want me to."

"Just . . . don't say anything," he said. "For now, let me handle it. I don't want anyone else to be hurt."

"Yeah," Gabi said. She met his gaze. "You seen Freya yet? In person, I mean?"

"No." He shuddered. "I've heard people talking about her."

"Bad things, I hope." Gabi wrinkled her nose. "She no good, Ry."

Ryan almost laughed, but he knew she'd take it the wrong way. "The war hasn't gone any better now that she's here?" he asked.

"Depends on what you mean by 'better.' But I don't trust her, and I don't think Mist does, either. My advice, just stay away from her."

"I plan to," Ryan said, wondering if he could keep that resolution. "Gabi . . . how is Dainn?"

Her eyes widened. "You don't know?"

A leaden weight settled in the pit of Ryan's stomach. "Did something happen?" he asked.

"Yeah," she mumbled, looking down again. "He's gone, Ry."

"Gone? Where?"

She told him. He had to sit down on the floor afterward, dizzy with the knowledge that he'd never so much as envisioned the scenario she'd described.

"I'm sure he didn't go willingly," Ryan said, arguing more with himself than with Gabi. "He was afraid of the beast taking over, hurting—"

"Mist was always ready to help him, no matter what he did." Gabi's voice rose in anger. "She should never have trusted him."

"But *something* made him do it. Something—" He broke off, remembering his last meeting with Dainn . . . how Dainn had let him go to Tashiro without trying to stop him. The elf had said he'd soon be incapable of harming Ryan. Did that mean he'd already expected to leave?

But then why would he tell Ryan to call him and Mist if he needed them? Ryan couldn't think of any explanation but that Dainn hadn't known exactly what was going to happen to him. He'd made one of those important choices.

There was something in play here that not even Mother Skye had anticipated.

"I'm sorry, Ry," Gabi said softly. "Maybe he thought he could help Mist by going to Loki. I don't know. But Freya . . . Ry?"

Freya. Ryan clenched his teeth together. Gods knew what the Lady had told Mist about Dainn.

"Does Mist hate him now?" he asked.

"She doesn't talk about him," Gabi said. "But I don't think so. Not the way she *should*." Gabi sighed. *"Ay, joder.* I know how you felt about—"

"Forget it," Ryan muttered. "Listen, you decide when you should tell Mist about Eir. I'm going to stay hidden until I know it's time to show myself." He shivered. "I'm really sorry, Gabi. And I promise I'll tell you everything as soon as it's safe."

"I know, Ry. I know." She bit her lip and lifted the Staff carefully, one hand on either side of the former break. "I'm never gonna be able to fit this back in the—"

All at once the smooth wood broke apart again, neatly and soundlessly, and Gabi was holding the two halves as if they had never been "healed" at all. Ryan couldn't tell if she was upset or relieved. She moved quickly to replace the pieces in their case and closed the lid, murmuring the sealing spell.

"You go now, Ry," she said, still chewing on her lower lip. "I'll check in on you later."

Ducking low, Ryan crept out of the building and started back for the infirmary. A figure moved among the shadows between two of the warehouses as he passed by, but he made himself keep walking and didn't look back.

5

Loki tossed his overcoat to the butler and sauntered into the marble foyer. There were very few real mansions left in San Francisco, but this house in Pacific Heights could truly be called one of the most expensive and elegant in the city. Indeed, in the entire state.

Not, he thought a little sourly, that he could choose any other place in California, even if he wished to. Though he'd abandoned his suite in his downtown headquarters five months ago, fully separating his personal life—and Danny—from his many business interests—he was still confined to San Francisco. Confined, that was, if he wanted full access to the bridges.

Which, at the moment, were still inconveniently unreliable in their functioning.

He reminded himself that the press conference had gone very well. The mayor relied on him so much these days . . . unofficially, of course. But Loki had helped transform him from an unpopular politician to one the plebeians respected, even though they should have despised him for his inability to control crime, to curb the excesses of overzealous law enforcement, and to share the wealth his administration had accrued with such rapidity.

But the citizenry was easily distracted with the little sops Loki arranged for them: civic pride celebrations, festivals offering generous free samples of fine food and wine, lotteries for big-ticket items, give-aways of every sort. All amounting to a pittance in expenditure. And then, of course, there were the new drugs, designed to keep a significant portion of the populace in a constant state of oblivious docility.

Panem et circenses, Loki thought. Give them what they think they want. Distract them, and then sit back as the world they know slowly crumbles around them.

With a wave of his hand, he indicated that Nicholas, his personal assistant, should precede him to his study to prepare the drinks, while the butler—whose name Loki hadn't bothered to remember—hurried off to inform the cook that a light supper was wanted. His "secretary," Scarlet, insinuated herself into the room and smiled invitingly.

He shook his head to dismiss her as Dainn came quietly up behind him. The butler returned quickly to relieve Dainn of his coat and scarf. Dainn nodded thanks—an irritating habit of acknowledging the services of the mortals in Loki's employ—and simply stood where he was, waiting. Waiting, like the rest of them, for his orders.

"So what did you think?" Loki asked lightly.

"Very effective," Dainn said, his voice as flat as always. "Your ability to entertain has never been in doubt."

"You're in a foul mood this afternoon," Loki said. He reached behind Dainn's head, freed the luxurious black hair from its neat tail, and twisted a lock around his finger.

"Life would be so much pleasanter for you if you'd simply give in," he said softly.

"I have no feelings for you," Dainn said. "Not of the kind you require."

As so often happened, Loki was torn between striking the elf and kissing him. He chose the latter. Dainn's mouth was cool and still under his.

Nine months—the time it took a mortal woman to bear a child—and nothing had changed. Every attempt Loki had made to make Dainn open up to him with his heart as well as his body had met with failure, despite all Loki's threats. And promises.

He still vividly remembered when Dainn had first come to Asgard, thousands of mortal years ago: a mysterious wanderer unfamiliar to any of the elves who frequented Valhalla. He had said little of himself, but Loki had felt his power—power he was sure not even Odin had suspected—and it had acted on Loki like the most potent aphrodisiac.

He had made it his business to learn, by mundane and magical means, who this mysterious creature truly was.

In time, he had realized that even Dainn didn't remember much of his own more distant past. It was almost as if he lived in an eternal present, and that had been Loki's greatest advantage. Dainn hadn't even realized what happened when Loki had worked the dangerous spell that had robbed the elf of the better part of his most potent source of magic: the Eitr—the mysterious substance of the universe itself. It had been *part* of Dainn, carried like the blood in his veins, and he had been as unconscious of its presence within him as he was of the air in his lungs or the beat of his heart.

Loki had felt some regret when he and Freya had seized the Eitr for their own use, knowing that it would change Dainn in ways not even he could imagine. Even so, Dainn had not lost the essence of what he was. He still had his elven magic. He had been calm and cool and wise as Odin's advisor, always a voice of reason. But in private . . .

In the seclusion of their bedchamber, when Dainn had believed he was fucking Freya, he had been more than adequately passionate. He had even declared his love for the Lady. Adoration Loki had wanted for himself, *as* himself.

It didn't matter that Loki couldn't return such feelings. He knew himself to be capable of a certain affection, and since Dainn had come to him here, he had treated the elf with great consideration.

Dainn had been far less than grateful. And certainly *far* from passionate.

But even the Rune-bringer, teacher of the ancient Alfar, couldn't hold out forever.

Loki stepped back and turned away as if he hadn't noticed Dainn's passive rejection. The elf followed him into the study, where Loki turned on the monitor of the remote camera that constantly surveyed Danny's room. Nicholas poured them both glasses of brandy. As always, Dainn didn't touch his.

"You drink too much," Dainn said, almost the only words he ever volunteered. "One day it will kill you."

Loki laughed and raised his glass. "Given what I've experienced at the hands of the Aesir, poisoning my drink isn't likely to produce the results you wish. However"—he settled into his favorite armchair, and gestured for Dainn to take his usual seat on the other side of the small table—"you seem to have done well enough working against me in other ways."

Moving with far less than his usual elvish grace, Dainn took the chair, his body folding in on itself like that of an injured animal attempting to conceal its wounds from a lurking predator. "I have no power to harm you," he said in a dull voice.

"Not with anything as crude as the beast inside you," Loki said, "or as elegant as the magic you lost due to your own unfortunate tendency to make decisions based on misplaced trust. But those are hardly your only tools." He signaled for Nicholas to refill his glass. "According to your most recent reports—or should I called them 'excuses'—Danny has made little progress in any of the tasks you were to help him perform." Loki sighed and stretched out his legs. "I fear that I will soon be driven to take more extreme measures in order to encourage your cooperation."

Dainn didn't react to the threat. "I have been unable to convey your desire that he create other portals to more distant regions of Midgard," he said. "It seems he lacks sufficient motivation to ease your Jotunar's search for the remaining Treasures."

"Because you have given him none."

"He *has* opened the bridges."

"Erratically. And for Freya as well as for me."

"It must please you to know that Freya cannot manage it herself, though she surely takes credit for it." Dainn leaned forward slightly, as if he were warming to the conversation. "I believe that this is a case of Danny's power working indiscriminately. It is a game to him. When he summoned me to help him retrieve Sleipnir on the steppes, he was not acting on your enemy's behalf. He was aware of his brother for reasons we do not understand, but he had no comprehension of the nature of this war, or its consequences. He seems to have forgotten everything that occurred before he returned from the steppes."

"Then why haven't you convinced him to play more of these 'games,' if that is how he perceives them?"

"Because his mind is far more powerful and delicate than you can imagine. He may not be capable of making complex moral judgments as yet, but this will cease to be a game if he begins to truly grasp what you are asking of him, and why."

"And you'll be sure to tell him that what I ask of him is wrong. Immoral."

"You continue to overestimate my influence on him. He still spends much of his time barely conscious of his surroundings."

Dainn glanced at the monitor, and Loki followed his gaze. Danny was sitting cross-legged on the bed, his seemingly ten-year-old face as expressionless as his father's, his wiry body rocking to a rhythm only he could hear. His nurse, Miss Jones, was temporarily away, but Loki knew that his manner seldom changed even when she was in the room with him.

"For most of the time I spend with him, he is as you see," Dainn said, echoing Loki's thoughts. "I have told you many times that Danny is not a tool to be manipulated like your other servants. He is still only half in this world, but if you push him, he may shatter."

Shifting in his chair, Loki scowled. "I know that you have a bond with him that I do not, and that was precisely the reason you were given charge of him. But he is not as disconnected from the world as you seem to believe. He can take images from our minds and create manifestations capable of acting as living beings. Yet he has not raised even a single one of the simple incarnations I have requested. Is that, too, a game you have failed to play?"

"All the shadows he raised in the past were familiar to you, or to me. These mortals you wish him to duplicate for your political machinations are hardly real to *you*."

"If that is the difficulty, I must simply take you to meet them. Given your affection for mortalkind, *you* will find them real enough."

Raw emotion flashed across Dainn's face, but Loki was unable to interpret it. Hope that he might find a chance to escape? Fear that Loki's suggestion might finally enable Danny to do what Loki wished?

"Why don't you just admit that you have attempted to convince him to spirit you both away," Loki said, "perhaps even to the camp of my enemies?" He smiled. "Oh, but that would hardly be wise . . . unless you wanted him dead."

Dainn didn't answer, but he didn't have to. *He* had been the one to tell Loki that Freya had intended to kill Danny on the steppes.

Loki remembered Freya's first meeting with Danny. He and Loki had been searching for a way out of the Jotunheim Shadow-Realm, and had encountered Freya engaged in the same activity. Even then, she had sensed what Danny might become.

"Perhaps you believe *Mist* would protect him," Loki said. "Apparently she has some affection for him. But as I recall, you said that she defended Danny against one of Freya's elves, not the Lady herself." He tipped his snifter to examine the last drops of liquor gleaming against the crystalline amber beads. "Odd, that. Mist would never believe that one of Freya's Alfar would try to harm him."

"Clearly, Freya has some Alfar who are willing to obey her without question. Mist simply assumed that her opponent was a Jotunn posing as an elf. She never realized that Freya meant to—" He broke off, clearly unable to finish the sentence.

Loki signaled for another refill and dismissed Nicholas. "You say that Danny doesn't remember her, or Freya. But what of the beast?"

The muscles in Dainn's jaws tightened. "He never saw it."

"Never? My Jotunar reported having seen it fighting at Mist's side at the portal."

His words clearly came as a shock to Dainn, but then Loki hadn't been entirely forthcoming about what his men had witnessed on the steppes.

"Danny was with Hild and Sleipnir then," Dainn protested, a little paler than he'd been a few moments before.

Loki set down his glass with great care and rose to stand over Dainn's chair. "Tell me," he said, "would you attempt to kill me now if the beast was loose?"

"You would destroy those I would protect, as well as mortal civilization."

"You truly believe that my dominion over this world will be worse than that of the Aesir, but I don't intend to rule as some sort of dictator once my experiment with this city is complete. There will be but one law. Every man for himself. Survival of the fittest. True, unfettered liberty."

"Chaos."

"Naturally."

"And then you will appear as the savior, to rescue mankind from itself."

"I certainly have no intention of allowing the species to become extinct. Mortals are far too amusing."

"Yet you claim this is a better fate than what the Aesir will bring?"

"The Aesir will rule Midgard with no more regard for its inhabitants than I. This Earth will become a new Asgard, with a population of properly subservient menials to cater to Odin's bottomless lust for veneration. That is, of course, if Freya allows it."

"Do you believe she would temper their rule?"

"You truly have no idea." He gazed at Dainn's averted face with bitter satisfaction. "Do you never wonder why Freya has failed to bring even a single one of the Aesir or Einherjar warriors to Midgard, in spite of Danny's 'assistance' with the bridges?"

Dainn didn't look up, but Loki knew he was listening intently to every word.

"Can it be that her access to Asgard's Shadow-Realm is still restricted, or could there be a more sinister reason?" He chuckled. "The Sow never told you the truth about our Hnefatafl game for Midgard, did she?"

"She told me everything," Dainn said, his body as rigid as if he were bracing himself against a physical attack.

"Oh, not everything, I think," Loki said. "You see, our agreement wasn't made with the approval of Odin or the other Aesir."

Dainn looked up. "What?"

"Freya desired to rule as much as I did, but not as only one among the gods. The one thing Freya and I always had in common—besides you, of course—was our opinion of the All-father as a blustering oaf.

An oaf with power and a certain cunning, yes, but an oaf nonetheless."

"You're mad."

"To the contrary. Odin was always the mad one, even if I was the only one to see it. When Freya and I met after the Dispersal, we agreed that she would use her magic to keep the other gods in a suspended state until we could determine which of us had the right to this world."

"Now you are lying. Freya hasn't that much power."

"Oh, I know you'd prefer to believe in my lack of honesty rather than accept that you took part in yet another betrayal of the Aesir and your own people."

Dainn released his breath and rested his hands on the arms of the chair. "If you made such a bargain, it was not while you were in Ginnungagap. Freya intended to take your part at the Last Battle, did she not?"

"I should have known better than to try to deceive you," Loki said with a mocking twist of his lips.

"And Odin sent his Treasures to Midgard before the end. He knew—"

"That Ragnarok, the Last Battle, would fail to bring the end of all things. *You* knew that when you came to Midgard. He intended to secure the Treasures for whatever future lay in store for the Aesir, and he knew that future would lie in this world. But he never suspected that others had access to the alternate prophecy that provoked him to take such actions in the first place."

"Alternate—"

"Freya hates Odin, but you know very well that she is not above employing her sensual talents to obtain what she desires. She heard of the second prophecy given to Odin, and determined to learn the truth of the rumor."

"She seduced him."

"Odd that it never happened before, in my opinion. It isn't as if Odin was ever faithful to Frigga, or any of his other wives."

"What else did this prophecy claim?" Dainn asked.

"If there was more to it, Freya wasn't able to find out. Or so she claimed." He shrugged. "Be that as it may, she was occupied with the All-father when we recognized how useful you would be to us, and I was more than willing to take her place in gaining your . . . 'cooperation.'"

Dainn was so rigid and pale that he seemed only another of Loki's flawless marble reproductions of exquisite Greek sculpture. "You have destroyed the Aesir," he whispered.

"Oh, they're still alive, if currently incapacitated. Sleeping, you might say. Though I believe Freya's work has cost her more than she expected."

Rising quickly, Dainn forced Loki to move away from the chair and paced aimlessly across the room. "So the gods cannot interfere with your plans, or Freya's," he said, "and Mist's hope of their coming—"

"Indeed," Loki said. "Mist is fighting for this world with no conception of the true odds she faces. And Freya is very unlikely to have to have told her, *n'est-ce pas?* It would certainly seem a worse betrayal than you ever committed." He paused dramatically. "Or would it? You never did inform Mist of the danger her mother presents to her, did you?"

The faint twitch of a muscle in Dainn's jaw was enough to tell Loki that he'd made a palpable hit. "But of course," Loki continued, "I distinctly remember your saying some time ago that Mist was too strong for Freya's possession, and that she'd cast the Lady out during the battle of Lefty O'Doul Bridge. I'm sure that must give you quite a sense of relief."

Dainn stopped abruptly and swung around to face Loki. "Why are you so certain that Freya will not decide that calling on the gods to defeat you is more important than ruling Midgard alone?"

"Because she'd rather die than submit to Odin again. But *you* must know what an evil fate that is."

The antique grandfather clock chimed, and Dainn flinched. "Do the Alfar know how Freya intended to betray the Aesir?" he asked.

"I doubt they would serve her if they did."

"And the Vanir?"

"She is, of course, much more favorably disposed toward her own kin. It was agreed that they might be brought over if I summoned my Children, which of course I always intended to do in any case."

"And you also intend to use Danny to—"

A flash of light from the monitor silenced Dainn, and Loki followed his gaze to the screen. Danny was standing on his bed, hands lifted and held wide apart. Between them, a formless, dark cloud spun slowly, the shifting gray mass pierced with tiny points of light. Connecting all of them was an enormous tree, its roots and branches extending to the ragged margin where the cloud ended.

Loki forgot to breathe. He recognized what Danny had summoned, though he had seen it in its pure form only a few times in his life: once, when he and Freya had stolen it from Dainn, and again when Dainn had come to kill him just before the Dispersal, calling upon lingering fragments of ancient magic—reawakened, perhaps, by the curse Odin had placed upon him.

Such magic was the only kind that could truly control the Eitr: life-giving, poisonous, extraordinarily dangerous in the wrong hands . . . or in ignorant ones. Now Danny displayed it for his parents to see, balancing the stuff in his palms as if it were a ball. A toy that could destroy the universe.

Glancing warily at Dainn, Loki tried to read the elf's expression. He had never been entirely sure how much Eitr had remained within Dainn after the theft. It was not the slightest comfort to him that Dainn had shown no sign of regaining control of the Eitr in Midgard.

Had Danny inherited the ability to hold it within himself in the way only Dainn had been able to do? Was this the true source of the boy's extraordinary ability, the ability Loki had never been able to clearly define?

Dainn made a sound in his throat, and Loki focused on the screen again. The tree within the cloud of magic had flung branches in every direction, stretching beyond the border of the amorphous cloud to every side and corner of the room. Wherever the branches touched, the walls and ceiling seemed to become liquid, fluid margins expanding around dark centers.

With a soft oath in a language spoken and abandoned millennia ago, Dainn started for the door. Loki was prepared to stop him and go to Danny himself when the energy between the boy's hands began to collapse, the branches withdrawing, the walls of his room becoming solid again. The cloud became transparent as the lights within it winked out one by one.

Then it simply vanished. Loki and Dainn stared at the monitor in shock. Danny dropped his hands and sat quietly on the bed, as if nothing unusual had happened. Vali stepped into the study, filling the entire door frame with his Jotunn-sized bulk.

"What is it?" Loki snapped.

Vali glanced at Dainn with a slight frown. "There's trouble in Civic Plaza, where you and the mayor held your press conference," he said.

"What trouble?"

"Some kind of protest, according to Hymir."

Loki hesitated. It was doubtful that Danny would be able to articulate what he'd done, but there was a risk in exposing Dainn to the Eitr if Danny chose to summon it again. If Dainn's lost memory was triggered in any way . . .

"Vali," he said, pulling the man aside, "inform Danny's guards that Dainn is not to enter his room under any circumstances."

Odin's son cast Dainn another uneasy glance. "Yes, sir."

Without addressing Dainn again, Loki strode from the room.

◑◐

Dainn realized that Loki knew exactly what they had just witnessed, just as *he* recognized that something extraordinary had happened in Danny's room. From the moment his son had summoned up that peculiar energy and balanced it so lightly between his hands, Dainn understood that the boy had found a new source of magic . . . or reawakened a hidden one that had been there all along.

Power, uncannily familiar. So familiar that Dainn had almost felt it move in his own body.

During Loki's revelation of his scheming with Freya in Asgard and Freya's purposeful betrayal of the other Aesir—and of Mist's vain hope of aid that would never come—Dainn had been numb with despair and self-contempt. Now he felt as if he had been sleepwalking and suddenly found himself on the edge of a cliff: a single step forward would either send him plunging to his destruction, or reveal hidden wings that would lift him toward the invisible sun. He felt more alive in this moment than he had in months.

Alive, and angry, as if he had just discovered that something even more precious than his elven magic had been taken from him by forces beyond his control.

He left the room ten minutes later, well aware that he would meet resistance from the Jotunar who guarded Danny's room. He found no one on the stairs. But when he faced the Jotunar outside the hall that contained Danny's room, they folded their arms across their chests and glared or smirked at him, contemptuous or resentful of his place as Loki's favorite.

"Let me by," Dainn said.

The smallest of the guards, all wiry muscle and sneers, snorted derisively. "We'll let you by when Loki tells us to. Go back to his bed like a good little she-elf."

Dainn didn't argue. The impulse came naturally to him, without thought or strategy behind it. He envisioned the energy Danny had summoned, closed his eyes, and reached out with his mind. He felt the swirling gray mist before he opened his eyes again, hovering before him just within his reach.

He plunged his hands into it, felt it coalesce around his fingers and seep into his skin. The shock was a physical sensation of brutal pain followed by sudden numbness. Through the fog he could see the Jotunar's eyes widen, their faces waxen like those of unpainted dolls.

"Let me by," Dainn repeated.

Moving like automatons, the guards stepped to the side. They stared at Dainn in confusion as he pushed past them and grasped the doorknob of Danny's room. Then the energy faded, and at once the Jotunar were behind him, reaching out to detain him with iron grips.

But not quickly enough. Light engulfed Dainn as soon as he

entered Danny's room, striking him full in the face and streaking past him to blast the Jotunar behind him.

Literally blinded, Dainn heard a chorus of yelps and curses as the Jotunar retreated. He slammed the door shut, leaned his weight against it, and lifted his arm to protect his eyes.

The area of the bed was the source of the light, but Dainn could barely make out the shape of the furniture, let alone find his son. He took a step away from the door, the radiance beating against him like the aftershock of a nuclear explosion.

"Danny!" he called.

"Dainn?"

The voice was so faint that Dainn could barely hear the word, let alone who spoke it. He pushed forward, calling Danny again.

But when the blinding radiance contracted to a tiny pinpoint and vanished, leaving the room cast in ordinary light and shadow, it was not Danny he saw first.

6

Mist sat on the bed beside the boy, her hands resting on her thighs, her grave gray eyes fixed on Dainn's. Danny's knees were drawn up to his chest, his gaze turned inward as if he were not even aware that Mist was in the room.

"He's all right," Mist said.

Dainn braced himself against the nurse's chair and stared at the Valkyrie. In every way, she looked as he had last seen her. In spite of the many battles she must have fought and all the responsibility she carried upon her shoulders, she was as beautiful as she had always been. Her hair was arranged in its usual thick braid, her jaw was set in stubborn determination, and her eyes saw through him as if he were made of glass.

In every way, she was *real*.

"Mist?" he whispered.

She rose from the bed. "I have a question for you," she said, as if they were in the middle of a discussion. "You know Freya as well as anyone. What does she really want of me?"

Struggling to find his tongue, Dainn glanced again at Danny. "I don't . . . understand," he said. "How did you—"

"You *must* know," Mist said. She took a step toward him. "She keeps insisting that I use my abilities. All of them."

Dainn's thoughts spun around each other too quickly for him to grasp. "No," he said. "You must go."

"Are you listening to me, Dainn?" Mist asked. She took another step, and Dainn felt his body go hot and hard, his pulse pounding in his throat as she came nearer. "My mother wants to join our powers somehow," Mist said. "But something doesn't seem—"

Suddenly she glanced over her shoulder—not at Danny, but at something only she was able to see. Dainn closed the distance between them and reached for her.

"Mist," he said.

She turned to look at him, a remote pity in her eyes. Her body caught fire, and her hair uncoiled from its braid, rising around her head like golden flame. Somehow, the strange energy was in *her*, too, taking a different but just as potent form. Dainn stumbled back, feeling his own flesh begin to burn.

And then she was gone. Danny was still sitting on the bed with his back against the headboard, but his eyes were wide open—not with fear, but with surprise.

"Papa?" he said.

Dainn forced his muscles to unlock and knelt on the bed. "Are you all right?" he asked.

The boy looked into his father's eyes with perfect comprehension . . . awake and alert, as he so often was not.

"Yes, Papa," he said. "I'm all right."

Dainn glanced up at the burned-out cameras over the bed. "Did you see her, Danny?" he asked.

"You mean Mist?"

Dainn released his breath, reminding himself to control his emotions. "Yes. Did you bring her here?"

"There was so much light," Danny murmured.

"Is that where she came from? Out of the light?" He dropped his hands to Danny's thin shoulders. "Did you open a portal?"

Danny blinked. "No," he said. He raised his hands and stared at them as if they belonged to someone else. "She came from here."

A manifestation. Dainn laughed silently at his own foolish hopes. He had been too dazzled to realize how bizarre her appearance had been. His heart had blinded him even more than the light.

Mist could not have penetrated Loki's lair easily, and if she had, she never would have come merely to question Dainn.

But now he knew that Danny *did* remember Mist. Or it might be that he had merely plucked the image, perfect as it was, out of Dainn's thoughts. As he could have done a thousand times in the past days and weeks and months, if he had wished to do so.

But he had chosen *this* time, just after he had revealed his new magic. And he had not merely re-created Mist; he had taken Dainn's own fears about Freya's intentions and given them voice and form.

But it wouldn't be necessary for Danny to share his father's emotions to do what he had done; he might simply have "replayed" Dainn's conversation with Loki, taking the words from Dainn's memory, guilelessly reinforcing the doubts Loki meant to sow in Dainn's mind. Merely an echo of something Danny himself might not understand.

"Danny . . ." Dainn began, hardly knowing how to begin.

Danny stared up at him, his lower lip trembling, his eyes welling with tears. "Do you hate me?" he asked.

"Hate you?" Dainn took Danny's face in his hands. "Why?"

"I made you sad."

"No," Dainn said, his heart making a concerted effort to pull itself apart. "No more than I could hate—"

He had almost said "myself." But he had hated himself all too many times since he had learned how Loki had used him in Asgard.

He took Danny's small hand and pressed it against his chest. "Danny, can you feel what I feel?"

The boy's brows drew down. "You *aren't* angry."

"What else?"

"You love me."

"Yes."

Danny sighed deeply. "You love *her,* too."

Utterly unprepared for Danny's words, Dainn found no answer.

"Do you love her more than me?"

"You are my son," Dainn said, gathering Danny close. "I could love no one more."

"But you don't love *him*."

Dainn stiffened. For all Loki's accusations, Dainn had never encouraged Danny to hate Loki, though he had on occasion tried to convince Danny to teleport both of them out of their prison. But he had guessed that Danny held no particular affection for his "mother," especially after he had turned a manifestation of Dainn's beast against Loki.

But there was still so much Dainn didn't know about Danny's true feelings. He had learned more in this single brief conversation than he had done in months of painstaking interaction.

"No," Dainn said, releasing Danny gently. "Do you?"

"He took care of me, in the other place. The Void."

"I know he did," Dainn said. "But he has—"

He broke off, realizing that he might finally have a chance to show Danny through his own thoughts and emotions what Loki truly was, what he had done, what he would do to Mist and all of Midgard if he won the battle. He might make Danny see, in a matter of moments, what this world was . . . make it real to his son as it had never been before. Make him understand that it must be protected, and that Danny had the power to help.

But if he made a mistake, if he showed Danny too much, and the boy's mind could not absorb or accept . . .

"He hurt you," Danny said, his eyes gone wide and strange as if something had broken loose inside him.

It took all of Dainn's will to hide his immediate and instinctive response. "That has nothing to do with you, Danny."

"You're lying," Danny said, his voice no longer that of a child. "You want to leave."

"I would not go without you."

"Does *he* love me, too?"

Dainn squeezed his scarred palm into a fist, remembering the foolish blood-oath he and Loki had made. How could he assure Danny that Loki was capable of such love? He had no way of knowing what Loki truly felt for his son. Or for anyone.

Small hands pried his fingers open, and he realized that the wound was bleeding, spattering the bedspread of cowboys and bucking horses with crimson drops.

"You hate him," Danny said as Dainn bound his hand with a strip torn from the bedspread. "*It* hates him. *It* wants to hurt us."

There was no mistaking Danny's meaning. The image of the beast swelled in Dainn's mind until his skull felt ready to burst.

"No," he said hoarsely.

Danny scrambled across the bed, putting its width between himself and Dainn. "I remember," he whispered. "*She* tried to make you hurt me."

The horror of that memory was like a Jotunn club crushing Dainn's sternum and driving deep into his chest, enveloping his heart in a crust of ice.

Danny *knew*.

"It can't hurt you now," Dainn said, pushing the words past the fist in his throat. "It's gone."

Danny shook his head almost violently. "It's hiding," he said.

"I will never let it touch you," he croaked. "Never, Danny."

The boy's eyes lost focus. He spread his hands, and the mysterious cloud of energy appeared again, swirling light and dark. The makeshift bandage wrapped around Dainn's hand began to unravel. As he watched in astonishment, the cloud seemed to pull blood from the wound in a thin stream and swallowed it like a hungry animal. Danny moaned, as if the energy were itself a beast, struggling to break free with teeth and claws.

But that, Dainn thought, was exactly what it was. Another kind of beast, with a mind and appetite of its own.

Dainn jumped back from the bed and closed his fingers over the wound. The bleeding stopped, but the red-gray substance Danny barely controlled reached toward him, stretching, thinning, straining to join with him. Dainn fell to his knees. The dark energy swirled around him, piercing his body in a hundred places. Danny slumped and folded in on himself as if the very thread of his life had snapped.

Struggling back to his feet, Dainn knelt on the edge of the bed. Danny was still breathing. He gathered Danny close and laid his hand over his son's heart. The seething energy seemed to flow out of him and back into Danny, leaving only a residue of magic that rapidly dissipated.

Danny opened his eyes, but there was no recognition in them. He sat up and pulled away from Dainn, refusing any help, and took up his familiar cross-legged position on the bed.

And then he began to rock.

Dainn watched him for a time, waiting for any change. Someone pounded on the door. He ignored the noise until he was certain that Danny was not going to wake again soon, and then rose to confront the Jotunar. His entire body ached as if the raw, dark energy had hollowed him out and left only flesh to hold him together.

The captain of the guards looked as if he wanted to strike Dainn with considerable force, but seemed to think better of it when he met Dainn's eyes.

"Get out," he growled.

"Something has happened," Dainn said, holding the Jotunn's gaze. "Danny should be watched carefully. Since Miss Jones is absent—"

"Don't worry your pretty head, Elf," the Jotunn said. "We'll watch him."

Given no other choice, Dainn brushed past the captain and the other Jotunar, who sidled out of his way with muttered curses. But he was wrestling with an idea he could hardly accept, one that made any conflict with Loki's resentful minions no more important than the quarreling of ants over a crumb of bread.

When he stepped out of the hall, he closed the door and stood frozen, wondering how he could have failed to understand when he'd first seen the thing Danny had created.

No, not created. It had always been there.

The Eitr.

Dainn descended the stairs like an automaton. Loki would immediately have recognized the physical form of the substance as soon as he saw it on the monitor, but Dainn had no idea how *he* knew what it was. He had no memory of seeing it manifest before, yet it seemed utterly familiar, like his own reflection in a mirror. The important question was whether or not Loki had always suspected that Danny could summon and wield the Eitr. When he'd glimpsed Loki's face after Danny's display, Dainn had seen genuine surprise there. That would be a normal reaction, given that Odin himself was said to have lost his power to wield it.

But Danny was unlike any other creature born of the Eight Home-worlds. Did Loki assume that the Eitr was the source of Danny's unusual abilities, the very fuel that fed his magic? Was that what gave him the power to open portals to other parts of the world, teleport himself and others, and create functional manifestations, even at a distance?

Whatever Loki might believe, he had never shared such thoughts with Dainn. And he had meant to keep Dainn away from Danny after their son's display.

Was it because he didn't want Dainn exposed to the Eitr . . . because he knew that Dainn would find it familiar even before he recognized its physical form?

That made no sense. Dainn had never touched the Eitr in Asgard. If he had called upon it when he'd confronted the Jotunar, he hadn't known what he did. Surely Loki couldn't have guessed that it would pierce him, consume his blood, and try to swallow him up.

Another kind of beast, Dainn thought, *with a mind and appetite of its own.* Why had it attacked him? Had Danny tried to pull it away from Dainn to save his father's life?

And what of the vision of Mist? Had that been connected to the Eitr as well?

Perhaps Danny did not truly control it, and Loki knew it. Did he hope to reconnect to it through Danny?

Dainn laughed, the sound echoing in the wide entrance hall. All his speculation might be utterly wrong. He understood nothing. It was all like a dream, except for that lingering sense of hollowness.

Dainn reached the bottom step and listened for Loki. Instead, he heard the voices of newscasters from multiple channels bellowing from Loki's media room, all chattering about "trouble" in Civic Plaza.

A "protest," Vali had said. If the citizens of San Francisco had begun to recognize what was happening all around them, it was all to the good.

Unless Loki chose to crush them.

ꙮ

"Loki's piss."

Mist rolled out of bed, slapping her hand down on the bed table as she searched for her phone. The alarm clock told her it was almost noon . . . only about five hours since she'd been fighting a dozen Jotunar in an alley off Grant Avenue and barely two since Koji had lured her into bed. She was almost too groggy to understand what the man on the other end of the phone was saying.

The man was Rick, Bryn's second-in-command among the bikers. "I think you should get down here," he said, his voice gravelly with the same exhaustion that plagued all of them.

"What?" Mist said, clearing her throat. "Where?"

"You near a TV?"

Mist fumbled for the remote and turned on the small set she kept in the bedroom. The TV was already set on one of the local news stations, and at the moment the screen was filled with images of shouting faces, raised fists, and the seething bodies of a crowd of very angry people. The news ticker at the bottom of the screen informed interested viewers that there was a protest going on in front of City Hall, where the mayor had recently held his press conference.

"Any of our other people there?" she asked Rick as she scooted off the bed.

"Hild, a few of us Einherjar, Taylor. We aren't having much—"

His voice broke off to the sound of a scuffle, a raised voice, and the racket of a cell phone flying out of someone's hand.

"Hey," Koji's drowsy voice protested from the other side of the bed. "Where're you going?"

"Don't worry," Mist said, hastily throwing a shirt over her tank and tugging on her jeans and boots. "I don't expect I'll be gone too long."

"*Chikusho*," Koji said, swinging his legs over the bed. "Is that what I think it is?"

"Someone got fed up with the mayor's excuses," Mist said, buckling Kettlingr, in its knife shape, to her heavy belt. "For all I know Loki's behind this. The crowd could be seeded with Jotunar. If that's true"—she shrugged into her jacket—"this would be the first time he's come right out and caused a major public disturbance."

"Why?" Koji asked, padding up behind her. "Why now? What is he hoping to achieve?"

She started for the door. "I guess I'll find out soon enough."

Koji stopped her as she was leaving the room. "What if Loki has nothing to do with this?"

"Then the people of this city are waking up a lot sooner than I expected," she said. "They have got plenty of reasons to be pissed, and they'll still need protection."

He touched her arm. "Just be careful, okay?"

"I always am." She gave him a lopsided smile and jogged down the hall as she called Bryn's number. Bryn didn't pick up, but Rota did.

"Grab as many of our most experienced people as you can, and send them to City Hall," Mist said. "Tell them to be prepared for trouble, but no open fighting."

"What—" Rota began.

"Check the news. Hurry."

The wind was blowing hard under the perpetually gray skies as Mist mounted Silfr and headed north. Freya wasn't picking up her cell, either, and she could be anywhere, taking care of her "business" for the cause. Her glamour, Mist thought, would be extremely useful about now.

Or you can use yours. Mist clamped her lips together and gripped the accelerator.

The situation was just as bad as the news made it seem, and Mist had to use a few spells and a lot of skill to wind her way among the police cars and emergency vehicles blocking every street around Civic Center Plaza. Cops in riot gear were bearing down on the crowd, which by Mist's hasty estimation comprised about two hundred people. There were nearly as many women as men, and even a few kids.

What in Hel were they thinking of, bringing their kids into this? Did they think the cops would be more restrained?

Mist parked the bike as far out of the way as she could and chanted a quick warding spell to keep the authorities from noticing her as she skirted the cordon and strode toward the shouting mob. Signs waved above the roiling mass of faces, calling for the mayor's resignation and investigations into government and police corruption.

It was too soon, Mist thought, too abrupt. But there was real rage behind this, and the protest was rapidly deteriorating into something much more dangerous, like an animal that had been pushed to its limit and was beginning to bite back. Some of the people were wild-eyed and well beyond reason, screaming incoherently, while others hefted boards, chunks of concrete, and rebar from unfinished construction projects.

Mist caught sight of Rick and former Marine Captain Taylor, among the first and foremost of her mortal officers, standing near the ragged margin of the crowd. She had to force her way among the people who were turning to face the cops as if they thought they were invincible.

"Mist," Taylor acknowledged in a low voice as she joined them. "A few of us were keeping an eye on the protest when it started after the mayor's speech." He cast a glance toward the advancing cops. "It was peaceful until a short time after you left. We weren't able to determine exactly what happened, but suddenly it exploded into this."

"Haven't seen Loki," Rick added, "but he has to be in this somewhere."

"Possibly," Mist said, continuing to scan the crowd. "That's what we have to find out. Rick, get your people looking for anyone who might be Jotunn. You all know the signs. We need to isolate them from the crowd without attracting attention. Captain, when our other people arrive, try to calm the crowd as much as possible. No force, just persuasion. We want to minimize the chance of violence."

"Can you deal with the police yourself?" Taylor asked.

"I've got a call in to Freya."

Rick snorted. "Good luck with that. She's probably watching this on TV in some bigwig's penthouse. She won't get her hands dirty."

"Just do what I told you. Captain Taylor, you're in command. Good luck."

Without waiting for any last-minute protests, Mist worked her way through the crowd toward the cops. Some of them were armed with riot guns, and she also saw canisters of tear gas. Loki could get around the no-firearms rule because these particular cops wouldn't be in his army.

But if Loki was behind this and anyone was really hurt, especially a child, it could backfire badly on him and his political cronies. Maybe Loki was hoping that she'd slip up and reveal herself, appear on the news or get herself arrested. But he couldn't be stupid enough to believe she'd allow *that*.

The bellow of police megaphones drowned out the shouts and cries of the mob, demanding that the protesters put down their weapons. The command had no effect. Mist found herself at one of the barricades and strengthened her spell, shifting the air around her so that she could become as close to invisible as possible.

The hastily erected barricades consisted of the typical "bike rack" steel fencing, with the rounded top bar less than two inches wide. Mist sucked in a deep breath and jumped to the top of the nearest segment, precariously balancing herself and looking out over the commotion.

The cops in riot gear were beginning to press in on the crowd, and the cries of protest became shouts of defiance. The police with riot guns and canisters waited for the signal to let loose. She had to halt them in their tracks, and not with her sword or risky offensive magic.

She knew what she had to do. But she couldn't maintain the "invisibility" spell properly when she was concentrating on other magic. Though none of the police seemed to notice her, a sharp-eyed newswoman had turned in her direction, gesturing for her cameraman to focus on a particular area of the barricade.

Working quickly, Mist began to weave Runes-staves of protection to form a veil—not opaque enough to hide her completely, but capable of preventing anyone from making a positive identification. The news cameras would see a figure at the barricades, and nothing more.

Blocking her rage at Loki and her own self-disgust, she turned toward the nearest cops and drew on the seductive, honeyed warmth of the glamour. It seemed to flow up from the soles of her feet, through her legs and into her torso, pulsing around her heart, reaching out toward her arms and fingers.

She spread her arms and cast the warmth out from her body, aware of it as an almost physical thing that settled like sunlight on the hats, helmets, and shoulders of the men and women ready to strike. Some looked around in confusion; others lowered their weapons, dreamy smiles crossing their grim faces.

Then the glamour failed, rushing back to her, into her, nearly lifting her off her feet. She fell from the barricade, landing hard on her knees. Every last trace of magic was knocked out of her, leaving her helpless and exposed.

"Having trouble, Daughter?"

Freya appeared beside her, dressed with surprising restraint in a long cashmere sweater, destructed skinny jeans, and glossy leather knee-high boots. She surveyed the crowd with interest.

"Oh, my," she said. "This looks most unpleasant."

Mist scrambled to her feet, her face hot with shame. "We need to stop this," she said, "or innocent people will be hurt. Maybe killed."

"Rather modest of Loki, don't you think?" Freya said, wrinkling her nose. "Couldn't he have found a more . . . dramatic display, if he really wanted to impress us?" She glanced at Mist. "You attempted the glamour, did you not? What went wrong?"

"We don't have time to discuss it."

Freya examined her daughter through hooded eyes. "You failed because you are still afraid. But if you allow your fears to rule you now, you will never be free of them."

"Whatever you can do, do it *now*," Mist said, gritting her teeth. "*Please.*"

The Lady's hair drifted outward from her face, forming a halo, and there was a terrible light in her eyes that belied her smile. "There is no better time than now for me to help you learn to use the tools with which you were born."

7

Freya extended her hand. Mist stared at the outstretched fingers, so delicate and fine and beautiful, nails glossy and perfect.

Red nails, like poison-tipped claws. Poison that would tear into Mist's skin if she touched them, replacing her blood with something hot and dark and full of rage.

Like the beast.

Illusion, Mist thought. A hallucination brought on by her own selfish fears. But she ignored Freya's invitation and stepped back, shaking her head.

"I can't," she said. "I'm not ready."

Freya's expression grew cold. "Will you sacrifice more lives because of your cowardice?" she demanded. "Will you forever be less than you were meant to be?"

"I need to be ready to fight," Mist said, flinching from the contempt in her mother's eyes. "This will be easy for you. We can try another time, when it isn't—"

"There *is* no time," Freya said. She crooked her fingers, and Mist felt the pull of the glamour, the power of distorted, incongruous love.

Acting entirely on instinct, Mist threw up a shield of forge-Galdr, steel polished to a mirror sheen that reflected Freya's magic back upon herself. The goddess swayed, her lips parting in astonishment.

And then she laughed. "Very well," she said. "Watch me, and learn."

Freya lifted her hands, and the magic that felt so unnatural to Mist rose to swirl around her like thousands of iridescent butterflies, trailing the scent of primroses. Golden light radiated outward from her fingertips, as intangible as a painting of the wind. It drifted down on the police at almost precisely the moment when the first riot shield was about to strike the first protester.

The effect was almost instantaneous. People on both sides of the line slowed to a halt, as if they were walking through cold honey. It didn't take long before weapons were lowered and signs and rebar and chips of concrete dropped to the ground, angry voices dwindling to a confused murmur. All the faces—of cops, protesters, even Mist's own soldiers—turned toward Freya with awe and wonder, rapidly verging on outright worship.

And Freya was eating it up.

"Thanks," Mist said, trying to grab her mother's attention. "But I think my people and I can handle it from here."

"Oh?" Freya didn't even glance down at her. "How will you disperse the crowd once I am gone? What if these police are still under Loki's—"

She broke off, and her face drained of color. Her skin seemed to sag, losing its resilience, as if she'd subjected herself to one too many plastic surgeries. Hard lines bracketed her mouth, and her hair turned the color of gray mold.

Mist was too shocked to speak. Freya cast her a frightened glance and began to fall. Somehow, Mist caught her in time and eased her to the ground.

There was no curse quite adequate to encompass the situation, but Mist did her best. She jumped back up on the barricade and tried to snatch the withering strands of Freya's magic out of the air before they, too, disappeared.

She caught them just in time, feeling the warmth and love and soft, nurturing light envelop and embrace her. She let the emotions and the light flow out to drift over the crowd like a gentle fog made of summer breezes and lullabies.

For a moment Mist was lost in her mother's magic, only vaguely aware of words floating like flower petals through her consciousness, encouraging her to open herself to all that was, all she could have again, all she could ever be.

And all she had to do was reach out and take it.

A strong hand gripped her arm. She looked down at the mortal standing below her, into light brown eyes and earnest, battle-worn features.

She recognized him. His name was Captain Antoine Taylor, and he had been among the first mortals to come to her after the fight with Jormungandr. Her legs began to give way beneath her, and Taylor helped her down from the barricade.

"Are you all right?" he asked.

"What did you say to me?" she asked. "'Not yet,' what?"

He took her gently by the jaw and turned her head toward the crowd. "You did it," he said.

Mist looked. The protesters—no more than seemingly harmless individuals again—began to scatter and drift apart, their purpose forgotten, as the cops put away their weapons and began to withdraw.

"What in hell happened to *her*?" Taylor asked.

Following his gaze, Mist felt a stab of alarm. Freya was sprawled inelegantly on the asphalt, her hair lifeless, her face ravaged as if by years in harsh weather. She was unconscious, but there were no signs of visible injuries.

And Mist didn't remember how it had come about. There was a blank in her mind that started from the moment she'd fallen from the barricade.

Had she turned to the ancient magic, and lost herself for a brief time? Would Taylor have recognized such a change in her?

"I . . . don't know," she stammered. "She was fine a few minutes ago." She ran her palm over her damp hair. "You didn't see anything?"

"I couldn't tell exactly what was going on up here. I assumed you were shielding yourself from view." Taylor crouched beside Freya to check her pulse. "Slow, but she's breathing okay. I never thought I'd see her . . ." He squinted up at Mist. "Did Loki do this?"

"If he could do something like this to her, he'd already have won the war." She knelt beside her mother and lifted her hand. "Gather your people and get her back to HQ. Maybe Eir can figure out what's wrong."

"We should keep this quiet, I think."

"Yes. It won't be possible to hide this from our people indefinitely, but we should try to buy some time for her to recover, or at least figure out what the Hel went wrong." She laid Freya's hand on her chest and rose. "I'll be back as soon as I can."

"You got it, Chief."

While Taylor put in a call to his lieutenant, Mist went looking for Hild, Rick, and the others. Her gaze caught on the figure of a man standing on the other side of the rapidly emptying plaza, an immovable object amidst the current of the dispersing crowd.

From a distance, he looked exactly like Vidarr.

Mist started across the plaza at a fast jog. No one had seen Vidarr since Orn and Anna had been kidnapped and escaped, and Loki had beaten him within an inch of his life. She'd figured that he was either dead, or in hiding.

If he was here, it couldn't be coincidence. And he had to know he might be recognized.

But he'd once said he'd be happy to stand back while Mist, Freya, and Loki destroyed each other. Presumably, he still had some divine magic to call on, but it wouldn't be enough to spark a riot like this one.

"Mist!"

Hild stepped into her path, forcing her to a sudden stop. By the time she dodged around the Valkyrie, Vidarr—or the man who looked like him—had vanished.

"Did you see him?" Mist demanded.

"Who?" Hild asked, looking over her shoulder.

Mist cursed under her breath. "Come on. Let's find the others."

Rota, Rick, a couple of the Einherjar, and three more recent recruits were crossing the plaza to meet them, while a third group, led by Bryn, were gathered at the corner of McAllister and Larkin.

When they were all together, Mist led them to a quiet area of Fulton beside the Asian Art Museum, well away from any potential eavesdroppers.

Mist was relieved that no one spoke up about Freya. Either the others hadn't seen her fall, or they thought better of advertising the fact.

"Did you find any Jotunar?" she asked.

"That's the weird thing," Rota said. "We didn't."

"Tall, blond hair and beard, shoulders like a linebacker?"

"Sounds like you're describing Vali," Hild said, dropping a weathered hand to the hilt of her sword, which, to mortal eyes, was no larger or deadlier than a small knife. "Did you see him?"

"I'm not sure who I saw," Mist said.

"If it *was* Vali," Rick said, "that would prove that Loki's involved, doesn't it?"

"Not necessarily. Something's off about this whole thing. It's lacking Loki's usual flair, and he wouldn't have done it just to show off. He'd have something specific to gain."

"He'd have known you'd show up for something like this," Bryn said. "He'd probably have expected Freya, too."

"A trap?" Hild asked.

"At this point, we have no idea if Loki was involved at all."

"You mean this thing just blew up for no reason?" Rick asked.

"There's plenty of reason for people to be pissed off," Rota said. "But if Loki didn't start it, he knows about it now."

"We'll talk about that when we're back at HQ," Mist said. "Bryn, you and your people spread out and make sure it's really over. Report anything or anyone unusual, no matter how trivial it may seem. Hild, take your team home. We'll debrief in two hours."

While the others separated to carry out their orders, Mist returned to the side street where she'd left her bike, Silfr. The news crews had already packed up and left, the cops had dispersed, and the plaza was as silent as if nothing had ever happened . . . except for the litter of signs and rebar and concrete the protesters had left behind them.

Mist knew cursed well that it wasn't really over.

Bending low over the handlebars, Mist accelerated as she wove through the freeway traffic, and wondered how things could get any worse.

The wind snatched the laugh from her throat.

◑◐

Gabi switched off the TV.

"Shit," she said. "That was close."

Anna shivered. "Close" didn't begin to describe it. She still wasn't sure how she'd been able to observe Mist and Freya when hardly anyone else in Civic Center Plaza had noticed them; even Gabi, who'd been with Mist almost from the beginning, hadn't really *seen* how mother and daughter had worked their magic to calm both the police and the protesters. It was as if they'd been completely invisible.

In fact, the reporter had made a big deal out of how the crisis had suddenly broken up for no apparent reason, and speculated that there must have been some quiet negotiation going on behind the scenes.

"If Loki's gonna start doing stuff like this right in the open," Gabi remarked, "it's gonna get bad even sooner than I thought."

"Is he that confident?" Anna murmured as Gabi got up to fetch them fresh cups of coffee.

Gabi swore in eloquent Spanish. "This *cabron,* his problem is that he thinks everyone else is stupid. But he didn't win, did he?"

No, Anna thought, he hadn't "won." But this could just be a test case, a warning shot to see how Freya and Mist would handle a more public conflict. If he kept escalating, the truth couldn't stay hidden long. People would begin to see things they wouldn't understand, and there would be no putting the worms back in the can.

"You been holed up in that computer room too long," Gabi said, returning with the replenished mugs. "You gotta get out and see what it's like."

"I haven't seen *you* go out much," Anna said, accepting her coffee with a nod of thanks.

Gabi set down her mug and held her hands up in front of her, wiggling her fingers. "There ain't enough time to learn everything I need to know, and—" Gabi broke off. "Did you hear that?"

Anna followed her gaze to the door on the other side of the warehouse floor. Because of the riot, the entire building was empty, including the walled-off sleeping areas, the various offices, and the infirmary.

"I didn't hear anything," Anna said. "But they'll be coming home now. At least no one was hurt."

"As far as we know." Gabi gulped down her coffee. "I gotta go. One of the Alfar healers said he'd let me try working on an elf with a minor wound, to see if I can use my abilities on non-mortals."

"That's quite an honor," Anna said. "And quite a vote of confidence in you."

"Yeah. Well, they ain't as conceited as they used to be."

Anna thought of Hrolf, whom she hadn't seen much at all since their return from Norway many months ago. *He'd* never been conceited. In fact, she'd liked him quite a bit.

But even if the feeling had been mutual, she didn't have time for personal relationships. She didn't want them. She'd lost someone she'd believed would never desert her, and she wasn't going to let that happen again.

"Don't work too hard," Gabi said as she finished washing out her mug in the sink and set it on the rack. "I don't need *you* to get sick, too."

"I'll be careful," Anna said. She finished her own coffee, her thoughts already on her work. She was sure she was coming close to locating one of the five remaining Valkyrie. If she could bring in another Treasure before Loki got to it, she could feel as if she was still worth something to the allies.

She had to do better. She had to prove . . .

She slowed as she approached the large office that housed the computers. The door was ajar, and she never left it open. The information squirreled away inside those computers was far too valuable to leave unattended.

"Hello?" she said, keeping her distance. "Who's there?"

A muscular arm wrapped around her neck from behind and began to drag her backward across the warehouse floor. She opened her mouth to yell, but her kidnapper slapped his other hand over her mouth and continued to pull her toward one of the factory's seldom-used side doors. His harsh, hot breath washed over her hair, but he held her at such an angle that she couldn't see his face. She only knew that he was big, strong, and easily capable of breaking her in half.

Like most of the Jotunar working for Loki.

Since muffled pleading wasn't likely to be effective, Anna let herself go limp. She certainly couldn't resist him physically, but if he thought she was easy prey she might have a chance to escape.

The Jotunn uncovered her mouth briefly as he opened the door. This time, Anna didn't try to scream. She relaxed all her muscles and forced him to carry her outside.

And then he stopped, as if he had nothing to fear from the mortal warriors and Valkyrie and Alfar who were bound to show up any minute. He pushed her against the wall and pinned her there with one huge hand on her shoulder.

She looked into his face.

"Vidarr!" she gasped.

Odin's son merely stared at her, expressionless, not so much as a glint of malice in his eyes. He didn't move, didn't speak, merely held her there as if he were waiting for something. Or some*one*.

She *hadn't* imagined seeing him in Norway. She'd thought she'd shot him, but here he was, and there was nothing of the menacing Nazi in him now.

Still, it took all her courage to meet his flat gaze. "I don't know how you got past the wards," she said. "But we're not in the wilderness now, and any second now this whole area will be swarming with people."

He didn't respond.

"If you let me go," she said, "I won't tell anyone I saw you. Everyone thinks you're either dead or hiding, so no one will think to look for you. I'll say—"

"Say nothing."

The voice wasn't Vidarr's, but it was more than familiar. Anna's heart thumped once, hard, and then accelerated into a fast, erratic beat.

"Orn," she said.

Abruptly Vidarr released her, and the raven took his familiar place on her shoulder, stropping his beak against her hair in an unmistakable gesture of affection.

"Orn," she breathed, reaching up to stroke his breast feathers. "I'm so glad you're back."

"I, too," Orn said.

"Where have you been? Why is Vidarr—"

"He cannot hurt you," Orn said, craning his neck to study her with one black marble eye. "He is nothing."

Orn's voice was clear, the words as distinct and deliberate and intelligent as they had been at his last meeting with her in Norway.

When he made the others forget, Anna thought, her own memory beginning to return. "You were hiding," she said, glancing to the left and right along the warehouse wall. "From Loki?"

Orn chuckled in a way that was eerily human. "Open your hands," he said.

Baffled, she did as he told her, holding her palms up. Something small and cool and hard dropped into her right hand.

The pendant. Instinctively she closed her fingers around it, feeling complete again for the first time since Orn had taken it away.

"Thank you," she said, tucking it into her pocket. "Orn, what's going on?"

"Much," he said. "You will see."

He cocked his head toward Vidarr, who stepped back several paces. There was still no life in his face, and he moved like a huge, remote-controlled robot.

Anna knew she should be happy to see him brought so low. But there was something deeply disturbing about seeing a man so full of life—even if it was nasty life—turned into a virtual zombie.

"What happened to him?" Anna asked. "Is he under a spell?"

"A spell, yes," Orn croaked, obvious amusement in his voice. "He is very obedient now."

"Then you're still working for Odin?"

"Always." He butted his head against her cheek.

"Do you know what's been going on with Loki? He's getting more powerful every day. He probably thinks the Aesir will never come."

"Odin is very near."

"Then Mist needs to know right away."

When he had taken the shape of a parrot, Orn had always been very expressive in spite of the limitations of his avian features. But *this* Orn radiated emotion in a way Anna had never experienced before.

And what he radiated now was menace. For the first time, Anna thought to wonder why he'd had Vidarr drag her out here as if she were a prisoner instead of choosing a less unpleasant way of attracting her attention.

"No," he said. "I need to see."

Anna swallowed. "See what?"

"You will watch Freya," he said. "And Mist."

"Watch them?" Anna winced as Orn's talons bit through her shirt. "Why?"

"Freya is not Odin's friend."

His meaning hit Anna all at once, and she was desperately glad that she had the wall at her back.

"I . . . I don't understand," she said. "I thought Odin and Freya were working together to—"

"No," Orn said, clacking his beak. "No."

Anna didn't want to believe him. It wasn't that she liked Freya; she most certainly didn't. The goddess was vain, dismissive of her "inferiors," and quick to use any means necessary to get what she wanted. She treated her own daughter little better than the rest of them . . . unless she needed something.

But if Orn was right, the implications were staggering.

She opened her mouth to ask all the questions bouncing frantically inside her head, but only one came out.

"Why Mist?" she asked.

"To be sure," he said. He began to croon, an aimless little melody more suitable for a songbird than a corvid. "Be sure of her."

Because Orn didn't trust her. Freya was not Odin's friend. And Mist was Freya's daughter.

Was that why he'd never given Mist the message everyone was so sure he had for her? Why he hadn't come back when he might have done so any time since Norway, or even before?

But when, after going to such lengths to find Mist the first time, had he changed his mind?

"Mist . . . serves the Aesir," she said, her thoughts beginning to drift along with Orn's odd little song. "She serves Odin."

"*You* serve Odin," he said. And suddenly she was back in Norway during the war, wearing a different face . . . in the interrogation room, refusing to tell them—tell Vidarr—where to find the bird, hiding the pendant, refusing to betray what she knew.

What she'd *always* known. Because if Mist were to fail, there would be another to help complete the plan.

"There is more," Orn said.

While she listened, numb and wired up all at once, he told her the other things she needed to do.

"I understand," Anna said. "But I can't promise I can get what you want."

"You will," Orn said. "Open your hand."

She wondered what new thing he was going to give her. But when she held her palm open again, he began to peck at it . . . not hard, but with just enough force to sting a bit. He continued to croon as he tapped out some kind of pattern or design on her skin, working with precision and concentration.

When he lifted his head, Anna felt as if some force had seeped from her skin into her bloodstream, pumping through her body and giving her a sense of strength she'd never experienced before.

Magic, she thought. Orn's magic.

"Three spells," he said, looking her in the eye. "Gleipnir, Jarngreipr,

Sleipnir. Touch the Chain and the Glove, and find the Steed. Choose carefully."

Though he didn't explain, Anna understood him. Orn needed her to get to two of the Treasures locked away in the vault: Gleipnir and Jarngreipr. All she had to do was gain access long enough to touch them with the pendant. But she knew that Sleipnir wasn't in the camp, and she had to find out where he was.

She had a pretty good idea where to begin.

"How do you want me to contact you?" she asked.

"I will find you," Orn said, "my Valkyrie."

8

"What did he tell you?" Loki asked, standing beside the living room couch with his arms crossed and a surprisingly serious look on his face.

He didn't seem to notice Dainn's makeshift bandage or the blood spots on his shirt, for which Dainn was extremely grateful. Eventually Loki would realize that the wound had opened again, but Dainn knew that this interrogation was likely to be worse than the last, and he had no intention of giving Loki more information than he was required to.

"What of the protest?" he countered, pretending to gaze out the expansive window at the endlessly spinning storm clouds that hung over the city.

"Oh, no," Loki said, strolling up behind him. "There's no squeezing out of this one, my Dainn. You disobeyed my orders and forced your way into Danny's room. I expect a thorough report, at the very least."

"There is little to tell," Dainn said. "I attempted to question Danny, but he was unable to answer, and fell into his quiescent state. I saw no further sign of this energy, or magic, or whatever it may be."

"Indeed. It seems strange, then, that my Jotunar were blasted by light which conveniently burned out the cameras."

Dainn glanced at the room's surveillance camera with its dark, empty face turned toward Loki's favorite armchair. "When did you decide to break our agreement that my sessions with Danny would not be monitored?" he asked.

"I made that agreement as an experiment, to see if you would be honest with me with regard to your progress. Your most recent lies—"

"I did not lie."

"Your recent *evasions* give me no reason to believe that leaving you to your own devices is anything but a disadvantage to me." Loki's eyes narrowed. "What was the source of the light?"

Thank the Norns, Dainn thought, that no one had seen the manifestation of Mist . . . or reported his use of the strange magic against the Jotunn guards. "It happened as I entered the room," he said. "I was blinded for a few moments, and so did not observe its source."

"The *source* is obvious. What else did Danny do?"

"Nothing."

Loki grabbed Dainn's shoulder and spun him around. "I am giving you one more chance to tell me the truth before I decide on the proper punishment for your recalcitrance. I suggest you take that chance."

"Punishment?" Dainn said flatly, jerking away. "What have I to fear now?"

"When you first came to me, I gave you the choice to leave without Danny. You stayed to protect him from me, fearing that I might use his abilities in a way that might harm him."

"And you would do that to him now, merely to punish me?"

"We observed something unusual today," Loki said, pressing one palm to the window. A delicate design of icy spirals unfurled from beneath his hand, quickly mutating into a jagged, abstract pattern that nearly covered the glass. "If you tell me what you know of it, there will be no need to question his future welfare."

Dainn was almost tempted to tell Loki that Danny had asked if his "mother" loved him, but he bit back the impulse. He would have to reveal just enough of the truth to convince Loki that he had neither the will nor desire to lie.

"Danny remembers Mist," he said.

Loki dropped his hand from the window, and tiny flakes of ice broke from the glass and tumbled to the carpet. "How?" he asked. "Did you tell him?"

"Not with words," Dainn said. He put a safer distance between himself and Loki, turning his back to hide his expression. "You asked me if I'd informed Mist of the danger her mother presents to her. I left a brief note for her when you permitted me to return to her one last time. I told her not to trust her mother. But my warning was not specific enough."

"And why is that, my Dainn? Why were you so slow to tell her the truth? Were you afraid how she would react when she learned that your betrayal went so far beyond what she'd ever guessed?"

"It doesn't matter now," Dainn said, looking away to conceal his shame. "We were speaking of Danny. I believe that he senses my concern for her."

"Senses?" Loki's footsteps whispered on the carpet behind him. "You mean that he reads your mind?"

"We already know that he takes the source of his manifestations from our thoughts. But on this occasion, Danny did more than acquire images from my mind. He absorbed my feelings as well. He read my *heart*."

"How poetic," Loki said, the words dripping venom. "You are suggesting that he has developed empathic abilities as well as the telepathic skills he already possesses. And evidently a much closer bond with you than you previously admitted."

"This has never happened before."

"So you say." Loki locked his hands behind his back and paced back and forth in front of the window. "Did he *speak* of Mist?"

"He did. His words were vague, but it was clear that he recognized that she is being threatened." Dainn hesitated, hoping his lies were credible. "He does not seem to remember Freya, nor did he refer to the beast. But whatever he may recall of his experiences with Mist, it is clear that he regards her in a favorable light."

"Because you do?" Loki came to a sudden stop. "Is this sudden change in his abilities connected in some way to his display of this new magic?"

"As I said, he showed no inclination to repeat what he had done. I saw no change in the room that might indicate what he was attempting to achieve, if he acted consciously at all."

Loki was quiet for a moment, though his steps quickened and his mouth was set in a hard, narrow line.

"What else has he gleaned from your emotions, I wonder?" he asked. "Perhaps your desire to see me fail?"

"If he had acted, even unconsciously, on such a desire," Dainn said, "then neither he nor I would still be here."

"And so you have run out of excuses. If Danny responds according to what he senses from you, you will be directly responsible for his failure to act on my commands." His lips turned down. "Why do you tell me what is so obviously of no benefit to you? Do you truly believe I would harm our son?"

"I know that not all your threats are empty." He went on before Loki could protest. "What if I could convince Danny to work directly against Freya?"

Loki's brows arched. "You take my breath away with these unexpected reversals. Why would you suddenly wish to turn him against my enemies?"

Dainn dodged the question. "If I can help Danny remember her, he may also remember what she tried to do to him. As I said, he is still incapable of making complex moral judgments—"

"Unless you make them for him."

"But he is mature enough to recognize a personal enemy, and the need to defend himself."

Orange flame danced along the perimeter of Loki's irises. "Against Freya, not Mist."

"It is Mist I wish to save."

Loki dropped onto the couch, assuming an air of boredom. "And I wish to destroy both of them."

"The mortals have a saying: 'If wishes were horses . . .'"

"Are you calling me a beggar?" Loki asked with deceptive amusement. "I have most of this city in the palm of my hand. Mist and Freya have . . ." He made an eloquent, dismissive gesture with his fingers.

"You are not yet a king," Dainn said. "You have power, and your allies outnumber Freya's and Mist's by a considerable margin. Yet when Freya came to Midgard in her borrowed body, their coalition of mortal and elven allies defeated your Jotunar and took Sleipnir."

"Conditions have changed considerably since then."

"Perhaps." Dainn moved closer to the couch, still wary of Loki's uncertain temper. "But Mist and the Lady worked closely together, using their powers in tandem. If Mist had known of Freya's intentions and confronted her mother with an accusation of filicide, it would have shattered the coalition, and their alliance."

With a deep sigh, Loki leaned his head against the back of the couch and closed his eyes. "From what my observers have reported, that alliance hangs by a thread even now."

"Mist will not abandon it without good reason."

"And that would mean convincing her that Freya truly means to destroy her. Are you now admitting that you doubt Mist's ability to resist her mother?"

"I deceived myself, yes."

Stretching his arms above his head, Loki chuckled. "At last, you admit to a lie."

"*You* seem uncertain of the truth. Have you considered how much Freya's abilities will increase once she has absorbed Mist's soul?"

There was a razor-edged blade hidden within Loki's toothy smile. "Mist has shown some ability, but I see no reason to worry about any contribution she might make to Freya's magic."

"You are lacking a few particular facts that may change your perspective," Dainn said. "When I was sent to Midgard, I was to prepare Mist for Freya's coming by opening her mind and destroying any defenses she might unconsciously turn against her mother. But I failed to perform my task. Instead, I determined to give Mist some means to resist." Dainn clasped his hands behind his back to keep them from trembling. "But as I did so, I encountered . . . certain talents even Freya was not aware her daughter possessed. I could not properly advise Mist on their use, but now Freya believes that she has more to gain from seizing Mist's soul than a strong, healthy Asgardian body capable of containing her power."

Loki sat up, narrow-eyed and alert. "Speak plainly," he said.

"Mist has done a few remarkable things, but there has been no consistency in her capacity to control her magic. She has the Galdr and Freya's glamour, but she has been unwilling or unable to call mortal allies as I urged her to do. In many ways, she is weak."

Loki rose, sauntered toward Dainn, and cupped his hand around Dainn's neck, pressing his thumb into the hollow of Dainn's throat. "You talk her down a little too eagerly," he said.

"I . . . merely meant that she is afraid . . . to strive for her full potential, of becoming like Freya or accepting her divine heritage. She will not use the authority her lineage has bestowed upon her."

"That, my dear Dainn, is precisely why I have no reason to fear her."

"But it is . . . very possible that the Lady can awaken these untapped abilities within Mist, as I could not, and join them with her own. She will not be . . . constrained by her daughter's fears, and what comes of that joining may well become far more than the sum of its parts."

"I presume you are trying to make a point," Loki said, tightening his fingers behind Dainn's neck.

"The point is . . . that Freya is already winning more influence in the city, with politicians and prominent citizens who oppose the policies you have set through the mayor and his cohorts. I have seen her more and more often on the news, flaunting her glamour and winning the hearts of people who could easily become your enemies. Once Freya gets what she wants, she won't hesitate to use that same glamour to summon thousands of mortals to her side. They will be cannon-fodder for her, as your mortal followers are to you. She'll use up as many of them as she must to defeat you."

"Which Mist would never do."

"And if Freya gains more power from Mist, she . . . will pose a direct threat you cannot dismiss."

"Can't I?" Loki's grip turned into a caress. "Your concern for me is deeply moving."

"There would be no need for concern of any kind if you rob Freya of her chance to steal Mist's soul."

"If all this is your way of asking for an opportunity to warn her again . . ."

Dainn closed his eyes, repulsed by Loki's touch. "I believe . . . I hope that Freya can only succeed if she takes Mist by surprise, or tricks her into dropping her guard. Mist will never let that occur once she learns the full truth. And Freya is facing a significant problem that would provide you with an additional advantage if you were to act quickly."

"Do enlighten me, by all means," Loki said, running his thumb up and down the side of Dainn's neck.

"Freya did not tell me what would become of Mist's body when she seized it, but this I do know: the shape the Lady wears now cannot contain her magic indefinitely." He swallowed. "It is only an interim solution, and I suspect that by now she is growing weak, no matter how well she conceals it. If she fails to take Mist's body soon, she will weaken still more."

"You *suspect*."

"She has shown no ability to create her own physical form, as she once claimed she could do. If she cannot take Mist or find another compatible body . . ."

"Warning Mist may lead to her mother's death."

"Or at least severe debilitation."

"But all this hangs on Mist's ability to resist her mother's impending assault." Loki pushed his face closer to Dainn's, his breath warming Dainn's skin. "You have taken great trouble to emphasize that Mist is afraid of rising to her full potential. Why should she have the courage to stand against Freya?"

"That is a different kind of courage, which Mist has never lacked. And even if she fails, her resistance could still weaken Freya to the point where your victory would be assured."

Loki twisted his hand. "You plot almost as well as I do, with that blandly innocent face of yours."

Dainn struggled to breathe. "The fact remains . . . that if you help Mist defeat Freya, it is unlikely that she could . . . stand against you, even if Freya's allies fight beside her."

"So I can easily conquer Mist."

Always couch lies in truth, Dainn thought desperately. "I don't know if it . . . will be easy. Only that you will suffer high losses if you face Freya, with Mist's . . . untapped talent at her command."

"And when I defeat our brave Valkyrie?"

"There is always . . . a chance that you'll allow her to keep her life."

Grasping Dainn's hair, Loki pulled his head back at a painful angle. "You won't beg me to spare her?"

"Even I know that . . . there are limits to your generosity."

"And yet you would risk this entire world for the sake of one female?"

"Yes."

Releasing Dainn with a sudden shove, Loki began to pace again. "The truth is that you hope Mist will rise to the occasion and defeat me, in spite of the odds against her. She'll forgive you and fall into your loving arms."

"I do not expect forgiveness."

"Is she aware that you are Danny's father?"

Dainn swallowed to ease the ache in his throat. "How could she? I have not seen her since you told me."

"How do you suppose she will react when she finds out?"

The mockery in Loki's voice was laced with anger. He clearly believed that Dainn would be ashamed.

And he *would* have been, before he knew Danny.

"If it will give you satisfaction, tell her," Dainn said. "Unlike the Lady, she would never harm him."

Loki did not misunderstand. A thin film of ice formed on nearly every surface of the room. "Freya will never have another opportunity to touch him," he snarled.

"Danny escaped you before, when he took me to Asbrew and opened the portal to the steppes. Whatever influence I may have on him, I cannot stop him if he chooses to leave again."

The frost thickened, glazing Dainn's hair. "So alerting Mist will protect him?" Loki asked. He stared at a Nicholas I Russian vase Dainn knew to be worth hundreds of thousands of dollars. Cracks formed in the delicate surface, widening into veins of ice that might have been beautiful had they not been so destructive. "Mist is unlikely to heed any further warnings from me . . . or from you, for that matter."

"Surely there is some gesture of good faith—"

"From Loki Scar-lip?" The vase burst apart, the pieces flying in every direction. One of them struck Dainn on the arm and might have injured him if not for the protection of his sleeve. He didn't move.

Loki expelled his breath and permitted the ice to dissipate into the air, leaving the furnishings and walls undamaged and Dainn's hair dry. Only the scattered shards of the vase remained as tokens of his anger.

"You asked about the protest," he said. "Perhaps what I tell you will alter your opinions."

There was a strange note in Loki's voice, as if he were about to reveal some unpleasant secret. Dainn's heart began to race.

"What happened?" he asked slowly.

"The peasants attempted a minor revolt, armed with rubble and illegible signs."

Dainn calmed himself with a deep, slow breath. "Why?" he asked. "Have they a quarrel with the current administration?"

Loki shot him an irritable glance and fell onto the couch again. "Something or someone provoked them into an act of rebellious stupidity."

"Freya?"

"She and Mist were at the protest, making a show of attempting to stop it."

"Attempting. Do you have evidence that Freya started it?"

"She would have much to gain if she suggested to her more influential mortal allies that the mayor was responsible for such a disturbance."

"What was Mist's part in this?"

"Didn't I mention that she arrived first? She tried to control the mob alone, and failed. Freya arrived shortly thereafter, and summoned the glamour."

Adrenaline rushed through Dainn's body. "Did she succeed?"

"According to my observers, Freya extended her hand to Mist, perhaps with an offer that they work together. Mist evidently refused, at which point Freya took her place. And that is where it becomes interesting." Loki's eyes brightened with malice. "As her spells began to have their effect, she fell, and Mist took *her* place."

"Fell?"

"Perhaps 'collapsed' would be the better word."

Suddenly Dainn realized how Loki had manipulated him. He had known all along that Freya had been weakened in some way. But Loki's revelation was significant in another sense, and it stunned Dainn into silence.

"Mist completed the Lady's work?" Dainn said at last.

"Indeed. My observers tell me that Mist seemed . . . not quite herself. In fact, her behavior was unusually grandiose. Perhaps her mother is finally rubbing off on her."

The room seemed to darken, and Dainn was compelled to concentrate in order to keep himself on his feet.

Not quite herself. But it couldn't have happened so easily, so quickly, under such unexceptional circumstances.

Could Danny's manifestation of Mist have been a warning that what his father most feared was already happening?

"You imply that Freya has taken Mist," Dainn said quietly.

"You never did tell me how the annexation is supposed to work." Loki tapped his lower lip. "I wonder if what my observers witnessed was a literal exchange of bodies, Freya taking Mist's and Mist briefly trapped in Freya's before she fell, mentally and literally."

"If you retained more intelligent observers, they might have been able to tell you."

For a very long few seconds, Loki studied Dainn with surprise rather than anger. "I must admit that you're doing an excellent job of pretending to accept the possibility that all your hopes have been destroyed."

"Possibility. You are not certain. It may be that *Freya* fell. Would that not be the simpler explanation?"

"I wonder if Danny might tell us?"

Loki turned on his heel, walked out into the foyer, and strode to the stairs. Dainn followed, his feet leaden.

When they reached the second floor, Loki ignored the nervous salutes of the new Jotunar guards and went straight to Danny's door. He paused just inside the room to study Danny, who sat in his customary position on the bed, apparently unaware of his parents' presence.

Forcing his legs to move, Dainn sat on the edge of the bed and spoke to Danny softly, using every method he had developed over the long months. He projected his emotions: his love for Danny, his fear for Mist, his hatred of the beast.

Danny didn't respond. He continued to rock, his deep blue eyes staring at nothing, his lips slightly parted.

"If this is an example of your efforts to communicate," Loki said, "it is no wonder you—"

"There is another way to get the information we seek," Dainn said, rising from the bed. "When will you be meeting Freya again?"

Loki's ginger brows lifted quizzically. "I don't make a habit of *meeting* with my enemies, unless it's to kill them."

"Yet you see Freya when you attend the same social functions, seeking the same allies among those mortals with wealth and influence."

"True." Loki circled the room and seated himself in Miss Jones's chair. "Though the pickings have grown sparser of late."

"And you still require Danny's help with manifestations that you will presumably use to frighten, blackmail, or bribe these potential allies. You suggested that you might take me to meet these men so that I might help Danny envision them." He paused. "I assume that

Freya will continue her social activities, regardless of what has become of Mist."

"And you want to meet her?" Loki said, holding Dainn's gaze. "Why?"

"Because when I see her, I'll know if Mist is still alive."

9

Loki shook his head. "I can determine that for myself."

"Perhaps not as easily as you believe. If Freya has taken Mist's body and power, she will require only a little magic to maintain an illusion of the appearance by which the people of this city recognize her. She will bend the remainder of her magic to concealing what she has done."

"But *you* will know," Loki said, lips curling. "'Love looks not with the eyes, but with the mind.' Your *feelings* will tell you."

Dainn knew it would do no good to protest. Loki was convinced that Dainn was "in love" with Mist, as the mortals so romantically put it.

He was not wrong.

"Of course, it should be easy enough to determine if Freya was damaged in the fall," Loki mused, smoothing one ginger brow with a long fingertip. "Her absence from the usual functions will tell us. But if what you most fear is true, you will suffer, and I will not be displeased to see it."

Dainn moved to stand in front of the chair. "If my suffering is inadequate to satisfy you," he said, "you may content yourself with the knowledge that I will do everything within my power to destroy Freya."

"Revenge?"

"By whatever means that do not involve harming those I once cared for."

"Your conditions are somewhat inconvenient."

"Those I desire to protect will be no threat to you when Freya is gone."

Loki rose, assumed a thoughtful expression, and walked around the room, pausing now and again to glance at Danny. "Suppose I permit you to see Freya, and you realize that she has not taken Mist after all?"

"My previous request to warn Mist still holds. And I will ask Danny to create the specific manifestations you requested."

"Even though you have no idea what I'll use them for?"

"As long as no innocents are harmed as a result."

"You would declare this entire world innocent."

"No," Dainn said. "Any mortal you believe you can corrupt is not likely to be innocent."

"Touché," Loki said. "I must say that I'm intrigued by this new ruthlessness. If I didn't know better, I'd suspect that the beast was returning."

Dainn pretended not to hear the comment. "You will take me to see her," he said.

"I will think on it. Your good behavior may influence my decision."

"I will do what is necessary."

"Yes," Loki said curtly. "Only what is necessary." He frowned, consulting some inner calendar. "There is a charitable function at the Fairmont in two days. That should do nicely." He tapped the wall intercom. "Call Miss Jones," he said to the Jotunar outside. "Inform the kitchen that we're ready to dine." He stepped away from the wall and took Dainn's arm. "I wouldn't have our pleasant little domestic life disturbed by Mist's family problems."

"Family," Danny said.

As one, Dainn and Loki turned to stare at the bed. Danny was awake again . . . awake, and with an expression on his face that Dainn had never seen before.

"What is it, Danny?" Loki asked, approaching the bed cautiously.

Danny turned his head to follow Loki's movements with eyes far darker than they should be. "I want my family," he said distinctly.

Family, Dainn thought, chilled by the obvious comprehension in

Danny's eyes. Loki's other children were the deadly enemies of the Aesir: Jormungandr, the giant serpent Danny had already manifested to attack Mist, at Loki's behest; Hel, Loki's daughter and ruler of the afterworld, Niflheim; and Fenrir, the monstrous wolf once destined to kill Odin himself.

But there was another, the one Danny had sought and found on the steppes. One with whom he had already formed a powerful bond.

Sleipnir, now in Mist's hands. Or Freya's.

"An excellent idea," Loki said, clapping his hands. "Can you fetch them for us, Danny?"

"No," Dainn said, moving toward the bed.

But there was something implacable in Danny's gaze when he looked at his father. Something that reminded Dainn not of Loki, but of the darkness within himself.

"I want to see Slippy," Danny said. "I miss him."

"Of course," Loki said. "We all do. Don't we, my Dainn?"

Dainn said nothing. Even if Danny remembered that Sleipnir had gone with the allies after the battle at the portal, surely he wouldn't understand the deadly consequences if Loki got his hands on one of the most important Treasures of the gods.

"Do you know where Sleipnir is, my son?" Loki asked, crouching beside the bed.

"I know," Danny said.

"Then why haven't you brought him here? You can move people from one place to another, just as you did with your father. Surely you can do the same with Sleipnir."

"Do you expect him to walk into your enemy's stronghold and snatch Sleipnir out from under their noses?" Dainn asked. "Would you put him directly into Freya's hands?"

"Of course not," Loki purred, his gaze locked with Danny's. "Why do you want him now, Danny? Why not before?"

"*He* is here," Danny said.

"Who?"

"Papa?" Danny said, looking at Dainn.

"Look at *me*, Danny," Loki commanded. He reached out to touch

Danny's cheek. Danny jerked his head away. Dainn grabbed Loki's shoulder before he could reach for Danny again.

Instantly Loki turned and flung Dainn against the wall with a blast of ice, pinning his shirt with jagged shards as if he were one of Danny's sketches.

Rage boiled over in Dainn's chest, surged up into his throat, and exploded inside his skull. For a moment the entire room flickered in yellow and red, seen through the eyes of a monster.

Hiding, Danny had said. The beast not gone, but watching. Waiting for the right moment to reappear.

The shock of the change turned rage to sickness, and Dainn struggled to keep the contents of his stomach where it belonged. Loki hadn't moved from the bed, but Danny continued to stare at Dainn, his eyes wide but unafraid.

"Never interfere between me and my son again," Loki hissed, his eye ablaze with orange fire. He released the spell that pinned Dainn to the wall, and Dainn staggered as the ice shards melted and frigid water soaked his shirt. He managed to keep his feet, but he remained where he was, still stunned by what he had experienced.

Not now, he thought. *Not with Danny.*

"I promise that we will retrieve your brother for you," Loki said to Danny as if there had been no interruption, "but we will need your help."

"How?" Dainn asked, shivering as rivulets of icy water trickled under his collar. "If you believed you could get past Freya's wards, you would have done it long ago."

"Now we have Danny's cooperation."

"You may have forgotten that Sleipnir is not a mindless object," Dainn said. "He will fight you."

"Sleipnir is also my son."

"Whom you gave to Odin. He no longer owes you any loyalty."

"But he *is* fond of Danny."

"Stop," Danny said abruptly. He stood up on the bed and turned to face the wall behind him. Light exploded like a flash bomb, and the wall began to shimmer, dissolving into a pocket of deep shadow encircled by icy gemstones that reflected a thousand colors at all once. The fine hairs bristled all over Dainn's body.

A bridge, he thought. A bridge to the Void.

Something burst through the opaline surface of the wall, all heavy black pelt, burning red eyes, and gaping jaws. It landed four-footed on the floor beside the bed, swinging its head toward Danny.

A wolf, twice as large as any known to man, with a pelt like a lion's mane and teeth as long and sharp as one of Mist's daggers.

Fenrisulfr. Fenrir, Loki's son. And utterly *real.*

Dainn moved before he could think, diving past Loki onto the bed and curling his body around Danny. Loki jumped up, facing his other son with astonishment.

Fenrir growled in apparently equal bewilderment, great triangular ears flat, head swinging from side to side as if he sought an enemy to which all his senses were blind.

Squirming out from under Dainn's body, Danny held out his hand and crooned a greeting. Fenrir tilted his head to look up at Loki, whose expression had reverted to one of familiar calculation. The Wolf tucked his tail under his belly and whined.

"My brother," Danny said to Dainn, a note of triumph in his voice.

As Dainn tried to make sense of what Danny had done, Fenrir slunk past Loki to the bed. Dainn grabbed Danny to hold him back, but Danny slipped free again, stretched out on his belly, and buried his hands in the Wolf's coarse mane. Fenrir licked Danny's cheek and fawned like a hungry cur.

"Well, well," Loki said. "Isn't this a tender scene."

Fenrir whimpered, but his slitted green eyes fixed on Dainn's, and there was no mistaking the hostility in them. Dainn felt a growl gather beneath his ribs. He held the Wolf's stare in challenge. And threat.

"No, Fen," Danny said. "No."

"Fenrir," Loki said.

Hanging his head, the Wolf backed away from the bed and crouched at Loki's feet.

"He said he was lonely," Danny volunteered, "and he wanted to be with his family, too."

"You have done very well, my son," Loki said.

Fenrir's black lips twitched up, revealing a wealth of sharp yellow teeth. "Father," he whined.

"I was not speaking to *you*," Loki said coldly. "You have displeased me a great many times, Fenrir. But you will have your chance to redeem yourself." He grinned at Dainn. "I think we've found a way to capture Sleipnir. And perhaps the right opportunity, as well."

Swallowing despair, Dainn took Danny gently by the shoulders and turned him around. Danny's expression was serene, but his eyes were very bright.

"It will be all right, Papa," he said. "It will be all right."

But Dainn knew it wouldn't. Danny was changing.

And so was *he*.

◑◐

Loki was no longer smiling after he sent Dainn to the dining room.

Oh, he'd achieved at least one victory. Danny had surpassed every expectation, with no apparent help from his father. For unfathomable reasons of his own, he had finally decided to cooperate.

So, it seemed, had Dainn. He badly wanted something only Loki could give him: an answer to the question of what had happened at the protest. An answer Loki wanted just as badly.

Returning to his suite, Loki put in a call to a certain highly placed public servant. "I want every man, woman, and child in or near the plaza questioned," he said, talking over the mortal's stuttered protests and apologies. "I don't care how difficult it is. Find a way. If necessary, I will speak to the mayor." He breathed a Rune-spell that silenced the fool on the other end of the line. "I would prefer not to become involved, but if I must, you will not be happy."

He hung up, made another quick call, and tried to relax on the couch. The news personalities on television were still jabbering on about the protest and how remarkable it was that it had ended with no casualties of any kind. Reporters were shown interviewing people who claimed to have been mere "observers," but none of them could account for what had happened.

It was possible, Loki mused, that Freya had fomented the protest merely to lay a trap for Mist, knowing that her daughter would inevitably become involved and might leave herself vulnerable as she attempted to stop it.

Irritated by the lack of information, Loki turned on the hastily repaired monitor in the living room to watch Miss Jones prepare Danny for sleep. The boy showed no sign that he remembered what he had done, and Fenrir was now confined to an isolated area of the house, where he wasn't apt to make any trouble. No one, not even Loki's most trusted servants, knew of his arrival, and Loki wasn't inclined to let Danny and the Wolf meet again until he knew what had triggered the boy's welcome but unexpected behavior.

As for Dainn . . . everything had changed. Again. Loki had watched the beast return to life suddenly and unexpectedly, between one heartbeat and the next—still trapped in an elven shape, but very near to breaking free.

That didn't mean that Dainn couldn't be of great help in taking Sleipnir. In fact, he might be far more useful than Loki had anticipated. It seemed that several disparate goals were converging all at once, and Loki intended to take full advantage of the possibilities.

He was still considering the next step when Nicholas informed him that Edvard was on the way up. The *berserkr* gave a slight nod as he walked into the room—the most respect Loki ever received from him—and seated himself in one of the armchairs without asking permission.

Unfortunately, the man was necessary as long as he possessed the herb that "controlled" Dainn's beast . . . a substance Loki had been unable to reproduce by conventional or magical means. During the time when he had ostensibly worked for Mist's Sister Valkyrie, Bryn, Edvard had offered the stuff to Dainn when the elf had been desperate to rid himself of his darker half. For a while, it had seemed to ameliorate the beast's savagery.

Until Dainn had consumed the last of his portion in a final, desperate attempt to destroy the beast. And along with it, his elven magic.

But whatever had become of Dainn's magical gifts, his bestial half wasn't really dead. And since Edvard had come to Loki, the mixture had been used to keep it out of sight and out of mind. *Dainn's* mind.

"You said it was urgent," Edvard said, scratching at the scruff of his week-old beard.

"It is," Loki said tightly. "Dainn's beast has broken through."

"Oh?" Edvard raised a shaggy brow. "Well, we knew that might happen."

"It happened in front of Danny."

"Bad timing. The herb acts like a drug, and you've been dosing him for months. He was bound to develop resistance sooner or later."

Loki examined the bear man with distaste. "I believe that Dainn's fear for the Sow's daughter triggered its resurrection."

"Mist?" the *berserkr* asked. "What's happened to her?"

"That's none of your concern," Loki said. "How much of the herb do you have left?"

"Depends on what you want." Edvard eyed him thoughtfully. "You sound pretty pissed off, but you're not as mad as you make out. Why is that?"

"I will tolerate a certain amount of impertinence from you," Loki said, "but not insolence." He brushed off his sleeve, as if the bear man had shed on his eight-thousand-dollar suit. "It may be that the timing is not so bad after all."

"Oh, so you can use the beast now? As a weapon?" Edvard shrugged at Loki's glare. "It's the obvious reason you'd keep that part of him alive instead of finding a way to destroy it."

"And likely destroy Dainn as well. No, I want it to remain under my control."

"Has he regained his magic as well?"

"The elf-magic?" Loki said. "No. But if it returns, he may attempt to hide it. I will know." He tapped his fingers on the arm of the couch. "Regardless of his magical status, I wish to present the creature as the entertainment at a very special event in two days' time."

"O-kay." Edvard dropped his chin to his burly chest. "It'll take a bit of finessing to make sure he's ready by then, but since he's already breaking free of the herb's influence, it can probably be done . . . if you're willing to take some risks."

"Such as?"

"First, stopping the herb cold turkey—completely cutting it out of the food you've been giving him—could do one of several things: kill him, make him too sick to move, destroy his mind . . . or, if you're lucky, release the beast without either one of you losing complete control of it."

"What are the odds?"

"No way of knowing. But he's strong. If you're lucky, you might be able to use small doses of the herb to help keep the beast in check. But it'll be pretty hard to do that without telling him what you've been doing to him."

"I don't need your advice on how to handle my elf," Loki said, dropping onto the couch. He continued to explain his plans for Dainn, and Edvard's eyes widened in the first real expression he'd shown in the past fifteen minutes.

"That's a little more complicated," the *berserkr* said. "But maybe your magic will be enough, if you work with the herb when you create your spells. I suggest you halve the dosage tonight. Tomorrow—"

"I will want instructions, as precise as you can make them, ready by tomorrow morning. You will remain here in the house to assist me for the next two days."

"Just so long as I don't have to see him."

"Ashamed?" Loki said, flashing his teeth. "Or just afraid he'll kill you?"

"I told you that giving him the drug when I rode with Bryn was a test to see if he was worthy. He failed. There was nothing personal about it."

"He may not see it that way, especially since you have decided that I will benefit your people more than Mist and Freya will."

The *berserkr* heaved himself to his feet. "If that's all for now . . ."

"Speak to Nicholas on the way out. He'll arrange quarters for you here until this experiment is complete. Oh, and one more thing."

Edvard stopped halfway to the door. "What?"

"You will personally attend the event I have arranged."

"Why?"

"You are involved in this up to your hairy neck," Loki said. "It's only right that you should be there to share my triumph."

Edvard swallowed and looked longingly at the door. "It's really not necessary. I'm sure you—"

"You *will* be there."

Three soft knocks announced the arrival of Scarlet, dressed as usual in her tight and very short skirt, open blouse, and spike heels. She ambulated into the room and inclined her head.

"My lord," she said, "Vali is here."

"Send him in," Loki said, sitting up quickly. "You can go," he said to Edvard, who shuffled out of the room much less impassively than he had entered it. Vali was looking over his shoulder as he passed through the door.

"Well?" Loki said.

"I saw Vidarr while I was at the plaza," Vali said, his broad, blunt features more than a little pinched.

Loki shot up from the couch. "Where was he?"

"Heading north on Powell Street, right after the protest."

"You told me he'd fled!"

"I thought he had, after that beating you gave him. He sure never contacted *me*."

"Did you follow him?"

"For a while. Then he just . . . vanished."

"Vanished, as in magically?"

"Looked that way."

After Edvard's provoking behavior, Vali's phlegmatic attitude was beginning to tell on Loki's patience. "Do you believe that Vidarr had something to do with the protest?" he asked.

"I don't know. But unless he's really been practicing up on his skills, I don't think he could control a whole mob of mortals that way."

Vali was right, Loki thought. Vidarr had once been a powerful god in his own right. But centuries among mortals had blunted his abilities, and he'd been helpless against Loki after he'd attempted to claim Dainn to satisfy his own desire for revenge.

No. That Vidarr had been present near the plaza was no coincidence, but he hadn't caused the problem by himself. If he'd been hiding in San Francisco all along, he'd certainly have been aware of the web Loki had been spinning across the city, and he was just smart enough to realize what would happen if he interfered.

His desire for vengeance would go unfulfilled, unless he had help. *Unless he serves a greater enemy.*

But that wasn't possible. Odin's messenger had never been found again. And the Aesir were still safely tucked away in the Void.

"Listen well, Odin's son," Loki said. "If you have any doubts about our agreement, or hold any lingering loyalty toward your brother or father, you will be of no use to me."

"Mist would never take me back," Vali said, shifting from one big, booted foot to the other like a child called to account before his elders.

"But 'neutral' is not an acceptable position," Loki said.

"I know that." Vali glanced at the ground and then met Loki's gaze. "Nothing's changed. You offered me a chance to be something more than a tool of the Aesir and my brother's lackey. If you stick to your part of the deal, that won't ever happen again."

"Oh, I intend to stick to it. But I won't hesitate to act lethally if I sense you might renege."

"You got nothing to worry about."

"Excellent." Loki rose and returned to the stairs. "It is time to make another move against Freya and her allies."

10

Anna rolled over to look at her watch, lying on the crate that served as a bed table. For a moment, her vision was blurred . . . not by sleep, but by that sense she'd had for so much of her life: that she was looking through someone else's eyes.

Oddly enough, she hadn't felt that way nearly so much since she'd met with Orn again. She couldn't really remember most of the conversation, except that he'd given her three tasks: to touch the two Treasures, to locate Sleipnir, and to watch Freya.

Mist, too, she thought, yawning in an attempt to clear her head. But she knew that Mist would never betray the All-father. Just like *she* wouldn't.

She turned her head to look at Hrolf. The elf's unusually pale hair was spread across his pillow with a natural kind of artistry, making her want to run her fingers through it again. One arm was draped over his head, the other across his chest, his wrist covering the mark Anna's hand had made.

Even with all the elven-magic Hrolf possessed, not to mention his extremely keen vision, he hadn't been able to see it. The design of interlocked Rune-staves Orn had pecked into her hand had transferred perfectly and painlessly to the elf's flesh.

She leaned over Hrolf's face to kiss him. He stirred with a low groan of contentment, and she felt a renewed sense of wonder that she was lying in bed with a being who shouldn't have looked twice at a little brown mouse like her.

And that hadn't even been part of the spell, though it could have been. She could have used the Runes to get him interested, the same way she'd tried to make him tell her where Sleipnir was hidden. But he'd responded to her overtures willingly, and it hadn't really mattered to her at the time if he wanted *her* or just the sex.

I don't want to do this, she argued with herself. *I don't want to use him, just as a means to an end.*

But Orn had called her his Valkyrie. And Valkyrie didn't give up.

Hrolf opened his eyes and stretched, his arm sliding off the invisible brand.

"What is it?" he asked.

"I just couldn't sleep," she said. "I kept having the same dream, over and over again."

"About what?" he said, beginning to sit up.

"About Sleipnir," she said.

His expression grew guarded. "In what sense?" he asked.

She pushed him back down and draped herself across him, tucking her head under his chin, and traced the staves on his chest with her fingertip. "Orn was trying to tell me something about Odin's horse . . . that there's a secret hidden inside him that could make all the difference in the war."

"But Orn is gone."

"Before he disappeared, we believed that he was sent with a message from Odin. Maybe a part of me glimpsed what he was trying to tell us, and now it's coming back to me in my dreams."

The elf's frown deepened. "But you cannot define this message?"

"I know it's important, Hrolf." She took a deep breath and propped herself up to look into the elf's face. "I just keep thinking that Orn knew Sleipnir was going to be found soon, and that I was supposed to . . . I don't know, find out if the horse had a message for me."

"Sleipnir cannot speak."

"But I know that I have to see him to understand the dream." She traced the staves again and again. "What if there is a way of communicating with Sleipnir, and he knows how to get in touch with Odin himself?"

The elf began to shake his head, but he never completed the motion. His eyes drifted half-closed, and his muscles went limp.

"Yes," he murmured. "Where would be the harm?"

"You know I'd never tell anyone," she said, kissing him again.

Suddenly he reared up, pushing her back, and stared into her eyes. "No," he said. "It is not possible."

Cold anger stiffened her body. "I serve the All-father," she said. "And all the Aesir and Vanir, including Freya, serve *him*. If you serve Freya, you must do as Odin commands."

"Odin is not here," Hrolf said, rising lithely to stand over her. "And until I receive orders to the contrary, I cannot tell you where Sleipnir is hidden." He tugged on his pants. "I have neglected my duties too long."

With short, almost angry jerks, he pulled on his pants and shoes and slipped away. Anna stared after him, shamed by her failure. A failure Mist would never have permitted herself.

She knelt, pushed aside the pile of her own clothing, and picked up the pendant hidden underneath. Once again, for a moment, her vision blurred.

And then, tucking the pendant under the crate, Anna dressed and went to look for Gabi.

She found the young Latina wandering among the rows of tents covering the parking lot nearest Illinois Street, her black hair whipping about in the wind, her chin bent to her chest. She glanced up at Anna with surprise and a sudden start, as if she had been caught in the midst of guilty thoughts.

But it was not she, Anna thought, who should be feeling guilty.

"What's wrong?" Anna asked, resting her hand on Gabi's shoulder.

"Everything," Gabi said, hunching her shoulders.

She told Anna about Eir. Anna was genuinely shocked and sorry, though her duty would not allow her to dwell on the loss too long. She let Gabi talk and held the younger woman's hand, slowly chanting the spell in her mind as she began to trace the Rune-staves on Gabi's palm.

In the end, Gabi was far more susceptible than Hrolf had been. It was almost easy for Anna to convince the young woman to show her the vault, and after that the spell took over, widening the crack in Gabi's resistance.

Once Gabi showed her what she wanted to see, Anna touched her pendant to Gleipnir and Jarngreipr. Gabi remained blind to Anna's actions as well as her own dereliction of duty, and when they left, the younger woman carried no clear memory of anything but speaking of Eir to a sympathetic listener.

Clutching the pendant, Anna could feel the new energy throbbing at its heart, almost too great for the small piece of stone to contain. The weight of the chain pulled on her neck and cut into her skin.

But soon it would belong to another. And Orn might be more willing to forgive her other mistakes.

She badly needed someone to forgive her.

◑◐

There were literally hundreds of them: men and women of every age, size, ethnicity and profession, all gathered on Illinois Street and waiting in silent expectation.

Waiting for me, Mist thought.

"I spoke to a few of them," Captain Taylor said. He stood beside her in front of the loft, as solid and unshakable as a rock. "It's the same as with all the others. They were drawn here, knowing they had to come but not sure exactly why."

And I didn't even try, Mist thought. *She* hadn't summoned them.

But you used the glamour at the plaza, she reminded herself. She hadn't sent out any kind of wide-ranging signal. . . .

Unless it had happened during that period she couldn't remember. And however this had come about—even if it was against her conscious will—she needed every person who'd shown up.

Loki's piss.

"What about Freya?" she asked, making sure no one else was close enough to hear.

"We took her to the loft," Taylor said, lowering his voice. "She's still unconscious, but otherwise seems stable. No visible injuries. I posted several guards outside and one inside at the door. I also sent someone to get Eir, but these people were already here when we returned, and I haven't followed up."

"I'll take care of that," Mist said. "For now, I want you to set up a station with as many of our people as you think can answer the recruits' basic questions. We know from past experience that they'll mostly be willing to accept what they're told, but we also have to assume they have no idea of the kind of commitment they'll be making."

"We've been fortunate so far," Taylor said, his gaze sweeping the orderly crowd, "but with so many, there are bound to be some who have commitments and relationships that will preclude their joining us."

"Of course I trust your judgment."

"I know you're overwhelmed right now," Taylor said. He laid his big hand on her shoulder, as familiar and sympathetic as a loving father or brother. "You still have trouble delegating, but that's what the chain of command is for. You can give your usual speeches and interviews after we've laid the groundwork."

Mist ducked her head. "Thanks for your support, Captain. It means . . . I'm grateful to have it."

"Stop being grateful, Chief. It's your right." He dropped his hand and glanced at the heavy clouds churning overhead. "We've got to get these people under cover. Looks like it's about to rain again."

More like snow, Mist thought. There hadn't been any this season . . . yet. But when the first real snowfall had come along two years ago—before she'd ever suspected the true cause for the radical changes in weather—it had started in October. This year, even the summer had been cold.

"If that's all, Chief," Taylor said, "I'll—" He broke off and looked toward the warehouses across the street. Mist followed his gaze. Gabi was approaching slowly, her feet dragging, eyes downcast.

"Something's wrong," Mist said. Forgetting Captain Taylor and

the strangers who were so intently watching her, Mist ran to meet
Gabi.

And skidded to a halt as if a Jotunn had swung a club full-force
into her belly.

"*No*," she said before Gabi could speak.

"I'm sorry," Gabi whispered, her eyes filling with tears. "Eir's
gone."

Mist took off again, hardly feeling the cold drops of stinging rain
that fell on her face and shoulders. She burst into the warehouse and
crossed the floor at a run.

One of the EMTs and a nurse were hovering over the cot. Both
mortals moved hastily out of Mist's path as she came to a stop.

Mist fell to her knees and slowly uncovered Eir's face. It was quiet
and untroubled in death, as if she were simply dreaming of some
happy moment in her long life.

"I'm sorry," the nurse said, coming to stand beside her. "Gabi said
she didn't suffer."

"But she looks so normal," Mist said, keeping her voice level in the
hope that if she pretended to be in control of her emotions, she actually would be. "So much better than she has for the past several
months."

"I know. Maybe you should speak to—"

"I'm here," Gabi said. She glanced at the nurse, who left her alone
with Mist. It was clear that Gabi had been crying; her eyes were
swollen and her nose was red.

So were her hands.

"You tried to heal her?" Mist asked.

"I . . . couldn't. . . ."

"When?"

"About two hours ago."

"Something must have happened." Mist latched on to her anger, so
much safer than grief. "Did she get the message about Freya?"

"I don't know about any message."

"Did she push herself too hard? Did she—"

"I don't know!" Gabi cried. She scrambled to her feet and stood facing Mist from several feet away, trembling as if she'd been struck. "I'm sorry!"

Gods, Mist thought, closing her eyes. Gabi had loved Eir, too. She didn't deserve to be punished this way.

"It's okay," Mist said. "Do you have any idea why she looks so much better now than when she was alive?"

Gabi hugged herself. "I did what you told me I could do if things got bad. I tried to use one of the seeds."

Mist nodded slowly and took Eir's cold hand. It no longer felt like bits of bone barely held together by wasted muscle, tendon, and flesh.

Something in the Apples had worked. Just not well enough.

"I know you did all you could," Mist said. She rose, kissed Eir's mouth and forehead, and then covered her again.

"What will you . . . do with her?" Gabi asked.

"She'd want to be given back to the earth where she lived so long," Mist said, thinking of the native spirits who had helped her and Mist fight Loki for possession of the Apples. "We can't take the time to do that now. But we we'll protect her body until we can."

"Where?"

"With the Treasures. She can guard the Apples again." She paced away from the bed, her hands locked behind her back. "I want you to rest. I'm pulling everyone back from patrol. We're going to try to avoid any fights for the next few days."

"I saw the protest on TV this afternoon. Did Loki cause it?"

"I don't know yet. But I'll find out."

"Okay. I'm going to lie down now."

"Good. And try not to blame yourself, Gabi, even though I know you want to."

"Are you gonna take your own advice?"

Before Mist could answer, Gabi rushed out of the infirmary. Mist remained a while longer, fighting with her grief until she was sure she had it under reasonable control. Then she went across the street to check on Freya.

Several of the Einherjar bikers and two other mortal recruits were watching the loft. They greeted Mist with worried looks and stood aside to let her pass, clearly bursting with questions but too well-disciplined to ask them.

Mist found the Lady in one of the spare bedrooms, but there was no guard at the door. Instead, two of Lord Konur's healers were with the goddess, murmuring to each other in Old Elvish.

"Lady Mist," the female elf said, inclining her head as Mist joined them beside the bed.

"Who sent you?" Mist asked. "Where's the guard?"

"We saw no guard," the male healer said. "Lord Konur witnessed the Lady's return. He asked us to observe her, and help if we could."

Funny, Mist thought, that the mortal guards hadn't mentioned any elves. She had a strong suspicion that the Alfar had slipped past them, and she wasn't happy about the deception. Especially since there was no apparent reason for it. It wasn't as if the Alfar, mortals, and Valkyrie hadn't been living, working, and fighting together—more or less—for the past nine months.

If circumstances had been different, Mist would have interrogated the healers then and there. But she wasn't prepared to imply a lack of trust in people whose help she badly needed, and she'd be talking to Konur soon enough.

She examined Freya, trying to see past that blank spot in her own mind where important memories should have been. Taylor had been right: no wounds, nothing to suggest a reason for the Lady's continued unconscious state except for the signs of aging in her face and skin.

Why don't I feel more? Mist asked herself. Eir's death had devastated her, but now it seemed that she was looking down at a stranger . . . a stranger for whom she couldn't spare even the most disinterested compassion.

You'll feel something if she dies, and you're stuck facing Loki alone again.

"You don't know what's wrong with her?" Mist asked, trying to shake off her disgust at her own icy pragmatism.

"We have been unable to determine the nature of this illness, or its source," the female healer said, "but we will continue to do what we can."

Mist left quickly, not even pausing to ask the guards outside if they'd seen the Alfar enter the loft. She was headed for the elven camp when she almost literally ran into Anna.

The young woman nearly jumped out of her skin when she recognized Mist, her skin flushed and her movements awkward.

"Are you okay?" Mist asked.

"Yes," Anna said quickly. "Yes, of course. I heard you just got back. Gabi and I saw everything on TV." She glanced toward the warehouse. "I guess no one was hurt?"

"Freya's suffered some kind of attack."

"An attack?" Anna's eyes widened, and Mist noticed perspiration beading along her hairline. "What kind of attack?"

"It happened while she was working magic, but we're still trying to figure out what caused it."

"Oh. Is she getting better?"

"She's got far too much of an ego to stay down long." Mist smiled to ease Anna's obvious unease. "Keep this quiet, okay? We don't want anyone to panic."

"I understand." Anna swallowed. "I just heard about Eir. I'm really sorry."

"She lived a good life. She died doing what she wanted to do."

Anna set off almost before Mist had finished speaking. Mist stared after her, wondering why the young woman seemed so particularly nervous when she usually kept her cool so well.

Maybe she was suffering from some of Horja's worst memories, or even Rebekka's. Mist certainly hadn't had many chances to talk privately with her and assess her state of mind.

Now was obviously not the time to start, especially since Mist could already feel her mask beginning to slip again. Gabi had been right to wonder if she could take her own advice and try not to blame herself for Eir's death.

The simple fact was that Eir had been as much her responsibility as all the others, from the youngest mortal to the eldest Alfr. But Eir had also been a friend. A Sister, to whom Mist hadn't even been able to say good-bye.

But Mist knew she couldn't let any of her troops see her paralyzed over one woman's death, and those few she might turn to for comfort had their own important work to do.

I've got to get out of here, she thought. Maybe a ride up to Twin Peaks, where she could look down on the city and pretend it wasn't on the verge of exploding into a battlefield.

What would happen if Loki knew that Freya was down?

Turning her back on every one of her vital responsibilities, Mist jogged back to Silfr and sped away from the loft, merging onto 280 south and following the curve in a wide semicircle to the west. She continued on O'Shaughnessy Boulevard, Portola Avenue and Twin Peaks Boulevard, stopping when she found a safe place to pull off to one side of the winding road.

Mist removed her helmet and shook out her hair. San Francisco *did* look peaceful, in spite of the ever-threatening clouds. Traffic moved in a steady stream over the Golden Gate and Bay Bridges, and the bay was calm. There could have been a hundred battles raging in back alleys all over the city, and you'd never know it up here.

A fierce gust of wind circled Mist like a seeking spell homing in on its target, and she zipped her jacket more for the comfort of the act than because she felt the chill. She could still remember the first time she'd seen the city, back in the fifties, when she'd been looking for a place to settle after the war. Then, she'd been seeking escape from the memory of other deaths, and from the burden of her own guilt and grief.

She'd found that escape, for a while. It had taken some years, but she'd finally settled into a "normal" sort of life, though she'd kept pretty much to herself. She'd become expert at forging fine replica swords, axes, and knives for collectors, which served the dual purpose of allowing her to maintain some link with her past—a past she hadn't yet been ready to surrender—and earn a living at the same time.

The past had caught up with her when she'd least expected it.

Mounting again, Mist took the road to the other side of the park and looked over Forest Hill and the Sunset District to the Pacific Ocean. Fog obscured the shore, though ordinarily the season would have been over this late in the year.

But "ordinarily" had become a meaningless word in San Francisco, while the rest of the world wallowed in ignorance. Across that vast expanse of water, no one had any idea what was going on in this jewel of the Pacific—a jewel that was only a single piece in a setting that would eventually encompass the entire planet, no matter which side was victorious.

"It does seem difficult to accept that the fate of this one city may determine that of all Midgard," a soft voice said just behind her.

Mist dropped her hand from the knife at her hip and turned. "How did you get up here?"

Konur gazed out at the ocean, unperturbed by her irritation. Like most of the Alfar—who had always favored bright jewel tones in Asgard and Alfheim—the elf-lord had adopted darker, less conspicuous clothing that made his tall, lithe physique seem even leaner. "I borrowed one of the mortal's motorcycles," he said. "Unpleasantly noisy and offensively malodorous, but it is necessary to adapt."

Looking past him, Mist saw the bike parked a few yards away and realized that if he'd been a Jotunn, she'd most likely be dead.

"You followed me?" she asked.

"Let us say that I was concerned about your mental state, and believed it would be better that you not travel unobserved."

"It never occurred to you that I might just want to be alone for a while?"

"It did, but your life is too important to risk."

"I can't be the person you and everyone else wants me to be. Not all the time."

The elf nodded, sympathy in his dark eyes. "You are Freya's daughter. Surely you are stronger than you believe."

"Did anyone ever tell you how Dainn used to lecture me?"

"In this particular sentiment, he was right."

"What is it with elves and their habit of dodging direct questions?" She narrowed her eyes. "You never met him before, did you? In Asgard?"

"No. After he arrived in Asgard as a mysterious wanderer, he visited Alfheim but once, and without notifying anyone beforehand. Only a very few saw him before he left again."

Mist remembered little hints Dainn had dropped about his dealings with his own people. She knew he'd never lived among the Alfar during his time as the All-father's advisor, nor had he been close to any of the elves who frequented Valhalla, Odin's hall.

Aside from that, she knew almost nothing about Dainn's past before the betrayal and curse . . . except, of course, for his affair with Loki—who had posed as Freya—and his reputation as a wise, level-headed, and rational counselor.

"You must hate him," she said, looking back out at the ocean.

Konur moved up beside her. "It is true that many of my people despise him for the shame he brought upon us, as well as for his betrayal. But there was a time when the Lady did trust him . . . and Loki most emphatically cannot be trusted."

"So?"

"Things are not always what they seem."

Mist started. Those were nearly the same words Dainn had written to her in his note. "You don't think he's a traitor?" she asked.

"I do not know. But this question still weighs upon your mind, and a time will come when you must meet him again."

"Let *me* worry about that, okay?"

"You say you cannot be what everyone expects of you, yet you refuse to share your burdens."

"I tried that once. It backfired rather badly."

"The tree that does not bend with the wind must break."

"Oh, sweet Baldr," she said. "Please don't do that."

"I will refrain." The elf gazed at her until she was forced to look at him again. "I know you do not confide in your mother, but—"

"Speaking of my mother," Mist interrupted, "did you send your healers to her without telling anyone else?"

As calm and self-controlled though he usually was, the elf-lord actually blinked. "I became aware of the Lady's affliction soon after she was returned to camp. Is there some difficulty?"

"Only that it seems strange that you wouldn't tell Taylor, since he's the one who brought her back."

"And he was occupied with the arrival of the new mortals," Konur said.

"Then why didn't the guards he set around the loft seem to know about the healers?"

"Did they not?" Konur's brows lifted. "I did tell my people to be discreet, since I assumed you would not want the Lady's state to become general knowledge as yet. Perhaps they were overly cautious."

"Taylor was going to send for Eir," she said thickly.

"Ah." Konur bowed his head. "I grieve for your loss."

"It was a loss for all of us. Eir might have figured out what was wrong with Freya." She took a moment to regain her composure. "If you didn't speak to Taylor, how do you know what actually happened to Freya? Did one of his people tell you?"

"No. I had hoped you could tell me."

Mist rubbed her arms and glanced longingly at Silfr. This, unfortunately, wasn't something she could run away from.

"All I can say is that it happened very suddenly," she said, "and it felt very much like a deliberate attack."

"It was my understanding that you and your observers detected no sign of Loki or his minions near the location."

"Right."

"Magic always leaves its signature. I believe you would have known if Loki had been the perpetrator."

"That's what I assumed. But there isn't anyone else in Midgard who could do something like that to Freya."

Konur slanted her a glance she couldn't quite interpret. But she wasn't really paying attention, because another very unpleasant idea was forming in her mind.

"What if her magic has failed?" she asked aloud.

"In what way?" Konur asked, his eyes intent on her face.

"She as much as admitted that the body she borrowed is giving out on her. Maybe this was the last straw."

The elf wore an expression of someone who'd just had his worst fears confirmed. "If this is true," he said, "then another vessel must be found for her. And quickly."

11

"You knew about the problem?" Mist asked.

"I was there when Freya attained her current body."

"You mean when the elf-woman donated it for Freya's use." Mist wrapped her arms around her chest. "She's still alive, isn't she?"

"She survives as the Aesir do," Konur said, "as a mind encased in a shape that appears physical only within the Shadow-Realms."

"But Freya said that she helped you and the other Alfar generate true physical forms in Ginnungagap, so that you could travel to Midgard."

The elf raised a brow. "Did you have reason to doubt her claim? I can assure you that it is true."

"She also said that making the Aesir physical bodies was much harder, and that she wasn't strong enough to pull it off yet."

"Indeed. And that is why, if her present body is no longer able to support Freya's magic, she must obtain another and return this one before it is no longer of use to its original owner."

Sick at the thought of what Konur was implying, Mist sat down on the brown grass beside the road. "Setting aside the question of *how* she's supposed to return it, just where do you think she's going to find an appropriate body? By traveling back to Ginnungagap and asking for another volunteer?"

"If she is as ill as she seems, that will probably not be possible."

"Then you're talking about finding a subject here in Midgard."

He crouched beside her. "Do you believe that to be so unlikely?"

"Let's put it this way. Even if you can keep someone's bodiless mind alive in the Void, it's not the same in Midgard. You can't just store something like that in a bottle."

"Not in a bottle, no. But surely, with the use of the right spells . . ."

He trailed off, and Mist recognized that even this wise, experienced elf-lord didn't know what the Hel he was talking about.

"You didn't plan for this, did you?" she asked. "Freya never expected she'd fall so far behind. She thought she'd have her true shape back, and all the Aesir here fighting with us."

"Her expectations do not change the current predicament," Konur said. He placed his palm flat on the weeds growing along the curb, and withered brown showed a flush of green life. "This problem is real, and we must take swift action."

"I'm not about to ask one of my mortals or Valkyrie to act as Freya's host without a guarantee that their minds will be safe and they'll get the rest back in undamaged condition."

Konur lifted his hand, and the weeds drooped and blackened again. "If many are willing to die to save Midgard," he said, "then they may be prepared to take this risk as well."

At that moment, Mist despised the elf and his cold-blooded pragmatism. "No. I think we should go back and see if your healers have learned anything useful before we start sacrificing lives on the Lady's altar."

"I know your relationship with your mother has not always been amicable—"

Mist snorted.

"—but you know we cannot achieve victory without her magic."

She turned to stare at him. "Let's be clear about this, Lord Konur. You and I have fought side by side. You've led the Alfar well, and done everything I asked of you. But I also know that you and Freya have been keeping secrets you haven't let me in on, and that doesn't exactly inspire feelings of good faith."

"What is it you wish to know?"

"During our last fight with the Jotunar, Freya said that you agreed to become her warriors for a very generous reward. What did she mean?"

Konur stood up quickly, his long overcoat swirling around his ankles. "She promised that the Alfar should take possession of large tracts of forested land on this world, after we defeated Loki."

Mist began to reply and stopped, thinking back to one of her earlier conversations with Dainn. The elf had said that the Aesir intended to build a new Homeworld in Midgard, and Mist had been forced to consider the very real possibility of gods sharing the Earth with humans.

Now Konur had given her a prime example of what was coming. No nature-loving elf would agree to stay behind in the Void if she had a chance at planting her feet in uncultivated soil again, no matter how polluted by elvish standards.

"Freya made this promise to you before you ever got here?" Mist asked. "Unilaterally? Or did all the Aesir decide this, and she was just the one who negotiated for your services?"

"We are not mercenaries to be bought and sold," Konur said, a cold note in his voice. "Is this so unreasonable a price for these Midgardians to pay for the survival of their world?"

"It is if they have no say in where or how the peoples of the other Homeworlds will settle here. It is if you toss the current inhabitants of those lands out on their ear." She calmed herself with a deep breath. "Will the Aesir impose some kind of dictatorship, the way Loki would?"

"I can speak only for my people," Konur said stiffly. "We wish no harm on mortalkind. Long ago, many of us made our homes here. But we must live, and we cannot exist in these places of steel and stone."

Mist ran her hand over her face. "I know," she said. "But I've also made my home here, and you can't expect me to forget all the years I've spent living with and fighting alongside mortals."

"I know you regard yourself as the spokesman for the inhabitants of Midgard, but do you truly consider yourself to be more one of them than of your own true kin?"

I don't know what I consider myself to be, Mist thought. *I never did.*

"Let's put it this way," she said. "Assuming I survive, what if I insisted that the mortals have some input when this is over? Would you listen to me?"

"*Would* you insist?"

"I might not give you everything you wanted."

"Then you would place me in a most difficult position."

"Why? I'm only half-goddess. I'd hardly be able to stand in your way if you and Freya opposed me."

"Are you so certain of that?"

It was such an odd question that Mist didn't quite know how to answer. "It's a moot point," she said. "I'm still Odin's servant. He'll have the final say, won't he?"

Or will I defy him if he insists on doling out the better parts of Earth to the Aesir and their allies?

Mist pushed the thought out of her mind. There was still no guarantee that Odin or any of the others would ever show up. Or that *any* of them would be alive to see the end of the war.

She jumped up and started toward Silfr, her jaw aching with anger.

"Mist," Konur called, striding after her.

Pulling on her helmet, she turned to face him again. "I need to get back. Can you find your way if we become separated?"

"I can."

Swinging her leg over Silfr's seat, Mist started the engine. She roared away without waiting to see if Konur was behind her.

When she reached the loft, Hild and Rota were waiting for her, their expressions solemn with worry.

"What is it?" Mist asked, jumping off the bike. "Freya?"

"In a manner of speaking," Rota said. She glanced at Hild, who offered Mist an open envelope.

It took Mist less than five seconds to realize why her Sisters looked so grim. "Loki?" she said in disbelief. "Loki wants a meeting with Freya?"

Konur's bike pulled up behind her. He dismounted and joined them, peering over Mist's shoulder at the bizarre invitation.

"What trick is this?" he murmured.

Mist handed him the note. He scanned it with a frown.

"'There are matters we must discuss,'" he read, and turned the beautifully engraved card over. A simple address had been written out in the Runic alphabet, along with a time.

"Another trap," Hild said.

"A test," Mist said, taking the note card back from the elf. "Lord Konur, you said that magic always leaves a signature, and we didn't detect Loki near the plaza. He may not have caused the trouble or hurt Freya himself, but I'm betting that he *does* know that something happened to her. And considering the location, he probably doesn't intend this to be a private meeting."

"You mean he's not really interested in 'talking' at all," Rota said. "He's trying to find out if she's capable of meeting him . . . and he'll be watching to see what we'll do if she isn't."

"But he can't expect Freya to come at his beck and call," Hild said. "Refusing his summons would prove nothing."

"He knows that Freya would want to test him as well—to find out what, if anything, he had to do with the protest," Mist said. "He also knows she'd want to rub his face in the fact that his ploy, if there was one, didn't succeed."

"Aesir and their pride," Rota said, her full mouth stretching in disgust.

"The point is that we can't let this go unanswered," Mist said. She tapped the card against her palm. "Where's Bryn?"

"With Freya." Rota read Mist's unspoken question. "No change."

"Since Bryn's been acting as Freya's social secretary these past months," Mist said, "maybe she can tell us if there's some significance to this meeting time and date. We have to make some kind of plan in case . . ."

In case Freya doesn't recover in time, Mist thought. Loki couldn't be allowed to find out how helpless she had become, or he'd strike at the allies when they were both demoralized and unable to call on the Lady's magic.

"It's still two days away," she said briskly. "The council will meet to discuss the problem, and we'll keep doing everything we can for Freya."

No one spoke. They only stared at her, soberly considering the alternatives just as she was doing. She didn't like the solution that was forming in her mind.

It would never work, she thought. But when she glanced at Konur, she knew that he'd come to the same conclusion. There was something like pity in his eyes.

"You would not be alone," he said, so softly that only she could hear. "I would accompany you."

"You don't know what you're asking," she said.

"I believe I do."

Then for the sake of every one of us, she thought, *we'd better hope that Freya regains her strength, magic, and beauty sometime within the next two days.*

◑◐

"This isn't a good idea," Koji said.

Mist cursed under her breath as Rota twisted her dyed hair into another knot. She felt as if every strand was being torn out by its roots, and that was probably going to be the *best* part of the day.

"Why work so hard to fix it," Mist said, wincing as Rota jerked a little too forcefully, "if I'm going to have to change everything else about myself? Can't I just make it look—"

"You're going to have enough to worry about with the coloring and eyes and face," Hild said, "not to mention the body. The more we can get you to look like Freya without relying on magic, the better."

"If you'd stop fidgeting," Rota said around the hairpins poking out of her mouth, "this wouldn't be so . . . difficult."

Not difficult, Mist thought. *Impossible. Crazy.* She still wasn't quite sure how she'd let Konur talk her into it.

If Bryn hadn't assured her that Freya had already planned to attend the reception at the Fairmont, Mist would never have consented to such a rash move. She might be her mother's daughter, but she was most assuredly *not* her mother.

Yet tonight she was going to have to try to be more like Freya than the Lady herself. She'd have to turn on the glamour in a way she never had before and outperform Bette Davis if she wanted to convince Loki that Freya was not only alive and well, but in top form.

"He'll be watching for deception," Koji said, standing before her with his arms crossed and an uncharacteristically grim expression on his handsome face. "You're giving him exactly what he wants."

"If we knew what he wanted, this would be easy," Rota said as she pinned up the thick coil of hair. "It's all a crapshoot."

"Set your mind at rest, Mr. Tashiro," Konur said, walking into the room. He stopped abruptly, one brow lifted, as if he was genuinely startled by Mist's altered appearance. "Mist has not only the use of her glamour, but my guidance as well."

"But you have no idea if Mist's glamour will work on Loki directly," Koji said.

Konur lifted his head, looking down his long and elegant nose. "I have every confidence in Mist's abilities. At the very least, Loki will be left as ignorant as he was before. He can only guess at our motives."

"The moment he recognizes her, he'll make the natural assumption that you're desperate," Koji said. He met Mist's gaze. "You'll need more than courage and magic. You'll need luck." He blinked, and Mist imagined that she saw a flash of silver in his dark eyes. "I'd like to come along."

Mist tugged at the straps of Freya's flimsy silk slip. "Konur was originally supposed to escort Freya, and it'll look pretty strange if her daughter's boyfriend shows up as her escort."

"I'll stay in the background."

"Sure. Koji Tashiro, of the San Francisco Tashiros. Not likely. And Loki knows you're on our side."

"You notice that he's never made a move against my family, or anyone connected with them."

"He still sees you as peripheral in this fight," Bryn said with her usual bluntness. "If you ever caused him real trouble, he might make some for you in return."

"What kind of trouble did you have in mind?"

"Try swinging that katana instead of shuffling legal documents," Bryn muttered.

"Bryn," Mist said, with a hard glance at her Sister. "I'm satisfied with Koji's work. If you have a problem with that, take it up with me when I get back."

With a sharp shake of her head, Bryn subsided. Koji sighed.

"I'm sorry," he said softly. "I never like seeing you risk your life."

"I know." She took his hand and gripped it tightly. "But even if I mess up, Loki's not likely to do anything dramatic like try to kill me. I may even learn something useful by getting an inside look at Freya's political and social machinations, not to mention Loki's."

"None of which will do us much good if Freya doesn't recover," Hild said.

"She will," Bryn said sharply.

"We've done everything we can for now," Mist said, forestalling another argument. "All our resources are focused on defense. We'll have to play it day by day . . . hour by hour if necessary."

For a time, no one spoke. Mist always wondered if her pep talks really did any good. How could she convince her friends and followers when she couldn't even convince herself?

Her ineffectual brooding ended when Rota held up the dress—a scarlet, very low-cut, figure-hugging confection with a slit up to there—and grinned at Mist.

"Prada," the redheaded Valkyrie said. "Just my style."

It certainly isn't mine, Mist thought. But it *was* Freya's, and that was the only thing that mattered.

Koji gave Mist a last, troubled look and walked out of the bedroom. Konur remained. Mist let Rota slip the dress over her head.

The silk was cool and luxurious on her skin. She felt overexposed and ridiculous, certain that the top, cinched tight as it was, would never hold the thing up over her chest.

"Wow," Rota said, beaming with admiration and pride. "The alterations are perfect. Fits like a glove."

"No kidding," Mist said, tugging at the seams on either side of her hips. "I can barely—"

"Stop that!" Rota said, slapping at her hands. "You'll pull it all out of shape. It's supposed to do that."

"Loki's piss."

"If you talk like that, you'll give yourself away in five seconds," Bryn remarked.

"I know. But if I can't let off some steam now . . ." She sighed. "Look, between you and Bryn and Konur I've had all the coaching I can take. If I can't do it now, I'll never be able to."

"Try the glamour," Konur said.

She did. It felt like a very small shift inside her, nothing like what she'd tried to use in the plaza. She wasn't moving people around like pieces on a Hnefatafl board or stopping a riot, and she didn't lose her sense of time. It was only herself she was trying to change.

But the magic must have worked, because Rota's mouth dropped open, Konur nodded approvingly, and even Bryn looked startled.

"It's perfect," Rota said. "You look exactly like Freya."

Mist reached up to pluck a strand of loose hair from her temple. "Black as any elf's," Hild said, taking the hair from Mist's hand and holding it under the light. "And your eyes are dark, too." She pursed her lips. "Body's right. I can't see any flaws."

"But do I *sound* like her?" Mist asked, clearing her throat.

"Exactly," Bryn said. Her nut-brown skin had gone more than a little pale. "As long as you speak the right words."

"You'll do fine," Rota said. "You won't be leaving for an hour. Use that time to relax. Meditate, or whatever it is you do in your copious spare time. If you need to talk, we'll be in the living room."

Mist nodded brusquely, and the three Valkyrie left. Konur lingered to stare at her a moment longer, but before she could ask him what was on his mind, he was striding out the door.

Mist released her breath and looked at her reflection in the mirror. She *did* look like Freya, to a frightening degree. Freya in her borrowed

elven body. The makeup, dress, and black spike-heel pumps only enhanced what was already a perfect illusion.

But she hated it. She wanted her jeans and boots and leather, her
familiar braid, the face people said was beautiful but had always
seemed comfortingly ordinary to her.

Even if she succeeded tonight, would she have to keep playing
Freya indefinitely, just to hold Loki at bay until the Lady came out of
her stupor?

She reached up to twist the braid that didn't exist, remembering
at the last moment that she was about to muss her artfully tousled
hair. "If it falls down, you'll look even more alluring," Rota had
assured her.

Alluring. Gods help me.

Turning her back on the mirror, Mist sat down on the bed—
carefully, so as not to split any of the seams—and kicked off the
pumps. She tried to meditate as Rota had suggested, and didn't realize she'd lost track of time until Konur knocked lightly on the door.

He was impeccably dressed in a formal suit, his long hair drawn
back in a neat ponytail, his handsome features solemn and quiet. She
stood and stepped into the pumps, patting her waist in search of
Kettlingr's comforting weight.

But even in its knife form, the sword would never fit in the tiny
clutch purse with its spray of minuscule diamonds.

"Are you ready?" Konur asked.

"I assume that is a rhetorical question," she said as she took Freya's
evening coat out of the closet.

"Not at all," Konur said. He took the coat from her and helped her
into it, making her feel even more foolish.

"It's what Freya would expect from her male escort," he said when
he was finished.

Let this be the one and only time, Mist prayed as Konur followed her
outside. *And let me not decide to bash Loki's face in with my spike heels
when I see him.*

By prior arrangement, only Bryn waited at the curb to see Mist off.
But as she climbed into the rented van, she saw Anna striding across

the street, her arms folded across her ribs and her chin pressed to her chest.

Mist couldn't imagine that Anna had seen anything incriminating, so she pushed her brief concern aside and settled into the driver's seat. When she and Konur reached the apartment Freya used as her "headquarters"—luxuriously fitted out to entertain potential contacts or allies—they would make the switch to the Lady's Maserati, the gift of one of her more amorous associates.

"Keep a close watch on Freya," Mist said to Bryn as she started the engine. She realized she wasn't going to be able to drive with the heels, so she pulled them off and stashed them behind the seat. "Call Konur if there's any change."

"I haven't forgotten," Bryn said. Her gaze was distant, as if she didn't really see Mist at all. "I'll take very good care of the Lady."

"Then wish me luck."

"*Lykke til, min venninne,*" Bryn said. But her voice was as remote as her gaze, and Mist found herself shivering as she pulled away.

❧

"There's always a chance that something will change," Vali said. "But Loki didn't extend this invitation to Freya just to find out what's happened with her. He means to keep her and Mist too busy to interfere when he sends his people after Sleipnir. And that'll keep him focused on other things while we carry out our raid of his mansion."

Perched on Asbrew's long-unused counter, Orn stretched out his wings and flapped them irritably. "Laufeyson knows where the horse resides, but neither you nor Anna can tell *me*. How did he learn this?"

"You know Loki doesn't always confide in me. He obviously didn't think that was important for me to know. And I'm sure that Anna did her best. She was able to confirm that Freya was still in seclusion as of this afternoon, and that tells us a lot."

"It does not tell us the state of her health, or of her magic."

"Loki will find that out at the party, and then we'll know, too." Vali kicked at the floor to dislodge a crust of mud acquired from the wet street outside. "If Loki manages to steal Sleipnir, I'm sure I'll be able to learn where he's hidden the horse."

"Laufeyson forgets who Sleipnir is," Orn said. "He may have given birth to the Slipper, but Odin's mount will not go willingly."

"And it's possible that if Freya or Mist figures out he's trying to distract them, they might get to Sleipnir in time to stop him."

Orn cocked his head, eying Vali appraisingly. "*Can* Mist stop him?"

"We still don't know exactly what happened at the protest." Vali stroked the side of his beard in a nervous gesture that belied his calm demeanor. "Even though Loki tries not to let it show, he's a lot more worried about her than he used to be."

"Then he will be more cautious," Orn said, pacing up and down the length of the counter.

"Maybe. But as long as he's got Dainn and the kid, he's going to believe he has good odds of winning tonight."

Dainn and the kid. Orn clacked his beak. He had known nothing of this child until Vali had informed him. He had not been pleased with what he had learned, but Loki's newest offspring had done little to aid his parent in recent months, and Dainn had been no more than a passive prisoner. According to Vali, neither of them was as easily manipulated as Loki wished.

Regardless of what happened at the reception, the elf would fall soon enough, and Danny might be of very great use to Odin. If Freya did not kill the boy first.

But Orn didn't believe she'd get the chance, even if her affliction was minor and temporary. He had gained many substantial advantages over both her and Loki. Laufeyson no longer considered him a threat. Orn had spies in each of the enemy camps. Mist possessed five of the Treasures, and Orn had already "touched" all of them, two—Gleipnir, the Chain, and Jarngreipr, the Glove—via Anna's pendant. His own followers, aided by Vali's technical expertise, had finally located and claimed two of the remaining Treasures for him. Bragi's Harp and Freyr's Sword, as well as their Valkyrie guardians Hrist and

Olrun, were now under his control. Each Treasure had restored a little more of his intelligence and magic.

Still, they were not enough. Now he must make physical contact with Loki's new acquisitions. The raid on Laufeyson's mansion would give him that opportunity. Though he needed Sleipnir in order to become fully himself, absorbing the power of Thor's magical weapons would increase his power and make it easier for him to take the horse when the time came.

Orn flew from the counter to the back of a chair, looking beyond Vali to the men gathered in the back of the bar. Some might have mistaken them for Jotunar in their more personable, mortal forms, but they were not frost giants. They had been selected long ago from among the most valiant warriors of Valhalla, and their strength, courage, and loyalty had been tested many times in the long ages before the Dispersal and the fall of the other Eight Homeworlds.

They were the *true* Einherjar, not some collection of scruffy mortal bikers.

"Go," he said to Vali. "Finish your preparations, and report to me when they are complete."

Odin's son rose and bowed, and the men behind him moved restlessly, eager for the fight.

Orn, too, was eager, but his face could not show it. He hopped up onto the tallest shelf behind the counter and imagined himself laughing, all the Einherjar laughing with him. Singing the Runes. Casting his Spear. Grinding his enemies beneath his heel.

Eternity would be his again. And this time, it would last forever.

❧

Ryan sat up, the vision still bright and painfully clear. Gabi's snores were so loud that, for a moment, he believed he was still in the midst of a battle.

"Gabi?" he whispered.

Throwing her arm over her head, Gabi mumbled into her pillow.

Ryan swung his legs over the side of the cot and stared at her. He wanted to tell her, but he couldn't. Ever since Eir's death, she'd been in a bad way . . . wandering around the camp in a daze, unable or unwilling to use her healing abilities, disappearing for long hours at a time.

He wouldn't put this on her now.

He got up very quietly and began to dress. He couldn't act just yet, but he couldn't sit still, either. And he needed to figure out how to accomplish what he had to do without letting Freya take advantage of his abilities. That could only lead to a disaster even greater than Eir's death.

He hoped that he'd be using his visions the *right* way for a change. Even if it meant killing someone else.

12

"High society just isn't what it used to be," Loki remarked as the limo let them out at the door of the Fairmont. "Mrs. Seaton certainly has come down in the world if she's taken up with that boy. Don't you agree?"

Dainn waited, rigidly silent, as the chauffeur made his dignified way to the passenger door and held it open for his employer.

"Not in the mood for gossip, I see," Loki said as the elf joined him on the sidewalk under the canopy. "But then again, you never are."

The doorman glided up to usher them through the door and into the marble-floored lobby, already occupied by a number of city luminaries gathering to exchange greetings before ascending to the Crown Room at the top of the hotel.

Loki quickly ascertained that Freya was not among them. With Dainn looming behind him like a bloodless ghost, he nodded coolly to the owner of a prominent real estate firm, whose mere two billion in assets made him hardly worth the effort of a greeting, and kissed the fair knuckles of the daughter of a software tycoon . . . whose father would, with the proper encouragement, be making a substantial investment in Lukas Landvik's newest project.

"And who is this?" Samantha asked, looking up at Dainn from under her thick, pale lashes.

"Forgive me," Loki said, straightening. "Dainn Alfgrim, one of my advisors."

"Of course," Samantha said, offering her hand to Dainn. "The mysterious gentleman everyone's been wondering about." She gave

Loki a disapproving glance. "Where have you been hiding him, Lukas?"

Dainn took the offered hand and shook it briefly. Samantha beamed at him, her perfect teeth flashing as she gazed at the elf just a little too admiringly.

"Dainn is of a retiring nature," Loki said. "He prefers to remain in the background. But he is indispensable when it comes to certain aspects of business, and so I persuaded him to accompany me this evening."

"Well, I'm very happy to see you tonight," Samantha said, gripping Dainn's hand a moment too long. "I hope you won't make yourself a stranger."

"Ah," Loki said abruptly. "There is a gentleman over by that potted palm I must see." He smiled at the girl. "You will forgive me, darling?"

With another lingering glance at Dainn, Samantha reluctantly murmured agreement. Dainn was already walking away.

"Even with that forbidding expression of yours," Loki said, catching up and seizing Dainn's arm, "you've charmed a very important mark. But don't make a habit of it."

Dainn stopped abruptly. "I did not intend to charm anyone."

"Are you quite certain of that? Perhaps you seek alliances of your own." He released Dainn's arm and beamed at the room in general. "This is no different from any other occasion when I've taken you out in public. You're my shadow, unless I require you to be otherwise."

"Then why begin introducing me here, particularly if you mean to present yourself as available to partners of the opposite sex?"

"How can you be so naïve? There are a refreshing number of mortals who enjoy a certain fluidity in their choice of playmates."

"I will not join in any of your games."

Loki shrugged. "There won't be time for games, especially if Freya makes an appearance." He nodded at the CEO of a top Internet auction site. "You *are* still eager to see her, aren't you?"

The elf's face went blank, and Loki reminded himself that he had complete control of the situation. However this played out, Dainn would come to hate Freya so fiercely that he would do anything to destroy her.

Whether Mist was alive or not.

Loki used a minor spell to move ahead of the guests waiting for the lift, and he and Dainn exited the elevator into a large room with golden carpeting, a dance floor, and open drapes revealing large windows overlooking the bay. A young man appeared to take their coats and Loki's hat and scarf. A woman similarly dressed in black trousers and spotless white shirt brought a tray of drinks before Loki could search out the bar.

"Don't say it," Loki said, selecting a glass of champagne. "I only drink tonight to be sociable."

Scanning the room, Dainn ignored him. "She isn't here," he said, his voice strained.

"Patience."

Loki found a convenient observation point near one of the large windows looking out over the bay. Dainn stood slightly behind him, his shoulder to the wall, oblivious of the stunning view or the "beautiful people" who drifted into the room, accepting drinks and pouring furs, cashmere capes, and Armani overcoats into the waiting arms of the attendants. The band struck up a bland playlist of smooth jazz.

The room was nearly full and every guest present when Dainn finally stirred.

"She is not coming," he said, relief in his voice. "She must be ill."

"That by no means suggests that Mist is safe," Loki said, still watching the door. "And you should not consider it a triumph that the only one of my enemies currently able to match me may be helpless to counter any move I make tonight, and possibly for . . ."

He trailed off as the room fell silent. Every head turned toward the door.

A lady walked in. She wore a crimson, floor-length strapless gown, stunning in its simplicity and perfect cut, and with every step the slit in the gown opened just enough to reveal a glimpse of thigh. Her black hair was piled high and loose, random tendrils artfully permitted to escape the arrangement as if the entire thing might come tumbling down with a toss of her head. She paused for dramatic effect, and Loki felt just a hint of the glamour flow into the room and circle slowly like lazy air currents on a long-forgotten summer's day.

For a moment, Loki was as caught up in the lady's spell as all the rest of the mortals. For a moment, he didn't know what he was seeing. He heard Dainn suck in his breath.

"It seems you were premature in your assumption," he whispered to Dainn, carefully controlling the tone of his voice. "But you did say you'd know right away if Mist was alive. Is she?"

ᘔ

Mist stood near the entrance to the room, momentarily frozen by the admiring stares and her almost painful awareness of lust, fascination, and envy that permeated the air. Instinctively she heightened the glamour, neither to draw nor repel but merely to soothe and quiet the high emotion "Freya's" appearance seemed to provoke.

They couldn't tell the difference. She had leaped the first hurdle. Now she had to find out if she could stay in the air.

Where are you, Konur?

Taking a deep breath, she did her best impression of a glide and moved into the crowd. Immediately she was surrounded by the elite, though somehow the men seemed to press in a little more closely. She could smell their perspiration, and the musk of arousal. Male and female both virtually dripped wealth and sophistication, from Louis Vuitton shoes to Fendi necklines and Charvet shirt-collars.

With every fiber of her being, Mist wanted nothing more than to turn on one narrow heel and stride out of the room. This was not her world, and these were no more her people than the highest of the Aesir and Alfar. She was still a common Norwegian Forest Cat dressed up in the sleek coat of a Siberian tiger, a kestrel hiding beneath a peacock's feathers. Her smile was painted on like the artificial shadows framing her eyes, and the glamour swirled around her head like noxious fumes.

But she held her ground, as she would do in any battle. Voices purred and chattered compliments and invitations of both the general and very personal sort, and fingertips brushed her arm and her shoulder and hip. She began to tense, remembered, and forced herself to relax again, hiding the subtle movement of her body with a sweep of her arm.

Somehow, she found the right things to say. Bryn and Rota's coaching took over, and she let it run like a computer program through her brain, detaching herself from the disgust she felt at this game she was required to play. A handsome man with graying hair took her arm in a proprietary gesture, and she knew without thinking that this was one of Freya's current lovers. A powerful entrepreneur, and one the Lady already had in her pocket and kept ready to sway the opinions of other men and women whose friendship would be required when the excrement hit the fan.

Mist refrained from wrenching free. It wasn't as if she'd have to take her impersonation to the limit. Her purpose here was clear and narrowly focused.

She scanned the room, holding her lips in a faint, mysterious smile. It took only one careful pass to find Loki, surprisingly and discreetly ensconced near one of the windows, and another second to recognize Dainn right behind him.

Her heart seized. Freya had never mentioned seeing him at any of the events and parties she attended. His appearance with Loki during the press conference had been the first Mist had seen.

He looked nearly the same as he had then: expressionless, pale, dark shadows under his eyes. He wore a black suit and conservative tie in vivid contrast to Loki's more eye-catching attire. When he met her gaze, she saw only emptiness.

Of course he believed she was Freya. Or so she hoped. She couldn't begin to guess what he thought of the Lady now, what he thought of anything.

Mist pitied him. She despised him. She . . .

"Freya," the Lady's lover said, his lips brushing her ear. "Can I get you anything? A glass of wine?"

Mist found her voice. "That would be lovely," she said, matching

Freya's cadence. When he was gone, she set her jaw, detached herself from her admirers, and strode toward Loki.

He met her halfway across the room, looking immensely pleased to see her. Dainn hung back.

"As always," Loki said, reaching for her hand, "Freya Ingrunn outshines every woman in the room."

Mist retreated a step. She had no idea if she'd fooled him, but one touch would probably tell him everything he wanted to know.

"How charming it is to see you again, Mr. Landvik," she said lightly.

"I'm most gratified that you accepted my invitation to talk," he said, carefully studying her face. "It has been so long."

"Not nearly long enough," she said with a gentle smile.

"Now, now," Loki chided. "Everyone knows that Ms. Ingrunn and Mr. Landvik are political and social rivals, but we must maintain at least the appearance of cordiality."

Mist laughed huskily and leaned toward him. "Very well. What is so urgent that you felt the need to exchange such pleasantries in public?"

"I knew you would never meet with me in private. I merely wished to assure myself that you are well."

"Why should I not be?"

"I heard certain rumors that you might have fallen ill while defending honest citizens from police brutality after the press conference."

It took a great act of will for Mist to stay relaxed. "However you provoked it," she said, stifling a yawn, "the protest was a strangely inept effort on your part. Just what were you hoping to achieve?"

"I?" Loki pressed his hand to his chest. "*I* had nothing to do with it. I would never be so crude."

"Of course not," Mist said, tossing her head. "But one of your minions might have become a little . . . overenthusiastic in your service."

A spiral of hair fell to her shoulder and curled into her cleavage. Loki stared at it, wetting his lips. Even now, with all that had passed between him and Freya, Loki could still be led around by his genitals.

"I can also assure you that none of my allies would have acted without my express permission," he said, catching himself.

"And why is it so important that I know these things?" Mist asked.

"Why did you come when I asked?"

Mist shrugged with an elegant lift of bare shoulders. "I would have attended this gathering in any case, as I am certain you are well aware."

"Or perhaps you simply did not wish me to believe that you might be vulnerable?"

He isn't even trying, Mist thought. *He's laying it right out in the open.*

But she still didn't know if he really believed she was Freya. If she made a single mistake . . .

"I do not know what you think you saw," she said, "but you were mistaken. I am as I always was."

"And what *are* you, my dear lady?"

He had to suspect, Mist thought. He was waiting for that single slip.

"Your superior in all things," she said. "And now, since we have both satisfied our curiosity—"

"But surely you have a few words for your former servant," Loki said, gesturing behind him at Dainn. "It would do him good to know that you do not hold his treachery against him."

Breathing silently through her nose, Mist tried to prepare herself. Konur appeared at her elbow.

"I apologize for my tardiness," he said, his gaze meeting Loki's. "Have I missed anything of importance?"

"Nothing," Mist said. Freya's current lover was approaching, carrying two wineglasses and napkins in his hands. He slowed as he saw Konur and Loki.

"Am I interrupting?" he asked with a hard stare at Loki.

Mist had to admire the mortal's courage, even if it was born of ignorance. "Mr. Landvik was just leaving," she said. She smiled at Loki. "It was . . . delightful to speak with you again."

Loki bowed. "Likewise, Ms. Ingrunn. Gentlemen."

Then he was strolling off, cool as you please, and Mist still had no idea if she'd fooled him. The mortal handed her one of the glasses.

"I have a little business to take care of myself," he said, glancing at Konur. "If you'll excuse me." With a slight frown, he gave the other glass to Konur and stalked away.

When Mist looked for Dainn, he, too, was gone.

"How many men in this room has Freya slept with?" she asked in an undertone, trying to distract herself from both relief and worry.

"At least half, I daresay," Konur said. "That is one of the hallmarks of her social success. How did it go?"

"I don't know." Mist continued to smile benevolently at everyone who passed, using just enough "anti-glamour" to keep anyone from getting too close. "He knows Freya was ill, as we expected. He also guessed that we came to prove that we aren't vulnerable. But he must think I, or someone else, could be impersonating her. He asked me outright who I am."

"Evidently he did not receive the answer he expected."

"He didn't receive an answer at all. You showed up at exactly the right time. Loki was about to reintroduce me to Dainn."

Konur must have heard the hardness in her voice. He touched her elbow gently.

"Maintain your pretense," he reminded her. "You cannot afford to abandon your concentration."

"Did you know that Dainn was here?"

"I sensed his presence, but did not expect Loki to bring him to Freya."

"Maybe that was part of his test. He hopes that Dainn will know who I am if he gets close enough to me."

"Then he will doubtless attempt it again."

"And I'll need to be prepared." Mist hooked Konur's arm and pulled him to the side of the room. "Can you tell . . . can you sense if Dainn has—"

"Gone into darkness?" Konur said. "Lost himself to this beast, or something worse? No." He took her hand between both of his. "He is deeply ill. Beyond that, I cannot tell."

"Then it's nothing we didn't know before. I need to stay away from him."

"If you hate him," Konur said, "it should not be difficult to continue playing the game."

But I don't, Mist thought. "We were close," she said. "We even touched minds. He might see things Loki can't. And Loki can probably read him like a book." She smiled vaguely at a woman across the room. "Do whatever you can to make sure he doesn't come near me."

"You will still require guidance and protection, should matters deteriorate."

"I seem to have done okay so far," Mist said. "You'll have to trust me."

Konur gave her a long, assessing look, nodded, and drifted away. Mist assumed Freya's mantle again, detesting the inevitable circulating she'd have to do, the insipid conversation she'd have to make, the aura of seduction she'd have to maintain.

And all for nothing, if Dainn gave her away.

Dainn watched her drift from one cluster of guests to another—laughing with her head flung back to expose the creamy length of her throat, tossing her black hair to send loose strands flying about her elegant shoulders, flashing white teeth at a jest. She moved as if a carpet of primroses carried her above the floor, and mortals gave way to her as if they knew precisely what she was.

But they did not. They had no way of knowing that the woman they adored was an impostor twice over.

When she had first entered the room, the sheer force of her presence had nearly shattered him. He had felt her glamour as if she had tossed a live grenade into the center of the floor, and the blast had caught him full in the chest.

And he had *known*. Known not only that Mist was alive, but that it was she and not Freya standing amongst mortals who hadn't the means to question what their eyes and senses insisted must be true.

His *heart* had told him.

Dainn leaned his cheek against the cold glass of the window. As he had continued to observe her, he had seen nothing of the Valkyrie in Mist's movements or what little he could hear of her speech. There was absolute confidence and self-assurance in her every action, with not so much of a trace of the uncertainty and vulnerability that had so often made Mist doubt herself and her own worth.

Perhaps some of that confidence was her own. He had been convinced that Freya had not found the means to seize her soul. The Lady *had* fallen, and Mist had completed her work during the protest. That meant Mist had indeed grown stronger . . . strong enough to take Freya's place tonight and maintain her mask of glamour with apparent ease.

If he had still been capable of joy, Dainn would have felt it in that moment of discovery. But Loki had shattered Dainn's conviction when he'd gone to meet Mist. There was contempt in the lady's eyes, but no rage. None of Mist's warrior's spirit, the fire that shone so brightly when she faced any enemy who could destroy what she loved. Doubt had burst within Dainn like a poisonous spore, eating away at his hope.

Moment by moment, Dainn's faith in his own judgment had begun to die. His *heart* had told him she was here, and alive. A heart which could not be trusted, no more than the beast could be.

When Mist and Loki parted, Dainn had shaken as if with fever, waiting for Loki to render his judgment. But Loki had simply instructed Dainn to meet him later and gone on about some other business. As if he had learned all he needed to know, and was unsurprised.

"A drink, sir?" one of the young servers asked, cleaving Dainn's thought with merciful swiftness. Dainn reached for a glass before he could think and downed the contents. It was only wine, but Dainn had not taken drink for many years, and he felt it burn though his body and begin to drown the poison.

He returned the empty glass to the tray and grabbed another while the bemused server looked on.

"Are you all right, sir?" she asked.

Dainn wiped his mouth with the back of his hand. "Yes. Thank you for the refreshment."

She backed away, steadying the empty glasses on the tray with one hand, and disappeared into the crowd. Dainn looked for the lady, but she, too, had vanished.

Shutting out the hum of voices and laughter, Dainn closed his eyes. He turned his senses inward, searching, reaching deep for the thing he hated.

"*If I didn't know better, I'd suspect that the beast was returning,*" Loki had said.

And it *had* returned, there in Danny's room when Dainn had faced Fenrir. The effects of the herb he had taken on the steppes had not been permanent after all.

He had sworn to fight its evil, even to his own death, if it attempted to reclaim its power. He would never allow Laufeyson to use the beast against Mist and the allies.

But it was still under his control. A voice was whispering inside him—the beast and not the beast, something still halfway between elf and monster. *It can tell you,* the voice assured him. *The beast has senses even you do not.*

There would be no guesswork. The torment of doubt would end. And if he learned that Mist was gone . . .

We will be one.

Dainn's eyes flew open, and he slammed the gate on the thing he had almost loosed. On the promises, and the threats. On the horror of what it offered.

Stumbling away from the window, Dainn wove through the knots of guests, staggering like a drunkard. *Perhaps,* he thought, *I am drunk.*

He turned in a slow circle, looking for the bar. Loki was there, sharing a drink with a woman Dainn had never seen. A few of the guests seemed to notice Dainn as if for the first time, but he knew himself incapable of speaking sensibly to any of them, not even for the purpose of discovering what they perceived of the woman in the crimson gown.

Panic caught at him with small, sharp claws. He could leave. He would not get far before Loki fetched him back, though it might take a little while for the Jotunar scattered around Nob Hill to find him.

As his gaze swung toward the door, he saw her. She had paused in an island of stillness, her head slightly cocked, her eyes alert.

And *Mist* was there again.

Dainn was aware of nothing else as he strode toward her, ignoring the grunts of annoyance and soft cries as he bumped a shoulder or jarred a hand cradling a glass of wine. She turned toward him as he drew near, and in her eyes he saw what he would expect of Freya's daughter: anger, consternation, confusion.

But not hatred. Not that.

Mist.

"Come no closer," a man said, stepping between him and the lady. Dainn glanced up, distracted, and froze.

The man was no man at all, but elf, and obviously a lord of his people. That was clear in his eyes, in his features, and in the easy authority of his bearing.

And he was also the very elf Dainn had begged to warn Mist about Freya after the battle at the portal. The one who had claimed that the elves who had almost taken Danny captive were not his.

Dainn had never known if the elf-lord had been telling the truth. But here he was, apparently guarding the lady, staring at Dainn with unmistakable hostility in his eyes.

"It's all right," the lady said, laying a hand on the elf-lord's arm. "Let me speak to the traitor, since he seems so eager to fling himself into my path."

The elf-lord inclined his head and stepped back, still within easy reach. The lady gazed into Dainn's eyes, her full, brightly painted lips curved in a mocking smile.

"So," she said softly, in a voice not even the nearest mortals could hear. "My once-faithful servant. I had not thought we would meet again under circumstances in which I could not destroy you."

"Mist," Dainn whispered.

"I wonder, Konur, if he has gone blind as well as mad," she said.

"He seems unable to distinguish ebon black hair from common yellow, and grace from gaucherie."

"Indeed," Konur said. "His poor judgment is such that I would gladly rid you of his presence."

The lady sighed. "Alas, Loki is too near, and will no doubt defend his prize." She leaned closer to Dainn. "Tell me, traitor . . . do you enjoy sharing his bed now as much as you did when you thought it was mine?"

13

Mist despised herself for speaking the words, but she knew she'd had no choice.

No choice, because suddenly she was vulnerable, more vulnerable than she had been when Loki had tried to bait her. Standing so close to Dainn, hearing him speak her name, was so much worse than she'd expected. She was aware of every tiny detail of his appearance and manner, every emotion that flickered across his face. She saw the muscles jump in his cheek, heard his breath catch, felt the agony of denial course through him as if it pumped in her own veins. Her emotions rose in response to his: her heart began to beat too hard and too fast, her skin to flush, her body to remember every touch they had ever shared.

If the beast was there, she couldn't see it. It had nearly killed Danny on the steppes, but now . . .

Think, she told herself. Konur hadn't seen any great darkness in Dainn. Freya had been so sure that Loki couldn't cure him, but what if he had? Was that why Dainn still remained with Loki, though he surely might have escaped many times? Could he feel bound by a debt he couldn't break?

Greater than the one he owes the Aesir? Greater than anything he ever felt for—

She parried the thought before it could cut too deep. Whatever Dainn's true reason, he hadn't turned the beast against Loki's enemies. He'd used no elven magic on Loki's behalf. What *had* he done against the allies, against *her?*

She desperately wanted to find out, to wrap them both in a circle of silence and finally learn the truth. But his eyes were still asking questions, dangerous ones . . . looking for proof, even the smallest sign, that his guess had been correct.

Had Loki sent the elf to test her again, as Konur had suggested he might? Or had Dainn simply seen her and *known*, as she would have known him in any guise, anywhere?

It didn't matter. Stopping him was more important than her fragile hope of reconciliation, of finding some way to forgive him. She couldn't afford the weakness of pity or compassion or hope. Not even for herself.

"I see you have no answer," she said. "Go slinking back to your master, cur, and perhaps you may leave this place alive."

Closing her eyes to shut out the sight of his face, Mist gathered her magic, infusing it with all Freya's arrogance and contempt. She turned it about and pushed outward, slamming Dainn with the "anti-glamour."

She heard him gasp, but when she opened her eyes she saw him braced against the magic like a deep-rooted tree holding fast in a savage storm. No one else in the room had been affected; none of the guests noticed the brutal attack.

But Dainn's eyes told her what she needed to know.

"Where is Mist?" he asked, his voice little more than a rasp.

Playing her role to the hilt, Mist pursed her lips in displeasure at the elf's continued defiance. "Why does it matter to you?" she asked scornfully. "Surely you know that she despises you even more than I do, and would gladly kill you just as swiftly."

Dainn took an uneven step back. "Then she still lives," he said.

Mist suppressed a frown of confusion. "Foolhardy Mist may be," she said, "but you may assure Loki that my daughter is still under my protection."

"Protection," Dainn said, his upper lip curling in a way that made the back of her neck prickle. "But for how much longer, Lady? When will you finish it? Or has she become too strong?"

The words made no sense to Mist, and she could see that Dainn regretted speaking them. He backed away another few steps, and Konur eased into the gap, placing himself between her and Dainn.

"Leave the Lady in peace, *nidingr,*" Konur said, haughty disdain in every line of his body.

"By all means," Loki said, coming up behind Dainn, "leave her in peace." He rested his hand on Dainn's shoulder, his fingers biting into the black wool of Dainn's jacket. "She has her business to attend to, and we have ours."

Dainn held Mist's gaze for a long, stubborn moment, refusing to be moved by Loki's hard grip. Konur stood directly in front of him and stared into his eyes. It seemed that something elvish passed between them—an unspoken message, a warning, a promise.

And then Dainn was turning to leave, wrenching himself free of Loki's hold. He strode away, head down, as if he didn't care where he was going.

Loki clucked his tongue. "I believe you have hurt his feelings, Lady Sow. Now I shall have to console him."

He strolled after Dainn, clearly in no hurry. Mist clenched her fists behind her back, wondering how much he had overheard.

Why would Dainn ask if Mist is still alive? she wondered. And why had he reacted with such hostility to the idea that Freya was protecting her daughter?

"What did he mean, Konur?" she murmured when he moved close enough to hear. "What did he expect Freya to finish? Why did he ask if I'd—if Mist had become too strong?"

"I don't know," Konur said, staring the way Dainn and Loki had gone.

But Dainn had warned her about Freya many times before. It almost sounded as if he'd expected Freya to *do* something to her.

Something that might even kill her.

Mist laughed aloud at her own paranoia, letting the sound rise above the drone of conversation. Now she had peoples' attention again, and men and women were converging on her, relieving her of the need to dwell on yet another ugly thought.

"I'll be all right now," she said to Konur as a group of local politicians wended their purposeful way toward her. "The mayor's circle of jerks is coming this way. I'll see if I can learn anything about the protest from them."

"Take care," Konur said. "Most of the men are Loki's, as is the mayor. Loki may have sent them to distract and expose you."

The elf-lord was gone by the time the mayor's hangers-on reached her. She was familiar with all their names, reputations, and recent activities, but had never met any of them in person. There wasn't a single woman among them. Two of the men—one a state senator, the other a member of the mayor's inner circle—were secretly in Freya's camp.

None of them, of course, knew that they were involved in anything more than a mortal struggle for power and control of a single city. The waters of Midgardian politics as a whole had become increasingly treacherous and difficult to navigate—a fact Loki had taken full advantage of—and reactionary ideologies provided sufficient rationale for the most extreme beliefs and behavior on the part of men like the mayor.

Pretending that they were all on the best of terms, Mist managed to make "appropriate" conversation with the men, parrying suggestive comments with ribald remarks of her own. Most of them were thinking more with their private parts than with their minds. The verbal foreplay came more and more naturally to her, and she could only assume that her use of the glamour had made it easier to slip into Freya's mind-set.

That wasn't something she was proud of. And in spite of her efforts, she couldn't learn anything new about the protest.

"Ah, *here* she is," a jovial male voice boomed as another man pushed his way in among the others. He was tall, a little portly, and on the fading edge of handsome, with a toothy grin and friendly manner.

But his eyes were hard, and Mist knew this man wasn't one Freya could twist around her finger, glamour or no. Mayor Walker was an opportunist who wouldn't be where he was today without Loki. He'd sacrificed both pride and independence for a shot at real power . . . at least until he had what he wanted.

That was how Loki controlled him. First the carrot and then the stick—allow this mortal to believe *he* was the one with all the bright ideas, and that the people of San Francisco were happy with the changes he'd brought to the city. Then the pointed reminders that without Loki, he'd quickly fall back into obscurity with the next election.

If there *was* one.

"Mayor Walker," Mist said, casting him a half-lidded glance. "I didn't know we'd have the pleasure of seeing you tonight."

He made a show of looking around as the other men stepped back. "'We'? I don't see any of your usual companions. Or did you mean it in the royal sense?"

"I should never wish to tread on the hem of your cape, Your Honor."

He took her hand and squeezed. It would have been painful if she'd been any less strong. Or prepared. "I hope we can maintain our truce a little longer, Ms. Ingrunn."

Mist squeezed back. "Oh, I think that would be very wise, Mr. Mayor. We wouldn't want to think that you make a habit of consummating your acts prematurely."

Someone snickered. The mayor's jaw bunched.

"I'd be more than happy to give you a private preview," he said.

"Oh, no. Please leave me the pleasure of my imagination. It's so disappointing when the final product doesn't live up to the hype."

Walker had enough self-control not to explode in front of the guests, a number of whom had gathered to listen in on the conversation. He was opening his mouth to answer when yet another man joined them . . . about twenty years older, with gray hair in a military crew cut, and a grim expression. He took the mayor by the arm and whispered in his ear.

"If you will excuse me, gentlemen," Walker said, pointedly excluding Mist, "there is a matter that requires my attention."

"Like that little protest in Civic Center Plaza?" Mist put in before he and the chief of police could walk away. "Are you certain you have enough law enforcement personnel and sufficient armaments to deal with a hundred men, women, and children carrying signs?"

The chief glared at her. "You're fortunate, Ms. Ingrunn, that you have my people to protect your pretty behind from the lawless elements in this city."

A few women in the vicinity gasped at his crudeness. Most of the other men had drifted away, obviously unwilling to confront the mayor or his cronies.

"Do you mean the young and poor being driven ever deeper into poverty and desperation?" Mist asked sweetly. "The ones falling prey to the aggressive drug dealers who have claimed nearly every street corner and lure children into addiction and slavery?"

Dead silence fell. The people in this room didn't have to deal with street crime. They certainly didn't want this kind of subject brought up at one of their gatherings.

"How is it that your forces keep growing and your jails overflow, yet this city is becoming a mecca for organized crime and sex trafficking?" Mist continued. "Who is paying the price?"

"Just what are you suggesting?" the captain said, pushing past the mayor.

Mist raised her hands and tossed the glamour at him like a net, halting him in midstride. Shock passed over his sharp-boned face. His knees trembled, and his eyes began to glaze over.

She held him there for one, five, ten seconds, a righteous anger deafening her to the startled voices around her. In those few seconds, the anger and magic blended into a perfect whole, and she knew again what it was like to be Freya, to wield such forces without the fetters of conscience.

He deserves to be punished, she thought. They all did, these savages, these defilers of all that was—

"Freya."

Konur's voice. Perhaps, had he been a mortal, she wouldn't have heard him. But he found some means of reaching her, and suddenly she was letting go, the rage draining out of her, the glamour withdrawing into her body and heating her blood like potent wine.

What have I done? She stared at the chief, who was in the process of getting to his feet. Everyone else was staring from him to Mist with varying degrees of astonishment, shock, and utter bewilderment.

"Let us go," Konur murmured, "before these mortals begin to imagine what truly happened."

Cursing herself silently, Mist let him lead her away. Her own knees were rubbery now, and she was grateful that Konur was able to negotiate the crowd in such a way that they could slip through without being stopped by the curious or admiring.

"I know," she moaned when she and the elf-lord were alone again. "I blew it."

"I doubt any of the mortals understood what they were seeing," he said.

"But if any of them have had exposure to magic . . ."

"The damage, if any, is done. Now there are more important matters that claim your attention."

"Loki?" she asked.

His gaze was stern. "What I show you will not be pleasant. But you must not use the glamour, or any magic that will call attention to yourself, no matter how greatly you are tempted."

"This sounds bad. Does it have something to do with—"

"Will you swear to me that you will do nothing to jeopardize Freya's position here?"

"Is someone being hurt?"

"Mist, you must not interfere. Not now. There will be other times."

"Show me."

Konur hesitated.

"Show me. Now."

With a last, long look into her eyes, Konur nodded. He led to the elevator, and they took it to another floor with a hallway closed off by a heavy door. It was locked by two dead bolts.

"A very private hall," Konur said. He grasped the doorknob and frowned. "Strange. This was unlocked when I first entered."

"What is going on, Konur?"

In silence he passed his hand over the doorknob and locks. Tiny, pale roots sprang out of the wood near the doorknob and squirmed into the cracks of the lower lock, wriggling and swelling, white turning dark as they grew. The lock began to swell, groaning softly as the various parts began to separate.

Sweat beaded on Konur's forehead, and he closed his eyes. Fresh roots began to invade the second lock.

"Stop, Konur," Mist said. "Let me finish this."

With a gasp of effort, Konur completed the spell, and the outer halves of both dead bolts thumped onto the carpet runner. There was a corresponding thump on the other side of the door, and holes where the locks had been.

Mist managed to grab Konur as he began to fall.

"Curse it," she hissed. "Conjuring roots out of a gods-know-how-old door? Do you want to make yourself useless?"

"I am not . . . useless yet," he said, straightening his shoulders as he pulled away. "But you must now set a ward to shield us. We do not wish to be seen."

"Now you've got me really worried," Mist muttered. She tried a basic deflection spell. It took nothing out of her, not even the usual temporary weakness or light-headedness that sometimes came with magic.

Considering that they were obviously walking into something bad, she was very, very grateful.

She kept Konur close, half-supporting him as they continued along the hall. Soon her ears picked up laughter: guttural, male, and probably drunk. She traced it to a door near the end of the hall even before Konur pointed it out.

Konur stopped her before she opened the door.

"Remember what I have told you," he said. "I might have hidden this from you, and prevented a possible battle we cannot afford." He stroked her cheek with his fingertip. "I must trust you now."

A peculiar sensation buzzed in Mist's nerves when he touched her, utterly different from what she felt when Dainn made physical contact. There was nothing remotely sexual about it, and yet she felt as if something powerful passed between her and the elf-lord. Something more potent than magic.

"Remember," Konur repeated, dropping his hand. Mist opened the unlocked door.

The suite was clearly one of the hotel's finest, luxuriously furnished and spacious enough for two dozen party guests. Five men were sprawled around the room in various states of undress, some snorting cocaine, others simply drinking.

Loki was sitting on a thickly padded armchair, watching the proceedings as if they amused him but were far too lowbrow to tempt him into participating.

She almost choked when she saw the four women in the room. None of them were laughing. Two of them, she knew.

Her Sisters—Skuld, guardian of Thor's Belt, Megingjord; and Regin, who had held Mjollnir, Thor's Hammer. They, like the other two women, were clad in diaphanous dresses that made Mist's form-fitting gown seem like a Puritan woman's all-encompassing black petticoats. One of the drunken men was pawing at Skuld, while Regin sat close to the coke table, staring into space.

Loki had gotten to them first.

Mist had taken a full step into the room before Konur grabbed her arm. "They do not see us yet," he said, "but it cannot be long before Loki senses our presence."

"What has he done to them?" Mist asked, her voice trembling with helpless anger. "Are they under a spell?"

"Is there reason to think that they might align themselves with Loki willingly?"

Mist clamped her fingers around Konur's wrist and pulled his hand away. "*Look* at them. Do you think they'd become the playthings of Loki's mortals?"

"No," Konur said softly. "I did not believe it. But you see that Loki is controlling them somehow, and he must have both Mjollnir and Megingjord."

Two out of three, Mist thought. If he could get Jarngreipr from Rota, he'd have all Thor's powerful Treasures.

"You are not in a position to free them," Konur said. "But now we know that Loki has been able to control two Valkyrie, and is bold enough to use them at his own convenience."

"And he didn't think I'd find out they were here?"

"Perhaps that is just what he intended. I caught a glimpse of Regin with one of these men while I was watching for Loki, and followed. Had he wished to conceal himself, surely he would have done so."

"He knows that Mist has a far more personal interest in the other Valkyrie than Freya does," Mist said. And if he had guessed that the "lady" was Mist, she thought, had he expected her to lose control and attempt a rescue, no matter what the cost?

"Of course this may also be a trap," Konur said, echoing her thoughts. "But I believed it was necessary for you to observe with your own eyes."

Mist backed deliberately away from the door. "We can't let this go on. One way or another—"

Loki cocked his head, turning it slightly toward the door. Regin got up and drifted across the room to stand beside his chair, playing with his hair and whispering in his ear. A moment later Dainn entered the room from another door, stopping some distance away from Loki and Regin. Loki called him, and he went to his master without so much as a glance at the Valkyrie.

Mist nearly lost control of her stomach. She staggered into the hall, doubled over, and covered her mouth with her hands.

"Let us go," Konur said.

"No," Mist said thickly. "We have to try to save Regin and Skuld."

He laid his hand on her back, and once again she felt that flow of comfort that seemed to dampen the nausea as well as the rage. "Loki has begun to sense something amiss, and I can be of little help to you."

But Mist had reason to doubt him when she found herself turning away, against every instinct, and retracing their path to the double-locked door. This time, Mist used the forge-Galdr to reassemble the locks, though they would never be fully functional again.

Loki would know they'd been tampered with, and by whom. But

that hardly mattered if Konur was right, and it had all been a setup. She just didn't want Loki to know she knew it.

Leaving Konur to follow at his own pace, Mist looked for the closest restroom and spent a good five minutes in one of the immaculate stalls, regaining control of her rebellious stomach. There was nothing more she could do here . . . nothing to save her Sisters, or act openly against Loki and his minions. She'd already risked too much. This wasn't her world, and she couldn't think straight, couldn't formulate any plans that didn't involve not only blowing her cover but also opening a Pandora's box not even the All-father would be able to close again.

Taking a deep breath, Mist left the restroom. Konur was gone, but someone else was waiting for her. Someone she hadn't seen since that last, open battle with Loki's Jotunar at the portal to the steppes.

He hadn't changed much physically over the past months, but he seemed fully conscious in a way he hadn't been during most of their adventure on the other side of the Earth. She and the allies had assumed that he was back with Loki, reclaimed by Laufeyson after he'd disappeared from the steppes.

But why was he *here,* of all places? Why would Loki have brought his son to this very adult event, where his enemies might get ahold of the boy?

"Danny?" Mist said, standing very still.

The boy looked up at her, his eyes alert and wary. "Who are you?" he asked.

She stiffened. Whether or not Danny had ever seen Freya on the steppes, Loki would have spent plenty of time and effort teaching his son to recognize and fear his enemies.

Opening her senses, Mist whispered a Rune-spell she'd seldom had cause to use before. She wasn't completely sure it was working until her subtle "push" suddenly broke through like an ax through soft butter. There was no resistance, no counter-spell of protection or obfuscation.

Only Danny. He was who and what he appeared to be. The tattoo on her wrist, concealed by a wide gold-and-gemstone bracelet, began to burn.

Danny stepped toward her and took her hand. A queasy moment later they were standing in an empty guest room, and the only sound breaking the silence was the hum of the fan blowing cool air out the vent in the ceiling.

Teleportation, Mist thought, battling another all-too-familiar bout of nausea. The same thing he'd done with Dainn when he'd rescued the elf from Loki and taken him through the portal to search for Sleipnir.

"You're Mist," Danny said, hopping up on the edge of the king-size bed. "You don't look right, but I remember you anyway."

The boy spoke with confidence, and Mist wondered if her magic had somehow worked both ways, opening her up to his mind and senses.

It wasn't going to do any good to lie to him now. "Yes," she said, "I remember you, too. You made the portal, and we helped you find Sleipnir."

Danny nodded. "He went away."

"I'm sorry," Mist said, wondering if he knew that she had Sleipnir. Would Loki have told him?

"How did you get here, Danny?" she asked gently.

"It was easy."

She understood his non-answer. Loki hadn't brought him at all.

"You did it the same way you transported me to this room?" she asked.

"Uh-huh." He continued to gaze at her intently.

"From Loki's house?"

He nodded again.

"Does he know you're here?"

"Uh-uh."

"Why did you come?"

"I couldn't help it," Danny said, his mouth twisting in frustration. "He was afraid."

"Who was afraid?"

"Papa."

Loki, afraid? "Of what?"

"Will you take him away?"

The boy was changing subjects faster than Mist could follow them. Was he so frightened that she would hurt Loki? Did he understand that much?

But he'd never seemed to care about his father when he'd been with her and Dainn on the steppes. To the contrary: he'd openly defied Loki by rescuing Dainn from Laufeyson at Asbrew.

That proves nothing, Mist thought. She didn't really know anything about Danny's life with Loki, before or after those events. From what Dainn had told her, she assumed he was virtually a prisoner, valuable to Loki only because of his powers.

Still, even Loki might be capable of some paternal affection. Maybe Danny, who seemed so much more focused now, returned those feelings.

But how much did he really understand of what was going on between his parent and Mist? Did Danny really have the maturity to recognize fear in his father and move on his own to ask mercy from an enemy?

Nothing he'd done in Mist's brief acquaintance with the boy suggested it. If Dainn were here in this room, maybe he could have told her what Danny was trying to say. He and Danny had been very close in that brief time they were together.

"Where do you think I would take him, Danny?" she asked.

Tears started in his eyes. "I don't know." He sniffed. "*He* will make everything bad."

There was something about Danny's emphasis on the "he" that seemed different from his talk about Loki. She felt a sudden chill.

"Who would make everything bad, Danny?"

The boy closed his eyes, and a gray cloud formed in front of his face. There was something inside it, something that flashed with sparks and streaks of lightning.

"They want to take it," Danny said, shaping the cloud with his hands like a sculptor molding an amorphous mass of clay.

Mist raised her hands as if to touch the vision, and it exploded into a shower of black feathers that disappeared an instant later.

Black feathers, Mist thought. Like a raven's. Her bracelet began to singe her skin above and below the tattoo.

"What are you trying to tell me?" she asked, biting back a cry of pain.

"I don't want to die," Danny whispered.

14

A thousand slivers of ice jammed into Mist's spine from neck to tailbone. "What do you mean?" She grasped his thin shoulders. "Danny, who is—"

But suddenly her hands were empty, and she found herself standing outside the restroom as if she'd never left.

As if Danny had never been there at all.

She lifted her hand and slid the bracelet off, pulling a little burned skin away with it. Maybe it *had* been an illusion . . . one of Loki's, something he could manage at a short distance.

But Loki's illusions weren't usually physical things, like Danny's manifestations. She'd *touched* the boy. And Danny himself had created some kind of manifestation.

But what in the gods' name was it? What did "they" want to take? And if Loki wasn't a threat to Danny, who was?

If the beast *had* returned . . .

Mist was just about to go in search of Konur, bare feet and all, when Danny ran into the hall and nearly collided with her.

"Danny!" she said, catching him. "Where did you go?"

He stared up at her, clearly terrified. "He's going to kill me!" he cried.

Grabbing his shoulders, she pulled him against the wall. "Is someone chasing you?"

"The monster!" Danny panted, looking over his shoulder.

Mist couldn't believe that Loki would allow the beast to roam unattended around these halls under any circumstances. He barely let Dainn out of his sight.

"Come with me," she said, taking his hand. "We'll find—"

He was gone again before she could finish speaking. She looked down the hall, but no one was coming. She sensed no threat.

Why hadn't Danny spoken directly of the beast before? Why had he been so vague, his speech so disconnected?

Of one thing Mist was certain: something was very wrong, and Danny had come to *her* for help. If he was still anywhere in this building, she'd track him down and get answers . . . without alerting Loki. Or Dainn.

The locks had been tampered with.

Dainn paused in front of the door to the private hall, his body still shaking with helpless anger. He had seen Regin and Skuld acting as playthings for Loki's mortal allies—dolls without volition or awareness—and there had been nothing he could do. Loki had made very clear that the consequences of any interference would fall, not on him, but on the Valkyrie.

And so, once he had put in an appearance as Loki had demanded for some unfathomable purpose of his own, Dainn had walked away. No one had stopped him. And now he discovered that magic had been worked on the hall door, magic with the distinct flavor of Freya's aristocratic elven escort.

Dainn laid his palm against the door. It shuddered, and the dead bolts and knob broke apart and fell to the carpet.

Whoever had broken the locks must have known that their intrusion would be discovered. Someone who might have witnessed Loki's private "party."

But Loki would have sensed the presence of enemies, and he'd shown no sign—

The door creaked on its hinges and swung open. Dainn jumped back, his body acting before his mind could prepare.

Danny stood on the other side of the door, wearing rumpled pajamas and an anxious expression.

"Papa?" he said.

Dainn looked beyond him into the hall. There was no one else there.

"Danny," he said, dropping into a crouch, "how did you get here?"

"I'm afraid, Papa," Danny said. "The lady wants to hurt me."

The lady. "Danny," Dainn said, reaching out. "How did you—"

His hand swept through empty air. Danny had spun around and was running away, pelting down the public hall in an awkward lope.

Dainn broke into a run, but within seconds Danny had disappeared, and Dainn could feel no sense of him. His heart raced, fueled by adrenaline and terror for his son.

She will kill him.

Dainn closed his eyes, struggling to block the other voice, the thing halfway between elf and monster. It was still weak, and it reached for Dainn with claws hardly more fearsome than a kitten's.

A kitten that fed on fear.

"No," Dainn said, his blood surging hot in his veins.

You have no choice.

"There is always a choice."

The claws lengthened and curved into scythes, and the voice grew stronger.

He will die.

A deep growl started up in Dainn's throat. His vision altered and his senses sharpened to painful clarity. He could already feel the beast's growing power swelling in his muscles, pounding in his chest . . . the terrible, familiar sense of losing himself to the creature that wanted nothing but blood and violence and death.

Our enemy's death, it said.

Freya's death. But as much as he despised her, he was almost certain that she had not yet destroyed Mist. The Lady was Loki's enemy, holding him in check until . . .

Will you contemplate the future while the boy falls?

Dainn pushed his forehead against the wall and raked gouges in the paint with his fingers. The beast knew his weaknesses. It knew what he would kill and die for. And when it faced the goddess who would destroy his son, it would not hesitate to act. It would give no thought to the consequences beyond what must be done.

And Dainn saw the trick.

You tried to kill Danny on the steppes, he said to the beast. *You said, "Take him, and we will be one." You demanded a sacrifice.*

The beast fell silent, withdrawing out of the reach of Dainn's rational mind as if it debated with itself.

I will not harm the child, it said at last.

I cannot trust you.

A terrible sound echoed inside Dainn's skull, a cry of terror that drove Dainn to his knees.

Danny.

The beast laughed again, its teeth flashing in its long, broad muzzle. And then it was gone.

Dainn scrambled to his feet, drawn by the cry echoing in his head. His senses were blurred and his muscles had lost all their strength, as if the beast's withdrawal had stolen everything that might have helped him save his son.

I will find him, without your help, he told the beast. *I will find him, and I will stop* her.

◑◐

The goddess woke up while Ryan was watching from the doorway. He slid out of sight, hoping she hadn't seen him, and held his breath.

"Mist?" Freya said, her voice more querulous than enticing. The sheets fell away from her chest, revealing full breasts covered by a thin nightgown that left little to the imagination. Though she'd been lying in the bed for two whole days, her black hair still looked freshly washed, and there wasn't a single crease on her face.

Ryan was extremely grateful that he was immune to her supposed charms. The fact that he couldn't be distracted by her appearance should have made it easier for him to figure out why he'd been stupid enough to come here, as if he could actually carry through with his plan.

Maybe it would backfire on him again, because misusing his abilities would make things even worse. *Who decides?* he asked himself. *Who decides if it's okay, if it's worth it to make one sacrifice to keep thousands of people from suffering?*

"Sometimes you will only see what is coming just as it is about to happen," Mother Skye had said. "Sometimes you will make mistakes. It is a hard truth, Ryan, that no one can protect you."

Like he couldn't seem to protect the people he cared about the most.

"Mist!" Freya called again, gracefully swinging her bare legs over the bed. She swayed a little, bracing herself on the mattress. Bryn walked in, stopped in surprise, and bowed. Ryan held his breath.

"Where is my daughter?" Freya demanded. "What has happened to me?"

"You've been very ill, Lady," Bryn said, pouring Freya a glass of water from the pitcher on the bedside table. "Please lie down."

Freya knocked Bryn's hand away when she offered the glass, causing water to slop all over the floor and the Valkyrie's sleeve. "What time is it? How long have I been here?"

"Two days, Lady," Bryn said, setting the half-empty glass back on the table.

"Two days?" Freya tried to rise, caught at Bryn's arm, and sank back to the bed.

"Do you remember what happened?" Bryn asked.

Freya rubbed her temples. "The squabble among the mortals. I—" She broke off, shaking her head slowly. "Tell me how I came to be here."

Ryan listened as Bryn explained what everyone in the camp already knew. The Valkyrie was diplomatic, but there was no getting around it: Freya had lost consciousness right in the middle of using her magic, and Mist had shut down a potential riot all on her own.

For about five minutes after Bryn finished, Freya didn't look particularly beautiful. Her face was red, her eyes were hard chips of blue flint, and Ryan was almost certain that she was going to do something like blast out the window of the bedroom.

But that wasn't the way she did things. Usually.

"And you say she is at the reception in my place?" Freya said.

Even the usually unflappable Bryn looked nervous. "Loki invited you to talk to him, and we couldn't let him think you were—"

"And how could you possibly believe that she could play *my* part?" Freya interrupted.

"Mist was able to create a perfect image of your elven form to disguise her body and features," Bryn said.

"She surely gave herself away the first time she opened her mouth."

"If anything had gone wrong, Konur would have let us know."

"Would he ever admit to any flaw in her?"

"His loyalty is still to you, Lady. Whatever she does, Mist will never be your equal."

Ryan was startled by Bryn's criticism. She and Mist were good friends, and Bryn had been the first ally to show up after Mist had met Dainn and learned that Ragnarok had never happened. Somehow, strong as she was, she'd fallen under Freya's spell.

Ryan spun around at the sound of heavy footsteps clomping down the hall. Rick was heading toward him, head down as if in thought. Ryan carefully closed the bedroom door and looked around quickly, wondering if he could get into the bathroom or the old computer room if he moved fast enough.

"Ryan?" Rick came to a sudden stop, an almost comical look of shock on his bearded face. "Where did *you* come from?"

Pressing against the wall near the bedroom door, Ryan tried to smile. "Uh . . . I just returned to camp."

Rick grinned, grabbed Ryan in a bear hug, and ruffled his hair. "You look okay, kid." He stepped back, and his mouth turned down. "The way you just disappeared, everyone was worried sick. Especially Gabi. That wasn't cool."

"I know," Ryan said, looking down at his boots. "I just had to get away, to figure stuff out. And I was causing everyone too much trouble."

"I wouldn't say that," Rick said gruffly. "You know Mist wanted you and Gabi to go because things were getting too dangerous."

"Yeah," Ryan said, pretty sure that Rick didn't know the half of it. He tried to listen through the door without being too obvious about it, hoping that Freya and Bryn weren't paying any attention to what was going on outside the room. "I . . . I've got everything under control now. I don't have those seizures anymore. I was just coming to look for Mist."

"You mean you haven't seen her yet? How long have you been back?"

"I wanted to . . . you know, kind of look things over first, make sure it was okay," Ryan said. "Or at least okay to talk to Mist about being here."

Rick grunted. "What about Gabi?"

"I've talked to her," Ryan admitted. "I made her promise not to tell anyone else I was back until I was ready."

"You know Eir's dead?"

"Yeah."

"She was good people. Helped a lot of us." He glanced at the door. "Mist ain't in there. She's out doing stuff for the Lady. Freya's resting because she—" He narrowed his eyes. "You didn't come back because you *saw* something happen, did you?"

"You mean like a vision?" Ryan said, hoping his voice was steady. "No. I mean, I just wanted to see if I could help, now that I'm not getting sick anymore. And I missed everyone."

"Well, you should keep a low profile until you can talk to Mist. Where are you staying?"

"I've been hiding out with Gabi."

"Okay. Mist'll probably be pretty busy when she gets back, so I'll get word to you when she's—"

The door opened, and Bryn stepped out.

"I heard voices," she said. She stared at Ryan. "Ryan?"

"Surprise," Rick said dryly. "Look, he don't want to let anyone know he's here until he talks to Mist, okay?"

Bryn blinked. "Freya's awake," she said to Rick.

"That's great!" Rick said, rubbing his beefy hands together. "Do you think it would be okay if I . . . just looked in on her?"

If the situation hadn't been so serious, Ryan would have rolled his eyes.

"I don't think that would be a good idea just now," Bryn said, lowering her voice. "The important thing is that she's recovering."

"And Mist is still all right?"

"We haven't heard from Konur. Whatever happens, she'll be back by dawn."

Ryan bit down hard on his lower lip. He couldn't wait to decide until Mist came back. If he was going to risk acting on what he'd "seen," it would have to be now.

Bryn looked at him again as if she'd only just noticed him there. Ryan braced himself for the same set of questions all over again.

But she surprised him. "I know you probably have a lot to say to Mist," she said. "But you haven't met the Lady, have you?"

She grabbed his arm and opened the door. Freya was in bed again, propped up on what looked like a dozen pillows. Her half-lidded eyes opened when she saw Ryan, and she sat up a little straighter, her black hair falling into naturally flattering lines around her neck.

There was something in her stare that scared Ryan half out of his wits. It was like she already knew. That she could *see* what he was.

Maybe Mist had told her about him while he was gone. Gabi hadn't mentioned it, but it didn't matter now. Bryn had made the choice for him.

"And who is this handsome young gentleman?" Freya asked in a husky voice.

"Gabriella's friend, Ryan," Bryn said before he could answer. "Our resident seer. Or he was, before he ran away. He has just returned."

"Oh?" Freya sat forward, and Ryan felt the push of something in his mind. Something that might have worked if he'd been someone else.

"He came to Mist when he saw something about the war in his dreams," Bryn said. "He understands what's happening."

"I see," Freya said, rubbing her lower lip with a flawless fingernail. "How fascinating." She smiled at Ryan. "Do you know who I am?"

"Yeah. Yes. Lady Freya. I knew about you before you got here, but I . . ." He licked his lips and stared, pretending to be overwhelmed by her beauty.

"Odd that Mist never mentioned you."

Ryan managed a brief bow. "Uh . . . like Bryn said, Lady Freya, I left. I did. . . . I can see the future sometimes, but it isn't always useful, or accurate. I wasn't really helping, so—"

"What did you see about the war?" Freya asked. The push on Ryan's mind grew stronger, but he could tell that the goddess knew her magic was failing with him. Her smile looked a little strained.

"It's hard to explain," he said. "Sometimes all I'd see was bright light. Or that danger was coming. Then I stopped seeing things at all. And I got seizures, so Mist wanted me away from anything that could trigger them."

"But you have returned," Freya said, cocking her head.

"Like I told Rick and Bryn, I don't get sick anymore. And I am . . ." He hesitated, wanting it to be just right. "I *am* seeing things again. I just don't know if they mean anything. That's why I came to talk to Mist before I told anyone el—"

"My daughter is very busy," Freya said. "Come, sit by me and tell me what you've seen."

"I . . . I think I should wait until Mist is back, shouldn't I?"

The Lady very nearly scowled. "I am the sole representative of the Aesir. Mist may lead the mortal forces in battle, but there is no hope of victory without me."

Ryan bobbed his head again. "I understand. I mean, I knew that."

"Did you have a vision of *me*, child?"

Ryan couldn't believe it was so easy. And he knew just what she'd want to hear. "After I first came here, I saw a . . . golden lady, leading an army of elves. She was using magic to destroy hundreds of Jotunar.

Loki was trying to fight, but he—" Ryan frowned. "That's all. I didn't tell Mist about it then, because so much else was going wrong."

"Was it me you saw?"

"Well, she had golden hair. She looked like Mist, but now that I'm here, I know it was you, even with the black hair."

"Where was Mist in your vision?"

"I didn't see her. It was like she wasn't there."

Freya sighed, but to Ryan the sound seemed less like disappointment than satisfaction. "You saw no end to the battle?"

"I'm sorry. That's the way it works. In pieces."

She seemed to relax, her eyes growing heavy-lidded again, and Ryan knew she was hooked.

That was why he still had hope.

"This is a puzzle," she said. "I should very much like to have all the pieces. Is this all that brought you to speak to Mist this night?"

Ryan pretended to hesitate, and then took a seat at the very end of the bed, as far from Freya as possible.

"I saw . . ." he began. He swallowed and started again. "Gabi told me that you have Odin's horse, Sleipnir. One of the Treasures."

"What of him?"

"I, uh, saw someone try to take him."

"What do you mean?" Bryn asked, moving swiftly to stand beside him.

"It's not completely clear," Ryan said. "I saw fighting, and there was something big and dark there, killing people. And elves. Enemies were stealing the horse."

"Do you mean Loki?" Bryn asked. She grasped Ryan's shoulder. "Was *he* there?"

"I didn't see him," Ryan said. "But there were Jotunar."

"When?"

"I'm not sure," Ryan said, wincing at the pressure of Bryn's fingers. "Soon, maybe even tonight."

"*If* this vision is true," Freya said. "Bryn, do you trust the boy?"

"It would be a good idea to check on it," Bryn said, releasing Ryan's shoulder. "It isn't happening now, or the guards would have called. But we've been wondering why Loki hasn't tried to do this before. If he knows you've been out of commission . . ."

"But did he know *before* he sent me the invitation?" Freya murmured. She addressed Ryan again. "What was this 'big and dark' thing you mentioned?"

That was the part Ryan hated thinking about. He'd seen Dainn's physical beast during the fight with Jormungandr, when Dainn had saved him—seen it not with his eyes, but with his inner sight.

It had wanted to kill him.

"I don't know," he lied. "But it was powerful. And none of the elves or humans could stop it."

Freya laughed softly. "*We* know what it is. Mist will be most distressed if the elf has finally succumbed."

To Loki, Ryan thought. Not just going over to the bad guys for reasons no one understood, but actually helping them fight the good guys.

Ryan still wouldn't believe it. And Freya certainly didn't seem worried.

"I'll go right away, take a dozen of my best fighters," Bryn said, moving away from the bed. "We'll keep watch until—"

"Until Mist returns?" Freya said. "Do you think *she* can stop this? She failed in her attempts to halt the protest before I intervened. She lacks control, and her magic remains unpredictable."

Ryan cleared his throat. "I'm sorry," he said, "but there was one other thing. I saw someone besides the elves fighting for Sleipnir. I thought it was Mist. But now I think it was you."

"And?"

He braced himself. "Lady, can I touch your hand?"

Staring at him through narrowed eyes, Freya extended her fingers toward him. He brushed them with his, gasped, and pulled away.

"You were winning," he whispered.

"Lady," Bryn said, "you can't get involved. You were in a coma, and you've barely come out of it."

There was a long silence, and Ryan could almost feel Freya thinking. She didn't have to take the bait. She didn't know him; she didn't know if his visions were true. She'd tried to work some kind of magic on him, and it hadn't succeeded.

Was it enough that Bryn believed?

"Look at me," Freya said, holding out her arms to the Valkyrie. "Have I changed? Do I look weak? Whatever happened during the squabble was a mere mishap, a fluke."

"We weren't sure you'd ever wake up," Bryn said.

"But I *am* awake, and there is nothing wrong with me. Sleipnir is important, and I can hardly permit my Alfar to die, or Loki to win without a fight."

"You don't have to," Bryn said. "Let me call Mist. At least she might be able to sense if something's wrong. She can go straight to Sleipnir from the party."

Freya sighed. "As always, you are the voice of reason. And Mist should be there, even if she is of little use to us."

Ryan thought frantically, wondering how he could convince Freya not to get Mist involved.

"No," he said suddenly, covering his eyes with his hand. "There's something wrong. Mist isn't supposed to be there."

"Why not?" Freya demanded.

It came to Ryan then that if she believed in his abilities, she might start wondering if he'd seen what she planned to do to Mist.

"I'm confused," he whispered. "It's all gray, now. I think . . . I must be wrong. About everything. . . ."

Freya studied him a moment longer and then climbed out of bed, rejecting Bryn's offered hand. "Send for Mist and Konur," she said. "If her intent was to make certain that Loki believes I am well and whole, surely she has accomplished that task by now. She can join us at the stable."

Bryn seemed about to speak, but Freya stared her down. "I will hear no arguments," she said. "Gather your fighters. We will leave within the hour."

Ryan closed his eyes. He'd succeeded in putting her at risk twice over: first by making her vulnerable to the consequences of listening to his visions of the future, and second by throwing her straight into the path of danger.

But now she was bringing Mist. And he couldn't be sure that anything else would go as he'd planned.

What if he was, at this very moment, causing the very thing he kept trying to stop?

15

Following Danny had almost been too easy.

Mist paused just outside the stairwell to the third floor of the Fairmont parking garage, listening. Her magic had led her to the lobby of the hotel, where she'd lost him, only to catch him running through the front door and down the street to the garage at the corner of California and Powell. A flash of red hair, a low cry, and he was racing up the stairs just as she reached the stairwell.

She'd followed him up to the third floor, but she couldn't see him now. There were no other people here, and hundreds of cars to hide behind if you were a boy afraid for his life.

But Danny wasn't an ordinary boy, and something didn't seem quite right. It didn't make sense that he'd have come to her twice and then vanished before she could figure out how to help him.

"Danny?" she called softly, as if she stood in an ancient cathedral rather than an ugly, utilitarian storage facility for motor vehicles. Her voice echoed hollowly. She tried again.

"That didn't last long," Loki said, stepping out from behind a pillar.

Mist cursed her own gullibility and prepared to defend herself. "What didn't last long, Slanderer?" she said in her silkiest Freya imitation.

"Your masquerade," Loki said. He leaned against the pillar, legs crossed at the ankle. "Freya would never expect Danny to answer her."

He wasn't surprised about Danny, Mist thought. The boy was probably here now, and Loki might have known all along that Danny had come to the hotel. He could easily have set another trap, in spite of Danny's claim that he'd come himself.

"Why?" she asked, still channeling Freya in the hope of finding out what in Hel was going on. "The boy came to me, asking for my help."

Loki laughed with obvious amusement. "And that statement, my dear Mist, reveals both your identity and your ignorance. The Lady won't be happy to know that you have failed to deceive me." He flicked an invisible piece of lint from his lapel. "How *is* your mother?"

Knowing the game was up, Mist shed the false front as if she were throwing off suffocating layers of too-tight clothing. "Fine," she said. "Busy."

"Then she has recovered from the incident during the protest?"

"There *was* no incident. Do you still claim to have had nothing to do with it?"

"Naturally."

"But you've been a busy little Scar-lip lately, haven't you?" Mist bit back the desire to tell him she'd seen Regin and Skuld, half-afraid that he'd gain some advantage by knowing it. "Did you force Danny to play a part in your sordid little game?"

"He's quite the rascal," Loki said. He began to stroll toward her. "I actually didn't realize he was here until a brief time ago."

Mist was startled by the admission. But, of course, Loki might be lying. That was always the safest assumption to make where he was concerned.

"Is Danny here with you now?" she asked.

"Very near. But he isn't safe. I must get him home."

"He's safe from *me*," Mist said, scanning the garage as subtly as she could. "He told me someone was threatening him. I must admit, you hooked me well and good."

Loki's brows drew down over bright green eyes, the outer rim of the irises flaring red. "Who threatened him?" he demanded.

He doesn't know, Mist thought in amazement. *Maybe that part was real, and Danny didn't tell him.*

"It's interesting," she said, trying to give herself time to think. "At first, Danny seemed worried that I'd hurt *you*."

A flash of real surprise crossed Loki's face, quickly hidden. He laughed sharply. "Now? And how would you do that?"

"He thought I would take you away."

"How interesting." He took a step toward her. "What were his exact words?"

"He said he had to come because his papa was afraid, and—"

Suddenly Loki began to laugh. When he stopped, his expression was a perfect mingling of scorn and amusement.

"His *papa*," he said.

Mist lowered her voice. "If Danny really has some affection for you," she said, "I'll be very sorry to take you away from him. But he'll be better off with almost anyone else."

"Will he? Who else can protect him?"

"I don't know how much you've told Danny about this war over Midgard, or whether you sent him here by manipulating or tricking him. But his fear is genuine. He said he didn't want to die. I think he believes someone really wants to kill him." She took a deep breath. "Let me talk to him."

Loki looked behind him. At first Mist expected Danny to step out into the light, but within a few seconds she realized that someone else was in the garage with them.

Jotunar. She couldn't tell how many, but there were more than a few. They'd been warded from her senses very skillfully.

"You don't really want a fight here, do you?" she asked.

"You tell *me*. Who is Danny supposed to be afraid of?"

"I'd say you," she said, "if he hadn't been so worried about my taking you away. And I don't think you'd ever hurt him deliberately. He's too valuable."

"Far too valuable. Who else? Surely someone among your allies would have excellent motive."

"Only a few people know about Danny, and they wouldn't hurt him any more than I would."

"Once upon a time, your naïveté held a certain charm. Now it is only one more weakness." He took another step toward her. "Did you ever discuss Danny with your mother?"

A spike of fear drove down into her belly. "Freya never mentioned him," she said.

"And you never spoke of him to her? Not even about his opening of the portal, and the bridges?" When Mist couldn't find an immediate answer, he said, "Perhaps you sensed how she might respond to such a potential threat."

Mist remembered Danny's wariness when he'd first asked her who she was. "You taught him to fear Freya," she said. "The first time he saw me, he assumed I was—"

"Your mother is far more ruthless than you are. Did it never occur to you that she might have met Danny before?"

Oh, it had. But Mist wanted to know what Loki knew.

"When?" she asked.

"Perhaps on the steppes, when you were otherwise occupied. Or possibly even earlier. She might have been reluctant to tell you, knowing of your sentimentality."

Mist ignored the spike of fear in her throat. "Enough of this," she said. "Danny said that 'he' with a capital *H* will make everything bad. If that's not you . . ." She took a deep breath. "We can clear it up in a few seconds if Danny—"

A car horn honked once, and without any warning at all Loki flung a spell at Mist, a unique combination of his ice and fire magic shaped into a frozen, flaming javelin. Instinctively she defended herself, falling back on the familiar, "safe" magic of the forge, the Rune-language of metal that came so naturally to her.

But she did it in a way she never had before, bespelling the closest car, lifting it easily off the concrete and suspending it in front of her. The javelin shattered on impact, and by the time Loki was ready to attack again she had dropped the car, torn off a door, and was already reinforcing it with Runes of protection and strength—Ox, Yew, and Elk.

Loki blasted pure fire at her, the flames transforming into serpents that tried to slither around her shield. She destroyed them with her own Jotunn command of ice and cold. Steam swirled around her, and she used its cover to work another lifting spell and hurl a Fiat at him. By the time she emerged from the cloud of vapor, Danny was standing in Loki's place.

They stood facing each other, boy and goddess, in the midst of metal fragments, melting ice and half-crushed automobiles. Danny's face was frozen in terror, and Freya held her hands out before her, ready to fling another spell.

She was trying to kill him.

Dainn took in the tableau, the seconds seeming like minutes, time that seemed to expand until nothing seemed to move, not even his own heart.

But the beast was there. It had clung to the inside of his skull like a hideous parasite as he'd tracked Danny to this place, hoping to save his son, to get him away before Freya found him and finished what she'd started on the steppes.

He was too late. When this moment of suspended time came to an end, he would move quickly. But not quickly enough. Not as he was now, an elf standing alone against the Lady.

Now you need me, the beast said.

Dainn's heart beat once. Again. He tried to speak, but his throat had been seized by an invisible fist.

I said I would not harm the child, the beast said.

Liar, Dainn thought. *Murderer.*

Long ago, you let me kill, the beast reminded him. *When you could not ignore me, you found bad men for me. For us.*

The memories were unbearable. Dainn had told Mist about those times, in a few brief sentences . . . about the victories he had won only to lose them again. Now the past had risen up to swallow him, and he recalled the faces: the rapists, the murderers, the beaters of women and children.

And Freya. She was bad. Evil, like those men he had let the beast destroy long ago when he'd had no other choice.

Every muscle in Dainn's body rebelled as he tried to take a single step away from the stairwell. Danny's face was still frozen, but it seemed to him that something had changed. Freya's fingers had flickered. The scent of magic rose in the stale air, a hint of what was to come.

"Papa!"

The single word was stretched out, as if distorted by a synthesizer. Danny's head had turned ever so slightly toward him, and his eyes were pleading. Begging.

Light filled Dainn's head, his chest, his entire being, and his rage burst like a suppurating wound left untended too long. The creature inside him cringed and whimpered.

Danny's fear. It gave him strength he couldn't remember ever having had before . . . magical strength to use the beast as a weapon. A weapon over which he had perfect control. He grasped the creature by its powerful neck and squeezed.

"*You will obey me,*" he said, "*or I will do far worse than kill you.*"

For once, the beast had no response, no threat to offer. It whined, hanging limp in his grip.

Then time started again, and Dainn let it go.

◑◐

"Danny!" Mist cried, struggling to find her voice. "What are you—"

A roar sounded behind her, and she barely turned in time to see the beast charge directly toward her and the boy.

"The monster!" Danny yelled, just as he had in the hotel hallway. "He's going to kill me!"

Acting without further thought, Mist summoned her inner Jotunn again and hurled a spinning disk of ice-spikes at the beast. The disk released its projectiles a few feet before it reached the creature, but they barely penetrated the heavy black coat, and the beast swept them aside with a hand-like forepaw.

Desperately seeking another spell, Mist put herself between the beast and Danny and stared at its face in horror. It sank its head between its shoulders as it stalked toward her, teeth bared, slitted eyes mad with rage. It was twice her size, and stronger than any Jotunn.

But she knew it. Better than she knew Loki, could ever know another living soul.

Dainn. Dainn was there behind those glaring red eyes. Not lost, not buried, but whole and aware.

And ready to kill.

"Run, Danny!" she yelled, and lifted her hands. The spell was only half-formed when the beast slammed into her and bore her to the ground, claws slashing at her shoulders.

"Dainn!" she said, gasping at the shock of searing pain.

The beast snapped at her face as if he—it—would silence her by ripping her jaw off. Ignoring the pain, she pushed up with all her strength. The beast tried to strike at her again, but she caught its massive wrist and twisted it aside.

"Dainn!" she gasped. "Stop!"

It stared into her eyes without recognition and wrenched its foreleg from her grip. In the strangely protracted moment between one second and the next, Mist wondered how it had come to this. How they had at last arrived at the moment when she would have to try to kill Dainn.

He's insane.

Gathering another Rune-spell, Mist wove staves of steel into a fine, flexible mesh and pushed it up against the beast's face, creating a muzzle to contain the vicious teeth. Then, as it pawed at its nose, she rolled out from under it and scrambled to her feet.

The beast raked the muzzle from its face and stood on its hind legs, swinging its head right and left. Searching. Looking for its prey.

But Danny was gone. Mist released an explosive breath and sorted through possible spells, wishing she'd had an excuse to bring Kettlingr to the party.

Maybe she could just slow the beast down. Loki had to be around somewhere. He could take Danny to safety while she—

No, she thought. There was something very wrong here. Dainn had been with Loki nearly the whole time he was at the party. Even if Loki didn't know that Dainn had tried to kill Danny on the steppes, he would have known the state of Dainn's mind, and what he was capable of, long before they had arrived at the hotel.

With a silence that astonished her, the beast charged. She was faster and more nimble, but even so it nearly caught her again.

If Dainn had truly gone mad, there was nothing she could do. But if there was still some way to reach him, keeping him down and quiet might give her the time she needed.

How, she thought, when even Gleipnir, the unbreakable Chain, hadn't been able to hold him? Basic Galdr wouldn't be enough. The forge-magic wouldn't be enough, or the glamour.

If she drew on the ancient magic, she might succeed. But she also might kill Dainn without meaning to, or become . . .

"Freya," the beast said, its deep, grating voice thick with hatred. "Afraid?"

Mist's heart jumped. She knew the beast was capable of speech when it was under Dainn's control, but she hadn't expected this.

Had Loki failed to tell Dainn of her attempt to impersonate Freya? If Dainn knew she was Mist, would he listen to her?

"I'm not Freya, Dainn," she said, as calmly as she could. "I'm Mist."

The beast flashed its teeth in a parody of a grin. "Lie," it said. Before she could take another breath, it had sprung across the distance between them, bounding on all four legs, and reared up again to snap at her neck. She fell back, stumbled, and snatched at the first defense she could find.

The concrete trembled beneath her feet as the limestone, clay, gravel, and sand began to come apart at her unspoken command, molecule by molecule. Car alarms began to shriek and wail, and water seeped from the floor.

Mist closed her eyes as the magic raced through her body, carrying her consciousness onto a higher plane. She felt neither fear nor anger, only a sense of complete freedom. Her purpose was clear.

And it was so easy. She could feel each element, drawn long ago from the earth, striving to reach her as the beast crashed onto its side, its dark fur streaked with pale dust. A crack formed under it, gaping like toothless jaws.

Like the street had cracked when Dainn fought Jormungandr. When the earth had almost swallowed him alive.

This time, he wouldn't survive.

And what becomes of those who will die when he does?

Her mind filled with images of fleeing mortals and crushed bodies, flattened under rubble from fallen walls and ceilings. Danny, blood leaking from his mouth, sightless eyes staring in a broken face.

Mist came back to herself just in time. She struggled to undo the spell, reversing the ancient magic, pushing the molecules back into place. The entire garage groaned, and Mist focused all her power on restoring its structural integrity.

The shaking stopped. The car alarms fell silent. Nothing moved except the beast, whose chest rose and fell violently as it coughed up powdered concrete.

Trembling with the effort, Mist got to her feet. She'd almost lost it. She'd snatched at the ancient magic, nearly killing Dainn—and almost destroying the entire garage along with him. Hundreds of lives at stake, because she had let herself . . .

The beast heaved itself to his feet and faced her, unfazed.

"Freya failed," it said.

"I'm not Freya!" She moved toward it, hands spread wide. "You know me, Dainn!"

Its ears flattened tight to its broad skull. "Kill Danny," it rasped.

"No. You won't hurt him." She sucked in a breath. "You've lost yourself. You're sick, Dainn. Like you were on the steppes."

The big body flinched, and the beast threw back its head like a wolf about to howl. "You kill him," it snarled. "*You.*"

And then she finally understood. The beast hadn't come to kill

Danny. It had seen what appeared to be the Lady preparing to attack the boy.

Because Loki set it up, Mist thought. Using his own son. Sending Danny to make Mist think that the beast might be after him, then giving Dainn reason to believe that Freya would kill the boy herself.

But if Loki had known that Mist was posing as her mother from the very beginning . . .

Timing, Mist thought. It would have had to be perfect. Dainn had to believe that Mist *was* Freya, and he had to be here at the right moment to see her as a direct threat to the boy.

But it wasn't Danny standing here a few moments ago, she thought, cursing her own carelessness. It had been illusion and a very tangible one. Loki's illusion.

Had she ever seen the real Danny at all?

Of one thing she was certain: Loki mustn't have believed that Dainn could kill her, or that she could kill Dainn. Or would want to.

He was half right.

Why does Loki want us to fight? Why here, and now?

"Dainn!" she said, backing away. "Listen to me. Loki's played a trick on us. I never intended to—"

With another roar, Dainn came at her. He was slower than before, and she jumped out of his path.

"I tried to kill you with the ancient magic," she said, circling the beast carefully. "I didn't even think about it, and I could have brought this entire garage down. If you keep pushing me, I might do it again." She ducked a sweep of its heavy foreleg. "Loki made himself look like Danny at exactly the moment you came in. I was trying to stop myself."

The beast paused in midstride, panting. There was a flicker of confusion in his eyes.

"She's lying!" Danny's voice shrieked.

Dainn turned his head toward the voice. Mist raced across the concrete to grab the reinforced car door she'd used during her fight with Loki.

"That isn't Danny!" she shouted. "Use your brain, Dainn! Listen to your instincts!"

But he wasn't listening. He leaped at her, and she swung the car door out, slamming it against him. Claws raked through her shield, severing Runes and metal at once. She was momentarily startled, until she remembered how Dainn, in beast form, had used some kind of bizarre magic to help drive Jormungandr back into the earth, and how he had healed Ryan of the wounds he himself had made.

Maybe he *could* kill her.

"That's enough," she snapped, pushing back with all her strength. "You betrayed me, Dainn. You betrayed all of us by going to Loki." She caught her breath. "Are you so far gone that you've forgotten everything we did together, everything we fought for? Everything in you that was ever sane or good?"

This time she made an impression. He retreated a few steps and stood, swaying slightly, staring at her. The beast's red irises deepened to elven indigo.

"Mist!"

Konur, somewhere across the garage. Mist didn't risk looking away from Dainn. She didn't dare move so much as an eyelash.

"You know who I am, Dainn," she said. "You know who *you* are. We both want to protect Danny. *Loki* is the enemy."

The beast shuddered. Mist thought she saw the heavy pelt begin to thin, the face to flatten, the posture to straighten.

He believed her. He was changing back.

Maybe there was a chance . . .

Dainn swung around, still poised between beast and elf. Mist followed his stare. Konur stood near an exit sign, holding another man by the collar.

Edvard. Edvard, the *berserkr* who had disappeared from the loft soon after he had confronted Dainn following Jormungandr's defeat.

Elf vanished, and the beast burst into a four-legged run. Mist caught a glimpse of Edvard's pale, panicked face as Konur lifted him and swung the *berserkr* behind him.

Mist knew Dainn wasn't after the elf-lord. And so, apparently, did Konur.

Remembering what she had done to the garage just minutes before, Mist hesitated. *All you have to do is stop him*, she thought. *He can be reasoned with.*

But no spell would come. Her voice refused to sing the chants, her fingers to shape the Rune-staves. She was failing, just as she had at the protest.

"Konur!" she shouted.

The elf raised his hands. Mist could feel him searching for the nearest source of living nature, but as he reached through the concrete toward the earth, she realized that even the smallest shift in the ground could cause the garage's structure to weaken again.

"No, Konur!" she shouted. He lifted his head, Dainn prepared for a final jump, and a small figure popped into existence halfway between beast and elf.

Dainn twisted in mid-leap, landing on his side inches away from Danny. The boy crouched beside him and laid his hand on the heaving chest.

A violent shiver wracked the beast from nearly invisible tail to gaping mouth. Fur gave way to a rumpled suit, pointed muzzle to pale elven skin. Dainn splayed his hands against the floor and pushed himself up, pausing to cough and gag. His long hair was a tangled mess, gray with dust.

By the time Mist reached him, Danny was gone again. Or Loki was. But would Laufeyson have tried to protect Konur and Edvard?

What in Hel was Edvard doing here in the first place?

Dainn climbed to his feet, twice losing his balance. He didn't look at her, and Mist didn't try to touch him. Konur watched him carefully, muscles tensed.

"Stay where you are, Dainn," Mist said. "We don't need to fight anymore."

"Where is . . ." His voice cracked, and he cleared his throat. "Where is Danny?"

"*If* he was here, I don't know. But I don't think he was ever in any danger." She kept her own voice neutral, neither accusing nor conciliatory. "Did Loki tell you that Freya planned to hurt Danny? Is that how he got you here?"

He shook his head. "Danny did."

"Then he was probably Loki in disguise. He managed to create a physical manifestation, and it must have taken all the magic he's got to pull it off."

Showing no sign that he'd heard her, Dainn straightened and stared at Edvard, who continued to hide behind Konur.

"Who is this man?" Konur asked Mist, tightening his grip on Edvard's collar.

"A *berserkr* who came with Bryn," Mist said, keeping an eye on Dainn. "He offered to help Dainn when—"

"*Help*," Dainn spat.

Mist flexed her fingers. "Dainn, it's over. Whatever problem you have with Edvard—"

"It isn't over," Dainn said. He glared at Edvard. "You betrayed me from the beginning. You knew all along that when the herb wore off, the beast would return."

"What herb?" Mist asked, painfully aware that she had no idea what elf and *berserkr* were talking about. "Where have you been, Edvard?"

"I caught him running out of the garage," Konur said. "I smelled Loki on him."

"You are working for Loki," Dainn said, taking a step toward him.

"It isn't that simple," Edvard said, his deep voice thin with fear.

Dainn took another step. "No one here can protect you if you do not tell me the truth. Did you give the herb to Loki, so that he could control the beast?"

Edvard swallowed several times. "He . . . fed you the herb with your meals, so the beast would stay quiet."

"But he stopped, did he not? And now you would turn me into a weapon for him. Was that always your plan?"

"You went to Loki willingly. You must have known—"

"My magic was gone. I was no threat to—"

"To Danny?"

Dainn froze, nostrils flaring, breath coming fast. "*She* told me to kill him." He looked at Mist, tears in his eyes. "Listen to me. Freya is—"

16

The words stopped, and Dainn's hands flew to his throat. Konur wore a look of intense concentration, and Mist knew that he had silenced Dainn, though she didn't know how. Or why.

"Let him finish, Konur," she said. "He said something to me during the party, when he thought I was Freya. I want to know what he meant."

"What he *says* does not matter," Konur said, his expression grim. "I know my own kind. Dainn is quite mad. His perception of the world has been warped through the eyes of the beast. He can destroy us with his lies."

Without warning, Dainn lunged at Konur. Fur sprouted from his body, covering and absorbing suit and elven flesh. Konur released Edvard and flung up his hands.

Mist propelled herself after Dainn, jumped onto his back, and locked her arms around his neck. No matter how hard she squeezed, his pelt protected him. He bucked like a bronco, trying to throw her off.

Her tattoo burned, and she remembered the bracelet. She tugged it off and, using forge-magic to enlarge it and reinforce the metal with Rune-staves of steel, created a collar large enough to fit around the beast's neck. She snapped the collar into place, welded it shut with another forge spell, and pulled it tight . . . tight enough to impair his ability to breathe without actually strangling him.

"Stop fighting," she said, digging her fingers into the dense fur on the sides of his jaw. "Give it up. You're not—"

Dainn reared and spun in one motion. Her hands lost their grip on the beast's fur, and she plummeted to the ground. Her sight dimmed, and she felt hot breath on her face.

By the time she could see again, Dainn the elf was lying on the floor, the collar still around his neck, his cheek pressed to the concrete. His eyes were closed. She fell beside him and put her fingers to his throat.

Alive. Breathing. He opened his eyes.

"Are you hurt?" she asked, quickly withdrawing.

His lips parted, but no sound emerged. He closed his eyes again, showing no inclination to move, let alone try to escape.

Konur joined her, along with a half-dozen Alfar who had arrived sometime during the last struggle.

"We must go," Konur said.

"Edvard?" Mist asked, getting to her feet.

"Escaped. But that is of no importance now. Loki is gone, and though I erected a ward to discourage mortals from entering here, it will not last much longer. Considering the damage—"

Mist scanned the garage, unable to hide a wince. She'd only destroyed two cars, but quite a few others had rolled away from their spaces and crashed into other vehicles.

The greater problem was that the entire structure had probably been weakened, and she was going to have to find a way to report the problem to the proper authorities without becoming directly involved.

"You cannot protect the mortals from such losses," Konur said. "If Loki wins, they will lose everything."

How many times had Mist heard some variation on those words? How many times had she told *herself*?

"Whatever Loki hoped to achieve by all this," she said grimly, "he must have been happy with the result."

One of Konur's Alfar spoke quietly to him in the Elvish tongue. "I am told that Freya has awakened," Konur said to Mist, "and that she has gone to the place where Sleipnir is hidden."

Mist felt a strange combination of relief and unease. If Freya had left the loft, she must have regained not only her consciousness but control of her magic.

"Do you know why she went there?" she asked. "She's never shown any interest in Sleipnir before."

"It is not clear," Konur said, after consulting with his aide again. "But apparently she was insistent that you should join her as soon as possible."

"Let me have your cell phone," Mist said. "I'll call her."

"I have tried," Konur said. "I cannot reach her."

Mist blew out her breath. "Can you and the others handle Dainn?"

"Is it safe to take him with us?" Konur asked, staring down at Dainn with icy hostility.

"We've got no choice. Get him back to the loft in one piece, but do it quietly. The fewer who know about his return to camp, the better."

"As you wish," Konur said, accepting her decision without any sign of reluctance. "Do we have your leave to do whatever is necessary to control him?"

"As long as you don't maim or kill him."

The anger in her own words shocked her, but she had felt herself slipping closer and closer to forgetting that Dainn was a traitor, both during the party and after the fight. Anger was the one sure way of fighting that kind of weakness.

"Do whatever you have to do," she said.

"We will see that he is confined in such a way that he cannot escape or harm anyone."

Suddenly Dainn pushed himself up and got to his knees, the muscles of his face bunched with effort. His mouth and throat worked.

"Are you keeping him silent?" she asked Konur.

The elf-lord shrugged. "Perhaps the beast has stolen his tongue."

Or it's the collar, Mist thought. It was snug around his neck, but it didn't look tight enough to cut off his voice.

Dainn reached for her, and a raw sound pushed out of his throat. Two of the Alfar grabbed him under the arms and pulled him to his feet, not gently. The others closed in around him.

Mist didn't look at him again. "I'm going to find a bike," she said. "I'll be in touch as soon as I find out what's going on with Freya."

Konur nodded to his men, and they half-dragged, half-carried Dainn toward the exit. Mist began looking for a bike she could "borrow" to get her to Sleipnir's hidden stable.

Halfway along the aisle, she saw movement and instinctively dropped behind the nearest vehicle. The figure was barely visible, but she recognized the clean-shaven man as none other than Vidarr Odin's-son.

The minute she saw him, he vanished again.

I did see him at the protest, she thought.

He couldn't be working for Loki now, but he had to factor into this somewhere. And chasing him down simply wasn't an option.

As she continued along the aisle, she could hear voices coming from the stairwell . . . mortals finally arriving to investigate the shaking and noise that must have carried over the entire block.

To be on the safe side, Mist followed the ramp to the lower level. She could see no obvious signs of damage. In a few minutes she'd found a Kawasaki Vulcan, thrown her bare legs over the seat, and started it with a Bind-Rune shaped to fit in the lock.

She used just a touch of the glamour to get past the toll booth and pulled into the street. At this hour, traffic was light, but the streets were clogged with the usual tourists, many of them returning to their hotels after visiting the junk-filled shops that had become fronts for underground clubs. The drug dealers were also out in force, along with young prostitutes whose heavy makeup couldn't hide their despair.

Mist forced herself to drive past them without stopping. Once she was on the freeway, she accelerated southbound toward Milpitas.

Timing, Mist thought. *Everything that's happened tonight has hung on things occurring at exactly the right moment. For Loki.*

Leaning over the handlebars, Mist gripped the accelerator until her hands ached. The fifty-mile ride seemed more like five hundred, even at a speed well above the limit. She coaxed every bit of power out of the Vulcan, wishing her mechanical mount could fly like Sleipnir.

❧

The Jotunar fell.

A quick seeking spell had told Orn that Loki had left nearly two dozen frost giants to defend his mansion, most of them doubtless charged with guarding the boy. None of them, however, was prepared to face Orn's magic, or his warriors.

They had spent centuries in Midgard training for battle, keeping themselves fit and ready for Odin's call, just as Mist and the Valkyrie had waited out the long years guarding the Treasures. Both warriors and women had hidden themselves among the mortals of Midgard, but the Valkyrie had never known they shared their adopted world with those whom they had once carried from the battlefields of Earth to the realm of the Aesir.

The foremost of Orn's Einherjar, Hrothgar, split his warriors into four groups, three to take on the rallying Jotunar and the fourth to look for the Treasures. Orn blackened the eyes of all the screens that watched the halls and chanted seeking spells. Loki's mortal servants were discovered in various parts of the house, and Hrothgar compelled one of them to turn off all the other electronic devices while the rest were quickly confined in a large closet. Soon one of the other teams returned with several Jotunar, and it took Orn very little time to learn where the Hammer and Belt were hidden.

While his other warriors continued to sweep the building and the air echoed with cries of shock, pain, and triumph, Orn flew ahead of Hrothgar to the stairs and glided up to the second floor. Ten frost giants stood fast in front of a heavy steel door, teeth bared and ready to fight.

They were clearly the most skilled and competent of Loki's resident Jotunar, for they quickly filled the room with a violent storm of ice-like chips of jagged glass, temporarily blinding the Einherjar. But the warriors forged ahead, shields raised, swords and axes swinging.

Orn found a perch, allowed his men to herd the Jotunar away from the door, and plucked a few black feathers from his breast. He held them suspended in the frigid air, blasted them into minute particles, and blew the ensuing cloud at the door.

Loki's Runes—the invisible staves he had used to ward the door against anyone but himself—sprang to life, outlined by the black powder. Orn struggled to speak the Runes aloud; the spell was complex, and not meant for a bird's throat to reproduce.

Still, in the end, the door gave way. It opened half an inch, groaning like the dying Jotunar. Of the ten giants, only two were still on their feet, and only three Einherjar remained, one too badly injured to fight.

"Hrothgar!" Orn said.

The warrior stepped away from the Jotunn he had just dispatched, put his shoulder to the door, and pushed it open wide enough for Orn to fly through.

There was a short corridor with several other doors just beyond. Orn settled on Hrothgar's shoulder and directed him to each of the doors in turn, feeling for the spell that would safeguard Loki's stolen prize.

Only the third door responded to his seeking. The inside of the room was neat and spare, equipped with a bed, chest, chairs, toys, and other items suitable to a young child. The child himself was not there.

But there were drawings pinned to the walls: crude images of Loki, Dainn, a dark-skinned woman, and Loki's children Jormungandr, Fenrir, and Sleipnir.

And of Odin himself.

"He must be hidden elsewhere," Hrothgar said, circling the room. "Would you have us search?"

"There is something else," Orn said. He half-hopped, half-flew from the rocking chair to the chest of drawers to the headboard of the bed, knowing he was close. Very close.

"Here," he said, pecking at the mattress. "Move the bed."

Hrothgar obeyed, pushing the bed against one of the walls. Beneath was a section of the carpet that covered most of the concrete floor. Hrothgar flipped it aside to reveal a cool, seemingly unbroken surface.

Orn knew it was not as it appeared. There was more than merely a Rune-ward here. He felt a flutter in his chest, as if his body had grown but his heart had remained the size of a bird's.

"Touch it," Orn commanded.

Hrothgar laid his palms on the floor. Orn hopped back at the smell of burning flesh, and Hrothgar cursed as he snapped his hands away from the concrete.

Fire-magic. Orn paced around the telltale spot. He did not have to see the Runes to know that the spell was powerful, and must have drained much of Loki's strength to cast.

Orn knew he could counter the magic at some cost to himself, and rely on the power he would gain from touching the Treasures to replenish what he had expended.

But there was another danger: if he had put so much effort into guarding the objects, Loki might have added a trigger to the spell, one that would alert him to any attempt to take the Treasures.

Tapping his beak gently on the concrete, Orn felt a jolt of pain at the base of his rump. He'd lost three tail feathers to one of Loki's frost giants when Loki had attempted to kidnap Anna and he had gone to her aid. At the time, he had lacked sufficient awareness to understand the significance of what Laufeyson had done.

The feathers had grown back, but if Loki had kept the originals and devised a way to use them . . .

Hrothgar's cell phone vibrated. "Our men at the Fairmont have intercepted Jotunar with the Valkyrie Regin and Skuld," he said to Orn when the communication was finished. "They were returning here. There's also been fighting between Loki's people and Freya's. We couldn't get many details without revealing ourselves."

"Who won the fight?" Orn asked.

"Unclear. The Jotunn we caught could tell us little, but we do not believe anyone was killed."

Then, Orn thought, it was possible that Loki would return to his mansion rather than seek out Sleipnir as he had planned.

"Leave me," he said to Hrothgar. "Let no one enter."

The Einherji hesitated, but a hard look from Orn sent him out the door. Orn shivered, shaking his feathers from crest to the tips of his tail feathers.

He had not used the Seidr for soul-travel since he had awakened; it was the most difficult work of all, save for shape-shifting, and he had not been prepared to leave himself so vulnerable before he had attained the greater part of his power. He was not complete, his soul not yet what it would become.

But he couldn't risk attempting to open the hidden cache by physical means. Preparing his mind as best he could, he began to pace around the warded place, turning his body in an awkward dance as he traced out Rune-staves with his feet. He let his thoughts grow dim, his senses become dulled to the world around him.

When his soul began to detach from his body, he sank down where he was and felt his muscles relax, wings and legs and neck going limp as if he had flung himself against some immovable barrier.

He knew immediately what that barrier was: the scattered ashes of his stolen tail feathers, just under the floor. A great sickness rolled over him, and for a moment his soul was in real danger. He fought with every counter-spell he knew, and at last the effects of the ashes began to wane.

His soul circled the cache as his body had done before, under his control once more, and slipped through the floor as if the concrete were a pool of still water. He found the objects within a case of ash wood, every portion of its surface inscribed with interlocking Rune-staves and dusted over with the ash. His control weakened again, and he almost lost his grip on the narrow cord that held his soul to his raven shape. After a long moment, during which he hung between life and death, he discovered the smallest break in the design and entered the case.

Mjollnir and Megingjord were laid out with care on the velvet lining, each one tied with spell-bound cord. Orn had no need to break the bindings. His soul touched Mjollnir, mingling with the wood and metal, drawing upon the spirit that dwelled within it. He moved quickly to Megingjord, repeating the act, and swiftly withdrew, rejoining his body with a painful jolt.

He felt the new power immediately, though it did not come without more pain. He staggered, unable to raise his wings, as the two new fragments rattled around inside him like sharp-edged puzzle pieces seeking their proper positions in the design.

A figure appeared before him, blurred by his cloudy vision. The boy stared down at him, ginger hair unkempt, dark eyes wide with surprise and fear.

"*You*," he said.

Orn tested his wings again. Soon, he would no longer need them. "Do you know me?" he asked the child in a voice nearly as clear and deep as the All-father's.

"You broke Papa."

"I have defeated Loki many times, child, but I have not yet broken him. That will come soon enough."

"You want to take *everything*," the boy whispered.

"I take what is mine." Orn cocked his head toward the closed door. "Come with me now," he said, "and I will permit your father to live."

"No." All at once the boy's eyes were full of purpose and adult understanding. "You *know* what he is. You're afraid."

"Of Loki?" Orn laughed as the door began to open very slowly behind Danny. "He was never anything but a coward and weakling."

"You will never get Sleipnir," the boy said.

The door burst open, and two Einherjar ran in, Hrothgar in the lead. With a well-coordinated burst of speed, Danny dodged the Einherji and raised his hands.

The room filled with darkness. Hrothgar fell and did not get up again. Pale, half-formed shapes resolved out of the dank mist, figures with empty eyes and faces sculpted by sorrow, suffering, and resignation.

A woman emerged from among them, her body black on one side and white on the other, alternately beautiful and hideous. She smiled at Orn and held out her hands.

"Will you not join us?" she asked in a voice almost as lovely as

Freya's. "Odin's son Baldr awaits you. Will you not enter Niflheim and be my honored guest?"

Orn fluttered away in disgust and horror. It was not possible that Loki had raised his daughter from the Underworld. But the boy . . .

"You are nothing but illusion," he said, seeking the child in the darkness. "Boy, end this game, or I will—"

Hel and her unwilling tenants vanished, Danny along with them. Orn took wing and circled the room in a flurry of rage while the other Einherji looked on in stupid bewilderment.

"The boy has fled," Orn said, his voice briefly descending into a croak again. "Release the mortal servants. I will finish."

Staring about him as if he expected Hel to reappear and carry him off to Niflheim, the Einherji bowed and left the room. Orn banked his anger and stared at Hrothgar's body.

The manner of his dying was unclear, but he was very clearly gone. Like all Einherjar, he should rise again after death. But when Hel or her minions chose to kill . . .

Orn refused to admit to such a disaster. The fragments from Mjollnir and Megingjord had been seamlessly absorbed into his soul. He felt a new strength, long anticipated, and knew his wait would soon come to an end. Once he had laid the spell to convince Loki that those who had killed his men and invaded his home had been sent by Freya, he need have no concern that he would be exposed before he was ready.

Now he must claim the most important piece of the puzzle. Then only one Treasure would remain, and when his men found it, the Horn would herald his victory.

Mist spun onto the Nimitz Freeway, nearly skinning her knee on the asphalt. Once she reached Milpitas and began hitting regular intersections, she whispered hasty Rune-spells to halt traffic and change signals in her favor, praying all the while that she wasn't too late.

The stable was concealed among warehouses along Fremont Boulevard, bordered to the west by the marshy land along Coyote Creek and various sloughs that led to the bay. It was well past nine p.m., and even in the dim light Mist could see the shimmer of magic rising like fog above the building—Alfar and Jotunn, distorted Rune-staves pushing back and forth at each other like two equally matched armies. Over it all hung a ward like an invisible dome, concealing what lay beneath from mortal eyes.

As Mist pulled into the parking lot and skidded around the corner of the warehouse to the back lot, she saw the real fighting in progress. There were far more Jotunar than Alfar, but no sign of Loki.

The elves had split into two groups, one guarding the stable and the other aggressively fighting the giants. The parking lot was slick with ice, and several Alfar were down with frigid spears piercing their chests. Others had drawn their magic from the marshland to the west—some calling up the waters, others the sodden earth and its resident animals, still others the rails, marsh sparrows, and yellowthroats. Shrews and mice and even foxes swarmed onto the asphalt, scrabbling for purchase on the bodies of frost giants who had donned mantles of ice, while birds dived at their heads. Mud rolled up and over the man-made surface and lapped at the Jotunar's heels, temporarily holding them in place.

Mist roared into the midst of the fight, dismounted, and looked for Freya.

"Mist!"

She turned around in time to snatch Kettlingr out of the air. Bryn met her gaze for an instant and spun to catch a looming Jotunn in the belly with a thrust of her own sword.

"You were slow in coming," Freya said behind her, drowning the smell of salt water and rotting vegetation in the scent of primroses as she sent a pair of small frost giants reeling away with a shot of "anti-glamour."

A weak shot, Mist thought, looking for another opening where her sword would do the most good. She wasn't sure about the efficacy of her own magic after the energy she'd expended at the garage, but she could tell from a single glance at Freya's haggard face that the Lady hadn't completely recovered after all.

"Why didn't you tell Konur they were attacking?" she asked.

"I did not know until we arrived," Freya said. Her voice was hoarse.

"Then why did you—" Mist parried the sweep of a frost-sword, snapping it in two and hacking into the Jotunn swordsman's arm. "Why did you come?"

"We received warning that an attempt might be made." Freya made a face that Mist assumed was meant to be a smile, luring another Jotunn close before thrusting a needle-fine dagger into his heart.

"Who warned you?"

"Your seer. But not well enough."

Seer. Ryan?

She didn't have time to consider what Freya's words might mean, or explain her theory about Loki's trick with Danny. She glanced toward the door of the stable warehouse, where several elves were desperately trying to prevent the entrance of four Jotunar armed with ice-maces, axes, and their enormous strength.

Mist ran to join them. One of the Alfar looked up just as a Jotunn crushed his chest with an ice-mailed fist.

Swinging Kettlingr high, Mist brought it down on the Jotunn's shoulder, crushing bone and driving him to his knees. She finished the job by removing his head, but her moment of victory was not to last.

A great, pale gray horse burst out of the door, silver hooves lashing, white teeth snapping at any Jotunn within reach. Steam erupted from his flared nostrils, and his eyes were wild. All eight of Sleipnir's legs were in constant motion as he danced around those who sought to take him, kicking and striking forward and back.

An instant later a huge dark form leaped out behind Sleipnir, claws scrabbling on the ice and great head swinging with a flash of bared teeth. It moved so fast that Mist couldn't see more than a long muzzle, black fur, and flattened ears. With a swipe of a huge paw, it sent another of the Alfar flying, leaving only two to stand against the Jotunar surrounding Sleipnir.

Mist was unable to move. The beast. Somehow it had escaped Konur, made its way here . . .

"Daughter!"

She snapped out of her horror to find Freya facing two frost giants, struggling and obviously failing to use her glamour on them. Sleipnir and the beast were circling each other, the horse shrilling anger and threat, the beast grinning and growling.

One of the frost giants, of the smaller and swifter breed, darted in with a rope to bind the horse as he plunged and bucked and squealed at his black-furred enemy. The remaining Alfar barely held off the other Jotunar. When Sleipnir reared on his four hind legs and tried to fling himself skyward, the beast leaped after him, closed its jaws around the horse's fetlocks, and pulled him down again.

Mist ran toward the Jotunar confronting Freya, yelling out a battle cry as Rune-staves danced on the edge of her sword. She felt herself begin to touch the ancient magic, knowing only that she had to protect her mother and get back to Sleipnir in time to save him from the beast.

The world telescoped around her as she felt the wind begin to howl, the earth to shake under her boots, the lightning gather to strike the ground where the Jotunar stood. She began to lose herself to the magic, surrendering to that primal self she had never been able to name.

And Freya was there, strengthening her and drawing on her magic at the same time.

The asphalt exploded under the Jotunar's feet, and when it was over only shards of bone and ice remained. Freya was unharmed, though no glimmer of a protective ward lay between her and the crater where the frost giants had stood.

"Sleipnir!" she called.

Mist spun around. The Jotunn with the rope had managed to throw a loop over Sleipnir's neck, and despite the horse's natural strength, the binding held. Dizziness and blinding pain gripped Mist's skull like a rock-Jotunn's hand. She staggered, half-aware of her enemies falling, Sleipnir wrenching free of the frost giant's hold. And the beast about to leap on the horse's broad back.

Strike! A voice in her head commanded. *Let it go!*

She almost did. She almost lost herself to the magic, but something drew her back from the brink. Her vision cleared, and she saw Sleipnir leaping skyward, all eight legs moving in concert as if he were galloping over a battlefield with Odin astride his back.

But it wasn't Odin riding him, but the beast, clinging with sharp nails and powerful legs, teeth entangled in the horse's thick mane. For the first time, Mist could see it clearly.

Not Dainn. Mist let out her breath in a rush and reached for the ancient power, but it had fled beyond her reach. The remaining Jotunar were fleeing, their work obviously done, leaving the dead in their wake.

Dead that included five of the nine Alfar who had been set to watch Sleipnir, and a dozen Jotunar.

Mist was exhausted from both the physical fighting and the magic, but she was able to call up the Rune-spell of the forge and turn the frost giants' bodies to ash.

With the Alfar it was more difficult. Mist watched the surviving elves gather around their own fallen in a circle of privacy and respect. She knew better than to interfere. In Alfheim, they would return one who had died to their own pristine earth, enhancing and accelerating the natural process of decomposition. But here, amid the workings and technology of mortals, they must either give the Alfar to the polluted marsh or carry them back to the elves' camp to dispose of the bodies there.

Worst of all, it seemed that they had died in vain. Sleipnir was gone. Odin's mount might throw off his "captor" at any time . . . if the rider hadn't been a magical creature itself.

For the first time, Mist had lost one of "her" Treasures to her enemy. And all she'd gotten in return was Dainn.

She had no idea what she was going to do with him. Or how she was going to get Sleipnir back.

17

"Daughter," Freya said, coming up behind her. Her voice had deteriorated to an almost ugly rasp, and her eyes were couched in deep shadow. She had never looked so ghastly.

"I have no idea . . . why I was unable to prevail against these frost giants," she said with a meekness Mist had never seen in her before.

"I saw you take several out," Mist said, torn between an instinctive desire to comfort her mother and the repulsive memory of Dainn's claim: "She *told me to kill.*"

Kill Danny. Didn't that explain his fear of Freya's intentions for the boy? Hadn't Mist herself always wondered if Freya might have seen Danny on the steppes?

Ask her now, Mist told herself. But how did she expect Freya to answer? Why would the Lady admit to knowing Danny at all, let alone to wanting him dead?

There had to be another way of learning the truth. And in the meantime, Mist knew that she couldn't allow her suspicions, no matter how terrible, to cloud her thinking.

"You know what happened to you during the protest?" she asked.

"Bryn explained," Freya said, a little faintly. "I had thought myself recovered."

"You'll have to go back and rest, as long as it takes."

"But we must recover the horse."

"When we've recouped and made a decent plan, yes."

Freya pushed a lock of lank, dull hair away from her face. "Loki will be bolder than ever. He will attempt to take the other Treasures in your keeping. How will you defend yourself?"

"Loki used tricks and illusions to keep me from getting here soon enough," Mist said, deciding to keep the explanations simple. "He's also got Regin and Skuld captive and serving as 'entertainment' for his mortal cronies, and they weren't doing it of their own free will." She took a long breath. "He's been using a Hel of a lot of magic, and I'm betting he won't find it easy to keep Sleipnir. As for our defenses, I'll be sending out a call for more allies, as I should have done long ago."

"That is wise," Freya said. Her expression softened. "Perhaps you are learning."

"I never wanted to learn *this*." She looked up at the sky, stormy as always but clear of wards or any signs of magic. "While you rest, I'll meet with my council and figure out our next move. At least we can be pretty sure that Loki will want Sleipnir close at hand, so he's not likely to—"

Before she could finish, six motorcycles and two SUVs pulled into the weedy parking lot. A dozen elves jumped out of one of the trucks while the bikers pulled to a stop a few feet from Mist and Freya.

"Where's the fight?" Roadkill asked, his gaze sweeping the lot. "Are we too—"

He subsided as several of the elves joined those who mourned over their fallen, and after a moment the Alfar carried the dead to the SUV. The bikers with Roadkill maintained a respectful silence.

Captain Taylor jumped out of the other SUV with four of his best fighters, all armed with swords and axes. He looked hard at Freya, who walked away. Not glided, not floated, but merely walked, her footsteps heavy on the asphalt.

"We just found out that Freya left camp with some of her elves," Taylor said, watching the goddess with a slight frown deepening the creases between his eyes. "One of the bikers heard that they were coming here. I don't understand why she didn't alert us."

"She says she wasn't sure if there would actually be an attack," Mist said, well aware of how odd the explanation must sound. "Had Konur returned when you left?"

"No. Was there a problem at the party?"

"That's putting it mildly. I'll fill you in when we're back at camp. Did you meet a young man named Ryan, by any chance?"

Taylor shook his head. "New recruit?"

"Not exactly new." She passed her hand over her face and told Taylor about Sleipnir. He was too well disciplined to swear in her presence.

"How did they find him?" he asked. "Do you believe that someone in our camp betrayed the location?"

"That, or Loki found it on his own. Either possibility is bad news."

"How did the Jotunar get the horse away?"

"They didn't. Loki sent some kind of animal to—"

Sweet Baldr, she thought. Some kind of huge, black, predatory . . .

"Animal?" Taylor prompted.

"I think Loki may have managed to get one of his other offspring across one of the bridges from Ginnungagap," she said.

"Who?"

"Fenrir. It's possible it was another manifestation like Jormungandr—"

She broke off again, wondering when she might discover how not to be an idiot. Who created the manifestations? A certain small boy who was much older than he appeared. The boy she might or might not have seen in the garage when she was fighting the elf who had seen her as a threat to that same child.

Danny had seemed deeply attached to Sleipnir on the steppes. Gods knew what Loki might have told Danny about Sleipnir's current situation.

But even a manifestation as real and dangerous as Jormungandr had been would find it difficult to make off with Odin's horse.

"—but I don't believe it was," she finished.

"So now we have to look for another possible traitor and contend with a giant wolf," Taylor said, rubbing the pommel of his sword with his thumb. "Anything else?"

"Oh, we don't get off that easy. We lost this fight in part because Freya isn't recovered from whatever happened to her at the protest."

"She looks like shit," Vixen said, coming to join them.

Mist and Taylor followed the biker woman's gaze. Freya was staring out into the marsh for all the world like any ordinary Midgardian contemplating her own mortality.

"Let's get back to HQ," Mist said, herding them away from the subject of Freya's health. "It's time for another council of war."

A war Loki had just taken another step toward winning.

◑◐

"Where is my son?"

Loki struck at the Jotunn kneeling before him, knocking him to the ground and setting the giant's hair alight with a fire spell. The Jotunn began to wail in pain and fear, unable to move his hands to put out the fire.

"How did they enter?" Loki snarled, bending over the writhing giant. "The whole place stinks of Alfar. Who among you admitted them?"

"No one, my lord," Hymir said, kneeling with the others in the small meeting room. "We do not know how they got in."

"They killed twenty of my best fighters," Loki said. He snapped his fingers, and the small flames in the Jotunn's hair went out. "Freya was *here,* and now my son is missing."

The smell of singed flesh set some of the Jotunar to coughing, but they quickly swallowed the noise. Only Vali had the courage to speak up again.

"None of us could have expected Freya to use Mist's impersonation as a distraction to raid the house," he said.

Loki barely restrained himself from breaking Vali's jaw. Freya's clever little plot was the least of his concerns. Among all the various plans he had made to detain Mist at the reception, not one had accounted for the actual presence of his son. Danny was to have appeared only as an illusion, a shape worn by Loki to deceive and provoke. Yet Danny had teleported himself to the hotel, though he should have been completely unaware of what was happening there.

His bond with Dainn, Loki thought. The elf hadn't known that

Loki had expected him to become the beast again. Perhaps Danny had felt his father's anguish, even from across the city.

And he had calmed the beast. He might even have helped Dainn resist the spells that should have given Loki better control of the beast during the encounter in the garage.

"I'm sure the kid's all right," Vali said. "Miss Jones says he was already back here before you returned from the reception. He would have seen the danger when Freya and the Alfar showed up. He could have escaped without thinking to warn anyone. And Freya probably only came for the Treasures."

"She always meant to kill Danny," Loki said through gritted teeth. "He may already be—"

To his astonishment, his voice broke. Danny gone. Dainn as well. Mistake after mistake. Even Loki could find no excuse for his own stupidity.

"The Treasures are still here," he said, mastering his rage. "And even if Danny avoided Freya, he could have gone seeking Dainn, and still ended up in her hands."

"But Mist tried to protect Danny, not hurt him. Do you think she'd let Freya do anything to him?"

"If Freya was powerful enough to breach my wards and kill my men, then she can—"

Take Mist's soul, he completed silently. In spite of what he'd said to Dainn, he had never dismissed the possibility that Mist's powers might significantly increase Freya's own.

Danny had to be found, and quickly. But there was one other place he might be. He had been most anxious to be reunited with his half-brother.

"Why have I not heard of Sleipnir?" Loki demanded of the cowering Jotunar. When no one answered, he called the leader of the Jotunar sent with Fenrir to capture Odin's Steed. Just as the call was about to default to voice mail, the giant answered.

"My lord?" The voice was raspy and faint, as if its owner was in pain.

"Have you seen Danny?" Loki asked.

"Danny?"

Loki cursed. "Where is Grer?"

"Dead." The giant coughed. "My lord, did you not receive our—"

"I received nothing," Loki said with deadly calm. "Is Sleipnir taken?"

"Fenrir was riding him, when we—" The Jotunn coughed again. "Mist came, but the Sow and her offspring did not succeed in stopping us."

So someone had guessed Loki's plans. Mist must have moved very quickly to get to the hidden stable in time to fight.

But *Freya* had been there. Even she could not be in two places at once. Without the Lady's direct participation, her Alfar could not have broken into Loki's mansion.

Who else could have done it?

"Inform me immediately if you see my son," Loki said, and ended the call. "Hymir, send all available men to watch Mist's camp and loft. If Danny is there with Dainn, I must know immediately."

"They won't be able to keep him if he wants to leave," Vali said as the Jotunn hurried out.

Loki shot him a poisonous glance. "I wonder if you had anything to do with this, Odin's-son. You and Edvard both knew of my plans, and now Edvard is gone. Traitor to one, traitor to all."

Vali seemed unperturbed by the accusation. "If you think that," he said, "why have you trusted me all this time?"

"Watch your insolence." He regarded the kneeling Jotunar with contempt. "Return to your posts. Vali, take two men and—"

Panting heavily, Fenrir slunk into the room, muzzle almost touching the floor. Loki strode toward him, and the Wolf rolled onto his back, belly exposed.

"Where is Sleipnir?" Loki demanded.

"Danny took him," Fenrir whined.

Loki closed his eyes. "How?" he asked.

"With magic. I could not stop him."

It was far from the worst news Loki could have received. He restrained himself from punishing Fenrir, as tempted as he was.

"Where have they gone?" he asked.

Fenrir sniffled. "I don't know. Please, Father . . ."

Loki turned his back on his son. "They may have gone to Mist," he said. "Hymir, send your men. We will find them."

With one of the surviving Alfar's help, Freya climbed into the SUV. Mist mounted the borrowed motorcycle and pulled out of the lot, the other bikers behind her. They took their time getting home in order to spare the injured Alfar, but she was hardly aware of the drive. There were far too many thoughts crowding her mind.

She knew how Loki had arranged to distract her from finding out about his attack on the stable, but why had he decided to go for it *now*? Because he'd believed that Freya might be incapacitated, or because he'd managed to summon Fenrir and knew he had a new advantage of surprise and strength? Had Danny been involved?

Maybe all of the above, she thought, sending the bike roaring ahead in a burst of speed. She was convinced that the "real" Danny *had* been at the party some of the time. But she didn't think he'd come at Loki's behest. And when he'd touched Dainn and stopped the beast . . .

Her mind shifted to thoughts of Regin and Skuld. If she'd had her way, she'd have taken some pretty big risks to rescue them. But that would mean raiding Loki's headquarters, and that simply wasn't possible. As much as it disturbed her, she couldn't help them until the chance came to do it without destroying the allies' other plans.

Then there was Ryan. Mist leaned low over the handlebars, feeling the wind tear at her gown. He was back, he still had his abilities, and he'd warned Freya that something might happen with Sleipnir.

Freya. Did she really want to hurt Danny? Was it because he was Loki's son, and she was desperate to gain some new advantage over Loki? She was failing even faster now, lending Konur's advice about finding a new body an unpalatable urgency.

And as Freya grew weaker, Mist found herself drawing on the ancient magic again, almost losing herself as she had so many times before.

Dainn would probably sense what she'd done as soon as she saw him again. What in Hel was she going to do with *him*?

Her grim thoughts had just trailed off into a tangled knot of emotion when she found herself pulling onto Illinois. To her surprise, she found Ryan standing on the sidewalk in front of the loft, his body illuminated by the streetlights. Bryn was also waiting. She ran up to Mist's bike as soon as she pulled up to the curb, the other bikes and cars rolling to a haphazard stop behind her.

"Where's Freya?" Bryn asked.

There was genuine fear in Bryn's voice. Since she'd begun working with Freya, she'd seemed not only protective but more a "daughter" to the Lady than Mist had ever been. Or wanted to be.

"She's in the SUV," Mist said, the tattered remnants of her slinky dress flapping around her as she dismounted. "She's all right, but she pushed herself too hard. You'll have to make her rest."

"And Sleipnir?" Bryn said, glancing toward the SUV.

"Gone."

Bryn cursed and, without another word, hurried off to help Freya out of the SUV. Mist turned to the teenager waiting nervously a few feet away.

"Ryan," she said.

He nearly jumped into her arms, burying his face into the crook of her neck. She gave him a quick hug and set him back.

"You've changed," she said. And he had. He'd filled out some, gotten a little taller, and cut his hair. His clothes were new. He almost looked like the rich kid he actually was, now that he'd presumably claimed his aunt's inheritance.

"Yeah," he said, rubbing his stubbled chin. "Feels like I've been gone a lot longer than nine months." He looked at Mist from under his straight, pale brows. "You dyed your hair."

"It'll be back to normal soon enough."

Ryan licked his lips nervously. "You mad that I came back?"

"I'm mad that you left without explaining why."

"I'm sorry. I . . . there was something I had to do."

"I gather it had something to do with your inheritance," she said, looking quickly over her shoulder at the Alfar carefully removing their dead from the SUV.

"Something like that," Ryan said. He stared at Freya as Bryn and Konur helped her hobble into the loft, and then quickly dropped his gaze. "I missed everyone. And I don't have those seizures anymore."

"No?"

"They just stopped. Maybe it's my age."

"But you still have the visions. Freya told me how you warned her."

He shifted with obvious unease. "It was sort of sudden, or I would have waited for you to come back." He glanced around. "What happened to Sleipnir?"

"He was taken by Loki."

"I'm sorry. If I'd only—"

Mist cut him off with a slice of her hand. "I assume that Gabi filled you in on everything you missed."

"Yes," he said, staring at the ground. "I'm really sorry about Eir. I know she was a good person."

"She knew what she was getting into," Mist said quietly. "Are you sticking around? You're welcome to stay as long as you want."

"I still can't always see what's going to happen, or be sure the visions are accurate," Ryan said, nearly tripping over his words. "If I could, I might have known for sure that Loki would get Sleipnir."

"I understand. No one expects you to read the future, unless that's what you want to do."

She hesitated, wondering how much of that was a lie. Could the allies ignore his ability to see major events just before they happened, even if there was a chance the visions might be wrong or distorted?

"I'm sorry to cut this off," she said, deferring the question, "but we have to—"

"I saw Dainn," Ryan said, his voice strained. "He's a prisoner, isn't he?"

"You know he went over to Loki?"

"There had to be a good reason. You don't know why he did what he did. Maybe it was for someone else. Whatever anyone says, he'd never turn evil, like Loki."

Studying Ryan closely, Mist wondered if he knew something. Knew, as in "saw." And if he would tell her.

"No matter why he did it, his beast is still alive," she said. "And it's dangerous as Hel."

Ryan's lower lip trembled. She almost felt like bawling herself.

"Can I see him?" Ryan asked.

"Not now. After I've finished questioning him, we'll have to keep him in isolation indefinitely." She blew out her breath. "I assume you've found a place to sleep."

"Yeah. Gabi did," he said, clearly eager to accept the change of subject. "Do you know where she is? I haven't seen her in a while."

"I've been—" *Too busy to pay the poor kid any attention,* Mist thought. "We'll talk more later," she said, giving him a little push in the direction of the warehouses. "I'm glad you're all right."

She just hoped he stayed that way, even if he never had another word to say about the future.

Konur emerged from the loft as Mist was about to call her lieutenants to another council of war.

"How is Freya?" she asked.

"Very weak." He shook his head. "The matter of finding her another body has only grown more urgent."

"We'll discuss it at the council meeting."

"That would not be wise."

"Everyone has the right to know what you're proposing."

"Will you also discuss the boy?"

"Danny," she said, bracing herself for the inevitable and dangerous questions. And answers she didn't want to hear. "Did you know that he's Loki's son?"

"No," he said. "But it explains much. He appears to be a remarkable child."

"You don't know the half of it."

"He was aiding his father in the hotel, was he not?"

"At least part of the time, Loki was posing as Danny. I know he didn't expect his son to show up."

"You did not answer my question."

"No, I don't think he was helping his father. I'm not sure that Danny has any loyalty to Loki at all. In fact, I know that his feelings are focused in a completely different direction." She considered how best to condense the facts so that Konur would understand and accept them. "It's true that Laufeyson may have compelled Danny to take action against us, but it wasn't of his own volition."

She told Konur how Danny had saved Dainn from Loki, opened the portal to the steppes, and led them to Sleipnir.

"A great mystery," Konur said. "Why would Loki's son solicit the assistance of his father's enemy, and put a potential weapon into that enemy's hands?"

"I can only say that the connection between Danny and Dainn was immediate and powerful, almost instinctive."

"Dainn spoke of Freya wishing to hurt Danny," Konur said.

"He actually said '*she* told me to kill,'" she quoted. "I think he was about to say more when you cut him off."

"I told you that Dainn is mad. He attempted to harm you, as well as this Edvard."

"Edvard is a *berserkr*, one of Bryn's Einherjar bikers. He disappeared from our camp following Jormungandr's attack. Before Dainn went to Loki, Edvard said he'd found a way to control the beast."

"The herb," Konur said. "I remember." He frowned. "Why did Danny put himself between the beast and the *berserkr*? If he was not trying to protect Loki's ally—"

"Maybe it was to save Dainn from himself." She caught Konur's gaze. "Danny's different in more ways than you can imagine, and Loki will use *him* as a weapon if we don't protect and guide him."

"Are you certain that the boy did not aid in Sleipnir's abduction?"

Konur's concern echoed Mist's a little too closely. "He might want to be reunited with Sleipnir," she said, "but he wouldn't help Loki to do it."

The elf-lord fell silent again, studying the pavement under his boots with great concentration. "He may not carry Loki's evil," he said, "but he is clearly dangerous." He looked up again. "You should know that we caught one of Loki's spies just outside of camp. He admitted that he was sent to search for Danny here, because the boy has apparently disappeared from Loki's home."

"Disappeared?"

"Evidently Loki didn't see him after the incident at the hotel. He is very concerned, which suggests that Danny has slipped his leash."

"He certainly didn't come *here*," she said. "But it is strange that Loki lost him around the same time that we lost Sleipnir."

"There is one other thing," Konur said. "It took considerably more effort to get the information out of Loki's agent, but it seems that Loki does not have Sleipnir, either."

"What?"

"At least not as of the time the spy was sent here. That may have changed."

"Where else would Fenrir go?"

"Danny is his brother."

"Are you suggesting that he'd take Sleipnir to Danny instead of Loki?"

"You know both Sleipnir and Danny better than I. Is it possible?"

At this point, Mist thought, just about anything was possible. If Sleipnir and Danny were together . . .

"Konur," she said. "I'd like you to let me know right away if Freya says anything about Danny."

Konur's eyes were as cold and dark as the bay at midnight. "I think you will find that your fears are unfounded, and that Dainn is . . ."

He trailed off, but Mist understood him well enough. "There's one other thing," she said. "I need you to personally make sure that no harm comes to Dainn. Whatever punishment it may seem he deserves, he's going to get a fair hearing. I want regular reports as to his behavior and anything he says when he can speak again. Will you do that for me?"

Bending his dark head, Konur sighed. "I will." He opened the door, walked through, and closed it behind him a little too carefully.

Mist stood still for a moment, feeling ill. Oh, Konur wouldn't let Dainn come to any harm. He'd given his word.

But she still didn't know whether or not he could be trusted where Freya was concerned. Or if *she* was crazy for believing that Dainn was telling the truth.

18

Longing for just a few minutes to grab a beer and talk to someone who wasn't up to his or her eyeballs in power struggles, conspiracies, and kidnappings, Mist followed Konur into the loft. She put her cell on the kitchen table and pulled a Guinness out of the fridge. Her hand was shaking as she opened the bottle.

Delayed reaction, she thought. And too much magic. The adrenaline was wearing off, and pretty soon she'd feel the exhaustion she'd been pushing away.

Maybe sleep was what she needed. Or maybe not. She stared at the phone, debating whether or not to call Koji. Usually he was one of the sanest among them, blessed with common sense and an easygoing attitude.

Until that afternoon, when he'd been so upset about her plans to take Freya's place at the reception. Was he developing feelings for her she'd never meant to encourage?

She didn't think she could deal with romantic complications on top of everything else.

Taking a final swig from the bottle, Mist set it on the table. A fifteen-minute nap was really all she could afford, but maybe it would get her through the meeting and talking to Freya and Dainn and calling new recruits and . . .

"Hey."

She looked up to find Koji standing in the doorway. He seemed more serious than usual, his dark eyes almost grave, and he was wearing a formal, expensive-looking business suit.

"I must really be slipping," Mist said, rubbing the bridge of her nose. "I didn't even hear you come through the door."

"I can see you've had a rough night." He looked her up and down as he joined her at the table. "I'm almost afraid to ask you how it went."

Mist glanced down at her now-filthy gown in surprise. The slits on the sides were almost up to her waist, and the bodice was barely hanging on.

"I guess I'd better change, huh?" she asked.

"I like the way you look." He moved closer, a little of the usual sparkle returning to his eyes, and bent to kiss her neck. She shied away, suddenly self-conscious about the grit and grime.

"Sorry," Koji said, stepping back quickly. "I should know better."

There was something in his tone that suggested he was talking about more than making advances when she was in no state to accept them. "It's okay," she said. "I'm just . . . a little confused right now. The party wasn't much fun. And then there was . . ." She sighed. "It's going to take a while to explain. I need to call a meeting, but if you want to stay up, I can tell you about it afterward."

He took a chair on the other side of the table and studied her face. "It really was bad, wasn't it?" he asked.

"Yeah."

"I should never have made such a fuss this afternoon. I'm just glad you're all right."

She pointed at the bottle. "Want one?"

Koji shook his head, as he always did when she offered him a beer. "I understand that Dainn has returned," he said.

She sat up straight. "You saw him?"

"I ran into Ryan on the street outside."

"I take it you didn't meet with him after he left camp last winter?"

"No. But from the look of him, he must have claimed his inheritance." He frowned a little. "He's very worried about Dainn."

"Dainn was at the party with Loki, and he's currently a prisoner with the Alfar. I'll be interrogating him soon."

"Do you hope he'll give you information you can use against Loki?"

"I don't know. I think he . . . Oh, Hel. I've begun to think his defection might not have been what it seemed."

"How so?"

"Bits and pieces of things he said when I . . . when we captured him. But I guess I'll find out soon enough."

"You still care for him, don't you?" Koji smiled wryly. "You never really stopped."

Mist jumped out of her chair, stalked around the table, and kissed Koji with all the passion she could muster. He began to respond and then stopped, his lips motionless under hers.

"Oh, gods," Mist said, scrambling backward. "I'm sorry. That wasn't . . . I don't know what to say."

"I should be flattered," he said, his tone a little too casual.

"No. You think I did that to prove I don't care about Dainn."

"Did you?"

"I don't know." She fell back into her chair. "Every time I think I have one thing figured out, something or someone pulls the rug out from under my feet." She laughed. "Sometimes I pull it out myself."

"It's okay," Koji said.

Mist looked at him quickly, trying to read his face. "I'm sorry," she repeated. "I wish I could explain things more clearly when we're together."

"We don't have much time these days," he said, tracing what looked like Kanji symbols on the table with his fingertip.

"I miss our talks," she said, watching his movements.

"I wish I could be of more help to you. I know how alone you are in all this."

"I'm not lonely, if that's what you mean."

Koji shook his head reprovingly. He didn't have to say anything; he knew when she was bullshitting. In that way, he was like Dainn.

Except under Dainn's deceptive calm and perception, the beast was always lurking. Koji didn't have any darkness inside him.

"Look," she said, taking a deep breath, "nothing is normal for me. Nothing *can* be normal until this is over."

"I understand," Koji said.

"Of course things may *never* be normal, not like they were before."

"Now you're joking," he said with a straight face.

"Okay. They *won't* be, no matter who wins. Even if *we* do, the Aesir will be here afterward. People are going to have some trouble dealing with that, especially the ones who don't believe in any gods and those who believe there's only one. And the gods themselves are going to need somewhere to live. The Alfar . . . well, they won't be going anywhere."

Koji finished his invisible writing and folded his hands on the tabletop. "If it were up to you," he said, "if you could keep this world 'normal' and stop any of the gods from interfering in any way, would you?"

"What do you mean, stop them?"

"You've never really talked about it, but it's pretty obvious that even the so-called 'good' gods aren't very different from humans in the way they act."

"If you mean Freya—"

"She's actually not at all like the mythology suggests."

"Mythology isn't exactly accurate."

"But if the goddess of beauty and love is so much less"—he hesitated, obviously searching for the right word—"less benevolent than she is in the stories, what about the others?" He leaned forward. "If you knew that even Loki's enemies would be harmful to this world, would you oppose them?"

He really wanted to know. She could see it in his eyes. And she didn't know what to tell him.

"My goal has always been to protect mortalkind," she said, dropping her gaze. "But I don't see why it can only be one or the other."

"And what if there are other gods, whole pantheons coexisting peacefully with humanity, who want to keep their freedom and the lives they've always known? What if the Aesir make trouble for everyone, not only human beings?"

She looked up sharply. "Other gods?"

Of course, she thought, feeling stupid. Gods like the desert spirits who had helped her fight Loki when she'd gone to fetch Eir and the Apples of Idunn in New Mexico. If "gods" was the right word.

But she'd never told Koji about that—just as, somehow, she'd never gotten around to telling Dainn.

"Do you know something I don't?" she asked, half-jokingly.

He smiled. "You know, Japan has its own kind of gods. We call them *kami*. Spirits of all kinds of things, from roads to wind and war, even foods and disease. They're not always nice, but they have no interest in ruling the world."

Mist remembered that Eir had said something very similar about the desert spirits. "You believe these *kami* are real?" she asked.

"I don't practice Shinto, but since the Nordic gods exist, I see no reason why the *kami* shouldn't be real as well."

"Would these *kami* resist other gods who *did* want to rule the world?" she asked.

His smile faded. "I don't know," he said. "It's all theory, isn't it?"

"Theory or not, I wouldn't let Midgard be destroyed in some war of pantheons," she said. "Not if I could do anything to stop it."

"And you won't let it happen in a war between Loki and the Aesir."

"I'm still only one—"

"—semi-divine, nearly unstoppable force of nature."

"I think that's taking it a little far," she said, trying for humor again.

"I'm not sure it is." He pushed his chair back. "Somehow, I don't think you've reached the limits of what you can do."

"I haven't changed, Koji." She touched her chest. "Not in *here*."

"But you have, Mist. And maybe that's not such a bad thing." He smiled to take the sting out of his words. "There was a time you wanted comfort, and I was there. But it was never meant to be more than that. I've known how you felt about Dainn since the first time I met him."

"I know you disliked him, but that has nothing to do with—"

"Maybe I *was* a little jealous, at the beginning. But I just wanted to make sure you'd be okay with him. Now I know you will be."

"It's not what you think."

"Trust what you feel. You never felt that for me. And you'll never stop feeling it for *him*."

"Koji, this really isn't the right time . . ."

"It's the *only* time, Mist." He got up from the table. "I should have said this as soon as I walked in, but I'm afraid I . . ." He sighed. "I let you distract me, and this is going to be harder than it has to be."

"What's going to be harder?" she asked, suddenly alarmed.

"I won't be seeing you again."

"What?" She rose and moved around the table. "I know what you've been saying about me and Dainn, but even if it were true, that's no reason for you to—"

"It isn't that." His usually pleasant, even voice cracked with distress. "I can't stay. I can't help you fight, and I can't stand by and watch you and everyone else risk their lives."

"But I've never judged you for not fighting."

"You will, when things get really bad." He met her gaze. "I wish I could explain more, but all I can say is that my family forbids me to get involved."

"Your family? The Tashiros? You've told them what's happening?"

"They already knew." He pressed his lips together and started for the kitchen door. "I've already said too much. Remember what I said about not letting the world be destroyed in a war between your gods."

"Wait!" She caught up with him halfway down the hall and grabbed his arm. "This is it? No more friendship, no legal advice, just good-bye?"

He turned, stood very straight, and gave her a formal bow. "Please forgive me," he said. "It has been my great honor to know you, Mist of the Valkyrie." The corner of his lips crooked up. "Please, promise me you'll rest between magical battles."

"Curse it, Koji—"

But he was already walking out of the loft. Just as she reached the door, she thought she saw a faint silver glow limning Koji's suit, a glimmer almost like the scales of a fish or a reptile. A long, whiplike tail coiled with a flourish behind him.

She rubbed her eyes, and the illusion was gone. He was just a man in a business suit, climbing into a silver Prius and waving to her one last time.

For a while she wasn't able to move, paralyzed by sadness and regret. *I took him for granted,* she thought. *This is my own cursed fault.*

But after a few minutes of self-reflection—and a little self-pity—she realized she was being foolish. Koji wasn't just going to disappear. She'd meet up with him again, and they'd hash it out properly.

If she could try to save a world, surely she could save a friendship.

As long as you don't keep fooling yourself, she thought. She'd told Koji she hadn't changed, but he'd known she was lying.

And so had she.

◑◐

Dainn sat on the floor, propped against the wall of the small office that served as his new prison. He judged that it was a little past dawn; they'd given him food and water, the Alfar who had locked him up here, but they hadn't looked at him, and their contempt was obvious.

How could he blame them? They rightfully saw him as a traitor to all they fought for, a personal affront to Alfheim, if Alfheim had still existed.

They remembered the way he'd been in Asgard, before the Last Battle. Before Loki. Wise, rational, Odin's very sane counselor.

He'd fallen as far as any being could. And they wouldn't let him forget. No more than *he* could forget.

Dainn touched his throat. He still couldn't speak. The collar wasn't the cause of his affliction. Nor was it the influence of the beast, which had gone dormant again . . . thanks to Danny.

The *other* Danny, the false one, had made Dainn believe that Mist was Freya, that she was hunting his son to his death. Laufeyson had deliberately provoked Dainn and the beast into attacking her.

But not to kill her. The altercation had served a very different purpose. Sleipnir had been taken, in spite of the real Danny's unexpected arrival at the hotel.

For a moment Dainn waited, listening. Waiting for the beast to make some mocking remark, a threat, a reminder of the perpetual shadow it cast over his soul.

But it was silent. Instead, another voice rang in his memory. Mist, defending Danny. Begging Dainn to recognize her. Telling him that Loki had tricked them.

Asking him if *he* was hurt.

And still he hadn't been able to warn her about Freya.

Dainn touched his throat again. Mist had asked Konur if he had placed a spell on Dainn. She had seemed to believe the elf-lord when he denied it.

But Konur had deceived her. It was the Lady the elf-lord served, even though he had ostensibly accompanied Mist to the reception in order to assist and protect her.

Did he support Freya's scheme to destroy Mist? If he did, he would have every reason to keep her away from Dainn, and find an excuse to silence Dainn permanently. Dainn had no choice but to consider the elf-lord his enemy.

He would have to escape without calling upon the beast. As long as it remained silent, he had a chance.

Closing his eyes, he turned inward and quieted his heart. He let his thoughts drift. What would Loki do with Danny, knowing that his son had interfered with his scheme and left the house without his permission? He wouldn't hurt Danny, surely, but he would doubtless try to find a stronger way to bind the boy so that he couldn't make another unauthorized venture into the outside world.

But an "unauthorized" exit from this cell was exactly what Dainn intended to make. He had worked magic—an inexplicable kind of magic—against Loki's Jotunn guards not long before the beast had returned. His magic and the beast had always seemed inextricably linked, and there was always the risk that any use of magic might strengthen his other side.

Nevertheless, he had to try. He called upon the abilities that came so naturally to his kind, seeking the weeds that had forced their way through cracks in cement and pavement outside the cell. He grasped at their tenacious life and built upon them, enhancing their strength until they burst through the floor of the cell and sent green tendrils crawling toward the door.

It was working. He flexed his fists and concentrated, urging the tendrils to invade the door's hinges, filling the smallest gaps between metal and wood. If he could weaken the hinges sufficiently, then he would be prepared when the guards changed shifts, or if the—

The door creaked as it swung inward, shattering the spell. The weeds contracted and disappeared into the tiny cracks in the floor. Dainn sprang to his feet.

"Wait!" a familiar voice whispered. "I'm here to help!"

Ryan. Dainn released his breath slowly and remained where he was, half-afraid that the beast might wake again.

"It's okay," Ryan said. He closed the door carefully and squatted a few feet away. "I know you can't talk, so just listen. I was here when they brought you back. I've been watching for a chance to talk to you."

Shaking his head with three sharp jerks, Dainn pointed at the door.

"They don't know I'm here," Ryan said. "I made sure of that."

Dainn opened his mouth. A hoarse growl emerged.

"I'm not in any danger," Ryan said. "But *you* are."

Touching his throat, Dainn tried again. "V—" he began. "Vis—"

"I don't need a vision to know that. Those elves out there don't like you."

It wasn't quite possible to laugh, but Dainn managed a reasonable approximation. Ryan didn't smile.

"Mist is in another council meeting," he said. "I found out last night that Danny escaped from Loki, and that Loki doesn't have Sleipnir, either. I thought you'd want to know right away." He glanced over his shoulder. "I can get you out of here now. It may sound strange, but I have a . . . a sort of new technique. I can predict people's movements just before they happen."

Dainn shook his head again, though his thoughts were running wild with speculation about Danny and Sleipnir.

"I don't have those seizures anymore," Ryan said, correctly inter-
preting Dainn's concern. "This technique isn't dangerous, as long as I
don't do it too often. We just need to get you out of the elves' camp
and somewhere safe."

"Mist," Dainn grunted.

"I know you're not the traitor everyone says you are, no matter
what you did. Mist needs you, even if she doesn't realize how much.
You have to talk to her again, in private."

Peering into the young man's eyes, Dainn wondered if Ryan, too,
knew of Freya's plans for Mist. If he did, it would be recent knowledge. Perhaps it had even brought him back from his self-imposed
exile.

Why, then, would he not tell Mist himself?

"Are you okay?" Ryan asked, his voice rising with anxiety. "I
mean—"

Dainn curled his fingers into claws, raked them across the floor,
and then drew a line through the invisible marks with his fingertip.

"Good," Ryan said with obvious relief. "Then all you need to do is
stick close to me. Every time I make a signal to move, like this"—he
raised his bent arm and clenched his fist—"you have to be ready."

Close on Ryan's heels, Dainn ran at a crouch out the door and into
the central area of the warehouse. No one had been guarding his
cell. He froze when he heard the whisper of elven footsteps, but Ryan
urged him on with a frantic gesture.

They continued toward the back door of the warehouse, keeping
close to the internal walls. Three times Ryan stopped abruptly, and
moments later Dainn would hear one or more mortals passing, sometimes speaking in soft voices, others on silent patrol. They had nearly
reached the door when Ryan abruptly stopped and pushed Dainn to
the floor. Five Alfar walked in, and Dainn heard his name.

"We have about thirty seconds to get out once they've passed us,"
Ryan whispered.

Dainn readied himself, and at Ryan's signal they ran toward the door.
Once outside, facing a wide stretch of broken concrete leading down
to an equally decrepit wharf, Ryan pointed east toward the bay. The air

was frigid in the filmy, early morning sunlight, and the water smelled of fish.

"There's an old pier you can hide under," he said. "I'll find a way to get Mist down here."

As he turned to go, Dainn gripped his arm and held it firmly. He smiled, and Ryan embraced him briefly but tightly before letting him go and setting off to the north.

He ran directly into Konur, who caught Ryan and held him easily. The elf-lord looked over the boy's head and met Dainn's gaze.

"Do not blame the young one," Konur said. "I knew of his feelings for you, and had him watched." He glanced down again as Ryan struggled in his grip. "You did well to come so far."

"Let him go, you fucking asshole," Ryan spat, utterly unlike himself. "I know Freya wants to kill him. I can stop—"

Konur released him, and Ryan staggered back, fists clenched. Dainn hesitated, listening for the beast.

It was there. He could reach it easily. But he was done making deals with the darkness. He felt his magic rise to his call, as eagerly as an arrow held too long in its quiver.

Dirt erupted through the cracks in the concrete, rushing toward Konur in a wave of rock, soil, and wood from an old landfill. The wave parted around Ryan and struck the elf-lord full-force.

When it collapsed on itself, Konur was still standing, his arms raised. A ward shimmered around him, drawn from Runes of air. He reshaped the Runes and hurled a great wind at Dainn. Again Ryan was untouched, but the wind knocked Dainn off his feet.

Air was the most difficult of all natural elements to control. Few Alfar possessed the knowledge, art, or natural talent to do so, beyond making use of simple seeking spells. Only a handful of the Aesir and Vanir could match Konur's ability.

Mist did, through the ancient magic. But Mist wasn't here.

"If you continue," Konur called, "you will release the creature again. I feel it even now. Can you control it, or will it rampage through this camp, killing everything that stands in its path?"

Dainn got to his knees and pressed his hands to the broken surface beneath them, letting the sharp edges cut into his palms. Ryan ran up to him and knelt beside him.

"Don't," Ryan begged. His voice was thick. "I'm sorry. I didn't see him coming."

"O . . . kay," Dainn whispered.

"Don't touch him," Ryan hissed as Konur came to stand over them.

"I will not harm him," Konur said, dropping into a crouch.

"Even if Freya tells you to?"

"Is this something you have seen in your visions, boy?" Konur asked.

Dainn stared into Konur's eyes, willing the elf-lord to remember what he had said of the beast moments before. And what it could do to *him*.

"The mortal will be safe, I promise you," Konur said, meeting Dainn's gaze.

"Who *are* you?" Ryan asked suddenly. "What do you have to do with the frost giant who attacked Mist at the loft nine months ago?"

The frost giant, Dainn thought. Svardkell, who had revealed himself to be Mist's father before dying of wounds received after he had been forced by Loki to attack his own daughter. Dainn remembered briefly speaking to Ryan about the captive Jotunn after the giant's death had abnormally affected the young man's mind, but he had given very little detail.

And *he* would never have linked a long-dead Jotunn with Freya's elf-lord.

"I do not understand you," Konur said to Ryan. But Dainn saw that his eyes had grown hard, almost threatening, and Dainn realized that Konur *did* understand.

Moving quickly, Dainn seized Ryan's arm and pulled him away from Konur. Ryan permitted himself to be dragged a few feet and then locked his knees.

"His name was Svardkell," Ryan continued, mouth tight. "I felt him die. I know you're connected with him somehow." He jerked up his chin. "Were you already here then? Did you kill him?"

Dainn tensed, ready to take whatever measures were necessary to protect Ryan. But Konur's expression changed to one of grim resignation.

"You are far more than you have led Freya to believe," he said. He glanced at Dainn. "There is something I would tell you. If you could speak, I would wait. But I am confident that my spell will hold as long as I require it to, and perhaps you will trust me when you understand."

"*Lie*," Dainn rasped, lunging forward. Ryan grabbed him.

"Why did you put a spell on Dainn?" Ryan asked.

"There are more important matters to discuss," Konur said. He turned to Dainn again. "Does the boy know that the giant was Mist's father?"

"Mist's—" Ryan released Dainn as if all the strength had gone out of his wiry body. "Dainn?"

Dainn nodded, trying to convey his regret with his gaze.

"Evidently he did not," Konur said. "Does Mist?" Dainn stared at him. "I see that she does." He met Ryan's eyes. "It must have been a terrible thing to feel a stranger's death. But given your close association with Mist . . ." He sighed. "I do not know how much else you may be aware of, but there are still secrets that must be kept. Secrets that, I assure you, will harm neither Dainn nor Mist."

"Why should I believe anything you say?" Ryan asked hotly.

"Perhaps you will believe that I, like Svardkell, am Mist's father."

19

Find the other fathers, Dainn thought, setting aside his shock. That was what Svardkell had told Dainn as he died, words which Dainn had never passed on to Mist.

He had no reason to believe Konur. But he did. It was obvious to him now . . . *now*, when he was helpless to act on the knowledge.

"Mist has *two* fathers?" Ryan whispered. "But that isn't—"

"We speak of a goddess, young mortal," Konur said. "I knew Svardkell. He was a good man."

"But he tried to kill Mist!" Ryan said.

"I did not know how he planned to reach Mist," Konur said, "but he sought to bring her a message. If he attempted to harm her, it was because he was coerced."

"Lo . . . ki," Dainn managed.

Konur's eyes narrowed. "Another crime for which he must pay, among ten thousand others. But now, perhaps, you will understand that I would never hurt my own daughter. I care for her deeply."

"You still haven't proven that you don't work for Freya," Ryan said.

"Have I attempted to kill your friend?" Konur said, nodding toward Dainn.

"Will you stop Freya if she tries to hurt Dainn or Mist?"

"What are you implying?"

"She—" Ryan turned bright red and clamped his lips together. That was when Dainn was sure that Ryan knew what Freya intended.

But it made no sense that he'd keep such knowledge to himself.

Perhaps, if Freya had somehow discovered what he knew, and threatened him . . .

But surely she would have had him silenced, permanently. Short of such foul measures, she couldn't stop Ryan from taking a risk, even a very dangerous one, to help a friend. He was not afraid for himself.

Dainn broke from his thoughts to find that Konur and Ryan were still speaking, Ryan asking questions and Konur clearly growing more angry by the moment. Calling on the attenuated natural life that still clung to the fragments of buried ships and old piers—once transported from other parts of the old city to extend the city's reach into the bay—Dainn drew that life into his body, and ran. With every pounding step his speed increased, until the beast began to rise, pumping his veins full of animal vigor.

Then the shockwave hit him, and he knew no more.

◑◐

"She is awake, and wants to see you," Konur said.

Mist raked her fingers through her loose hair. She'd barely slept, and she longed for a shower the way Odin's wolves Geri and Freki hungered for meat. But it had been nearly twelve hours since she and Freya had returned from the battle for Sleipnir, and all that time Mist had been haunted by the question she had never quite found the right moment to ask.

She'd hoped she'd think of another way to learn the truth. Freya still had no reason to admit any complicity in Danny's attempted murder. And once the accusation was made, there would be no going back.

Pushing the pile of reports across the table to Roadkill, she got up and tried to clear her thoughts of names and numbers and locations. It had been remarkably quiet on the streets since Sleipnir's abduction; the Jotunar bully-boys who drew Mist's warriors into alley fights and midnight battles had all but vanished.

If both Danny and Sleipnir were lost to Loki, at least for the time being, it made sense that he wouldn't attempt any kind of assault. Considering that Mist had managed to put off her "mass summoning" of mortal allies once again, she wouldn't be ready if Loki decided he could afford to throw all caution to the winds. She wondered if she should go to Ryan and learn if he'd foreseen trouble in the near future.

But she'd promised him she wouldn't ask. And he wasn't talking. As she threw on her jacket, Mist realized that she hadn't laid eyes on him or Gabi since just after Ryan's reappearance.

She hadn't talked to Dainn since his recapture, either. He'd been unconscious when Konur brought him back, and she hadn't even taken the time to make personally sure he was okay.

She put that thought out of her mind, along with all the others. "Give me a few minutes, Konur," she said. She took the shower, restoring her hair to its natural color, and followed Konur across the street.

Bryn met her at the front door—Bryn, alight with vitality for the first time since she'd voluntarily taken on the job of Freya's personal assistant. Her brown eyes sparkled; her skin and hair, nearly the same tone, were glossy with health. Her petite, wiry body seemed to shed raw energy like a storm about to break.

"Mist!" she said, holding out her arms.

It took Mist about another three seconds to realize what was wrong. She stopped abruptly, and Konur nearly ran into her.

"Where's Bryn?" she asked, her voice beginning to shake.

"I see I didn't deceive you," Freya said, lowering her arms. "No matter. Bryn is perfectly well. She lent me her body for a time, but her soul is quite safe."

"Where?"

"Because of her generosity, I had the strength I needed to secure her soul in one of the Treasures . . . the one she once carried for the Aesir." She touched her chest, and Mist saw that the Falcon Cloak hung in its tiny feathered pouch from a cord around her neck. "She will be safe here, against my heart."

"What happened to the body you occupied before?"

"I have placed a spell upon it, to hold it in stasis until it can be properly healed and returned to its rightful owner in Ginnungagap."

"You had no right to take Bryn," Mist said, still caught up in a fog of denial and disbelief.

"It was her choice," Freya said with an air of impatience. "I hear that Sleipnir is in the wind. I thought you would consider it a priority to regain him and retrieve the Aesir."

"You think you can manage that now?"

"Bryn has a remarkable store of power she has never been able to tap," Freya said. "I will be able to do many things."

"Bryn has power?" Mist asked. "Magic?"

"I always sensed it, which is why I kept her near me."

"You always intended to do this, didn't you?" Mist took a step closer to Freya. "What else have you tried to do without mentioning it to anyone else? What about—"

"Mist," Konur said, laying his hand on her shoulder. She felt a spell coursing through his fingers and into her body, and turned sharply to face him.

"What are *you* afraid of, Konur?" she demanded.

Say nothing.

The voice was in her head, the way Dainn's had been more than once before the beast had begun to interfere. The way Freya's had been when she and Mist had fought for Sleipnir, telling Mist to strike. To *let go*.

She stared at the elf-lord defiantly, prepared to disobey his unspoken command. But it was as if the mental contact had extinguished all her doubts about him. If he'd placed a spell in her mind, she couldn't detect it.

"Konur is afraid of very little," Freya said, as if there had been no pause in the conversation. "Now, I suggest we waste no time in beginning the search for the Steed. Of course, we must work closely together. I would not wish to overtax this body as I did the other."

Mist took a deep breath. "You want to join our powers," she said.

"And our minds. If you had not resisted this joining in the past, we might easily have stopped the protest without speeding the deterioration of my other body, and prevented Sleipnir from being taken."

Might, Mist thought. Or might not. But with so much at stake, she had no sound argument to offer against trying Freya's method. And if she could see into Freya's mind, she might learn what she wanted to know.

And Freya could do the same with me, she thought. All her doubts could be exposed. Everything she knew about Danny, and Dainn, and other subjects she'd chosen not to broach with her mother.

"I'm willing to try," Mist said. "But only if there's a way we can blend our abilities without invading each other's thoughts."

"That would require a fine degree of control," Freya said, displeasure in Bryn's husky voice. "But children must always keep secrets from their parents. We shall attempt it."

Mist inclined her head, the most gratitude she was willing to extend. "When do you want to start?" she asked.

"I am ready," Freya said, spreading her hands wide. "If you are presently free of obligations . . ."

"I'll talk with my advisors and make sure I'm covered. We need privacy, I assume?"

"I would suggest the small warehouse you have not yet refurbished. We will not be disturbed there."

With a brief nod of acknowledgment, Mist asked Konur to select an elven guard to stand watch over the unfinished warehouse. While she arranged to have council members assume her regular work—enjoining them not to tell anyone else that she'd be temporarily unavailable—Freya prepared the warehouse's interior to her liking. Mist finally dropped by the Alfar camp to make sure that Dainn was well and left without seeing him. Joining magically with a mother she didn't trust seemed more palatable than confronting Dainn face-to-face.

Returning to the loft for a hasty snack, Mist found Anna waiting in the kitchen. Her face seemed strange to Mist, and not only because they hadn't talked much in the past few weeks. There was less delicacy in Anna's features: the bone structure seemed more pronounced, the jaw firmer, the brow stronger.

But it was Anna's soft, hesitant voice that asked her about Sleipnir.

"Have you found him yet?" she asked, twisting her hands together at her waist.

"Sit down," Mist said, pointing to a chair. "It's only been a little over twelve hours. What's got you so upset? Worrying about Sleipnir isn't part of your job description."

"Everything seems to be going wrong," Anna said. She stood behind the chair but didn't sit. "Now that almost all the Treasures are accounted for, I'm not much good to anyone."

"That's not true," Mist said. She leaned over the table, trying to make sense of Anna's mood and remembering that she'd seemed equally disturbed when Mist had returned from the protest. "You and the other IT people are doing important work by monitoring what Loki and his followers are up to around the city. Just because we haven't acted on all the information doesn't mean that—"

"I'm failing him," Anna whispered.

"Who?"

Anna seemed not to hear Mist. "Why didn't Fenrir take Sleipnir to Loki?"

"I don't know," Mist said. "But we're going to find out."

"You have to bring him back."

Mist circled the table. "Anna, do you need help?"

The young woman blinked, and the odd changes Mist had seen in her disappeared. "I'm sorry to have bothered you," she said.

"It's never a bother. I'm just sorry we haven't talked more."

"It's not your fault. I know the responsibilities you carry."

"You deserve better," Mist said, touching Anna's sleeve. "If you need me, you just have to ask. I'll make sure to be there."

With a vague nod, Anna wandered into the front hall. Mist considered following her, but decided to respect Anna's ability to decide if or when she needed help. And everyone in camp had good reason to be worried about Sleipnir.

If we're lucky, not much longer, Mist thought. But she didn't feel lucky. Not at all.

◑◐

"The Seidr," Freya had said, "will be our best means of finding what we seek."

Sitting opposite the Lady on a pile of cushions artistically arranged over the bare floor, Mist kept her body relaxed. She had a slightly better idea of what soul-travel entailed, now that Freya had taken the time to explain.

The explanations didn't make her feel any better.

"Traveling apart from the body is the most dangerous aspect of the Seidr," the Lady said, "and it burns magical strength quickly."

"Aren't you worried about Bryn's body?" Mist asked, breathing slowly and deliberately.

"Of course. And that is why you must follow exactly where I lead, so that nothing goes wrong."

Everything could go wrong, Mist thought. Especially if she found out that Freya was hiding ugly secrets that could alter the fate of Midgard.

"Are you ready to begin?" Freya asked.

Mist glanced at her watch, noting the time. She took Freya's hands. There was a moment of disorientation, as if the world had tilted sideways, and then Mist could feel her soul separate from her body—not as it sometimes did when she used the ancient magic, but in a way that felt almost physical, as if an actual cord stretched between the spiritual and corporeal realms.

Let it go, Freya said, her thought entwined with Mist's. *Release your hold on the world, and let me guide you.*

It was a heady thing to fly free, connected to Freya by a bond more real than any that tied parent to child. The Lady spread falcon wings, the tips of their feathers brushing Mist's cheek. She felt no anxiety as they rose as one above the floor of the warehouse, through the ceiling, and into the sky.

She looked down on the encampment, on the other warehouses and the parking lots and her own loft, a peculiar joy rising in her. Joy like she hadn't felt in so many long months.

You see, Freya said, *how simple it is.*

Euphoria overwhelmed Mist, and some distant part of her recognized it as the Lady's glamour. She didn't fear it. It was impossible to fear anything. She felt Freya's love, all-encompassing but soft and warm, like a mother's womb.

They flew higher, sweeping over Dogpatch with the storm swirling above them. *Open your senses,* Freya said. *Open your mind to the spirit of Odin's mount.*

Mist remembered seeing Sleipnir for the first time on the steppes, magnificent as an emperor, bending his head to touch Danny's—

A veil of confusion wrapped around the memory, smothering it into silence. A mass of energy enfolded Mist, cradling her in its heart, at the same time soothing and stinging her intangible flesh. It seemed to sing of the ancient magic with ethereal voices.

The soul of the universe, Mist thought dreamily. If she touched it, she wouldn't lose herself. It was the missing piece she had been looking for.

The Eitr. Vaguely, she remembered Dainn explaining it to her. But now she needed no explanation. She felt it. She *knew* it.

It was the answer. To everything.

Mist! Freya shouted in her mind.

Mist faltered, and she felt herself begin to plummet, spinning toward the streets far below. But something caught her, holding her up in strong arms made of living wood, branches that stretched into infinity on every side. The entire tree was itself made of magic, sinking roots deep into the earth and beyond, reaching far above the atmosphere.

Yggdrasil, Mist thought. *The World Tree.* But Mist saw that it was only a physical representation of the immense energy that bound the universe together. *Concentrate, Daughter!* the Lady said. *I feel my strength beginning to wane. Give me your magic!*

Rising up like a flame, Mist felt a sword in her hand . . . not Kettlingr, but one that might have belonged to the mortal God's avenging angels. Like an angel, she soared with wings of fire, the branches of the World Tree interlocking and rising with her, unsinged. She had endless power to share, an abundance of love and righteous fury, and she poured it into the goddess.

More, Freya urged. *A little more, and I will find him.*

Yes, Mist thought. Freya reached for her again, and Mist turned the sword, about to pass it into hands that were not really there.

A bolt of lightning shot from the tree branches writhing around her, striking at the Lady. The universe reverberated with a shriek of pain and rage. The sword fell from her hand, and as it spun away she glimpsed reflections of faces in its perfect blade—some strange, a few she recognized. Svardkell and Konur were among them.

Then her mind went dark, joy turning in on itself, twisting to become its opposite.

Hatred. Jealousy. Fear. Raw images of battle, of sex, of plotting in dark corners. Asgard in ruins. The Void, jaws wide to swallow all life.

And then the struggle. Dainn and the beast. Treachery. Sorrow beyond bearing.

There were too many thoughts in her head, but she understood what Freya had hidden so well. The Lady had betrayed Odin and all the Aesir. She had known of a prophecy that negated the one that foretold Ragnarok, and had intended to seize rule from the All-father in order to save Asgard. She had met Danny with Loki in the Void, and she really had intended to kill the boy.

And Dainn had conspired with the goddess to seize Mist's body and soul. He had lied to her from the beginning, setting her up to die.

Forget, Freya whispered. *Surrender, and be at peace.*

Unable to bear the horror of what she had seen, Mist nearly gave up. She rejected the energy, the power, the World Tree and all it contained. She wheeled on blackened wings to return to the warehouse.

A blinding white light speared into Mist's mind. Freya's weapon, carrying all her will, her ambition, her desperation.

Mist tried to block the spear as it plunged toward the center of her being. She batted the shaft aside before the blade could touch her, Freya's raging face before her . . . an image of the true goddess, flawless features framed by golden waves of hair.

You were always mine, Freya said.

Wheeling back toward the warehouse on singed wings, buffeted by the endless storm, Mist fled. Freya's spear never ceased its inexorable progress. Lightning arced from one cloud to the next, and Mist called to it, opening herself to the ancient magic, letting it consume her.

She didn't hear the thunder. She was barely aware when the spear snapped, and Freya began to scream again.

Bryn will die! the Lady cried, clawing at Mist with invisible fingers.

Mist heard her, but felt nothing but the will to survive.

I am your mother! I gave you life! Freya began to shed tears of molten gold. *Loki will destroy you!*

Lightning struck Freya through the heart, and she tumbled earthward, her wings folded tight to her body, her hair flying around her. Mist watched her fall. A great, surging triumph filled the emptiness inside her, and she laughed.

When she snapped back into her body, it was lying far from the pillows, and her joints and bones and muscles ached as if she had plunged to the concrete floor from a great height.

She lifted her head, wincing as the faint late-morning light from the high windows struck her eyes. Freya lay near the far wall—Bryn's body again, unnaturally twisted. Her eyes were closed, brown lashes sweeping her tanned cheeks, and she wasn't breathing.

Forcing her aching body to move, Mist struggled to her feet and stumbled across the room. She fell to her knees beside her mother and touched her throat.

There was no pulse. No life. The body was dead. And the spirit . . .

Mist searched. She knew Freya's soul as well as her own now, would know if it still existed.

It did not.

Mist had killed her, and Bryn's body with her.

The room spun around Mist as she got up and wandered around the echoing space, remembering bits and snatches of what she had done. What Freya had tried to do. The floor danced, and random flashes of light struck the walls and vanished almost instantly. The ancient magic spilled from Mist's fingers, thick and warm as honey, and circled her head as if she were a Christian saint. More magic than her body could possibly contain.

She shouted a Rune-spell and flung it at the wall. A gaping hole appeared, scattering rubble and rebar.

Her power had not diminished by one iota. She tried again, directing her fury at the ceiling. It evaporated, and she felt the magic continue up, meeting no barrier, until it reached the clouds. Lightning plunged down to meet her, and she absorbed it without the slightest pain. Absorbed it, and knew her mind and body could accept no more.

She fell to her knees and crawled back to Bryn's body. Her fingers felt for the Cloak in its pouch. It tore from its cord as she collapsed.

Go away, she chanted silently. *Go away.*

Freya vanished, body and soul.

⚭

Consciousness came and went like the shadows flickering over her closed eyelids. Sometimes she heard voices; sometimes the voice was her own, shouting denials and rage and madness.

Once she woke to find Koji beside her. He smiled and stroked her hair as she looked up at him.

"You're doing much better," he said. "When you've—"

He vanished, and didn't return. Later, the healers were there, frowning in concentration. Then came the elf-lord, whose name she couldn't remember, and Rota, and Hild, and various mortals in succession. She had no sense of time. The struggle went on as her body fought to absorb the infection that had invaded her, a disease no physician, not even the greatest in Asgard, could ever heal.

When she finally came to full awareness, Konur was beside the bed, holding her hand. His expression was grave, but his gaze was gentle.

She surged up, tensing to escape. Konur eased her back down before she collapsed again.

"You must remain quiet," he said.

"No," she whispered.

He squeezed her fingers gently. "Something happened to you when you were with Freya, something no healer has been able to determine. You have resisted every effort to wake you, but it seems that the power that has been burning in you like a fever has finally subsided."

The power. All at once Mist remembered. She turned her head on the pillow, beginning to gag.

"Drink," Konur said. He cradled her head and offered a glass of water. Without meaning to, she found herself gulping it down, begging for more as soon as the glass left her lips.

When she'd drunk three glasses, she lay back and closed her eyes. "How long have I been out?" she asked.

"Three days."

Her throat seemed barbed with thorns. "Is everyone all right? Has Loki—"

"He remains quiet." Konur eased her down again. "There have been few fights with the Jotunar, and the camp continues to run smoothly, thanks to Captain Taylor and your other officers."

"And . . . you?"

He gave a subtle, very elvish shrug. She almost asked him about Dainn, but then she remembered. Panic pushed her heart into a frantic rhythm.

"I have to get out of here," she said. "I can't just—"

"I know you will wish to return to your work as soon as possible," Konur said, "but you must not tax yourself too soon." He hesitated. "What has happened to Freya?"

Suddenly she was weeping. "No," she said, tears leaking from the corners of her eyes.

He stroked them away with the pad of his thumb. "Do not fear me," he said.

"I don't," she said, despising her helplessness.

"Then tell me what has become of her."

"Where is the pouch?"

To her surprise, he produced the Falcon Cloak and laid the pouch on her stomach. "This was in your hand when we found you."

After she'd ripped the roof off. The whole camp must have seen . . .

She covered the pouch with her hand and commanded the tears to stop, remembering when Konur had mentally urged her to "say nothing" when she'd tried to question Freya about Bryn and other things the Lady might have kept from her.

If she asked him what he'd meant, would he tell her now? How much had he known of Freya's evil intentions? Had he prevented Dainn from warning her about her mother?

If he *hadn't* known, would he believe what Freya had tried to do, and why Mist had been forced to kill her?

I can't, she thought. She couldn't tell Konur the truth. Not until she was sure. Sure of him, and of herself.

So she told only a small part, and nothing of the Eitr or the World Tree. "We tried to do what Freya wanted to," she said. "But once we were . . . mentally joined, something went wrong. Freya just—" She covered her eyes. "There was a . . . kind of darkness I'd never seen before. It sucked her in, and she just disappeared. When I woke up in the warehouse, she wasn't there."

"Not even her body?"

The image of Freya-Bryn lying on the warehouse floor was forever burned into Mist's mind.

I destroyed her. Nothing is left. Nothing.

"Did you see one?" she snapped. She exhaled slowly and dropped her hand from her face. "I'm sorry. Whatever I felt about my mother, I never thought something like this could happen."

"You are most fortunate that you did not follow her into this darkness," Konur said. There was no grief in his voice, only calm acceptance. "The Aesir and Vanir are not mortal, but they can be killed. Bryn . . ."

"I'm afraid her body is lost," Mist said. She touched the pouch again. "If her soul is still in here, maybe we can bring it back in a body that no longer has a mind of its own."

"As long as the essence of her spirit is safe, we can but hope." He rose. "We will speak more of this later," he said. "You may feel recovered now, but the shock will not have passed so quickly."

"Don't worry about me," Mist said. She met his gaze. "What do *you* feel about Freya being gone? You had a past together, didn't you?"

At first she thought she'd overstepped. He stared at her, a grim set to his mouth. "We all respond to such tragedies in our own ways," he said, rising. "Rest now. I will be drilling my Alfar away from camp, so do not be alarmed if I am absent for a few days."

Almost as soon as he was gone, Mist began to weep again. When she finally slept, her dreams were crowded images of violence, and she felt herself being literally torn apart, Freya tugging on one arm and some invisible force pulling the other. Then she fell, endlessly, screaming with Freya's voice. Calling for Dainn, who only watched with his most expressionless face.

Dense darkness closed in around her again with the surreal terror of a nightmare, and suddenly Freya was alive within her mind, her eyes glittering with malice to equal Loki's. She extended her hands as she had when they had joined, but they were covered in blood.

You know, she said, laughing at Mist's anguish. *You cannot live without the force I gave you the power to wield. You must be whole, or you will end. And all you fight for ends with you.*

"Why did you betray me?" Mist cried. "Why did you hate me?"

Because you were to be mine in all things—my weapon, my champion, my other self, the one to wield the power even I could not. You overcame my will. But hear this, Daughter. No matter how far you run, you will always carry me within you.

20

When Mist woke again, it was gone. The grief, the guilt, the horror over what she had done. Her body surged with new energy, driving her out of bed, compelling her to ignore the healer on duty, who drew back in shock when Mist all but pushed him aside.

She showered, put on clean clothes, and called to convene a council meeting within the hour. When she walked out of the loft at noon, her mind was already racing with ideas.

Her "advisors" were waiting for her in the smaller meeting room across the street from her loft. Roadkill and Vixen were nursing beers, while the Alfar, excluding the absent Konur, sat quietly in meditative poses. They all rose when she walked in.

"Brooding, my friends?" she asked, laughing at their expressions.

Rick stared at her. "What the hell has been happening?" he asked. "You've been sick ever since you got back from trying to find Sleipnir. We heard you were in some kind of coma."

"I'm fine now," Mist said. "Unfortunately, we were unable to locate Sleipnir, and Freya has left us to carry out work only she can do."

Glances were exchanged around the table—some troubled, some relieved, others unreadable.

"Where did Freya go?" Rota asked, her round face drawn with worry.

"Were you offended that we didn't include you in our discussion, Sister?" Mist asked lightly.

"We thought you were dying," Hild said.

Mist found herself becoming annoyed. "Do I look as if I am

dying?" She lifted her hands and felt the World Tree reaching down with branches of energy, winding about her arms and sending fresh power into her body. "We have made new plans, and now we can proceed."

"You've already proceeded without us," Rick said. "What's the point of being in your council if you don't bother to—"

Mist moved the floor under the mortal's chair, and he jumped out of it just before it toppled. Everyone stared, and then slowly returned their attention to Mist.

"*I* make the decisions," Mist said, staring at each of the Valkyrie, mortals, and Alfar in turn. "Sit down, Rick."

Eyes wide with confusion, Rick righted the chair and resumed his seat.

"I shall tell you where Freya has gone," Mist said, moving to the head of the table. "She has discovered the means to stabilize the bridges to Ginnungagap so that their function is no longer so erratic. She has returned to the Shadow-Realms to make another attempt to bring the Aesir to Midgard."

This time, there was a little hope on some of the faces turned toward Mist. A pinprick of guilt prodded her heart and was quickly gone.

"Where's Bryn?" Hild asked.

Mist had forgotten about Bryn entirely, and the question only increased her irritation. "Bryn is also on assignment," she said, "which will remain confidential. In her absence, you, Rick, and Captain Taylor will divide responsibility for the mortals under her command. Unless, of course, you choose to sit in a corner and sulk like a child denied his piece of the birthday cake."

Shaking his head with a quick jerk, Rick clamped his jaws together. Perhaps, Mist thought, she was being too harsh, though it was difficult to forget the inferiority of these short-lived, fragile creatures.

"You will all be given new commands and assignments," she said. "Prepare to work harder than you ever have before. It is my task to summon a true army of mortals to join in our fight, which I shall begin immediately."

Rota raised her hand. "How can you keep attending Freya's social events and gather an army at the same time?"

"There will be no need for more 'social events,'" Mist said. "We have waited long enough. We are taking the war to Loki."

❦

Over the next few days, the mortals came singly, in their dozens, and their hundreds. Mist cast her net of glamour wide, and the magic poured forth like the waters of some ancient flood sweeping over the city.

Most of those who arrived were neither dazed nor bewildered by the compulsion that had brought them to the ever-expanding camp. They already understood why they were there, and the new administrative staff Mist had already appointed to prep the newcomers had little difficulty in organizing and transporting them to the various buildings in the area that Mist had purchased as additional dormitories.

Just as she had intended, a significant majority of the new recruits were physically and psychologically capable of fighting and even killing for their world, and Mist's officers—including Captain Taylor, Hild, and the bikers Rick and Tennessee—quickly assigned each prospective fighter to a squad for training in the use of bladed weapons and the skill of Jotunn-killing. Medical personnel were sent to the Alfar healers, and those with essential administrative skills to Roadkill. Since Anna had apparently hidden herself away, Mist appointed a new manager for her expanded IT team.

On the fourth day, she called another meeting to hear reports from the council. Konur was still absent, a fact that might once have troubled her but now merely annoyed her, since she had easily been able to put lesser Alfar lords in his place. Captain Taylor was clearly exhausted, as were Rick and the other bikers.

But Mist was unable to suppress her satisfaction. Everything was proceeding exactly as she had planned.

"You have all done very well," she said, beaming at each of the familiar faces with impartial benevolence. "I will continue to expect daily reports, but you and your lieutenants will deal with any but the most significant problems. I expect our new recruits to conform to the discipline necessary to build our army. We must be one body to overcome Loki."

It was Rick who stood first, bracing his hands on the meeting room table. "You're talking about human beings here, Mist," he said, his rough voice almost a whisper. "They may understand more or less what they're getting into, but they didn't come as one organized group ready to work together. We've handled some fights already. There're gonna be more."

"Then stop them," Mist said. "I have given you the authority."

"And what about the ones who obviously aren't going to work out?" Rota asked. "The first couple of days, you had us send you the recruits who were obviously not going to be much help to us, so you could blank out their memories. More of them are coming all the time, and the troublemakers tend to show their true colors when we start teaching them how to fight. What do we do with the psychopaths who just like to kill?"

"If they kill Loki's allies, what do their reasons matter?"

A stunned silence fell over the room. Mist laughed. "Come, now. You surely exaggerate the numbers of these deviants. If you can't handle them, send them to me. But see that you send only the worst. I don't have time to deal with every little problem."

Vixen rose to stand beside Rick, who seemed frozen in place. "My God," she said. "You sound like Freya."

"And how well did you know the Lady?" Mist snapped. "How often did you speak to her?" She swept her gaze around the table. "I see that I shall have to be frank with you. Freya will be working entirely in the Shadow-Realms from now on. She will not be returning."

"What the fuck," Tennessee growled.

Mist stared at him, and he sank deeper into his seat. "There is no cause for concern," she said. "I am her daughter, and she taught me what I needed to know. I told you we would take the war to Loki, and

I will deal with his more powerful allies in my own way. And make clear to any others who might join him that they will face painful consequences if they choose incorrectly."

"How?" Vixen asked. "You plan to assassinate them or something?"

Mist didn't answer. Rick sat down heavily. Someone cursed.

"The corruption of the government will be exposed," she continued. "We will hunt out the Jotunar and the gangs that support them. We will shatter the foundations of the edifice the Slanderer has built, and when the final battle comes, we will watch it crush him as it falls."

"You talk as if this will be easy," Rick said. "Even with hundreds more fighters . . . thousands . . ."

"And Alfar," Mist said. "As soon as things are more settled with the new recruits, I will open the bridge to Alfheim's Shadow-Realm."

"But I thought Freya was the one who was supposed to—"

Mist silenced the mortal with a sweep of her hand and faced the nearest wall. It was so easy, so natural to call on the ancient magic now, not only to control the elements, but also to touch the Void. The surface shimmered and an aperture opened in the wall, expanding from the center as if it were a sheet of paper touched by a match, the first tiny scorch mark burning rapidly outward.

Framed by the aperture, the Void—Ginnungagap—roiled in shades of black and gray like a storm-tossed sea.

"*This* is what Freya and I have done," she said, setting aside her reluctance to share any credit with her late mother. "It only remains to see if Freya has completed her task and made the Aesir ready."

"Let's *hope* they're ready," Captain Taylor muttered, speaking for the first time.

Mist smiled at him with remote affection. "I have every confidence. Again, I must rely on all of you, and those you appoint, to carry out our other preparations without question or doubt."

"What about Sleipnir?" he asked.

"I assure you that we will soon have him safely back with us." She rose from her chair. "Are there any more questions?"

No one spoke. One by one the council members drifted away.

Mist was pleased. Such meetings were still necessary, but soon she could concentrate on her real work. The work only a goddess could accomplish.

She strode out of the building. Sunlight had cut through the cloud cover, and Mist basked in its warmth as she surveyed the camp. Mortals scurried about, some already organized in marching columns, others intent upon business of a less martial nature. Useful tools, flawed though they might be.

A few noticed her and turned, instinctively recognizing her though she had met only a handful in person. She would walk among them later, in the cool of evening, and remind them whom they followed and why they had come to sacrifice their freedom and their lives.

"Not all of them are here willingly," Captain Taylor said, coming up behind her. "Not the way they should be."

She glanced at him. "What is will?" she asked. "They understand enough."

"Understanding doesn't protect them from death."

"Neither does ignoring the peril their world faces," she said. "If a few were compelled, it is a small enough price for mortalkind to pay."

"Isn't that the kind of logic Loki would use?"

"Loki desires chaos. I will give them—"

She caught her breath, and the sunlight winked out. The world darkened.

I will give them a benevolent ruler, and Midgard will finally be at peace. No war, no violence . . .

No freedom.

"Mist?"

She focused on his voice, hanging on to it like a mountain climber clings to the crumbling edge of a cliff. "Taylor?" she said.

"I'm here." His broad hand clamped on her arm. "What has happened to you?"

The question cleared her mind like a thunderclap. She shook him off.

"Captain Taylor," she said, "I would suggest that you reexamine your priorities, or you shall be of no further use to me."

"Yes, ma'am," he said, straightening to rigid attention.

His formality softened her heart. "This is no time for allies to quarrel," she said.

He gazed at her, his brown eyes bewildered. "No," he murmured. "This isn't right."

"Do not presume to question me again. Go."

The captain gave her a stiff salute and stalked away. Mist frowned, some vestige of foreign emotion passing through her mind. She dismissed it.

In the end, Taylor was no different from the others. He would obey. If he did not, she would make a necessary example of him.

But not until she had made very clear that treachery would be punished. For the sake of the world she loved.

❧

"Make yourself ready. *She* wants to see you."

Dainn sat up. He didn't recognize the elf who had spoken; at first his guards had been of Konur's band, not friendly but not openly hostile.

That had changed when the new mortals had begun to arrive. Dainn had listened intently to the few conversations held within his earshot. Konur and his Alfar had apparently been assigned elsewhere—though Dainn had his doubts that Mist had been involved in that "reassignment"—and he'd had no word of Ryan, let alone of Sleipnir and Danny. There was new activity in the camp, a buzz of excitement, the overwhelming sense that something had changed.

Mist, they said, had changed.

Scrambling to his feet, Dainn lost all awareness of his filthy clothes, the stench of his unwashed body, the misery of thirst, and the humiliation of the spell that still kept him silent. His limbs were heavy as the guard stood aside and she swept into the room.

She *was* different. He saw it in her bearing, the lift of her head, her eyes, the cruelty in her smile. There was no doubt in her, no uncertainty of power or purpose.

"So," she said. She glanced around the room, her nose wrinkling with distaste. "In the absence of a permanent visit to Niflheim, this seems almost a fitting prison for a traitor of your considerable merit."

The words, the cadence of her voice, even the sentiment were not Mist's. She might have deceived every other elf or mortal in the camp. Even Mist's father, if she had seen him. Perhaps even Ryan.

But she could not deceive *him*.

Freya had finally succeeded. Konur had not protected his daughter, and Ryan hadn't warned her. That which Dainn had feared for so long had finally come to pass.

This was no longer Mist pretending to be Freya, as at the reception, but Freya within Mist's body. Not daring, yet, to reveal her true self, because it was still possible that she had not learned to wield Mist's power well enough to control any who might object to the murder of her daughter.

A great roaring filled Dainn's head, unimaginable grief, the agony of loss. But he didn't let her see it. She had to believe that he, too, had fallen for her trick.

She would be his means of leaving this cell and searching for Danny. Nothing else held any meaning for him. Or ever would.

"No words of greeting?" Freya asked. "Oh, but of course. You can't speak."

He touched his throat, letting his eyes plead for him. "Mis—" he whispered.

"Konur should not have lied to me about placing this spell upon you," she said, "but he did me a service. I have no desire to hear your excuses."

Then why are you here?

Freya flinched, and he realized that he had projected the thought. They had communicated that way a hundred times when Freya was still confined to the Void and he had acted as the Lady's voice in Midgard.

But it had not happened since her arrival on Earth. And he could not let it happen again.

"Unfortunately," she said, as if she had not heard him, "I must question you before I decide your fate. I may find it in my heart to end it painlessly if you tell me all you know of Loki's plans." She gestured with her forefinger, and Dainn felt the spell released, his throat open again. He coughed, spitting blood into his palm.

"I can . . . tell you very little," he rasped.

"You went to Loki of your own free will."

He sat up on his knees. "I did it to . . . protect you. The beast had no power then. My magic was gone. I didn't believe I could be turned against you and your allies."

"A pretty lie," Freya said. "You cared nothing for me. For any of us."

"However it may have appeared to you," he said, coughing again, "I was never incapable of feeling."

"Love, perhaps?" she asked mockingly. "The way you loved Freya in Asgard?"

"I was a fool," he whispered.

"You were *always* a traitor, shifting with the slightest breeze."

Dainn croaked a laugh. "Did your mother tell you how she and Loki schemed to betray Odin in Asgard?" he asked. "Can there be any greater treachery than that?"

"Betray him?" Freya asked, much too lightly.

"Loki may lie about many things, but in this he told the truth."

"And he told you many other truths, which I *will* have from you." A weight of air pressed down on Dainn's shoulders, heavy as steel bars. "Down, traitor."

The concrete rose up to meet Dainn, and he toppled. He knew at once that it was not common magic, but touched on the ancient, calling upon all the elements at once.

And there was a darkness in it, pain that rushed into Dainn's nostrils and mouth like noxious gas. The wound in his palm split open, and blood spiraled up into the air.

Just as it had with Danny in his bedroom. The *Eitr*. Freya controlled it, wielded it, as she had previously been unwilling or unable to do since her physical arrival from the Shadow-Realm in Ginnun-gagap.

Now it was poison, swirling through vein and artery, heart and gut. His body fought to expel it, and as he struggled he felt the nature of the stuff change inside him, as if his organs had taken the magic and leached it of all malignancy. Almost . . . *almost* he could grasp it, like a weapon to be turned about and hurled against its original wielder.

But he stopped before he could follow the instinct, because as the Eitr changed it also gave up the secret it had been hiding, the unique signature he would have known even to the end of all things.

It did not belong to Freya. The Lady had *failed*.

Moisture flooded Dainn's eyes, and he kept his face averted. Freya was gone. He felt emptiness where a connection had once existed, and wondered how he ever could have mistaken it for the living goddess.

Did Mist know what had happened? Did she understand the horror of what had almost been done to her? Had she fought for her life, forced to destroy before she was destroyed?

Dainn didn't dare ask her now. Mist's mind was sullied, murky with dark dreams. Freya's presence might have vanished from the world, but a part of the Lady was still with Mist: a ghost, a shadow, a malign revenant that had not yet been fully dislodged. As long as she remained . . .

Fixing his eyes on the ground, Dainn clenched his bloody fist. Mist had to be shocked out of her dream before the malignancy grew and made her a mirror image of her mother.

"Who are you, Lady of Darkness?" he asked.

She struck him with a little more force than he had anticipated. He wiped the blood from his cheek and grabbed her callused fingers.

"Whose hand is this?" he asked as she tried to pull away. "Does it belong to the goddess who mated with both Jotunn and Alfr to produce a daughter fit to be her sword against the All-father? Did she even understand what she was creating?"

"What . . . Alfr?" she asked, squinting at him as if her vision were failing her.

"Konur. He told the secret to me and Ryan after the boy came to find me and tried to help me escape. You have two fathers."

"It isn't true," she said, wrenching her hand from his. "You have said enough."

"But I thought you wanted a confession." He rose onto his haunches. She didn't stop him. "Look into my mind, Mist. I know you are capable of it, as you are capable of controlling your magic as you never could before."

He felt the slight push from her mind, instinctively resisted, and then gave in. He let her see what was necessary, and when she was finished she rocked back on her heels, her eyes the color of ice.

"What will you do with this knowledge, Mist?" he asked, relentless in his fear for her. "Will you accept it, or will you escape into Freya's malicious influence to avoid what you cannot face?"

The shock of his words did as he had hoped, and he was prepared for the attack. The ancient magic, swelled by the Eitr, reared up again to punish and consume, but he cast it back and aimed his thoughts to strike at the very heart of her being, as he had done months ago when he had first sought to break down the mental barriers that prevented her from accepting his help and recognizing her magic.

You are not Freya, he said. *You can never be.*

Her fingers blackened and burned like live coals in a fire pit, and she raised her hands to fling the fire at his face. He leaped at her, holding the beast in check with all the magic that had been restored to him along with it.

They came together in a tangle of limbs, and he dragged her to the ground. He pinned her there, and a flash of memory took him back to that moment when he had driven Freya from her body with a kiss. He wanted her, even as she met his gaze with disgust and hatred.

But he could never touch her again. He had been tainted—not only by the beast, but by his months as Loki's captive. He had let himself be used in every way imaginable. His love for Danny held no cure for what he had become. Only now, as he saw the contempt in Mist's eyes, did he realize just how deep the corruption had reached.

He rolled away, and Mist sprang to her feet, panting harshly. Dainn rose and put his back to the wall.

"Konur is your father," he said. "He served Freya, but he chose you."

21

Mist sank back to her knees, no longer raging but bewildered and lost. "What do you mean he chose me?"

In a matter of seconds, Dainn relived the confrontation behind the warehouses, when Konur had spoken of secrets that must still be kept. When he'd promised not to hurt his own daughter.

"Over the Lady," Dainn answered slowly, watching Mist's face for any sign of rejection. "He must have known that only one of you would survive."

Her skin blanched, and she raised both hands to her mouth. "Sweet Baldr," she whispered. "I killed her."

It was not a sudden realization, Dainn knew, but a fresh acceptance. She remembered everything, and he felt the shock of that memory in his own mind.

"She is gone?" he asked.

"I . . . destroyed her body. But not all of her. Not until now."

"She was powerful," Dainn said. "Her spirit was strong, and—"

"You *knew*," Mist said suddenly. "I saw it in her mind. You knew what she planned all along."

Dainn closed his eyes. "Yes," he said.

"You always intended to help her." She scrambled up, stumbled back, and slammed into the door, leaning against it heavily. "*That* was why you were sent to me . . . not for the Treasures, or because I was supposed to lead any kind of resistance against Loki."

"I was wrong," he said, striving to keep his voice level. "I realized it not long after we met. But I was too much a coward. I feared you would cease to trust me." He swallowed. "For a long time, even when I was with Loki, I convinced myself that you had grown strong enough to hold your own against her. Only after the protest, when you—" He broke off. "I made an unforgivable mistake."

Mist shook her head wildly. "No. At the garage, you *did* try to warn me. Konur silenced you."

It was, Dainn thought, as if she were grasping at any excuse to absolve him. He was unable to speak.

"You said he chose me, but he let me fall into Freya's trap," she said, a bitter edge in her voice. "My own—"

"I know Konur will have a reason for his actions," Dainn said, though in that moment he hated Konur as much as he hated himself. "He had ample opportunity to do more than silence me. Perhaps he always knew you would win."

Mist began to laugh, a strange, high-pitched moan. Someone approached the door from outside, and she pressed her palms flat against the door. It turned to ice.

"Konur was with me, after it happened," she said, the laughter dying. "I was in and out of consciousness for days. I told him that Freya was lost when we were working together to find Sleipnir—he was in the room when she asked me to do it. He didn't seem to grieve for her at all." She seemed to notice what she had done to the door and tucked her hands under her arms. "You're right. If he knew, he must have thought I would—Gods." Mist dragged her hand over her face, smearing tears across her cheeks. "Is there anyone left I can trust?"

"You must make your own peace with Konur," Dainn said, bowing his head. "I will tell you what little I know of Loki's plans, though he did not often confide in me. I will not ask for your forgiveness."

"Still the noble elf," she said, though her contempt rang hollow.

"Never noble," he said. "There were many times I wanted to die. I told you once that the beast would not permit it. But the creature was gone almost all the time I was with Loki, as was my magic."

"In the garage, you said—"

"I said that without the herb, the beast would return."

"And Edvard provided you with that herb, before he left us."

"He claimed it was used by his people when one of them suffered an illness that interfered with their control of their own beasts. For a short while, when I was still with you, the herb was effective. But on the steppes—"

"The beast tried to kill Danny. At Freya's command."

"Yes. I feared I could not stop, so I took the remainder of the herb I had brought with me, and it silenced the beast. When I was with Loki—" He slid down to the floor and wrapped his arms around his knees. "They continued to feed the herb to me without my knowledge, waiting until Loki found some use for the beast again. But even if I had known, I would have taken it willingly."

"Odin's balls," Mist said, teeth clenched. "Why did Edvard go to Loki in the first place?"

"I do not know. I never saw him at Loki's house. I only realized the part he must have played when I saw him in the parking facility, and understood that they wanted the beast to create havoc while they stole Sleipnir." He bowed his head. "I believed you were Freya. I meant only to protect Danny."

Mist ran her hands through her hair. "Loki knew I was Mist all along."

"He would have schemed for any eventuality, but he told me that Freya might have . . . already taken you at the protest, when she seemed to fall. I asked to attend the party to learn the truth."

She gave a hoarse laugh. "Did *he* always know what Freya wanted, too?"

Dainn winced. "I believe he discovered it when you fought him at his first apartment."

"She tried to do it then, didn't she? I used the ancient magic, and when I fell into the fugue state, it was really her taking over. *You* got rid of her."

"I did not know what had become of her after she vanished. Not until Loki told me that Freya had placed the other Aesir under a spell, and that she had never intended to bring them to Midgard."

"I know," Mist said. She clamped her hands around her head. "I know everything she did and meant to do. You said it. I was supposed to be her champion against Odin. I was supposed to have power she didn't, because I was . . . *bred* to be different."

"But she rejected you in Asgard, failing to see how well she had succeeded. You overcame all the magic she sent against you here, and now you have access to more power than you could have imagined. She tried to create a weapon, but it turned in her hand."

Mist straightened and met his gaze, dry-eyed and sober. "I think this power has always been inside me, like the ability to use the ancient magic."

"Because one is dependent upon the other," Dainn said slowly. "You have discovered the Eitr." He leaned forward, engaged in spite of himself. "You were always able to touch it, Mist. The eldest magic manipulates the source of all life, the beginning and end, the sickness and the cure, all the elements in perfect concert. Without the ancient magic, the Eitr is almost impossible to control. Odin once wielded it himself, but was said to have lost the skill over the millennia. Freya and Loki both held it for a time—"

"Freya still had it, when she tried to take me," Mist said. "But how could she, if Odin didn't?"

"I do not know. But Loki depleted his, and Freya . . . she could not still have possessed it in any measure when she tried to take you, or she would have destroyed you."

Mist was silent, and Dainn thought of Danny. His excitement evaporated. If Danny returned to Loki, Laufeyson would use the boy's access to the Eitr. And he would use it to destroy.

"Mist," he said, "I heard that Danny escaped from Loki. Have you learned anything more?"

"No. But I wonder if he could be with Sleipnir now."

"It is possible," Dainn said. "But Danny is still in great danger."

"I'm as worried about the kid as you are," Mist said. Dainn took a long, deep breath. "You still believe that Danny is an innocent," he said, watching her carefully.

"Loki's used him as badly as he has anyone. Maybe—" She glanced at Dainn with a slight grimace. "Maybe even worse."

"Yes. That is why I ask you to withhold judgment when I tell you that it was Danny who asked Loki to take Sleipnir."

Mist stopped in midstride. "He *asked*?"

"He craved a reunion. And Loki believed the time was right."

"We saw Fenrir. Did Danny find *him*, too?"

"Danny has a little more understanding since you saw him on the steppes, but his motives remain a mystery, even to me." Dainn gathered his courage. "I said I left you for Loki because I did not believe that he could use the beast to harm you, and because I feared what I might do to you if I remained. But those were not the only reasons, Mist. There was another just as great. I feared for Danny, for what Loki would do to him. I believed I could protect him."

"How could you protect a son from his own father, especially a father like Loki?"

"Because Loki is not his father.

"I am."

ॐ

It all made a horrible kind of sense.

Mist found herself leaning against the door again, her mind busy sorting through memories and bits of conversation and all the clues that should have told her the truth long ago. Danny's rescuing Dainn from Loki and demanding his help in finding Sleipnir on the other side of the portal. Dainn's seemingly immediate affection for the boy. The bond that had been so evident between them from the beginning.

And all the time Dainn had been with Loki in Asgard, believing his intimate partner to be Freya.

"How long have you known?" she asked, stumbling over the words. "Was he . . . was Danny born in Asgard?"

"No," Dainn said, his haunted eyes focused on something Mist was glad she couldn't see. "He was born in the Void. I knew nothing of him until Loki told me, after I gave myself up to him."

"Loki's fucking piss," Mist said, remembering to breathe. "But some part of you *did* know, didn't you?"

Dainn didn't answer. It was as if he didn't want to give her any excuse for letting him off the hook.

As if she *could*. As if she would ever forget all the lies he'd told, knowing she would lose everything when Freya came for her.

And he'd still betrayed his mistress in the end.

"Did Freya know?" she asked quietly.

He shook his head. His eyes were wet. She looked away.

"I'm sorry," she said. "What Freya did to you on the steppes—"

"I gave her power over me. There is no excuse."

She dropped into a crouch. "What am I supposed to do with you now? You knocked Freya out of . . . whatever part of my mind she still controlled, like you did before. I'm grateful for that."

"It was my responsibility."

"I'm responsible for myself."

"Then I repeat my request. I cannot protect Danny now. Once Loki recovers Danny—and he surely will, if he is not stopped—he will still try to turn my son's abilities against you."

"Have you been keeping Danny from helping him?"

"Loki permitted me to work with him, believing that I could reach through the barriers of Danny's mind and convince him to act on Loki's behalf. I did what I could to discourage him." His voice dropped to a hoarse plea. "You must find him. Please."

His desperate humility made her feel ill. "I promise that I'll try. I just don't know if I can—"

"Once you have truly learned to control the Eitr—"

"Didn't I almost kill you a few minutes ago?" She swallowed. "Have you forgotten that you called me 'Lady of Darkness'?" He didn't respond, but she knew there was no easy answer. There was and had always been a shadow inside her that her battle with Freya had tapped, not created. She had known it ever since she had used the glamour on Koji last winter. She'd behaved exactly like Freya that time, too.

If she were as noble and pure as the champion she should be, Freya's corrupt influence could never have touched her.

"*There is no evil in you,*" Dainn had said, ages ago. But he had been wrong then, and he must know it now.

"Dainn," she began.

But he no longer seemed to be listening. He slumped over himself, forehead to knees, and Mist noticed for the first time how much he resembled the "homeless man" she had found in Golden Gate Park on the day she had met the Jotunn Hrimgrimir and realized that all she had believed of the past was a lie.

"Don't," she said. She moved toward him as carefully as she would approach a dangerous animal backed into a corner and wondered if, in his desperate fear for his son, he would call on the beast. "I can't blame you for doing everything to save your son."

He looked up, and his pain became hers—his shame, his self-contempt, his horror at what he had become. The beast was no part of that horror, though his hatred of it had never left him. The anguish she saw now was only a tiny fraction of the torment he endured every moment he was alive.

And he had concealed it. From Loki, from Danny, from her, even from himself. His captivity had nearly shattered him, but it was *her* presence that had finished the job.

There was nothing more she could ever do to punish him more than he had already punished himself.

"Please," he whispered. "If you cannot help Danny, at least remember to trust no one but yourself, and doubt any thought that craves power or urges you to belittle the mortals for whom you fight."

"I doubt everything," she said, reaching toward him. "I need to know—"

He jerked away violently, huddling in the corner like a prisoner seeing light for the first time in a decade. She retreated, her legs barely carrying her to the door. She stumbled on the threshold, and the elven guard caught at her arm.

"Do you need assistance, Lady?" he asked. "Did the traitor do you harm?"

"No," she said. "I'm fine. Bring him fresh clothes, water, and decent food. After that, he isn't to be disturbed."

Whatever the elf might feel about Dainn, he took his cue from the tone of Mist's voice, bowed, and moved quickly to follow her instructions.

Dazed by the horrors of the past week, Mist stepped out of the warehouse. The same men and women scurried about, the same troops marched, and the sun struck down out of the clouds.

But everything had changed. Freya's influence was gone, and Mist felt no satisfaction, no pride in what she had accomplished. She remembered what Taylor had told her about calling mortals who might not have been willing, what Rick had said about fights and conflict within the ranks. She remembered treating her own advisors and friends like servants. As Freya had done.

She touched the pouch, hanging from a new cord around her neck. Bryn was still trapped. She hadn't seen Gabi anywhere, Ryan was missing, and so was Konur. And Danny was Dainn's son, who had to be saved.

She faced a chaotic situation she had helped create, and she alone could make it right. She had to confess what she had done to her mother, and why. She had to learn who among the mortals shouldn't be here, for any reason. She would have to rely even more on her commanders and administrators and advisors.

Even then, there was no guarantee that she wouldn't fail, and take every one of the allies down with her.

The sunlight faded again, as if it knew she wanted nothing to do with its promise of victory over the darkness. A warm hand closed around hers, and she jerked her head toward the one to whom it belonged.

"You're scared," Anna said, squeezing Mist's hand. "You don't need to be afraid." The young woman smiled, and it was not Anna's smile. "I know someone who can help you."

All at once Mist recognized what was different about Anna's voice and the way she smiled. Both voice and smile were those of a child, secure and happy and oblivious to the chaos around her. The agitation, the furtive behavior, and inexplicable fear were gone.

"Come," Anna said, tugging on Mist's hand.

Mist allowed Anna to guide her past the occupied warehouses toward the one where Freya had died. Mist stopped when she saw where they were going, her heart turning over beneath her ribs.

"It's okay," Anna said. "He isn't mad. He understands."

"He?" Mist said blankly.

"He's waiting," Anna said. She tugged again, and Mist shuffled after her like a zombie on Valium.

Only when they reached the door and stepped into the roofless building did her tattoo begin to burn again, and she felt the force of the magic: not Freya's or that of any elf, but a blast of pure masculine energy, the essence of primal dominance and virility. The broadshouldered figure was limned in light, half-solid but very real.

"Odin," Mist said.

The All-father smiled down on Mist, his single eye very bright, his broad, muscular body flickering in and out of focus.

He's not all here, Mist thought, though thinking at all required considerable effort. But this was no illusion, no manifestation.

Odin had come to Midgard. Odin: Lord of the Aesir; Father of Men; Flaming-eye; Spear-shaker; Weather-maker. Odin, who had sacrificed his own eye for knowledge of the Runes he had passed on to the Aesir. Odin, whose magic was greater than that of any of the other gods, and who had never been defeated.

"All-father," she whispered. "How—"

His laughter boomed, bouncing off the walls and surging toward the sky like a jet breaking the sound barrier.

"You have seen me before," he said. He smiled at Anna, who gazed up at him with love and awe. He opened his fist, and black feathers exploded from his hand to circle around his head.

Orn.

Mist rose slowly, beating down the anger she had no right to feel. "You were . . . hiding?" she asked in astonishment.

"Hiding." Odin turned his head and spat. The feathers fell like stones at his feet. "Anna."

The young woman approached him, bowed, and held up her hand. The raven pendant hung from a chain clasped between her fingers. Mist felt a second jolt of shock, as if she hadn't seen the stone since she'd first given it to Rebekka seventy years ago.

"Take it to Mist," Odin said.

Anna obeyed, offering the pendant to Mist. She took it and cradled the flat stone in her palm. Her tattoo seemed ready to sever her hand from her arm.

"You were meant to hold this for me," Odin said, his voice stern again. "Yet you gave it away."

"All-father, I—"

"It is fortunate that the child Rebekka, and Anna, kept it safe for me until I led her here, for it was the pendant that tied me to this world and held the means by which I would regain my true form."

"You . . . were in Midgard since the Last Battle?"

"Within the raven, yes. And in the parrot, which allowed me to conceal myself in the sight of mortals who might wonder at a child keeping a raven as a pet. For many years I forgot who and what I was, but I protected myself, and even now my enemies remain ignorant of my survival and my plan for the restoration of the Aesir."

Mist glanced toward the door. Odin laughed. "We are well warded. Only you and Anna can hear or see me, until I choose otherwise."

Sorting through her disordered thoughts, Mist struggled to find the right questions. "Why did you come to Midgard in the first place?" she asked. "How did you know what would happen after the Last Battle?"

"I learned a second prophecy in Asgard, one that offered hope of escaping the doom of Ragnarok."

The second prophecy, Mist thought. When she and Freya had joined, the Lady had also thought of such a prophecy.

"Did you not learn of it when you destroyed the bitch goddess?" Odin demanded.

"You were . . ." she stammered. "You saw—"

"I did not have to see what passed between you. Her destruction echoed throughout this world as Thor's Hammer strikes down our enemies."

Mist locked her knees, hoping she wouldn't fall. "You *knew* this was coming," she said.

"I knew the Last Battle would not destroy us. I did not know what would become of the Homeworlds until the moment we were flung into Ginnungagap, but the prophecy made clear that Midgard would be spared."

Yet he hadn't told his Valkyrie why he sent them to Midgard with the Treasures, Mist thought, or why he believed they might one day be reclaimed.

"When Freya called to the elf Dainn Faith-breaker from the great Void," Odin said, speaking over her silence, "she woke me from my long sleep. I sensed where to find you, and I influenced Anna to move to this city. Even the bird's dim intelligence understood that I must warn you of the Sow's machinations."

"You mean her bargain with Loki to keep the Aesir from interfering until either she or Loki conquered Midgard?"

"So you *did* learn something from Freya's addled mind."

"But if you were already on Earth . . ."

"Immediately after the Dispersal, I had a single line of communication open between me and the new Shadow-Realms. It did not last, but before I began to lose my memory, I learned that Freya held the Aesir in a state not unlike death. I was able to create a simulacrum of myself, and the All-father she bespelled in our Shadow-Realm was but a puppet made to deceive her."

"But Orn . . . *you* came to me after Dainn lost contact with Freya and the Void," Mist said. "And when she returned, you went into hiding again, without ever giving me a message."

Odin frowned. "I would not face her until I regained enough power to meet her on *my* terms."

And in the end, Mist thought, he hadn't had to face Freya at all.

"You knew Freya was my mother, didn't you?" Mist asked.

"Of course, though she concealed your kinship from everyone else.

I chose you as my champion long before the Last Battle." He chuckled at Mist's expression. "I was aware that Freya attempted a spell at your conception that would give you the magic of all the races."

Mist released her breath. What did he mean by "all the races"? Did he realize that the "spell" had involved creating a child of two fathers?

"In Asgard, Freya believed that her efforts had failed, and she abandoned you in childhood. I knew you had great potential, and so I turned you to my service as my Valkyrie. I sent you to Midgard knowing that you were loyal only to me, and if Freya survived to turn against me, you would stand against *her*."

Mist's head began to pound in time to the throbbing of her tattoo. "You never told me what she would try to do to me here, in Midgard," she said. "If she'd succeeded . . ."

"She made those plans for you after the Dispersal. I knew nothing of them. It took time for me to regain enough intelligence to observe and understand the circumstances of your life here, and when I recognized the influence the traitor elf had over you, I knew that I could not yet reveal the Sow's original scheme and her relationship to you."

The traitor elf, Mist thought, barely hearing the rest of Odin's explanation. Odin himself had condemned Dainn in Asgard, and there would be no mercy in him now. Dainn was in terrible danger.

But Odin spoke in the past tense. Could he be unaware that Dainn was within this camp?

"What happened when Vali abducted you and Anna?" she asked, eager to distract him. "Why did you let him take you to Vidarr?"

"Because there were things Orn needed to learn." Odin bared his teeth. "He discovered how thoroughly Odin's sons had betrayed him."

"I never recognized what Vali was capable of," Mist said. "I—"

"Vidarr had already betrayed me, when he sought the Treasures under the guise of a mortal soldier during your so-called World War."

Anna's memories of Horja being interrogated by Nazis, Mist thought.

"I had sent him and Vali to Midgard to await my coming," Odin continued, "but even then I knew that Vidarr craved more power than I had ever granted him in Asgard. And Vali eventually became his willing lackey . . . until I gave him another chance to avoid his right-ful punishment."

"Vali is working for you?"

"Posing as one who hates me enough to become Loki's loyal servant."

"Then you have a way of knowing what Loki's doing."

"To the extent that Vali is taken into the Slanderer's confidence."

"And Vidarr is still alive."

"He serves me, but he is . . . not quite himself." Odin smiled unpleasantly. "He fulfills a purpose by observing and doing what I believe mortals call 'odd jobs.'"

And he had been in the garage, Mist thought, however briefly. Odin had to know about the party and its aftermath.

"You knew about Sleipnir," Mist said slowly.

"Of course."

"But you did not intervene."

Odin's heavy brows met above his eye and eye patch. "I was other-wise occupied, and I thought I could trust you with Sleipnir's safety. But Loki deceived you, and you failed to protect what is mine."

Mist tried not to flinch. "He's not in Loki's hands yet, All-father. It's only a matter of time—"

"There *is* no time. I am still not fully within this realm, or I would have acted to end this farce myself. I must have my mount and the Gjallarhorn to be complete."

"I don't understand."

"The true worth of the Treasures does not lie in their value as weapons to be used against Loki, or by him against me. Each one of them contained a part of my soul."

22

Mist was grateful that she still had full control of her body, because shock was pushing her toward a very humiliating collapse.

"Do not berate yourself too harshly for failing to see it," Odin said. "It is evident that Loki has also remained ignorant as to the Treasures' true worth."

Or he would have spared no effort in taking the ones *she* had found, Mist thought. "How do you . . . regain your soul?" she asked.

"I must come into contact with each Treasure, as I have done with the ones you now hold." He nodded benevolently toward Anna. "This my servant has done for me."

"But Loki has two of the—"

"While you entertained him at your party, I entered Loki's mansion and found where he had hidden them."

Mist almost laughed. Loki's scheme had backfired in a way she had never anticipated.

"You have his Treasures?" she asked.

"Touching them was enough. I led him to believe that Freya had broken in to find them, but failed."

"Did you find Regin and Skuld?"

"They were also at the mansion. They are mine again." He flashed another grin, casting a spell as powerful as Freya's glamour had ever been. "I already have Bragi's Harp and Freyr's Sword."

"Hrist and Olrun?" Mist asked, a little faintly.

"Yes. And when I take Sleipnir from Loki, he will be all but finished."

Finished. Finally, Mist understood what the obvious truth her astonishment and awe had prevented her from seeing. What she'd hoped for all along, ever since Dainn had dumped the unwanted and unanticipated responsibility into her lap.

She wasn't alone now. She would no longer be in charge of a seemingly endless holding action, waiting with growing pessimism for Freya to act, for the Aesir to arrive.

The All-father would take the burden from her.

"Who else knows about the Treasures' real purpose?" she asked.

"None but you, this girl, and Vali. And no one else may know until I have come into my full power."

"I understand." She hesitated. "What of the other Aesir? Have they awakened? Can you bring them here?"

"The spell Freya cast against them is a powerful one, and I will need Sleipnir before I attempt it. Freya was never weak, though her spirit was corrupted long ago." Odin's one-eyed gaze grew distant. "I remember a time when she was very different."

A Lady of Light, Mist thought . . . a goddess of passion and fertility and life. But she had never known *that* Freya.

"What changed her?" Mist asked.

"The thirst to take what was not hers," Odin said. His face hardened. "Now she has paid for her crimes."

I made *her pay,* Mist thought. She bowed her head. "All-father," she said, "I have made many mistakes, and there is still so much I don't understand—"

"It is enough for you to know that your mistakes can be rectified. Your magic will help us to regain Sleipnir." He extended his arm. "Show me your right hand."

She did. The tattoo around her wrist was black and red, as if live coals burned in the wolf-and-raven design.

"When you obtained this tattoo in Asgard, it was no random impulse," Odin said. "I made certain that circumstances led you to the decision, and that the spell I placed in it would respond to your use of magic." He took her wrist and turned it up. "In this is recorded every instance of when you pushed beyond the simplest Rune-magic."

Mist flexed her fingers. "Recorded?"

"Because of this mark, I know that your abilities can serve me."

He knew what she was capable of? Did he know about her ancient magic, and her use of the Eitr?

"All-father—" she began.

"You already know what it is to join souls and magic with another. Now you will give me complete access to your spirit, and this time Sleipnir *will* be found."

☊

It was all Mist could do not to shake her head, back away, refuse.

Yes, she knew what it was to "join souls and magic with another." She knew what it was to lose her way, lose herself, to almost *become* her mother.

And Odin was more powerful still. He could obliterate her mind with a stray thought.

"I see your fear," Odin said, almost gently. "There is no need." He laid his hand on her head. She barely felt the touch, but it filled her with joy in the way Freya's embraces had never done.

"It is only in obedience and recognizing your purpose that you will help me save Midgard," he said. "You will be well rewarded. Soon we will have the true paradise promised us after the Last Battle." He lifted her chin with his fist. "The retrieval may well be easier than we anticipated. Vali tells me that a child may have stolen Sleipnir away. Loki's son."

Mist concealed her shock. She had been afraid that Freya would find a way to kill Danny, but she hadn't even considered what Odin might know about the boy.

It had always been said that the All-father could observe the Homeworlds and the doings of their inhabitants from his throne in Asgard, and that his ravens Huginn and Muninn brought him news of all nine worlds every evening. But if he hadn't known about Danny in Asgard or Ginnungagap, Vali would have told him anything he needed to know by now.

That meant he'd also know that Dainn was one of Danny's parents. He might even have seen Danny when he had raided Loki's mansion.

"What do you know of this boy?" Odin asked, dropping his hand.

"He ran away from Loki twice, and one of those times I spent a few hours with him," Mist said, taking great care with her words in case Odin knew the circumstances of their journey to the steppes. "He is very much like an ordinary child."

"But he possesses power, does he not? The ability to create manifestations, and open portals from one part of Midgard to another?"

So he knows that, too, Mist thought. "Loki forced him to act against us in the beginning, All-father," she said, "but he has done nothing for many months."

"Hasn't he?" Odin stroked his beard and studied Mist intently. "Is it true that he previously led you to Sleipnir?"

"Yes."

"Vali suggests that you may bear the child some affection, in spite of his parentage."

"Not all children are like their parents," Mist said, praying that her gaze was as steady as her words. "He doesn't seem to have any use for Loki."

"And Loki? Does he feel affection for the boy?"

"I don't know, All-father. With Loki, it's impossible to tell."

"Ah," Odin said. "But Loki has always been capable of feeling— sometimes too much to be *skoruligr,* manly." He shook his head, as if at some private memory. "The child might be of some use as a hostage, but it would be better still if you can convince him to turn his power to our service. And since he is seemingly in hiding with Sleipnir, we may take both before the Slanderer can find them."

"Yes, All-father," she said, concealing her despair. *Odin would never hurt him,* she told herself. *He'll be safe from Loki. He'll be safe. . . .*

"Then we are in agreement," Odin said, as if he required her assent. "It will please you to know that once we have Sleipnir, you will ride with your Sisters again."

"Eir is gone," Mist said, fighting a fresh wave of grief, "and Horja died years ago. Sigrun has chosen a path that has taken her far from us. Kara and the Gjallarhorn are still missing. Rota and Hild are well, but Bryn—"

"I feel her," Odin said, touching the pouch that hung against Mist's chest. "When my magic is fully restored, I will restore her as well."

"Thank you, All-father."

"You may show your gratitude by using every means at your disposal to summon as many mortals as you can in the next few days, while I make preparations to seek my mount. I grow weary of waiting. These mortals must be trained quickly to attack Loki on many fronts when we take the war to him. Even those unable to fight can serve their purpose."

Mist had a terrible idea what he meant by "purpose." Cannon-fodder, perhaps? Convenient "diversions" whose deaths would be considered no more than collateral damage?

But hadn't she been thinking the same thing before Dainn had "knocked" Freya's ghost out of her head? She'd been willing to compel mortals into service, even if they didn't understand what they were getting into. Even if they had to die without knowing why.

Odin seemed to read her thoughts. "You question my judgment," he said, disappointment in his voice. "Have you become weak, living among these mortals for so many years?"

Mist shivered. Loki had said nearly the same thing to her on several occasions. He had been mocking, but Odin was deadly serious.

"I will be patient with you, my Valkyrie," Odin said. "I have my own army of Einherjar, planted on this world when I sent you here with the Treasures."

Einherjar? Mist thought numbly. He could have no more loyal warriors than those who had died on mortal battlefields, only to rise again in Asgard as ageless as the gods.

I'll have to tell Vixen and Rick, she thought. *If they keep calling their club the Einherjar . . .*

"Do you hear me, Mist? I will not waste my men on minor skirmishes. It will be your duty to make your mortals and Alfar understand that as they serve me with absolute obedience, they fight for their own survival and a worthy place among my Einherjar when Loki is defeated."

Absolute obedience by men and women who might never even have heard of Odin All-father? Doubt pinched Mist's gut like scouting microbes paving the way for a long and unpleasant illness.

But Odin was the cure. She *had* been weak, and he was right. The world had to purge itself of evil before it could be safe again, no matter what the cost.

Whatever Freya had planned for her daughter, Mist had always served Odin. And always would.

"I will find the mortals we need," she said.

"I never doubted your loyalty." Odin's body began to grow hazy around the edges. "And do not cease searching for the Gjallarhorn."

Within moments, he was gone. Anna, who had been so quiet that Mist had nearly forgotten her, stared at the place he had been, as if his disappearance had left her without purpose or volition.

Mist wondered what had happened to change Anna so much. She'd been deeply connected to Orn, and Orn had been Odin all along. His transformation from raven to god would be enough to mess with anyone's head.

Had she become no more than another one of his servants, after all she'd done to protect him? Was Horja's influence coming to the fore? Did Anna remember "becoming" Rebekka when she'd come to fetch Mist?

Pressing her lips together, Mist crouched to pick up one of the raven feathers left scattered on the floor. "Odin's gone for now," she said gently. "But we have a lot of work to do. We have to redouble our efforts to find Kara and the Gjallarhorn. You can help with that."

She waited to see if Anna understood. After a pause, the young woman shook her head.

"I'm sorry," she said, "I have to stay with Orn. You understand."

Mist suppressed a shiver. She remembered the pendant, clutched forgotten in her hand. "You should take this back."

Anna covered Mist's hand with her own and folded Mist's fingers around the stone. "I'm glad you have it again," she said, only the subtlest trace of sadness in her voice. She turned and rushed out of the building without a backward glance.

Mist was still staring at the open door long after Anna was gone, trying to prioritize the tasks she had to perform in addition to fulfilling Odin's commands. One of them was finding Konur and Ryan. She had a few stringent things to say to her second "father." And she had to see Dainn, to warn him that Odin had finally come.

The pendant bit into her hand, and she opened her fingers. It would be rank disloyalty to help Dainn escape, a betrayal as terrible as any Dainn himself had committed. But he had never been the irredeemable traitor the Aesir and Alfar had declared him to be.

The cold, hard fact was that she still didn't understand Dainn, or what lay hidden in the deepest shadows of his mind. And she didn't know how much Odin knew about Dainn's part in Freya's plans or the depth of his relationship with Mist.

But if she didn't protect Dainn, Odin would almost certainly decide to rid himself of Freya's former servant as soon as he had questioned the elf about Loki.

At least if Odin caught her, Mist thought, she knew that the Allfather could lead the allies to victory without her.

∞

Freya is dead.

The explosive words that had stupefied Mist's councilors nearly paralyzed Loki as well. As the Alfar and mortals began to file out of the room, he adjusted his position on the wall, twitching both forelegs and antennae in an elaborate pattern, drawing cold out of the floor and spinning Rune-staves that crept like fingers of hoarfrost toward the feet of his enemy.

For a few seconds, Mist was too preoccupied to notice them, even when one icy finger touched the heel of her boot. Then she looked down, and Loki withdrew the spell back into himself, turning his dark exoskeleton ghostly pale and stiffening his joints. When he could move again, he nearly flung himself against the bottom of the door.

Freya was dead. And Loki understood what he had felt when he had flown under the wards . . . the magic he had followed across the camp, the sense of something new and dangerous.

"*There may be as yet untapped abilities within Mist that only Freya can awaken,*" Dainn had once told him, with complete and prophetic honesty.

With a furious beating of fragile wings, Loki fled the warehouse. His laughter emerged as the faintest buzz. Heedless of those who might notice a particularly handsome and unusually purposeful fly, he launched himself toward the nearest border of the ward, passed through the barrier, and flew on until he could fly no more. He plummeted onto the lid of a rubbish can left in an alley and fell to the asphalt, spinning helplessly on his back until he found the strength to regain his true shape.

As weak as he was, he found the energy to pull his cell phone from his jacket's inner pocket and called Vali. Odin's son came himself, appearing a little less offensively unflappable than usual.

"Boss?" he asked, helping Loki to his feet while the other Jotunar and the black limousine waited at the mouth of the alley.

"Were you aware that Orn has returned?" Loki demanded.

Vali blinked, giving the impression of a mindless, cud-chewing cow suddenly confronted with one of Odin's ravenous wolves. "Odin's messenger?" he asked.

Loki brushed off his leather pants and cast Vali a withering look. "There have been no raven sightings lately?"

"No, boss. Where did you see him?"

"I didn't. But I know he has returned, and is involved with Mist again."

"That ain't good," Vali said.

Loki straightened. "How stunningly perceptive you are," he said. "I would almost think you're playing stupid because you have a guilty conscience."

"You mean I should have known that Orn came back? I don't have any connection to him now. Aside from you, I'm the last person he'd come to."

Batting Vali's arm away, Loki started toward the limo. "Now I know it was not Freya who infiltrated my house."

"Orn?" Vali asked as Loki climbed into the rear of the limo, wincing at sore joints and aching bones. "He worked a spell that strong?"

Loki opened the minibar and selected a glass. "He was unable to take the Treasures, but he has power he did not possess before. And I believe I know why." The glass shattered in his hand, and blood spattered the smooth leather of the seat.

"Odin is here."

When they arrived at Loki's mansion, he took the back stairs to the second floor and opened the heavy doors, bypassing Danny's still-empty room and continuing to the end of the short hall.

The last room hadn't been used since just after Loki had purchased the building. Now the door swung open with an ominous groan, rather like the dead bewailing their fates.

As it happened, the dead were not in view, but their mistress certainly was. Hel sat on a throne built of bones and draped with skins of questionable origins, her face—half-dark, half-light—beautiful and ugly and utterly cold.

"Father," she said in her hoarse, brittle voice. "At last you deign to visit me?"

Loki closed the door. "My dear," he said, "I do not mean to keep you prisoner, but it wouldn't do to let our enemies know that you are among us."

"The ones who came here believed I was an illusion," she said with a bitter smile.

"And you told me it was Freya you saw," he said. "It was not."

She lifted a pale brow. "So I have been told." She raised her hand, and half-formed figures drifted out of the darkness behind her: the recent dead, distinguished by the expressions of horror on their faces.

Confined though they were to Niflheim, they could be given solid form in order to kill . . . and to die again.

"This," Hel said, gesturing to a tall mortal, "was one of the Einherjar who accompanied the thieves."

Loki smiled. Odin's eternal warriors were not so eternal when Hel's minions took them down.

"What is your name?" Loki asked the Einherji.

The man's mouth moved stiffly, as if he were only just becoming used to his phantom bones. "Hrothgar," he said.

Loki peered into the pale, tormented face. "Who brought you to Midgard?"

"The All-father," Hrothgar whispered.

"When?"

"My guests have no sense of time, Father," Hel said with a roll of her bloodshot eyes.

Loki was reminded how like him she could be. The comparison did not particularly please him.

"Did Orn see my son?" Loki asked the warrior.

With a breathy wail, Hrothgar collapsed to the floor. "I should not be here," he whined. "Take me to Valhalla."

"There is no Valhalla," Loki said. "No lovely afterlife of swilling mead, swinging swords, and swiving beautiful women. But you will have many more of your comrades to keep you company soon."

Hel leaned forward, searching Loki's face. "Are we finally to have a proper battle?"

"Can you summon more of the dead?"

"The way is open," she said, "thanks to my little brother, though I do not believe he understood what he did. I will need your help."

"You will have it after you have proven your loyalty to me. The wait will be worth it, I assure you."

"But how can you doubt my devotion, Father?"

"Fenrir failed to pass a most basic test of his competence by allowing Sleipnir to escape. I hope that you perform better than your brother."

"I will not disappoint you." Twitching her fingers, Hel dismissed

Hrothgar. He faded back among the others clustered behind Hel's throne. Loki turned toward the door.

"Father," Hel said. She rose from the throne, and her robes parted, revealing the rotting flesh of her legs. "Do send me more bones. I am exceedingly hungry."

"And I should not want my beloved daughter to die of starvation," Loki said. "Make yourself ready to aid me when I call you."

◑◐

Ryan broke away from the Alfar and stared across the vast expanse of parking lots, astonished by what Mist had done in less than a week. Every free square foot of concrete and asphalt was occupied with people—mainly humans, with a healthy portion of Alfar—marching in columns like soldiers, practicing with swords and axes, all in constant motion.

Mist was finally building a real army.

Ryan heard Konur come up behind him and steadfastly ignored the elf-lord. He didn't know what pissed him off more: the fact that Konur had known what Freya planned for Mist and hadn't warned her, or that he'd kept Ryan a virtual prisoner since he and Dainn had fought on the waterfront.

But at least Freya hadn't won. Konur had told him that the fight was over—though he hadn't said *how* he knew—and that Mist was alive.

Ryan had allowed himself to wonder if maybe his warning Freya about Sleipnir had brought about the consequences he'd hoped for, and actually led to her defeat. But he knew he couldn't take the credit. Mist had done it, just like she'd brought all these people together to fight for their world.

Of course Sleipnir was still missing, but at least some of the other news was good. According to Captain Taylor, Dainn was okay, even if he was still a prisoner, and Loki hadn't tried anything for days.

The bad news was that Gabi had been making herself scarce while Ryan was away, and no one knew where she'd been. Soon after Eir had died, she'd claimed that she couldn't heal anymore, and Ryan was more than a little worried that she'd gone back to "spying" on Loki's gangbangers and drug dealers the way she had before he'd gone to Mother Skye. She'd been using her ex-con brother, Ramon, as a contact, and that was dangerous work. But if she didn't think she could help any other way . . .

Something tickled the corner of Ryan's vision, breaking the train of his thoughts, and he looked up. The raven was back, just as he'd known it would be.

Mist was waiting for them near the small unfinished warehouse, arms folded across her chest. She gave Konur a cool, unreadable glance, and Ryan thought of the excuse he and the elf had concocted to explain their absence. Ryan had only agreed to the deception because he didn't have the guts to tell Mist that *he'd* never found a way to warn her about Freya.

Only he couldn't have told her even if he'd been brave enough, because apparently she wasn't ready to admit to anyone in camp what had really happened. Why should she, when revealing what Freya had tried to do would only raise all kinds of questions and make her job that much harder?

"Captain Taylor," Mist said, dismissing the former Marine with a brief nod before turning to Ryan. "Are you all right? When Konur sent word that you'd had another seizure—"

"I'm fine." Ryan flushed and ran his hand over his left sleeve, as if it were still coated in dirt and crumbled concrete from the back lot of the warehouse. "I'm sorry. I thought they were over with."

"Now that we know they aren't, you're going to have to be a lot more careful." She frowned at him. "Konur said you saw something about me in the future, and that you tried to force a vision. That was a bad idea. I'm glad that Konur and his healers were able to help you recover."

"Are *you* okay?" Ryan asked quickly.

"Why shouldn't I be?" Her eyes narrowed. "If what you saw was something bad, I don't want to hear it. I don't want you to think about it for one more second. Agreed?"

Ryan clamped his lips together and nodded. Mist looked up to watch Konur approach.

"There is something you can tell me," she said. "When you were with him, did he say anything about being my father?"

At least I don't have to lie about that, Ryan thought. He didn't know who had told her, but he suspected Dainn. It wouldn't have been an easy thing to talk about. Or to accept.

"Konur told me," he admitted.

"And did he happen to mention why he felt the need to take you so far from camp to help you?"

There was definitely suspicion in her voice, and Ryan thought it was exactly what Konur deserved. "He *told* me that letting me stay near camp when I was already sick was—"

"It would have been most inadvisable," Konur said, coming up beside Ryan. "But I should have informed you from the beginning." He scanned the parking lots. "It seems that my lieutenants have done well enough in my place."

He and Mist gazed at each other, and Ryan wondered who was going to be next to speak.

"I know who you are," Mist said at last.

"Yes."

"Ryan," Mist said, "would you mind giving us a little privacy for a few minutes?"

Grateful to get away, Ryan put a good six yards between himself and the two of them. He could hear them speaking, maybe arguing, in low voices, but the words were too soft for him to hear, and neither of them showed much emotion.

He'd learned that elves tended to be that way. Not Mist, unless she was really upset.

She was obviously really upset.

The conversation lasted about five minutes. When it was over, some of the tension had gone out of Mist's shoulders. Konur touched her sleeve ever so briefly and then walked away, graceful and aristocratic as always. And not in the least bit guilty-looking.

Ryan wished he could say the same of himself. He was going to have to admit the truth sooner or later: that he'd tried to help Dainn escape, that he'd seen what Freya planned to do, that warning Eir had probably hastened her death. And that there would always be that kind of risk attached to any vision he revealed.

The *truth* was that he had too many questions and not enough answers.

"I have to get back to work," Mist said, "if you're going to be all right."

"I am." He hesitated. "What did Konur say about hiding Freya's intentions?"

"He admitted that he knew what Freya was up to," she said darkly, "but he felt he still owed her some kind of loyalty. He was also convinced that I would win, as Dainn guessed. He was willing to take some pretty big risks based on that belief, like keeping Dainn quiet when he tried to warn me."

"So he never *really* betrayed you."

"I can either toss him out on his ear, or accept his explanations and keep him and the Alfar in this fight. There's not much of a choice."

"But you forgive him?"

Mist nodded curtly. "If there's nothing else . . ."

"There *is* one more thing."

"Go ahead."

"I've seen *him*."

She started. "Who?"

"Orn."

A short puff of air escaped her lips. "It's not exactly a secret." She smiled, and a shaft of sunlight beamed out of the sky to turn her hair to gold and her eyes the color of clear water. "Something has happened that will change everything."

Ryan didn't have a single doubt about that.

"You probably want to know about Dainn," Mist said, her gaze already focused on something across the parking lot. "He's all right, but I'm trying to keep his presence here as quiet as possible. I've listened to his story, and—"

"You don't hate him?" Ryan asked anxiously.

"No."

The response was terse, but it untied the knot in Ryan's stomach. "Will . . . will you let me see him?" he asked.

"Later. And that's enough for now. This is an order—don't force anything where your visions are concerned. We don't want any more seizures."

Ryan nodded, knowing that was the best he was going to get. "Have you seen Gabi?"

"Not recently." She sighed. "I don't know what's gotten into that girl, but if you see her, try to talk some sense into her. I want her here, where it's . . ." She chuckled grimly. "Where it's as safe as anywhere else in Midgard."

"I will." Mist walked away, and Ryan chewed on his lower lip, wondering if Midgard would ever be safe again.

Everything hung on the will of two people who had to accept what they were meant to be.

23

Dainn ran.

The beast was swifter than the elf, but he had no difficulty in resisting the temptation to call upon it. He had already gone well outside the ward and beyond the reach of those who might immediately notice his absence. Mist had efficiently distracted his Alfar guards and concealed his escape with a touch of the ancient magic and the unseasonable fog that had pushed its way across the city from the Pacific Ocean.

He had worried when she had told him how she planned to help him escape. But in the last moment before he'd left her, he had seen no deterioration in her nature, no sign that Freya's fading influence had touched her again. They had stood together behind the warehouse in the pre-dawn darkness, silent and apart. Not even a brief mental farewell had passed between them.

But their last exchange of thoughts had seared itself into his brain like Loki's knife had bitten into his palm when he and Dainn had made their preposterous oath. It wasn't her decision to save him from Odin, who had so miraculously appeared to claim her obedience, or her willingness to forgive his many misdeeds.

It was the emotion she had fought to conceal from him, as he fought to conceal his own from her.

He didn't know if he had succeeded. He knew she had sensed his shame. But when she had tried to touch him, and he'd jerked away . . .

That had hurt her. And no amount of self-contempt could change his visceral reaction, his inability to accept the contact.

Dainn paused to catch his breath, leaning against the trunk of a tree. At nine p.m., Golden Gate Park was quiet save for the usual vagrants settling in among the shrubbery and a pair of young mortals who had braved the cold and wind to kiss on an isolated park bench.

This was where it had begun. Where Mist had found him. Some might think to look for him here.

But here there was magic . . . not only the magic of the living tree that flowed into his fingers and seeped from the brown grass, but of memory. Mist's stern face staring down at him as he recovered from Hrimgrimir's attack. Her impatience when he had tried to explain his purpose, and his mockery of her because, even then, he had realized how difficult it would be to carry through with Freya's commands.

He hadn't realized then that he loved her. That it would be as impossible for him to stop loving her as it would be to reject Danny or refuse to fight even Odin himself for the safety of his son.

Find him.

Curling his fingers against the bark, he closed his eyes, feeling the wind whipping his hair around his face, the insects scurrying under his feet, the sap sluggish in the tree's heart. His elven magic had begun to return. And this was the test to see if Konur had been right . . . if the beast would rise with every attempt to call on his abilities, as it had done in the past.

Dainn opened his eyes and looked up at the needled branches overhead. The boughs rustled, and small birds hidden among them twittered and chirped. They felt him, and he felt them: their simple thoughts of comfort and food and sleep, of mating and offspring and flight. He called them, and they fluttered out of their shelter to settle on his head and shoulders, peeping and fluffing their feathers.

One had a damaged wing; he stroked his fingers across it, and the air around him suddenly seemed almost solid, sliding in and out of his lungs easily enough, yet heavy with vitality and magic.

He knew what it was, and flinched away. Mist had used it as a weapon against him in his cell. But the Eitr spun slowly around Dainn, not touching, and he remembered when his body had changed the poison to an inert energy that he almost, *almost* believed he could use himself.

It seemed now that he only had to reach out and take a handful of the substance, gather and manipulate it as he would a shapeless mass of clay, making it conform to his will.

The thought froze his heart. The Eitr was not his to wield. This must be a freakish manifestation, a lingering trace of Mist's magic. Hadn't he told Mist that the Eitr and the ancient magic were interconnected?

It is real.

Dainn tried to ignore the voice, but it would not be silenced.

Do not deny what is yours.

How many times had the beast said such things to him, tempting him to violence and evil?

Do you not remember when you healed the boy?

The boy. Not Danny, but Ryan . . . *after* the beast had almost killed the young man during Jormungandr's attack. There had been a great struggle, Dainn against the beast, and . . .

Did you think this ability came from nothing?

Dainn forgot to breathe. His heart rattled under his ribs. It was impossible that he should possess such a gift and not know it.

Your body knows it.

The voice was so rational, almost soothing. It was as if the Eitr itself had changed the beast, transforming its savagery to reason.

And what it said accorded with everything Dainn felt now. The injured bird nestled deeper in his palm, trusting and unafraid. *It* felt no evil, no discord.

It trusted him as he did not trust himself.

Instinct told him to use the tools he had already mastered, and so he began to sing . . . hesitantly, softly, weaving a spell around the Eitr like a bird constructing a nest. He invited the Eitr into the sanctuary he had made, drew it into himself, breathed deeply and slowly. Light burst behind his eyes, and he felt a seed germinate in his mind— twigs and branches stretching out and down through muscle and tendon, the rich sap of life filling his veins and arteries. His feet took root in the soil; leaves rustled in his hair. His hand grew hot, and the bird seemed to sigh.

The park fell silent. A timeless moment passed, and then the bird stretched its newly healed wing and darted up into the tree. Another moment, a single heartbeat, and then everything shifted.

Under Dainn's feet, roots shriveled. Pain doubled him over as the branches interlaced with muscle and bone began to rot and wither. The poison was too great for his body to counter, the dark side of the Eitr too vast for his mind to compass. A pool opened up under his feet, blackened grass giving way to crumbling, sterile earth.

He stumbled. A great shadow began to swallow him whole as he grasped at the crumbling edges of the pit. It was not some Christian Hell below him, nor the underworld of any mythic tale, but the complete negation of all things. Not even the beast could survive it.

Danny's face came to him then—open, laughing, full of joy and complete comprehension.

"It belongs to us," he said. "To all of us."

Then Dainn began to lose his grip, and the black reached up to take him.

Someone caught Dainn by his shoulders and pulled him—back, up, out of the pit, and onto solid ground. He found himself gasping and bathed in perspiration, a mantle of pine needles and dead grass covering his head and jacket.

But there was no one with him. The Eitr had vanished. Even the beast was gone.

So was the pain. But the pit in the earth was still there, an open wound slow to heal. He pushed himself to his knees and looked over the edge. He sensed a bottom; it did not sink into an endless darkness as he had imagined. But the stink of rot rose up from it, and he knew nothing would ever grow there again.

Still, the rot had not spread. Scooting back, Dainn leaned against the tree trunk. One of the birds, perhaps the healed one, uttered a soft peep.

Dainn took comfort in the company. He assessed his condition. His body was weak; his use of the Eitr had exacted a price. He had floundered like a child with his first spell, and it had nearly destroyed him.

But he had survived, and something had been given to him in return. He turned up his scarred palm. A substance like healthy sap was smeared over the wound, and he could feel a change in his flesh, as if new vessels had grown throughout his body to carry something far more potent than blood.

"*It belongs to us,*" Danny had said, as if he had been there with Dainn, encouraging him as the beast had done, and Dainn realized that boy and beast had sounded nearly alike.

That was impossible. Danny and the beast were utter opposites. But their message had been the same. And he could not ignore it.

He pressed his hands to the tree trunk. The Eitr was beyond his reach now, and he understood the risk should he move too quickly. But if he could call on any lingering power, foreign though it might be to him, he had to take the chance. And Danny's face, his presence, was still fresh in Dainn's memory.

Closing his eyes, he began to construct a complete image of Danny in his imagination: Danny smiling, happy, sketching Sleipnir with a gray crayon on fine white drawing paper. He saw Danny on the steppes, laughing as Sleipnir bounced him on the Horse's broad back. He remembered Danny asking to be reunited with Sleipnir again.

Once the pictures were firmly established in Dainn's mind, he sang the Runes in the language of the elves as he sketched Rune-staves into the dirt before him—Laguz for life energy and Dagaz for awakening. The earth erupted around the staves like oil from a derrick, its flow controlled and shaped by Dainn's song. Within a minute, the earth had taken the shape of a small human figure, and began to develop fingers and toes, features, and even hair.

A small, inebriated man in an oversized trench coat emerged from a dense thicket of shrubs, stared at Dainn and the earth-figure of Danny, and staggered away. Dainn made certain he was gone before he completed his spell. The staves crumbled and became one with the soil, raising fresh green grass.

The Danny-figure smiled at Dainn and offered its hand.

"Show me," Dainn said.

The crude, miniature figure of a horse rose out of the earth beside

Danny, and Dainn knew that that boy and Steed were together. Had Danny convinced Fenrir to let Sleipnir go, or had he used the Eitr to steal Steed from Wolf?

"Where are you?" Dainn asked.

"It's hardly polite to leave me out of this," Loki said, appearing suddenly behind earth-Danny. "Especially since I have a friend of yours who undoubtedly wishes to keep his life."

"I'm sorry," Ryan said, hanging limply from Loki's grip on the collar of his jacket. "I only followed you a little ways outside the ward, but he was—"

"There is no need for apologies," Dainn said, meeting Loki's gaze. "How did you find me?"

"A fly on the wall told me."

Dainn spoke a stream of words even he didn't understand, and Loki blanched, swung Ryan around, and held the young man like a shield in front of his chest.

"I don't know what you just did," Loki said, "but try it again and I will give this boy to Hel."

Dainn knew that he wasn't in any position to fight Loki now, and all he could do was bluff. "You won't kill him," he said, "because he has the ability to predict the future."

Loki stared into Ryan's face. "This is the *spamadr*?"

"Yes," Dainn said. "And I do not believe you will rob yourself of such a valuable resource."

Loki's lips curved unpleasantly. "Should I test his worthiness now? Or will you take me to Danny?"

⁂

The All-father rose from his chair as if it were his throne, Hlidsjalf, looking down over all the worlds from his hall Valaskjalf.

"We have delayed long enough," he said. "Set aside your worries, Valkyrie, and know you are strong enough to serve as my anchor to the world."

It was a compliment to match the others he had bestowed on Mist, but she didn't take any pleasure in it. He had told her what was expected of her: merely to hold herself steady and let him draw on as much of her inherent magic as he needed to stay connected to the real world while his spirit conducted the search for Sleipnir.

The problem was that holding herself steady wouldn't be enough. She'd have to be actively working to keep Odin from sharing her thoughts. She'd told Dainn about Odin's return, and Dainn had understood that once Odin was aware of Danny's identity and abilities, the boy would become a pawn to be used by whoever got to him first.

So he and Mist had agreed that Dainn would "escape," find Danny, and—with luck—hide his son until Odin and Loki were fully engaged with each other.

What Dainn needed now was time. He'd been gone about six hours, but that didn't seem like nearly enough. She would have to bury her most private thoughts where even the All-father was unlikely to reach: within the Eitr. It was a guess, an experiment that might fail . . . but Dainn had told her that Odin had "lost" the means to work the Eitr. She hoped to Ymir that he was right. She walked a blade's fine edge between treason and compassion, between what she knew of Odin's dread responsibilities and what she didn't know of his innermost thoughts.

Whatever favor he might have shown her, she understood that she was never *meant* to know.

That was the greatest danger of all.

"Take my hand," Odin commanded.

She laid her hand in his. Immediately she felt the crushing grip of his broad fingers. The pressure lasted only for a moment, and then she became aware of Odin's consciousness as it linked with hers.

The joining was nothing like it had been with Freya. There were no demands this time, no desperation . . . only Odin's supreme confidence. She felt a warmth in him she had never found in her mother. There was no golden light or scent of primroses, but the call of one warrior to another, a true respect for her strength of will and purpose that she hadn't expected and wasn't sure she deserved.

"There are circles of magic within each being that wields it," he had told her, reminding her that he was a teacher as well as a warrior, that his wisdom was as great as his pride. "Circles within circles, and only the most powerful of gods and Alfar—and you, my Valkyrie— possesses more than one. The outer circle is that magic closest to the surface, easiest to summon, requiring the least effort to wield."

She felt a sudden tug when Odin touched that outermost circle, the simplest Rune-chants she had known even as an "ordinary" Valkyrie. She sensed his power as if it were a burgeoning storm, drawing energy from the charged air around it.

His consciousness expanded as he called on the next circle, the more sophisticated Galdr, the forge-magic she had built from her knowledge as a maker of swords and knives. Instinctively she created a strong scaffold from Rune-staves of iron and fire to anchor the densely woven filaments that bound the essence of Odin's spirit to his incomplete body, and felt him gradually drawing away from her as he reached for the third circle.

That circle was the Seidr, the magic of soul-travel which Mist had never truly learned. Odin knew it well, however, and he found the remnants of magic that Freya had employed in her failed union with Mist, using the scraps to strengthen the soul-cord as he played it out.

It was the fourth circle she had to hide from him, shielding it from his consciousness without faltering in her grip on his soul. A single moment of inattention on her part might have alerted him, but he was deep into his search by then, and he passed by the circle without noting its existence.

Odin drifted farther away, and Mist allowed herself a moment of relief. It didn't last. Someone screamed outside the warehouse, and she bounced back to full consciousness. The scaffolding that moored Odin's soul began to dissolve. She snatched at the soul-cord, gripping it with all her mental and magical strength.

Odin plummeted back as the cord retracted, and the semi-solid figure of the All-father shuddered violently in his chair, still unaware of the world around him. There were more screams, cries of shock and agony, dozens of voices united in terror.

Leaving Odin where he was, Mist drew Kettlingr and ran outside.

It was already dark, the stars and moon mostly obscured by the perpetual cloud cover, but there was a shadow lying over the camp that would make an ordinary night seem as bright as noon.

Hel had come to Earth.

Swinging Kettlingr before her, Mist sang Rune-spells of battle as she clothed herself and the sword in heat and light. The phantoms appeared out of the murk, caught in the glare, and shrieked their own fear, abandoning the bodies of those they had already claimed for their mistress of Death. Mist chased them, knowing that few of the sleeping mortals had the means to defend themselves from the dead. Driven by rage, she called upon the ancient magic and infused her sword with the Eitr. Wherever Kettlingr struck, a shadow-soul shattered into dust.

Alfar joined her, along with Hild and Rota, each wielding her weapon and singing her chant. Death was the Valkyrie's province, and though these souls belonged to the mistress of Niflheim, they fled from the Choosers of the Slain.

In minutes the last of the army of the dead were fleeing, leaving a thick coating of ash and dust and powdered bone in their wake.

With a cry of anger, Mist ran after the creatures. She cut them down as she reached the stragglers, swinging wildly and without thought as they passed through the wards, unaffected by spells that were only meant to stop the living. She didn't care if she fought alone; all that mattered was the killing. She followed the dead as they swept onto Twenty-Second Street and reached Third, where a few mortals waited at the light rail stop to catch the last train. The dead swept over them, and they toppled to the ground like felled trees.

Mist stopped. The dead, too, had come to a halt. From among them walked a woman in sweeping black and red robes, her body divided into dark and light, eyes red with a narrow rim of green.

Hel.

She smiled at Mist. "Valkyrie," she said, inclining her head. "My father has so often spoken of you, and I have been eager to welcome you to my halls."

Searching the ancient magic for a weapon against the goddess,

Mist laughed. "I know you resent me and my Sisters, Mistress of Corpses, because we rob you of your prey when we carry the souls of heroes to Odin's hall."

"Ah, yes," Hel said, sounding all too much like her father. "The glorious Einherjar. But you have been sadly lacking in employment since Valhalla ceased to exist."

"Oh, we have employment," Mist said, hearing the footsteps of her Sisters drumming behind her. "And right now it's sending you back to wherever you came from."

"But Niflheim was destroyed with all the rest of the Homeworlds, save this one."

"You must have your own Shadow-Realm—"

"Yes. But at last I have been set free by the boy you sought to protect."

"What boy?" Rota asked.

Mist lost track of her spell-seeking and searched Hel's hideously beautiful face. "The daughter of the Father of Lies can easily lie herself," she said.

"But I don't. My brother is a child of many accomplishments, and he was only defending his home from attack by intruders."

Defending his home? Mist thought. Was Danny unaware of what he had unleashed? Dainn had said that he didn't always understand what he did. If the boy had acted purely on instinct . . .

Odin had admitted to being the intruder, leaving a trail that would implicate Freya. He had never mentioned seeing Danny.

"I see that this disturbs you," Hel said. "Perhaps now you will admit that my little brother belongs among his true kin." She smiled, treating Mist to a clear view of her rotten teeth. "Think instead on what you will lose if you continue to send your warriors against Loki. I will claim all those whom my guests have slain today, all they kill tomorrow, and every other mortal who falls in this war. Do you wish such a fate on your followers?"

Almost before Hel had completed the question, Mist found what she was looking for. The Eitr surged up inside her, all light untainted by even a hint of darkness.

"I don't think so," Mist said, and cast the light toward her enemies. Hel's face became even more hideous as the magic of life battered against her, and the dead around her began to howl in pain.

All at once there was a scuffle among her minions, ghost turning on ghost as dull swords and axes and daggers appeared in their hands. Mist stepped back, Hild and Rota on either side of her, trying to make sense of the bizarre spectacle.

Hel vanished. The battling dead remained behind, until suddenly one faction broke apart and began to run. Rota started after them, but Mist held her back.

"Wait," she said.

The phantoms who had lingered laid down their crumbling weapons, indicating surrender. One of them moved toward Mist, limping as if he had taken a wound like any living creature.

Mist raised her sword, but the specter halted several yards away. His blurred face began to resolve, features coming into focus.

Features Mist knew, as she knew the texture of his hair and the weary smile.

"Geir," she whispered.

"Mist," he said, his voice as dry and barren as Hel's heart. "I've been waiting a very long time to see you again."

24

Mist raised her hands palm-out as if she could block the sight of him. "You can't be here," she said.

"But I am," Geir said, deep sadness in his dull blue eyes. "I am dead, Mist."

"You can't be with *her*," Mist said, letting her hands fall. "Not with Hel."

"But I died of old age," he said. "Of sickness and my body's failure. I was never bound for Valhalla."

She tried to touch him, but her hand passed through him and emerged coated with ash. "You were never a follower of the ancient religions," she said.

"I was Norse," he said. "And Hel took many who should never have gone to her."

"Took from where? The Void?"

"I do not know *where* I was before. The laws of life and death are out of balance, and there is no means of telling where any who die will come to rest."

"Out of balance?"

"Hel can claim nearly anyone she chooses, including every mortal who dies in this war."

His story was so unexpected that Mist could hardly accept it. She had always assumed that those who died following any particular faith would go to the place they believed in, though she had often hoped that there would be some justice for the good and evil.

This was wrong. Terribly wrong.

"I can get you out," Mist said. "I can—"

"Bring me to life again?" He raised his hands, revealing layers of skin and muscle and bone all visible at once. "Even with the abilities of Freya's daughter, you cannot restore life. But *we* can help *you*."

She looked beyond him to the twenty or so phantoms who waited unmoving, their faces indistinct. She couldn't even tell if they'd been men or women in life.

"You just slaughtered dozens of my people," she said, blinking to clear her vision.

"*We* did not," he said, gesturing behind him, "though Hel was too busy to notice those who hung back." His eyes flickered with something like hope. "Once you and I fought side by side, resisting the Nazis. There is another rebellion brewing among the dead, and we are part of it."

"Rebellion? Against Hel?"

"We have no wish to fight for Loki against the living. We cannot destroy Hel, but we can reduce the numbers of her willing followers, to whom she has promised great rewards."

"If what you say is true, Hel must have thousands, millions . . ."

"Yes. But numbers never stopped us before." He lifted his hand and dropped it again before Mist could be reminded that he wasn't capable of touching her, embracing her, loving her. "We must go. I will—"

He never finished, for a voice booming Rune-spells fell like a net around the dead, sweeping them up, flinging them high, scattering them like seeds thrown carelessly onto fallow earth.

There was no trace of Geir and his fighters when Odin strode up to Mist, pushing Hild and Rota aside.

Mist was too numb to move. "All-father?" she whispered.

"Did I give you permission to abandon our search?" he asked.

Hild and Rota gaped at Odin and fell to their knees. He ignored them. Murmurs and oaths rose from the Alfar behind them.

"What did you do to Hel's dead?" Mist said, staring at the place where Geir had been standing a minute before.

"The slayers of my servants? I gave them true death. Loki has made his move too soon." His eye narrowed. "How did he set her free?"

Mist knew she couldn't answer his question, or Danny would be in even greater danger. She looked from Hild to Rota with a plea in her eyes, hoping they understood. Rota still didn't know anything about Danny, and Mist had asked Hild not to speak of him to Freya. But if they told Odin what Hel had said . . .

"Hel said that Loki knew you'd raided his mansion," Mist said, "and he brought her through from Ginnungagap."

"Then he has advanced further than I thought possible," Odin rumbled. "Who was this phantom with whom you spoke?"

At least now she could tell the truth. "There's some kind of rebellion among the dead," she said, "a group that doesn't want to follow Hel or Loki against you."

"Indeed?" Odin's ferocious expression began to clear. "What more did it say?"

"He . . . it and its companions didn't have anything to do with killing—" She clenched her teeth and turned back for the camp. "I have to get back to my people."

"*Yours?*" Odin said.

"Some victims may still be alive," she said, hardening her heart. "With your permission, All-father. . . . Rota, Hild, please see to the mortals at the light rail stop. If they're dead, we have to dispose of the bodies."

"And witnesses?"

"Will anyone else believe what they might have seen?"

"We'll take care of it," Rota said, giving Mist a long, probing look as she and Hild got to their feet.

"Valkyrie," Odin said, "Alfar. Say nothing of my presence here. The time has not yet come to reveal myself."

Hild and Rota exchanged glances, but they bowed acknowledgment, and the Alfar murmured agreement. They scattered, leaving Mist alone with Odin again.

"This attack was no coincidence," Odin said, glaring at Mist as if she were responsible. "Assign others to see to the fallen. You and I will resume our search at once."

No one saw him return to the warehouse. Mist hung back. Alfar and mortals were already walking among the dead, checking pulses and counting the losses.

Captain Taylor found her and spoke softly in her ear. Forty-six. Forty-three mortals and three Alfar driven from their bedrolls, their bodies gaunt and leached of color, their eyes unrelieved black.

Shaking with impotent rage, Mist returned to the warehouse, and she and Odin began again. He passed by the circles of Mist's magic without pause, and this time there was no incident to interrupt his work.

When he returned to his physical body, he was smiling in a way that chilled Mist to the core.

"It is done," he said. "I have found him."

Arrangements were made quickly. It was obvious that Odin could no longer maintain his invisibility among the troops he chose to accompany him, so he summoned eight of his hidden fighters . . . the Einherjar he had been so reluctant to waste on "minor skirmishes." Mist was grateful that she didn't recognize any of them from her years in Asgard, especially the warriors she'd whisked away from mortal battlefields centuries ago.

Unable to think of any way to delay Odin further, Mist braced herself for the worst. But as soon as she, Odin, and his guard reached the deserted crack house in the mission, Mist realized that the Allfather had made a rather crucial mistake.

Danny and Sleipnir were there, together. But they weren't alone.

For a handful of seconds, Mist shared the advantage of Odin's concealing spell and caught a glimpse of a strange tableau, frozen as if in the flash of a camera. Sleipnir was tied up at one side of the filthy room; Ryan was trussed like an underfed turkey on the other side; and Dainn, his hand resting lightly on Ryan's shoulder, watched Loki speak urgently to Danny beside a sagging couch in the center of the stained and littered floor.

A dozen thoughts flashed through Mist's mind in those few seconds: who had found Danny and Sleipnir first, Dainn or Loki? What had happened to Fenrir? How had Ryan gotten himself mixed up in this Nornsforsaken mess? And why in Hel wasn't Danny doing anything to get himself, his father, and the horse out of this place?

All eyes, even Sleipnir's, snapped to Mist as she moved forward, breaking the spell. Dainn met her gaze, his eyes filled with misery, anger, and shame. She understood what he was trying to tell her; he wasn't with Loki willingly, but Ryan's situation had tied his hands.

Loki's face betrayed genuine shock, and she realized that he hadn't expected to be found here. She gripped Kettlingr's sheath, a profound hatred seething in her gut.

"Welcome, Freya's daughter," Loki said, rising quickly as Danny broke away to huddle beneath Sleipnir's massive forelegs. "What an unexpected pleasure. May I offer my congra—"

He broke off as Odin made his grand entrance, clad in a literally gleaming shirt of mail, Gungnir in hand and his Einherjar behind him. He paused to stare at Loki in surprise, which quickly turned to calculation.

"Slanderer," he said. "Did you really think to stop me with a few hundred of Hel's minions?"

This time, Loki did a better job of hiding his consternation. "Allfather," he said with a very slight bow. "How I have missed our little chats."

"You will miss them even more when you are dead," Odin said.

"I shall regret not sharing the paradise you will create out of this world," Loki said. "How many of Midgard's people must die to make it suitable for the All-father?"

Mist wondered if Odin would throw caution to the winds and attack Loki here and now, when the enemy was alone and vulnerable. Loki was clearly preparing to repel a magical assault. But Odin seemed to dismiss his enemy as he would a yapping mongrel. His gaze swept over Dainn and Ryan and came to rest on Sleipnir, who tossed his head and snorted.

"Come, my pretty one," he said, holding out his free hand.

The horse danced away on his eight legs, and Danny, who had been staring at Odin with wide, fearful eyes, clutched at the trailing ends of the horse's mane and retreated with him.

"Ah," Odin said. "And here is the child. Do you remember me, boy?"

Mist started. Odin *had* seen Danny before. Loki's eyes narrowed.

"I don't think my sons wish to see *you* at the moment," he said with a little too much nonchalance, his eyes darting back and forth between Odin and Mist. "They are engaged in a private conference."

"It is not honorable to teach your children to ignore your guests," Odin said, hooking his thumbs in his wide leather belt. "But Mist assures me that you turned this boy against her and my other servants, and that he is innocent of your evil." He smiled through his beard. "She also suggests that you may have some affection for the child. Now you have the chance to spare him the fate that will befall the children of Angrboda."

"Your arrogance outpaces your wisdom, Lord of Gallows," Loki hissed.

Odin's lid dropped over his eye in an expression of boredom, and he looked at Dainn. "How did this treacherous mongrel come to be here?"

Dainn stepped away from Ryan, head lowered and eyes dark with hatred. Loki spoke before Dainn could open his mouth.

"I took him from *her,*" he said with a poisonous glance at Mist. "Or didn't you know he was Mist's prisoner?"

"Oh, I knew," Odin said, neatly disabusing Mist of her hope that he had been unaware of Dainn's presence in camp. "Do you expect me to believe that *you* set him free?"

"No," Dainn said quickly. "I escaped myse—"

"You do not guard your resources adequately," Loki said, interrupting Dainn and letting Mist off the hook for reasons she couldn't fathom. "Or perhaps you are simply too arrogant to value them. I knew the elf could find my son, since he and Danny became fast friends while he lodged with me."

"Fast friends," Odin said, as if he found the notion amusing. "Perhaps the boy's *friend* can save his own life by convincing your son to return my mount. I would be reluctant to harm the child."

"You will never touch—" Dainn began.

"Dainn cannot help you," Loki said, talking over him again. "The Steed is no longer yours, Murderer of Children."

Mist knew that Loki was referring to the Aesir's killing of his own Jotunn son, Narfi, in Asgard. The taunt was effective. Odin advanced on Loki, Gungnir raised.

Sleipnir reared, thrashing the air with his forehooves. Dainn started toward Danny, paused, and looked back at Ryan with eloquent distress.

"All-father," Mist said, stepping in front of Odin, "there will be time enough to kill the Slanderer, and make him suffer before he dies."

A heavy hand struck out at her shoulder. The blow was painful, but Mist had achieved her purpose. Odin stopped.

"Watch Laufeyson," he said coldly. He stared at Dainn. "You. Bring the horse to me, or I shall kill you and take the boy."

"No," Dainn said.

"*No,*" Mist said at the same moment.

Odin looked down at her, brow furrowed. "No?"

"Do you think I am incapable of defending my own?" Loki snarled. He raised his hands, and fire danced at the tips of his fingers. Odin bared his teeth, the muscles of his arms bunching to lift Gungnir again.

"Are you ready for war?" Mist said, looking from god to trickster and back again. "Here and now, in such a place, without your armies behind you, or any hope of glory?"

Loki scowled, but Odin's laugh nearly knocked her out of her boots.

"My Mist," he said. "I would not wish to disappoint you." He smiled at Loki. "You are fortunate to have such a champion," he said with heavy irony, "though I suspect it is not you she wishes to defend." His gaze fell on Dainn. "Why, I wonder, when you would have betrayed her to Freya?"

Defiance flared in Dainn's eyes. "I am not what I was, All-father."

No, Mist thought, he was not. Odin had cursed him, Freya and Loki had used him, and the beast had stolen his will again and again. But his loyalties were as clear as his dislike of Odin, and Mist realized that he'd reached the limits of what he could or would endure without taking a very foolish risk.

She knew of only one way to reach him.

Convince Danny to let Sleipnir go to Odin, she said, projecting her thoughts into his mind.

Dainn blinked and glanced from Loki to the All-father. *Can you protect Danny and Ryan from Odin?* he asked bluntly.

I will, she promised. *There is no other way for this to end without violence.*

She drew a mental image of Dainn giving way to the beast and attacking Odin. Dainn grimaced and released his breath in a sharp burst of air. He started toward Danny and Sleipnir.

Loki spun around, ran to Ryan, and dragged the young man to his feet. He held a dagger to Ryan's throat. Mist lunged toward them, but she stopped when Loki nicked Ryan's neck with the blade.

"Help Odin, and you know what happens to this mortal," Loki said.

"Don't . . . listen," Ryan said, his Adam's apple bobbing against the dagger's edge. "You have to live . . . for all of us."

"A prophecy?" Loki asked, grinning at Dainn. "How trustworthy is your seer?"

Mist moved as if she were going after Sleipnir, but at the last moment she pivoted and went straight at Loki. Laufeyson shoved Ryan away and moved to parry Kettlingr, a slender silver sword of ice in his hand. As their blades clashed, Odin advanced on Sleipnir.

Mist was too busy defending herself to see what happened immediately afterward. She heard Sleipnir's defiant squeal and a wail of protest from Danny, then caught a glimpse of Dainn streaking toward his son.

A moment later Dainn was pulling Danny away from Sleipnir, who was unable to escape Odin's iron grip on his jaw. Odin's Einherjar formed a cordon around horse and god. Loki broke free and began to chant, fire encircling the green of his irises.

The air turned cold enough to deaden Mist's fingers, and she almost lost her grip on Kettlingr. Loki cast a net of ice-rope at Dainn, who raised his hand and shattered it with a touch. Magical energy burst around him, gone as soon as it appeared. He ran to Ryan, shifted Danny onto his shoulder, and began to tear at the young man's bonds.

Take Ryan and go! Mist told him.

Dainn stopped with the rope still in his hands, his face a mask of concentration. Mist could feel some interior struggle going on between him and his son, and another within Dainn himself. Danny didn't want to leave Sleipnir, and Dainn didn't want to leave *her*.

Paralyzed by doubt, Mist sheathed Kettlingr and glanced at Odin. Sleipnir's eyes were glassy, his skin twitching as if he were being bitten by clouds of flies. Odin's expression was stuck somewhere between bewildered and dumbfounded.

"All-father?" Mist said.

He didn't so much as glance in her direction. It came to her that he was locked in some kind of spell . . . and *not* one of Loki's making.

But Loki had not been idle. Every one of the Einherjar was trapped in a shell of ice.

"Shall we cry truce," Loki said, flexing his fingers, "or shall I kill Odin while he is unable to defend himself?"

Mist felt the Eitr gathering around her. "I don't need Odin's warriors to stop you, Scar-lip," she said.

"Why should you try to stop me?" Loki asked. "He'll kill Dainn, and undoubtedly our son as well."

"He has what he wants. You let Danny, Dainn, and Ryan go, and I won't stop you from running."

"You've become much better at bluffing," Loki said, "but whatever you may have gained from Freya's death, you are still not my equal."

"Don't test her," Dainn said. He pressed Danny's face into his shoulder. "You have no idea what she may unleash."

"And *she*," Loki said, "has no idea—"

Before he could finish, Mist called on the Eitr and reached into the floor under Loki's feet, splintering wood and shattering concrete. She reshaped both into manacles that closed around Loki's ankles, locking him in place.

While he cursed and struggled, Mist strode up to Dainn and touched his cheek. His skin felt hot, and her inner senses recognized a change in him she couldn't identify or define, a current of energy both strange and familiar.

Like the Eitr. And the beast. Like both, and neither.

"Listen to me," she said, searching his eyes. "Take Danny and Ryan while you still have the chance."

"And what will become of you if Odin realizes you let us escape?" Dainn asked softly, gripping her free hand.

"Dainn is right," Loki said, kicking one foot free of the floor. "If you fail Odin in even the smallest matter, he will make you suffer for it."

Mist burst into a laugh. "Go on, Slanderer. By all means, try to convince me."

"You have to be together," Ryan said.

They all turned to stare at him. His eyes were as unseeing as Odin's.

"Who?" Loki asked Ryan, freeing his other foot. "You're not very specific for a seer."

"Brother," Danny sniffled, quiet in Dainn's arms.

"*You*," Ryan said, blindly turning his head from Dainn's face to Loki's and then Mist's. "Many as one."

"Well, that's a good deal of help, isn't it?" Loki said. "Perhaps we should march away, arm in arm, one happy family, and make our own little world."

"I'm only interested in a world without *you*," Mist said. The Eitr rose again, hot and murky, clouding her thoughts and filling her skull with thunder. The walls began to shake, the decrepit furniture to rattle.

"No," Ryan moaned. Danny whimpered.

"Mist," Dainn said. His fingers tightened on hers, reminding her how strong he had always been. "I feel what is in you now. Remember the Lady of Darkness. Remember the poison."

"I stopped Hel with light, not darkness," she said, struggling to focus on his face.

"It can change between one moment and the next." He stroked her knuckles with his thumb, his voice almost hypnotic. "I *know*, Mist. This is not the way."

Loki chuckled. "Don't discourage her, Dainn. Perhaps she'll bring the walls down around the All-father's ears."

"And kill everyone else in the room," Dainn said, holding her gaze. "She can take this entire building apart, if she chooses."

"At least give this poor condemned prisoner a last chance to speak," Loki said.

The conversation seemed to come from far away, but Mist heard enough of it to grasp the danger. She squeezed Dainn's hand as if he were her sole anchor in a vicious hurricane and called back the Eitr.

Immediately the room stopped shaking. Mist released Dainn and turned toward Loki. "I'll hear no more of your lies, Slanderer," she said.

Dainn wrapped his arms around Danny, the pulse beating fast in his throat. "For Danny's sake," he said to Loki, "go while you still can."

"I think you'll want to hear me out," Loki said, raising his hands in an exaggerated gesture of surrender. "We haven't much time."

"You mean *you* haven't," Mist said, glancing toward Odin's guards. The ice encasing them was beginning to melt. "I won't betray the All-father for your sake."

"Listen to him, Mist," Ryan said, shaking off the loose ropes. "Please."

Ryan seemed himself again, and Mist couldn't dismiss the plea in his voice. If he'd *seen* something important . . .

"Talk fast," she said to Loki.

"In private."

"Loki—" Dainn began.

"Watch Odin," Mist told Dainn. "If he starts to wake . . ."

Dainn nodded, and she jerked her head toward the far corner of the room. Loki followed her.

"You've got as long as it takes for that ice to melt," she said, gesturing toward the guards.

"Are you finished with threats, or will you listen?" Loki asked.

"Your daughter killed forty-six of my warriors. Just give me one more reason to—"

"Do you know why Danny fled with Sleipnir?" he interrupted.

The question took her off guard. "He wanted to get the Hel away from you," she said.

"Not at all. He wanted to get away from Dainn, and Odin's mount wanted to get away from Odin."

"You'll have to do better than that. Odin wasn't . . . Sleipnir had no contact with Odin after we brought him through the portal, and Danny isn't exactly trying to get away from Dainn right now."

"Danny is a trifle confused. But wouldn't you be, in his place?" His smile was more bitter than mocking. "He doesn't seem to like me, in spite of all the care I've lavished on him. He loves Dainn, but he's deathly afraid of the beast. Which is a perfectly understandable reaction, considering."

"I saw Danny in the garage. He stopped the beast. If Danny's afraid, it's because of you. As for Dainn, after what you've done to *him*—"

Loki sighed. "I see you've forgiven him. But we can discuss what I've done to Dainn another time, in as great detail as you wish. I'm sure he hasn't been quite so forthcoming."

Mist drew Kettlingr again and carefully placed the tip at the base of Loki's sternum. "One more word—"

Delicately pushing the sword away with the pad of his forefinger, Loki shook his head. "Let us return to Odin and Sleipnir," he said. "The All-father did tell you how he scattered pieces of his soul all over Midgard?"

"How did you—"

"Danny told me, right after Dainn and I found him and the horse. You see, Sleipnir knows what will be taken from him, and as he has become far more than he was before Odin gifted him with a portion of his divine spirit, he isn't eager to become a slightly-above-average horse again."

25

Loki's claim confused Mist so much that she had to take a few moments to digest his words. Odin had never said anything about hurting Sleipnir when he took back that portion of his soul.

"How could one of *your* children be average?" she asked bitingly.

"Sleipnir's father was an above-ordinary horse, not a goddess or giantess. Now the Slipper possesses a true soul of his own. Losing it to Odin will be the same as if Danny were to lose all ability to communicate with the world, including his father."

"I'm sorry for Sleipnir," Mist said, meaning it, "but I won't—"

"Danny is trying to protect Sleipnir," Loki said. "Can't you see that he's doing it even as we speak?"

Mist turned to stare at Odin. He and Sleipnir were still locked in some kind of stasis. She looked at Danny, unusually quiet in Dainn's arms. His face was screwed up with intense concentration, and she felt his power even though she understood neither its source nor its purpose.

"I do not know what Danny is doing to help his brother," Loki said, reading her expression, "but I'm quite certain even he can't keep it up forever. Odin will destroy him when he finds out who has interfered with his high purpose."

Suddenly Mist's lungs couldn't seem to hold enough air. "I sent Dainn to find Danny and get him away. They can still—"

"Believe it or not, I know what it is like to be torn apart by conflicting loyalties. But you should have all the facts. You must realize that Danny is not the only one in danger. As Loki explained, Mist found herself fighting harder and harder to draw a full breath. And when he was finished, she couldn't breathe at all."

"You're wrong," she said. "Odin would never commit genocide against mankind to remake Midgard."

"Wouldn't he? Where is that green, fertile land the first prophecy promised? Among these steel buildings and dirty streets, befouled by humankind?"

"I don't believe you."

"Odin is and always was a tyrant, and he will give no more thought to the lives of your mortals than he would to a hill of ants."

"He has favored many mortals in his time," Mist protested. "He honors Thor most among all his children, and Thor is the protector of Midgard. They will—"

"They respected your mortals in the old days," Loki said. "But nothing is as it was."

"You speak of ants, but mortals are less than insects to you. You'll let them devour each other, and set Hel to rule over a world of corpses."

"How many times have we discussed this?" Loki asked. "I will give mortals the ultimate freedom."

"You'll destroy all law and let the criminals and those who feed off the weak and helpless have their way. The corrupt and powerful will rule without any check on their greed and cruelty."

"At least the strong will survive, and I will honor them."

Mist spat at Loki's feet. "You honor no one but yourself."

"Neither does Odin, but you're too blind to see it. Just as you were blind with Freya."

His words were like a fist to the jaw. "I won't stop Dainn from going with you," she said. "But I—"

"Mist!"

Odin's voice was strangely thin, and she as she turned, he began to fall. Four of his guards, free of Loki's spell, caught him before he hit the ground. He thrust them away and stood with his feet braced apart, fury burning away the fog in his eye.

"Loki," he shouted. "What have you done to my mount?"

"He thinks *you* stopped him," Mist said to Loki, "and I'm going to give him every reason to believe it." She strode toward Odin, and the All-father roared Laufeyson's name again.

As light on his feet as a dancing flame, Loki sprinted toward Dainn. Dainn let Danny slide down to his feet and raised his hands, chanting in some language she had never heard in her life.

Loki skidded to a stop as if he had run into an invisible barrier. Odin lifted Gungnir, his face red and his body shaking. He took aim.

"Remember, Mist!" Loki cried. He ran lightly to Ryan, a knife in his hand, and slit the young man's throat. Gungnir hurtled toward him, and all at once there was a fly where Loki had been. It shot upward just as the Spear's tip penetrated the wall, and a tiny fragment of one nearly transparent wing drifted to the ground. Odin's Einherjar, dripping wet, found no enemy to fight.

Dainn pushed Danny into Mist's arms and ran to Ryan, cradling him as he collapsed. The red line at his neck had begun to bleed profusely. Dainn clamped his hand over Ryan's throat and closed his eyes.

Clasping Danny tightly to her chest, Mist tried to keep her head. Time slowed to a crawl. Once again Dainn spoke the strange language, the words she didn't understand. Magic scented the air, tasting of the Eitr and yet subtly different because it wasn't hers.

It came from Dainn. And as she watched, the blood pumping from Ryan's wound slowed, trickling sluggishly from between Dainn's fingers, and then stopped.

Panting heavily, Dainn eased Ryan to the floor. He removed his hands. There was a faint scar where Ryan's wound had been. The young man was unconscious and his skin was pale, but his breathing was steady.

"Dainn," Mist whispered.

He looked up, and smiled. For her. "He will be all right," he said, his voice rough with exhaustion.

For a handful of seconds there was no Odin, no Einherjar, no Sleipnir, no fate of the world hanging in the balance. She and Dainn gazed at each other, bound by their relief and their astonishment. And feelings . . . so many more than she could ever . . .

Danny's body went limp in her arms. She shifted him and looked into his face. He wasn't breathing.

"Dainn!" she cried.

He stumbled to her side and took Danny from her. "He's empty," Dainn whispered, and put his mouth over Danny's, sharing his breath and singing without words or voice.

Danny jerked awake, eyes wide and frightened. "Papa?" he whispered.

Taking Danny's little face between his hands, Dainn kissed Danny's forehead and both soft cheeks. Mist was drawn in, as if she had been part of the miracle, part of father and son. Amid the fear and confusion was a sense of wholeness she had felt only a few times in her life.

But she had no opportunity to make sense of what had happened. Suddenly Odin was there, and Dainn had carried Danny a safe distance away, leaving Mist as chilled as if Loki had encased *her* in ice.

There was no chance for Dainn to get away now.

"So he is a healer as well as a traitor," Odin said to Mist, staring balefully at Dainn. "He may still be of use to us. And since you failed to stop Loki, my Valkyrie, you will personally see to Sleipnir." He glanced at his warriors. "Einherjar, take the elf and the mortal."

Sleipnir's skin was still twitching, but he had begun to move again, jerking his head and flaring his nostrils. Danny began to squirm in Dainn's arms, but Dainn spoke to him softly, and he subsided. Two of Odin's soldiers went to Ryan, who was just beginning to stir.

"Take care with him," Dainn said.

Odin raised his hand to strike. Dainn stared at him, and he lowered his hand before Mist could intervene.

"You have no voice here," Odin spat. He nodded to the Einherjar, who closed around Dainn. Dainn met Mist's gaze and inclined his head.

We will survive.

Sleipnir was docile when Mist looped a piece of rope around his neck and led him from the building, but he refused to go anywhere near Odin. Mist was careful to keep herself and the horse between the All-father and Dainn.

For now, it was the best protection she could give him.

◑◐

At noon the next day, Dainn was confined in his cell, Ryan was resting in the infirmary, and Sleipnir was housed in a makeshift stall in one of the warehouses—with Danny, because the Steed was unmanageable in his absence. Mist had finally informed Rota and Hild about Danny and his origins, hoping for their acceptance. Fortunately, they'd both dealt with the revelation very well, and promised to help keep an eye on him.

Meanwhile, Odin—still invisible to most of the camp, Alfar and humans alike—brooded in Mist's confiscated bedroom while carpenters, electricians, and roofers swarmed to remodel the small warehouse he had chosen as his "hall."

The sun had managed to squeeze out from among the clouds, but Mist knew it wouldn't last. The weather was an omen, just as it had been last year and for the better part of this one, with temperatures more fit for Siberia than San Francisco.

Ironically, it almost felt like spring when Mist and Captain Taylor made a complete tour of the camp, trying to quiet the rumors circulating among the recruits who hadn't directly observed the previous night's massacre by Hel and her minions. Mist took more time with the survivors, of whom there were few enough. There wasn't much she could do to help them.

"You can't do everything," Taylor reminded her as he pushed a cup of strong coffee into her hands. "There are hundreds of recruits. You can't see every one of them in person."

Mist knew he was right, but his advice wasn't of much comfort. The image of Hel's victims wouldn't leave her mind, and she was haunted by the idea that every one of them had gone to the goddess of death, swelling her ranks by nearly four dozen more "tenants."

The last thing she wanted to do now was send more of her people into Hel's waiting arms. Still, she knew that Taylor and the other instructors were doing everything they could to keep that from happening. Troops were drilling constantly, more and more of them every day as Taylor and his lieutenants tested and passed new recruits. Some were already fighters . . . soldiers from wars as recent as Afghanistan and as far back as Vietnam. Good men and women, the captain said.

But they were in the minority. Most of the newcomers needed at least several weeks of training before they'd be ready for battle, and some would never be ready at all. Mist had quietly disregarded Odin's instructions and sent the weakest away.

And that wasn't the only area where she found herself in conflict with Odin's wishes. While Odin's Einherjar guarded Sleipnir and Dainn, Mist had her own people watching the watchers. Odin didn't attempt to interrogate Dainn or Danny, however, and he didn't approach Sleipnir.

That left Mist with a little time to think once her rounds were finished. She knew better than to try to see Dainn when Odin's warriors were observing every move he made in his cell, so she had no way of finding out what had been going on in his mind when he'd healed Ryan, or why Danny had become ill immediately afterward. And Ryan wasn't in any shape to elaborate on his most recent "prophecy."

Only one other person might understand the things that were bothering her, and she didn't particularly want to see him. But he was an elf like Dainn, and so, at the end of the day, she went to find Konur.

He was inspecting his Alfar troops, calling out quiet commands as they practiced their hand-to-hand combat and knife-work. Mist had learned enough about elves to know that they detested war in all its forms, fought only with magic when they were compelled to make war, and considered the use of weapons to be barbaric. But they'd learned to set aside their scruples quickly enough when they'd faced Loki's Jotunar, and realized that their use of magic was heavily restricted in the cities of Men.

Konur was already waiting for her before she got within shouting range, dark shadows under his eyes and deep lines bracketing his mouth.

"How may I serve you, Lady Mist?" he asked with a respectful bow.

"Why all the formality, Lord Konur?" she asked. "Don't you want me to call you 'Dad'?"

Konur averted his eyes. "I have made many mistakes—"

"I'm not here to hold your feet to the fire again," Mist said wearily. "I understand why you didn't tell me that I had two fathers, or that Freya created me to be her champion and then decided I'd make a good permanent residence. I know why you felt you had to stay out of the business between me and Freya for the sake of the other Alfar. If you'd taken sides, it could have provoked a conflict among your followers, and you were smart to realize that wouldn't help me."

"There were many who believed that Freya commanded our absolute loyalty," Konur said. "But I can assure you that it was no pleasure to know that my own child might be fighting for her life."

"At least you had 'faith' in me," Mist said, trying without success to swallow her lingering bitterness.

"Yes," Konur said, "for more reasons than you can imagine." He signaled for one of his lieutenants to take over and gestured for Mist to walk with him. "Let us go to my tent. There is still much I would tell you, if you will hear me."

"Actually, I was coming to you for advice."

"I am gratified."

"You're the one most likely to be able to answer my questions about Dainn."

"Ah. I still know far less about him than—"

"It's not anything personal." They reached his tent, and Konur lifted the flap for Mist to enter. "It has to do with several things that happened when we found Sleipnir."

"I have heard rumors," Konur said. He offered her wine, which she declined. "Even the Einherjar have been known to speak unwisely."

Mist was willing to bet that they hadn't gossiped about Odin's failure to claim Sleipnir. Like several of the officers in camp, Konur knew about Odin and his warriors, but even he wasn't aware of the soul-bits-in-the-Treasures business, and Mist hadn't been authorized to tell him.

Then again, she hadn't been authorized to do a lot of things.

"Did they mention that Loki slit Ryan's throat, and Dainn healed him?" she asked.

"Something to that effect." Konur gestured toward one of the two camp chairs and took the other. "I did not realize this was among his current skills."

His voice was dry, and Mist felt her anger rise. "It's not the first time he's healed Ryan," she said sharply. "Only last time, the beast was involved. Now . . ." She lowered her voice. "It came from somewhere else. He used spells I've never heard before."

"Elven spells?" Konur asked, his eyes alert.

"That's what I don't know. I'm not sure that even Dainn understood what he was saying at the time. He used a language I'm not familiar with, and it called up some powerful magic."

"Can you remember any of this language?"

"I'll try." She closed her eyes. "Tell me if any of this sounds familiar."

She repeated what she remembered of the words, and Konur reared back in astonishment.

"That is what he said?" he asked.

"That's what I heard, though I'm sure I got a lot of it wrong." She leaned toward Konur. "What is it?"

"A very ancient language," he said.

"I figured as much. Ancient Elvish?"

"Older." He rested his chin on his interlaced hands and frowned down at the carpet of grass that covered the broken asphalt. "Older than the coming of the first Runes. So old, in fact, that it is not even taught to our children, though a few survive who remember having learned some small part of it."

"But not you?"

Konur shook his head.

"Then why would Dainn know it?"

Konur looked up. "Dainn came to the Aesir's Homeworld from some other realm, and said he had been wandering for many years. We all assumed that he was one of the eldermost of Alfar, though not an Elder according to our customs."

"I know," Mist said, remembering all too clearly what Loki had told her. "But it isn't normal for your Elders to speak this forgotten language?"

"Not even among themselves."

"Then what are you getting at, Konur? Are you saying he's older than all the other Alfar?"

"I do not know." Konur rose and moved with agitated steps around the tent. "You say that he did not know what he was doing when he spoke these words?"

"That's how it seemed to me."

"Then asking him about it may do no good. I only wonder if it is true what some in Asgard said, that he had lost part of his memory."

Mist remembered when Dainn had admitted to her that he'd come to Asgard with no memory of where he'd originated. She was rapidly wading into waters well out of her depth. "I'm more concerned about what it means *now*," she said. "I'm afraid that Dainn is changing, and I don't know how or why."

"I am sorry," Konur said, obviously sincere in his regret. "I wish I could tell you more. The All-father is among the most ancient of beings, born soon after the creation of the world. It is possible that he may understand what I do not."

And I'm not about to share this with Odin, Mist thought.

"Thank you," Mist said, getting to her feet. "I'm sorry to have disturbed you."

"Wait," Konur said, stepping smoothly between her and the tent flap. "I would speak to you of the Eitr. It is important that you understand what it means now that you possess the power to wield it."

Mist stiffened. "How do you know about that?"

"I did not realize that you had access to a more ancient magic when we Alfar first arrived, but it became more and more apparent as

I continued to observe you. After what happened when you found Sleipnir, there can be no doubt of it." He cleared his throat. "When you told me what Dainn had said about your having two fathers, there was much more that I should have told you. Please, sit."

"I can hear what you have to say standing right here," she said, though her legs felt more than a little wobbly.

Konur, too, remained standing. "You know that both Loki and Freya had some access to the Eitr in Asgard, though it was not widely known at the time."

"I was told, yes."

"Freya occasionally spoke of it when she and I . . . when we knew each other in Asgard. I learned of Svardkell's part in Freya's scheme before the Dispersal, but I came to realize that he understood much more than I ever did. Freya's ability to control the Eitr, no matter how tenuous, led her to attempt something she had never done before, that none of the gods had ever considered."

"Let me guess," Mist said. "Blending magical genetics with the abilities of a Jotunn and an elf."

"No," Konur said softly. "It was not so simple. Svardkell and I were not your only fathers."

"What?"

"There were five."

Mist laughed and kept laughing until she realized that Konur was serious. She remembered what Odin had said: *I was aware that Freya attempted a spell at your conception that would give you the magic of all the races.* At the time, she hadn't known what he meant.

Now Konur had given her an explanation. One she could barely accept.

"Do I get to know who these fathers are?" she asked when she could speak again.

"One male of each race," Konur said, turning away so that she couldn't see his face. "Elf, Jotunn, dwarf, mortal, and god."

Mist wished she'd taken Konur's advice and sat down. Instead, she grabbed one of the tent poles and hung on. "Did she seduce them all at once, or one after another?"

"I knew nothing of the others, until I met Svardkell and we put certain facts together."

Mist swallowed. "Where are they?" she asked. "*Who* are they?"

"We of the Alfar's and Aesir's Shadow-Realms have never made contact with the Dwarven realm. We can only assume it exists in Ginnungagap, beyond our reach."

"And the god?"

"I do not know. The mortal, of course, would have died long ago." He sighed. "I did not intend to wait until after Freya's death to tell you."

Mist shrugged. "What's done is done. I suppose I'll find out who the god was once Odin brings the Aesir to Midgard. Or maybe not. I don't really care as long as it's not Thor. I never liked him. Baldr would have been a nice father, if he hadn't—" She broke off. "Loki's piss. Odin knows that Freya had plans for me in Asgard. I never found out if he knew I had more than one. But *this* . . ."

"Perhaps it would be better to wait before broaching the subject with him. He carries the fate of the world on his shoulders."

Yes, Mist thought, he carried that burden, and she'd been glad for it. In Asgard, he had been all that was noble and wise. But he was also ruthless, capable of great cruelty and harsh judgment.

"*Odin is and always was a tyrant,*" Loki had said, "*and he will give no more thought to the lives of your mortals than he would to a hill of ants.*"

"I don't know what to think anymore," Mist said, feeling light-headed. "I must be doing something very wrong."

Konur turned back to her and held out his arms. She fell into them, letting herself be weak for a few ragged breaths, and then pulled away.

"Thanks for being honest," she said. "I still don't understand, but at least I have a better idea of why I still haven't figured out who or what the Hel I am."

"There are answers, if you will but be patient."

"I can't begin to tell you how tired I am of being pa—"

"Mist." He gazed at her very seriously, and she knew he was about to say something important. "Remember this. We Alfar serve Odin as we once served Freya, but we serve you even above him."

Mist slipped from the tent before she lost all self-control, her heart clenched into a knot and hot anger pumping through her veins. She didn't want to be patient. In fact, at the moment what she wanted to do most was bang a few Jotunn skulls together, and to Hel with the consequences.

Without consulting Odin, she spoke with Vixen, the head of her spy network. The woman had been receiving an unusual number of tips about Loki's illegal operations from someone who didn't want to take credit for the information.

"It might be someone from the enemy camp," Vixen admitted, "but so far all the tips have been good, and we've shut down a number of sex trafficking rings and drug labs."

"That's good," Mist said, "because tonight we're taking out another one."

Once she'd chosen the target, Mist put out a call for fighters. She made clear that this was only an unofficial strike, a chance to test the waters following Loki's flight from the crack house.

She had more volunteers than she could handle, including nearly a dozen Alfar. She chose four of them and six mortals, experienced soldiers she wouldn't need to worry about as she would the newer recruits. Tennessee and Vixen were among them.

They reached the drug lab just after sunset. It was a professional operation, run by a powerful gang under the supervision of a Jotunn boss and three lesser frost giants. Mist and her fighters made it to the steps of the false storefront before the lookouts knew they were under attack.

Elves and mortal warriors fought beside Mist as she drove the guards through the door and into a room filled to the brim with lab equipment, chemicals, and stacks of clear packages. Someone inside had come up with the brilliant idea of tossing handfuls of the white powder into the air, but Mist's mortals had come prepared with masks, and the Alfar were unaffected.

The thuggish mortals who stood guard over the frightened workers put up a strong defense while the Jotunar prepared to attack, but the gang members still weren't completely accustomed to using bladed weapons instead of their usual semiautomatics. When the Jotunar finally joined in the fight, wielding clubs and axes as well as ice-magic, Mist countered with forge-magic to warp the metal tables, twist the rebar inside the walls, and turned the floor under the enemies' feet to hot slurry. She froze half of the chemistry equipment with her Jotunn magic while the Alfar danced around their opponents, bobbing and feinting and striking with fists, feet, and knives wherever they could. The mortal fighters, carrying heavier blades and axes, moved in where the elves left an opening.

It was nasty work, but Mist wasn't remotely interested in taking prisoners. Two of her mortal troops had fallen by the time they had taken out the Jotunar. At that point the room was like a meat locker, with frost coating every surface and the Jotunn bodies frozen to the walls with their own blood.

Mist paused to sing a protective spell over her fallen warriors, a Rune-chant she hoped would preserve their souls from being claimed by Hel. Afterward, they found the lab workers huddled in a room in the back. All of them wore cheap surgical face masks, eyes wide above the white fabric. Their brown skin was coated with the powder, and some were coughing.

"Surely *these* are not criminals," one of the elf-women said.

"She's right," Vixen said. "They're the victims here."

Mist stared at the cowering workers. Like so many of the poor and the recent immigrants, they had been exploited by men who had been emboldened by the mayor's cuts to legitimate law enforcement and his lax handling of organized crime. Some of these people were here because they couldn't get better jobs, even at minimum wage, and city officials and politicians certainly weren't trying to do anything about it.

Because this is exactly the way Loki wants it, Mist thought. Desperate people pushed to their limits. Another move in his game of chaos.

"It's all right," she said in Spanish. "We're not here to hurt you. You're free to leave." She repeated the words in Tagalog and Cantonese. Some of the workers edged toward the back door, others remained hunched against the wall, too beaten down to expect anything but abuse.

"No, Ramon!" a young woman shouted from the dark hallway running along the back of the building.

Mist swung around to face several young men led by a Latino youth with a scarred face and dark, angry eyes.

"You not supposed to be here," he said to Mist, his gaze taking in the Alfar and mortals around her. "No one's supposed to hit this place."

"Ramon!" the woman's voice repeated, and Gabi ran out from behind the men, throwing herself between Ramon and Mist.

"Gabi?" Mist asked in astonishment.

"Don't hurt him!" she begged, flinging her arms wide like a shield. "No one was supposed to come here! It was part of the deal, so that Ramon wouldn't get in trou—"

"What deal?" Mist asked. "Why are you here, Gabi?"

"Ramon works for Loki," Gabi said, gasping for breath. "He's been getting info from Loki's people and passing it to me. This place was his cover. Long as he kept making the drugs . . ." She turned to face Ramon. "Go! No one will tell, I promise!"

"You try to betray us, Gabriella?" Ramon asked, his voice heavy. "After all I done for you?"

"The anonymous tips," Vixen whispered. "But I didn't know about any deal!"

"He's my brother!" Gabi cried. "You have to let him go!"

"Shut up," Ramon spat. "If I don't fight, they kill me anyway." He nodded to his men, who drew knives and spread out. Every one of them looked prepared to die.

"Stand clear, Gabi," Mist ordered. "You," she said to Ramon, "you were trying to help us?"

Ramon laughed. "Not you, *gringa*. Gabi's *familia*."

Then he came straight at Mist.

26

Mist didn't want to hurt him. To the contrary: knowing he was Gabi's brother, and that both of them had secretly been working to get the allies information to use against the enemy, made her all the more determined to keep Ramon and his men alive.

But Ramon had decided otherwise. Maybe he was genuinely afraid of what would happen if Loki discovered that he was a traitor, or perhaps it was some code of honor Mist didn't understand. But he moved to kill, and she simply didn't think. The Eitr acted for her before she could even draw her sword, and flung Ramon and the others back like pins in a bowling alley. They crashed against the walls and into the floor, and when it was over, none of them was moving.

Gabi screamed and raced to Ramon. She put her hands to his throat, began to weep, and gripped the cross around her neck.

Mist ran to kneel at Gabi's side and felt Ramon's pulse. It was silent. She took Gabi's fisted hands in her own. They were barely warm.

Yesterday, Dainn had found a way to heal Ryan. Today, Gabi couldn't heal at all.

"I'm sorry," she said, sickened by what she had done. "You must believe that I didn't mean to hurt them."

"He wasn't a good guy," Gabi murmured, the tears running down her cheeks. "He hurt people. I tried to make him *help*. *I* wanted to help." She scraped at her face with her sleeve. "I can't heal no more. Ramon's dead. I messed up."

"Gabi," Mist said, "none of this is your fault." She saw the wild look in Gabi's eyes and thought quickly. "You've been away from camp," she said, "so you probably don't know that Ryan was taken hostage by Loki. He'll be anxious to see you."

"Is he all right?" Gabi asked, sniffing hard.

"Yes. You need to talk to him, show him you're all right." Mist called over her shoulder, "Tennessee, check on the others. Vixen, make sure the workers are okay."

As the two bikers hurried to obey, Mist helped Gabi to her feet. "Come home now," she said. "We'll make sure that Ramon's body is taken care of, too, however you want us to—"

"I have to go," Gabi said, jumping to her feet. "I have to tell *mi abuelita*."

"Gabi—"

The girl took off like a shot, bursting into a run down the hall. Vixen appeared beside Mist.

"Let her go," the biker said quietly. "I don't know what the hell just happened, but she lost a brother, even if he *was* a bad guy."

"I did this," Mist said, staring down at her hands.

"You're a warrior. Your body uses whatever tools it has to defend itself."

"And what if I turn it against the wrong person?"

"You won't," Vixen said. She laid her hand on Mist's shoulder. "Two of Ramon's men are still alive. We'll get the rest back to the—"

Tennessee nearly ran into them, his breath sawing in his throat. "I think you better come outside," he said. "It's Hel out there."

⌾

The second prophecy had said nothing about the child.

Odin sat on his throne in the room in his newly renovated hall, half-listening to the constant hum of voices and the clash of steel that had continued well into the night. He had already taken advantage of part of the prophecy by making the necessary preparations to take Midgard after the Last Battle, and at the same time, had fulfilled the promise that "many as one" would settle Midgard's fate by sending pieces of his soul to the Earth with his Valkyrie.

But the second prophecy had been far more vague than the first, which had predicted Ragnarok, the destruction of nearly all the gods including Odin, and the coming of a new paradise. Odin intended to create that paradise in Midgard, no matter what he had to do to achieve it.

Anna understood. She sat on a cushion beside him, ready to provide him with anything he should wish, as the Valkyrie had done in Valhalla when they were not riding over a mortal battlefield.

She was the one he could rely on, the one whose loyalty was absolute. Mist . . .

He shifted on the throne and frowned at the floor, covered with a rug he had been told was very fine but seemed little more than a scrap of cotton rag. Mist. He should be able to trust her absolutely . . . her above all others.

But her behavior since his awakening had roused many suspicions. First there was the elf's escape. Mist could easily have helped him. And then, when they had found Sleipnir, she had been far too protective of the traitor, discouraging Odin from killing him.

Afterward, Odin had been caught in a mind-numbing spell even as he attempted—and failed—to regain the most important part of his soul from his former mount, and neither he nor his guards had any memory of what had transpired for the next fourteen minutes.

At first, Odin had thought the spell was Loki's doing. But now he knew it had been the work of the creature who had summoned Hel for Loki.

The boy. Danny, whom Mist had cradled in her arms with all the tenderness of a mother. The child who held the Eitr in his little hands, when Odin could not even touch it.

It was amazing good fortune that Loki hadn't utilized his son's abilities to more devastating effect. But there was yet another factor Odin had never considered, and it was the most infuriating of all.

Dainn had used the Eitr. Odin had heard the voice, the most ancient tongue even he did not remember. He had watched Dainn heal the hostage of a mortal wound as easily as he might bind up a shallow scratch.

Father and son, both possessed of the magic of life itself. Both must be controlled. Both must be made to give up what was Odin's by right.

But first he must have Sleipnir.

"My lord?" Anna murmured.

Odin smiled. She always knew his moods, as she had known them when he'd been no more than a simple bird.

"I have a task for you," he said. "I have much work to do, many spells to prepare. You must wait outside the door and see to it that I am not disturbed, no matter what you may hear. Do you understand?"

"Yes, my lord."

He watched her go, wondering how far he might be driven to claim what was rightfully his.

It hardly mattered. In the end, he would take it, and neither life nor death would stand in his way.

◑◐

There were six dead mortals on the street outside the store. It was not a good neighborhood, and it was well after dark. Two of the dead were dealers, one an unfortunate vagrant, another a prostitute, and two of what Mist presumed to be johns. Every one of them had died the same way, and they all had the same staring eyes.

Mist knelt beside the prostitute. She was hardly more than a kid, in her early teens; her face was plastered with makeup, but she couldn't conceal the gauntness of her face or the thinness of her body under the short skirt and skimpy top.

She must have been freezing, Mist thought. She removed her jacket and covered the girl's face, trying to get a handle on her rage.

"Where is Hel?" Mist said, getting to her feet.

"*We* know," one of the elves said. "Follow."

They broke into a run. It took less than two minutes before Mist knew where they were going.

The Financial District should have been deserted on this cold night. The office buildings and high-rises were empty save for cleaning staff and a few overworked employees huddled at their desks behind lit windows. The restaurants, except for a few scattered clubs and bars, were closed.

But the district wasn't completely abandoned. There had been tourists who had wandered away from the nearly constant activity of Market Street, office workers heading for buses and home, inebriated clubbers scouting out their next drink, a dozen drug dealers and their customers, and a few scattered homeless people huddled in recessed doorways.

Some were still alive. Most of the survivors were kneeling on the pavement in a state of shock, half-dead themselves. Others were weeping. Mist's people scattered, doing what little they could.

"Most of them can't speak," Vixen said. "I've seen a lot of terrible deaths since all this started, but this beats them all."

Because it's Death herself we're facing, Mist thought. Hel's soldiers could have taken all of the mortals easily enough. She hadn't, and that meant that this was a warning.

No, not a warning. A taunt. A dare. *Come and find us, or more mortals die.*

Too soon. Odin still wasn't ready to lead a concerted attack against their enemy.

"We can't just call an ambulance," Tennessee said, joining Mist and Vixen. "They'll take one look at these people and there'll be cops and fire trucks and people thinking this is some kind of weird infectious disease. Someone's going to leak this for sure."

Mist beckoned to the others, who quickly gathered around her. The Alfar wore grim expressions, and few of the mortals could conceal their horror.

"I know what you're feeling," she said, working to keep her voice level and her face calm. "But this isn't the time for a reckless attack on an enemy we don't have the means to fight. I want all of you to go back to the drug lab and collect our fallen. Hide the bodies of the other mortals as best you can. I'll take care of them later. Once you're out of the area, call the police anonymously and tell them that there've been multiple casualties."

"You sound as if you're staying here," Tennessee said.

"I'm going to have to dispose of these bodies."

"You mean they'll just disappear," Vixen said. "Their families will never know what happened to them."

"It's that, or citywide panic," Mist said. "I'll keep their identification. After this is over, we'll find a way to get word to their relatives."

"And the living?" one of the elves asked.

"By the time the EMTs get here, they'll look like victims of a gang attack."

"You're not actually going to hurt them?" Vixen asked.

Mist gave her a hard look. "I won't touch them. Most of it will be for show."

"She does what she must," the elf said. "Let us go."

They left, slowly, one or two of them looking over their shoulders. Mist threw up a ward and went to work, the rage feeding her magic. When she finally set out after Hel, bloodied mortals with glamour-induced amnesia sat or lay on the sidewalk, and every trace of the dead was gone. The wailing of sirens drowned the roar of her pulse throbbing behind Mist's ears.

∂∘

Dainn leaped out of his cot, aware only that someone had entered the cell.

"Dainn Faith-breaker," Odin said. He stood near the door, the edges of his powerful body blurred, the faint outline of the door visible behind him.

The beast stirred. Dainn pushed it down. He could hate; he could long for the chance to kill Odin for lying to Mist, for threatening Danny, for what the All-father had done to *him*.

But the king of the Aesir still had Danny.

"You come very late," Dainn said coldly.

"You know why I am here," Odin said.

"No."

Odin laughed softly. "One might almost believe that you are still the inscrutable advisor I once permitted to stand by my throne and speak words of wisdom into my ear."

"I was never a traitor."

Odin leaned against the wall, becoming more solid as he relaxed. "You *were* a traitor, of sorts. You made the error of falling for Loki's tricks while Freya believed she was seducing me. I knew all along that they were conspiring against me."

"Not from the beginning," Dainn said, "or you would have done far worse to Loki than bind him beneath the serpent to suffer from its venom until the coming of Ragnarok. And Freya would never have escaped unscathed."

"What I did not know, you told me when you came to me to warn me of their schemes. And there was much I understood that you never did."

Dainn's heart pounded behind his ears. "Is it your intention to enlighten me, All-father?"

"Have you begun to remember?"

"Remember what?"

"The time before you came to Asgard. The magic you always claimed not to possess."

Suddenly Dainn grasped Odin's meaning. The All-father had seen Dainn's "new" ability to heal, heard spells chanted in a language he did not know. He had witnessed the use of magic Dainn still did not fully comprehend.

The ancient magic, pulling the Eitr into Dainn's body.

"I remember no such magic from a time before Asgard," Dainn said with desperate honesty. "I always had the magic of my people—"

"But this is not elven magic," Odin said, his teeth flashing through his beard. "For millennia I held the Eitr, but it was lost to me along with the spells to wield it. From the moment you came to Asgard, you burned with its light. I showed you great favor, stranger that you were, waiting for you to transmit your knowledge and power to me."

"You never asked for such knowledge," Dainn said. "*I* saw no light. How could I—"

"Why should I *ask*?" Odin snapped. "I gave you everything, and expected so little in return."

"I had nothing to give you."

"And yet you have access to the Eitr now, do you not?" Odin asked. "Where did it come from, Alfr? Have you always denied its presence, even to yourself?"

"If I had such abilities, you would have destroyed them when you cursed me with the beast."

"A beast you cannot control without my help."

"You would help me control the thing you created to punish me?" Dainn asked with a short laugh. "Perhaps I no longer require assistance."

"Even if you believe you have mastered it now, do you truly believe it will not escape again?"

"Are you suggesting that you will remove the curse?"

"I am the All-father. I can undo what I have done."

For a moment, Dainn was almost tempted. Tempted enough to believe that Odin might be telling the truth.

But the price would be too high. And as long as the All-father didn't know that Mist possessed the ancient magic, as well . . .

"You know the spells, the chants to obtain and control the Eitr," Odin said, his words almost wheedling. "You will teach them to me."

"I do not *control* the Eitr," Dainn said quietly, praying that Odin would accept the half-truth. "If I drew upon it, I did so in extremity, not because of any discipline or true understanding. What I do not understand, I cannot teach."

"If adversity inspires you, it can easily be arranged. Your son—" Odin laughed. "Yes, I know he is your son, Faith-breaker. As I know that he, too, has the use of the Eitr."

Nearly choking on the bile that rose into his throat, Dainn clenched his teeth. "You are mistaken," he said.

"He has placed a spell on Sleipnir to bar my access to my own soul, and my patience is not without limit."

Dainn suppressed a shiver. From the moment Danny had fallen

into a state so near death, he had been certain that the boy's desire to protect Sleipnir had greatly weakened him. The fact that Dainn had been able to revive his son was of little comfort, given that Danny obviously maintained the spell even now.

Through Rota, Mist had assured him that Danny would be closely watched—as yet, most of the allies, elf and human, knew only that an unknown boy had been brought into camp—and that any sign of illness would be dealt with immediately. Dainn never doubted that she would do almost anything to save Danny. But as long as Danny continued to protect Sleipnir from Odin, he was as much at risk as if Odin directly threatened his life.

He will have Sleipnir's soul by any means necessary, Dainn thought.

But he would *not* have Danny.

"You want me to convince Danny to release the spell," Dainn said.

"Convince or compel, yes. But then you and I shall begin working together, as Mist and I did when we sought Sleipnir. You will let me into *your* soul, Faith-breaker, and show me what you claim you cannot teach."

Shadows closed in around Dainn, exuding a thousand tiny needles that stabbed through his clothing into every raw nerve. His palm flared with pain.

"You do not know what you ask," he rasped. "You cannot take the Eitr by force."

"But you will *give* it to me. If saving your son is not enough motivation, you may also think of Mist. Or are you prepared to sacrifice her to your own arrogance?"

Blood began to drip sluggishly from between Dainn's curled fingers. "Why should Mist suffer because of me?" he asked.

"Her loyalties are divided. She has some affection for you, and for your son. I can easily do without her if she—"

"But you cannot," Dainn said. "You will fall without her at your side."

Odin strode up to him, seizing his wrist. "The oath you swore with Loki," he said, Dainn's blood running over his hand. "Why does it bleed?" He twisted Dainn's arm. "What do you *see*?"

Dainn bared his teeth, and the beast stirred under his skin. Odin jerked back, scraping his bloody hands across his pants. Struggling against his darker half, Dainn calmed his emotions and let the beast fade away.

"I will ask Danny to release Sleipnir," he said. "But I warn you. The Eitr can destroy as well as heal, and it will not be compelled. Take great care, Odin All-father."

"I suggest you follow your own advice, Faith-breaker."

Making a great deal of noise about it, Odin stomped out of the cell. Distantly, Dainn heard the All-father's hoarse commands. He exhaled slowly.

The door to the cell was open.

The Alfar guards ignored him when he walked out, wrapping a scrap of one of his clean shirts around his hand. He made his way to the stable, his senses taking in everything around him, gathering information he might need when he went to warn Mist. The shadow of the Eitr nipped at his heels like a beast still hungry for his blood.

Sleipnir laid his ears back and pawed the ground when Dainn opened the stall door. Danny was already on his feet. He seemed healthy and alert, bearing no mark of his trauma.

"Danny," Dainn said, his voice cracking.

"Papa," Danny said. There was wariness in the word, as if he already suspected why Dainn had come.

And why should he not, when Dainn had tried to do it before?

"I'm sorry, Danny," Dainn said, crouching just out of range of Sleipnir's hooves. "You have to let Sleipnir go."

Grabbing a handful of Sleipnir's long mane, Danny shook his head. "No," he said.

Dainn looked up at the horse. "I know you understand me," he said. "You have permitted Danny to aid you, at some cost to him. If you do not give yourself to Odin, you will only postpone what must be, and surrender the life of the one who protects you."

Nostrils flared wide and ears twitched forward and back. Sleipnir understood him well enough.

"I beg you not to fight it," Dainn said. "I beg you to save my son."

Sleipnir lowered his head, his muzzle nearly touching the ground. It was a gesture of agreement, of sorrow, of defeat.

"No, Slippy!" Danny said.

The horse dropped to his knees and rolled onto his side. Danny draped himself over Sleipnir's barrel. Dainn felt a sense of release, as if a boat had come unmoored from a pier. Fresh blood soaked through his bandage and into his sleeve.

"Danny," he said, hiding his hand behind his back.

With strange, almost jerky movements, Danny straightened. He lifted his head to meet Dainn's eyes.

"You've made a mistake," he said. "You've given Odin everything, and left yourself with nothing."

"Loki," Dainn said. He scrambled to his feet. "Where is my son?"

"Here." Loki reached behind his back and pulled Danny out from behind him. The two were identical in every possible way, but Danny was limp, as if lost in a deep sleep.

Dainn considered for less than a second. "Can you take him with you, now?"

Loki's mocking expression was a travesty on Danny's face. "You'll give him back to me?"

"To save him, yes."

"And hand me the victory." He laughed. "I knew this would come, if I remained patient. You were never anything but transparent, my Dainn."

"*Loki*," Odin's voice rumbled from the doorway. "I did not believe you had the courage to come here without Hel's skirts to shield you."

The All-father's voice sounded strangely uninflected, almost mechanical. But Loki responded before Dainn could get between him and Odin.

"You have no hope of killing me without Sleipnir," Loki said, "Danny still protects him."

"No," Dainn said, edging closer to the unnatural twins. "Sleipnir is yours, All-father. Laufeyson, take Danny and go."

"I never expected anything but treachery from you, Faith-breaker," Odin said. He sketched Rune-staves in the air with callused fingers:

Merkstaves, Wunjo reversed, joy turned to *berserkr* rage and frenzy. "Again, I curse you."

Dainn endured a moment of terror, and then the beast took him. His body expanded as if it would fill the entire room, heavy black pelt covering taut muscle, claws and teeth like daggers.

The sacrifice. The fading, rational part of Dainn understood, then. The beast considered Danny a threat to his existence. Danny could stop him, control him, prevent him from becoming what he believed he was destined to be. He was the darkness seeking to smother the light.

There was no room for both boy and beast in Dainn's soul. Losing the last of his rationality, he sprang at Danny. At the last moment he turned and bore Loki to the ground, seizing the false child's neck in his jaws and shaking until it snapped. Sleipnir screamed, rolling to his feet, and lashed out at the beast, kicking him hard in the side. The beast caught Loki's foot and dragged the godling with him to the corner, half-whimpering, half-snarling as he stared up into the eyes of the All-father.

But Odin made no move toward the beast and his slaughtered prey. His pale eye stared into the stall, where the horse whinnied over and over again like a weeping mother.

Dainn's consciousness flared inside the beast's skin. He felt the Eitr eating its way through his misshapen body, the taint of poison that fed the evil within it.

But the space between the beast's paws was empty. No blood, no broken body. Loki was gone. A boy lay on the mat a dozen feet away, his small form sprawled and his lifeless arm stretched as if he were reaching for something he would never touch.

Acting without thought, the beast leaped up and flung himself at Odin. He struck the wall hard where the All-father had stood an instant before and slid to the floor, the air knocked out of his lungs.

When he opened his eyes, the beast had left him, and Danny . . .

Crawling on hands and knees, Dainn found his way across the floor, unable to make a sound. He reached Danny and touched the still-warm body with a bloody hand.

There was no other sign of injury on the boy, no broken bones, no torn flesh. Yet he was as dead as if the beast had torn him apart.

I killed him.

Dainn pressed his face to the mat, listening to the horse kicking at the wall until it began to crack. He clung to Danny's ankle, struggling to find his voice. One blow from those iron hooves . . .

He lifted his head. The little body didn't move, but something remained within it, something very small. A mote of life Dainn could almost feel passing from Danny into himself.

And then it was no more.

Dainn pulled Danny into his arms, cradling his son and crooning words he didn't understand. Sleipnir slumped against the wall, his legs buckling, and stretched his neck toward Danny.

"He's gone," Dainn said, stroking Danny's hair away from his forehead. "He's gone."

Sleipnir wept.

27

Mist knew that Hel could outrun her. She knew that the goddess of death could simply disappear if she wished. Mist had already seen it happen.

It was not so easy for the dead.

At least a hundred loped ahead of her toward North Beach, abandoned by their mistress, given physical form and the prospect of a permanent extinction. Mist might have pitied them, knowing that many had probably been forced to obey, and that others, like Geir, were rebelling.

But there was no way for her to separate the good from the evil, and she could only hope that Geir and his resistance had been able to do it for her.

And hope that *she* could save the living who got in the way of her enemies.

Running as swiftly and lightly as an elf, Mist had almost caught up with the stragglers when clawed fingers seized her heart, stopping its beat and robbing her of breath. She fell to her knees, overwhelming grief and denial drowning out the horror that lay just ahead of her.

Someone had died. Someone close to her, close to her heart and yet beyond her reach.

No. Light and smoke seemed to fill her skull, and she felt the burning elation of the Eitr, life-giving and lethal, stretching across the city from the allies' camp. Dainn's mind was crying out in that ancient tongue, and Danny . . .

Neither dead nor alive, but poised somewhere in the middle, caught in the Eitr like a fly in amber. But Dainn grieved as if he believed that Danny was gone, his emotion carried to her along invisible currents that linked her mind and his.

Go to him, her heart insisted. The Eitr insisted. But Mist pushed against the pavement with the palms of her hands, fighting the pressure to return to camp, filling her mind with images of the dying only she might save.

Blinded by tears, Mist burst into a run. Hel's minions were rushing past the corner of Kearny and Columbus Avenues, flowing like smoke over the pedestrians wandering amongst lounges, restaurants, and clubs that beckoned with colorful signs, fancy drinks, and late hours.

Mist felt the fear before she heard the cries of shock and horror. Several people had already died by the time she reached Columbus, and there were dozens of unsuspecting mortals just ahead of the deadly wave. Hel floated behind her servants, observing without participating.

There was no sign of law enforcement of any kind, but Mist knew that emergency personnel would have been slaughtered just as easily as the people they tried to protect. Well aware that she couldn't get ahead of the dead in time to stop them, she envisioned the choppy waters of the bay half a mile to the west and found a song as unfamiliar as Dainn's ancient language. She magically sought, gathered, and transported wood and metal from nearby piers, and constructed giant water tanks. She directed the tanks to fill themselves, and used the forge-magic to heat the water to a temperature above the boiling point. She pulled the tanks through the air and over the buildings to hover just above the section of the street the dead were about to reach.

With careful precision, Mist opened the tanks and let the scalding water fall on the dead without touching the onlookers frozen on the sidewalk. Moans and muffled cries announced the annihilation of Hel's minions, who disintegrated to ash before the mortals' disbelieving eyes.

The carnage sent most of the mortals running into the nearest open buildings they could find, but a few, curiosity outweighing sense, remained to record the scene with their cell phones. Without warning or explanation, the mobile devices turned black and disintegrated in their users' hands. Some of the dead rushed onto the sidewalk to snatch up the would-be photographers, while others invaded the clubs, dragging the patrons nearest the door out into the street.

Mist unsheathed Kettlingr. Six of the dead charged, and she cut them down, enhancing her sword-work with all the magic she had at her disposal: Galdr, Jotunn, and Eitr, Rune-staves forged into missiles flung by the invisible winds of the Void amid hails of ice and snow. Another nine or ten dead came at her from two sides, and she managed to take them down as well.

But she quickly realized that the magic she had used to destroy the first wave had enervated her to the point that it was becoming more and more difficult to wield Kettlingr, especially when she was so keenly aware of the mortals who were very likely to die if she didn't think of a more permanent solution.

And still no police showed up, no ambulances. The hundreds of mortals cowering in the clubs and lounges must have called 911 by now, even if the people on the sidewalk hadn't succeeded. For the first time, Mist wondered if Hel had created a kind of "dead zone" to keep anyone from entering or leaving the neighborhood. If she could do something like that, she was even more powerful than Mist had realized.

Luckily for her, the dead seemed to have lost their momentum. Hel screeched at them, a sound so hideous that Mist almost dropped the sword to cover her ears. A dozen more of Hel's hosts started forward, while those who had taken mortals from clubs and restaurants lined them up along the sidewalks like grotesque mannequins.

The dead made no further attempts to kill, and after a time some of the unaffected mortals began to creep out of their hiding places to stare and take more photos. Their devices disintegrated as well. None of them dared to help the hostages, who seemed to be in a kind of trance, unable or unwilling to escape.

Mist glanced at her watch. It would be dawn in less than an hour.

The dead must lose some of their power during the day, and once Mist could call for reinforcements . . .

"You have stood in my way too long," Hel croaked, rising out of the asphalt near Mist's boots. "Stand aside."

"Fat chance," Mist said, meeting Hel's penetrating stare.

"You are alone, with no one to help you," Hel said. "Though your trick with the water tanks was impressive, I can feel that you have weakened. Soon you will no longer be able to destroy even a few of my hosts without suffering injuries yourself."

"Let me worry about my own health, Fenrir's Sister," Mist said through her teeth. "The one thing I don't get is why Loki sent you *here*. If it was a trap for my allies, it didn't work. And these mortals aren't fighters or anyone who can hurt him. If Loki wants to terrorize average citizens, why aren't you letting people and calls go through so that this gets out to the whole city?"

"I am not subject to Loki's every whim."

"You mean he didn't order this strike, and you just wanted to come out and play?"

"Perhaps I merely wish to swell my ranks."

"You've presumably got millions already at your command. I wonder if you're really just showing Loki that you have a mind and will of your own?"

Sweeping her robes around her legs, Hel hovered in a tight circle like an angry wasp. "Do not presume to know me, Valkyrie," she hissed. "But perhaps we can reach an agreement. I take a few dozen mortals to join my host, and then I will leave the survivors in peace."

"Until tomorrow, you mean?" Mist tipped Kettlingr toward Hel's semitransparent neck. "I don't think so."

"But I can never be destroyed, and I cannot return to my realm, since it no longer exists." She spread her hands. "A place must be made for me in Midgard, or I will go on wreaking havoc on your innocent mortals."

"So this *is* about you. Loki won't be happy if you go on rampages without his permission."

"Must my father be happy?" She smiled. "Must yours?" She glanced to the east. "Night wanes. But I was never confined to darkness, whatever Midgardian legends may claim." She lifted her arms with a terrible ululation and opened her robes. More dead rose around her, emerging from beneath her gown, tumbling over each other in their haste to reach the watching mortals. A miasma of rot and putrefaction came with them. Mist found her own arms almost too heavy to lift, her strength rapidly waning as if she were soon to be among the dead herself.

She closed her eyes, remembering her own darkness—not only Freya's legacy, the desire to rule at any cost, but the power to destroy that had always lain within her since she had first used the ancient magic.

All she had to do was accept it, and she might still save the mortals facing a most horrible death. *I can destroy Hel*, she thought. Suddenly the answer was clear, and red mist swirled behind her eyes, the blood of the Eitr pulsing hot and hungry. *I can only kill evil with evil.*

But her body resisted her mind's commands. It began to tremble, and her hand went numb on Kettlingr's hilt. Hel's dark cloak flared wide like a cobra's hood. A great moaning rose up over the neighborhood, and the sky overhead turned black.

But as dawn broke over the hills across the bay, forging a narrow path through the clouds, it brought with it a powerful man on a white, eight-legged steed, wielding a spear that sang as he raised it to strike. Behind him ran six Valkyrie—Rota and Hild, Hrist, Regin, Olrun, and Skuld, the latter four carrying Treasures: Bragi's Harp, Freyr's Sword, the Chain Gleipnir, and the two halves of Thor's Staff, Gridarvoll.

And behind them came tall men, warriors in dark leather, bearing axes and swords only the strongest of mortals could wield. The true Einherjar, Odin's resurrected warriors . . . his hidden army, set loose at last.

Odin swept past Mist, unseeing, and cast his spear at Hel. It struck her in the chest, and she shrieked, her body seeming to collapse in on itself like the Wicked Witch of the West beneath her black robes. Clouds boiled and simmered overhead, smothering the weak rays of the rising sun.

The other Valkyrie caught Mist up among them, and she raised her sword, fresh energy pouring into her arms and legs, the reckless, mindless heat of war filling her veins with fire. She cut down the dead in their dozens, cleaving and hacking and chopping at half-living flesh until there was nothing left of her opponents to stand and fight. There were screams amid the shouts of battle, but to Mist they were music, like the sounding of trumpets, like the Gjallarhorn itself.

And now, *now* the darkness came. The shadow-side of the Eitr rolled before her like a hard wind before a storm. She called up Rune-staves of the forge and twisted them, reversed them, cast Merkstaves that reduced the dead to ash. She dropped Kettlingr and pushed her way through bodies of the once-living, laughing as they crumbled in her wake. Only as she reached the last line of Hel's warriors did she feel the joyful fury begin to subside. There was no hope for them; the Einherjar were already among them. Though many had fallen to "permanent" death at the hands of the dead, they continued to fight with reckless courage, their blows severing gaunt heads from half-wasted bodies.

Mist paused to catch her breath and grinned at Rota and Hild, who had stopped to stand beside her. Rota's red hair was loose around her face, and Hild was smudged with ash and blood.

A single, pitiful beam of sunlight brushed Mist's eyelids. She blinked to clear her eyes, and the darkness was gone.

"Mist," Rota whispered.

The street was littered with dead. Not only the ash that was all that remained of Hel's minions, but at least twenty Einherjar and two dozen men and women, mortals all, some struck down by the same warriors and magic that had destroyed the enemy.

"*Yzhas,*" Hild swore. Mist closed her eyes and opened them again.

It was no illusion. Odin sat on Sleipnir, erect in the saddle, Gungnir braced against his thigh. The Einherjar stood around him, weapons leveled as if they expected the dead mortals to rise as they themselves had done, ready to fight for Hel.

But the mortal dead remained silent. Mist walked to the nearest body, an elderly woman with a grocery bag of vegetables torn open on the ground beside her. Her eyes were staring, but they were an ordinary brown. Mist knelt beside her and passed her hand over the woman's face.

"Sweet Baldr, welcome and protect her," she whispered. Surely no one else in Hel would. If that was where her soul had gone. The idea of this old woman with some ghastly weapon in her hand, slaughtering her own kind . . .

Mist rose, her jaw clenched so tight that she felt the bones would split her skin. She made her way through the ash to Sleipnir—past Valkyrie who had been lost to her so long—and stared up at Odin, seeing nothing but a halo of reddish light.

"Mist," he said, reaching down to touch the top of her head. "Well done."

But there was something wrong about his voice, and suddenly Mist could see him properly again: only a god on a horse, a strange look in his blue eye. He smiled, and the look was gone.

"If all our victories are so easy," he said, "we will win this city within a week." He kicked Sleipnir's barrel, and the horse picked his way among the bodies without a single twitch of his ear.

The Sleipnir she had known was gone. And Odin looked down at the dead mortals with as little interest as he would show a can of beer crushed under the horse's hooves. With hardly a glance in her direction, the Valkyrie Odin had claimed—Olrun, Hrist, Regin, and Skuld—marched at his heels. Einherjar ran out into the street to collect the bodies of their own fallen.

Mist turned aside and retched. Rota laid a plump hand on her shoulder. "It was not . . . what we thought it would be," she said in a very quiet voice. "We never expected so many innocents to die."

With a grim look, Hild folded her arms across her chest. "All is not well in the camp," she said.

"Danny," Mist said, the sickness threatening to turn her stomach inside out. "I felt—"

"He is dead," Hild said. There were tears in her eyes. "It was an accident."

Mist swayed on her feet. "Who did it?" she asked.

"I'm sorry, Mist. It was Dainn."

∞

Dainn wasn't in his cell when Mist returned to camp. He was chained up to a pile of rebar-laden rubble tossed outside one of the refurbished warehouses, his clothes filthy and a bloodstained bandage wrapped around his right hand. Four Alfar surrounded him, alert and well-armed. One of them blocked Mist's path with his spear as she approached. She looked him in the eye, and he bowed and raised the spear, stepping out of her way.

If he hadn't, Mist thought, she would have punched him in the face.

She knelt level with Dainn, her empty stomach still heaving, and tried to get him to look at her. He didn't. In fact, everything about him reminded her of Danny when he was in his detached state.

But it wasn't ordinary grief that had turned him silent and expressionless. He'd been that way many times before. Even horror and guilt weren't enough to cause this emptiness, create this hollowed-out husk that felt as dead to her as any of the mortals she'd seen lying on the street.

Neither Rota nor Hild had been able to tell her who had witnessed the death, or how it had come about. She didn't need the details to know what *hadn't* happened.

"I don't believe it," she said softly. "They say it was the beast, but you had it under control."

Dainn continued to stare at some spot on the cracked concrete a dozen feet away.

"I felt something, when it happened," she said. "I felt that he wasn't really dead." She shook Dainn's shoulder. "Dainn, listen to me."

"He will not speak," said the Alfar with the spear, his tone respectful and apologetic. "Would you have me try to wake him?"

"He's not asleep," she said. She looked up at the elf. "What is your name?"

"Styfialdr, Lady."

"You know why Dainn is here?"

"It is said that he killed his own son."

So, Mist thought, someone had informed the camp about Danny's identity. She wondered how the humans and Alfar had reacted to the revelation, and how much they actually knew.

Why did she still feel as if he wasn't dead at all?

"Where is the body?" she asked the elf.

"I do not know. I have heard that it disappeared."

Mist digested the information with narrowed eyes.

"Do you think he killed his son?" she asked.

"Odin himself witnessed it," Styfialdr said. "They say the Faith-breaker was mad, and the child was Loki's."

Odin witnessed it, Mist thought with a sinking heart. He had to be wrong. He *had* to be.

"Dainn loved Danny more than anything else in the Homeworlds," she said, pushing the words past the lump in her throat. "What does the All-father intend to do with him?"

Glancing at his companions, Styfialdr hesitated. "Lady, he has said that he is too deadly to live."

"Then he plans to execute him."

Again, Styfialdr lowered his gaze. Mist could think of only one solution short of violence.

"Konur said all the Alfar will follow me now," she said.

"That is our duty."

"And does your duty include obeying me, even if what I ask directly contradicts Odin's command?"

The elf met her gaze. "What would you have us do, Lady?"

She told him, and a few minutes later he and the other guards had disappeared around the corner of the warehouse. Mist looked for the locks on the several heavy chains that held Dainn pinned to the rubble like Loki under the serpent. She didn't believe it was coincidence.

Odin must really think that Dainn was unable to fight, Mist thought as she broke the locks. Or that no one would fight *for* him. The beast could snap these bonds as easily as a daisy chain.

But when she'd freed him, he still didn't move. He continued to stare at that same spot until she hooked her hands under his arms and pulled him to his feet. She thought she would have to carry him, but after she'd walked him a few feet away from the rubble, he stood on his own.

"Good," she said, as if she were talking to his son. "Just walk with me. You don't have to do anything."

He went with her, never speaking, moving his legs as if they belonged to someone else. There was a small, unrefurbished factory on the other side of the fence, and she led him to it, slicing through the chain links with a murmured spell and mending them seamlessly behind her.

The only useful object in the room was a torn, sprung couch someone had left lying on the factory floor, butted up against defunct machinery. Mist eased Dainn onto the couch and arranged his arms and legs. He "helped" her just enough to keep his full weight off her arms.

She crouched before him and put her hands on his knees. "I know you're in there," she said. "I know you're grieving for him. I—" Her eyes teared up. She stopped them with a fresh upwelling of anger. "I've never had a child, so I can't know what it's like for you. But I . . . I love him, too. I want to help."

His head moved just enough for her to notice. She squeezed his knee gently. "I need your help. Odin won a victory over Hel. But he was responsible for . . . *we* were responsible for a lot of unnecessary deaths. Innocent people died just because they were in the way, and no one bothered to separate friend from enemy." She closed her eyes. "It was dark, Dainn. Dark and ugly. I was part of it."

When she opened her eyes, Dainn's lips were slightly parted, though his eyes continued to stare at nothing.

"I'm going to try something, Dainn," she said. "We've shared our minds and our thoughts even when we've been far away from each other. I think you're very far away now. Try to listen."

I'm here, she said into his mind. *Can you hear me?*

There was a vast, terrible silence where Dainn should be. She wandered through his mind, hearing the echo of her own thoughts, knowing he had to be hidden away in some dark corner where he didn't have to think or feel.

You can come out, she said. *You're safe with me.* She listened for an answer, and after a span of uncounted time she caught a breath of sound, a distant howling.

The beast, she thought in panic. *That's all that's left.* But she followed the sound to its source, and it was no beast. The child looked exactly like Dainn, with his long black hair and indigo eyes. A bandage was wound around his hand. He clutched a black-haired stuffed animal close to his chest as he lifted his tearstained face to hers.

This was the being who could speak a language older than the oldest Elvish tongue, and he was utterly helpless. She knew instantly that she didn't dare ask him how Danny had been hurt. The question would destroy any hope she had of reaching him.

"Dainn?" she said. "I've come to take you back."

The boy said nothing. She knelt and held out her hand.

"I know it hurts," she said, "but you can't hide forever." She hesitated. "I need you, Dainn."

"It's dark," Dainn whispered. "I can't see."

"I can see for you. I know the way."

"There are monsters."

"I have a sword. See?" She showed him the imaginary Kettlingr. "And you're very strong, Dainn, even though you've never believed it."

"You never believed it, either," Dainn said. "*You* can't fight it."

At first she didn't understand him, but the connection between their minds filled with an image, a sensation that couldn't be mistaken.

The Eitr. Not the bright healing magic, but the destructive force, the poison that had claimed her during the battle with Hel. It spun around her now, as if she were at the center of a hurricane, still quiet in the midst of chaos.

Dainn *knew* she had lost control. Suddenly he threw the stuffed animal to her. She caught and looked into its blunt-muzzled face.

The beast. Small, harmless, not even alive. But the dark Eitr converged on it like a swarm of flies on a corpse, and the stink of rot rose from torn seams.

Evil. Yet the ancient magic conveyed another message, and she realized as she held the toy that it was no separate being trapped in fake fur and fiberfill. She felt the invisible cord binding it to the center of boy-Dainn's chest.

Slowly, Mist began to understand. The revelation was as startling as the knowledge that Dainn himself was not aware of it, though the truth lived there within his own mind, so deeply buried that only her outsider's eyes could detect it.

The beast was not the creation of Odin's curse. It was a manifestation of the dark Eitr, as much a part of Dainn's being as the elf. When he fought it, he fought that darkness . . . and the forces that made it what it was. Yet each time he used magic, especially the Eitr, he was at constant risk of literally giving way to his other half.

It was very old, this unwilling symbiosis. Yet the beast could not be destroyed—only denied, driven back, crowded into a small space where it had no power.

For a long while, before Freya had found him in Midgard, he had kept it caged. Emotion and conflict had broken down the walls. And *Mist* was as much responsible for that as anyone else.

"He was very bad," Dainn said in a small voice.

What could she say? Even this child-Dainn knew what the beast had done. The guilt . . . the terrible, searing self-contempt . . .

"I have it now," she said, clutching the stuffed animal more tightly in spite of her loathing. "It's safe."

"No." He shook his head wildly, dark hair snapping around his face. "*They* made it worse."

The onslaught of memories assaulting her mind nearly bowled her off her feet. She could see the men he spoke of: the big one with a single eye, red-blond hair shot with gray, a full beard and mustache, and undeniable authority; the other a slender young man with bright red hair and green eyes, ever mocking.

Odin and Loki. Both had pushed Dainn even further past his limit, Odin with his threats and contempt, Loki with—

Gods. Until this moment, Mist had only witnessed Dainn's shame, felt it in his thoughts. She had never *lived* it. Now, as the child Dainn cowered in his corner, she knew exactly how he had felt every moment he had remained Loki's captive . . . helpless, abused, without hope. Unable to protect the one he loved most.

She saw the scene in the stable play out as if it were on a movie screen: Loki taunting Dainn, making himself look like Danny for Norns knew what reason, and then Odin striding in . . .

The rest became a blur. But *Loki* had been there. Odin had seen him.

What if Loki was ultimately responsible for Danny's death? He could have used a spell on Dainn . . .

To kill his own son?

Dainn whimpered. Mist cut off the terrible thought.

"I'm sorry," she whispered, gripping the plush toy until the stuffing seemed near to bursting out between the seams. "I should have tried harder to understand, to see . . ."

Dainn stood up. "I want to hurt them," he said.

The words were flat, almost matter-of-fact. They would have been obscene coming from the mouth of a real child.

But now he is *a child,* she thought. As innocent and deadly as Danny.

"No," she said gently. She held her free hand palm-up and summoned a soft bed of glowing coals that warmed but didn't burn. "You always said I could learn to master the ancient magic, and you can do the same. Maybe we can help each other walk through this darkness. Together."

Dainn stared at her for a long time, unblinking, weighing, judging. He didn't trust her. He didn't trust himself. She was about to offer her hand when an explosion of magical power pummeled her like a vicious north wind, parted around her, and howled through the emptiness behind her. Strange Runes appeared in the air between her and Dainn. She tried to sound them out, but they tore apart and flew away like scraps of shredded paper.

The toy beast leaped in her hand, and she felt it fighting to return to Dainn. Acting on instinct, she pulled several strands of hair from her head, sang them into steel, and wrapped them around the toy's neck, tugging until they formed a snug and unbreakable collar. The beast seemed to shudder, and then went still.

"You don't need to be afraid now," she said, tucking the toy under her arm. "It can't hurt anyone."

Dainn gazed at the toy, shivered, and held out his hand. She took it and led him back the way she had come, into the light. Just as she felt the dream-world grow dim, she thought she saw a shadow behind Dainn—another child, trailing behind him. The shadow laughed, and a gentler wind blew past her, ruffling her hair.

She opened her eyes. Dainn was huddled on the couch, deep, wracking sobs shaking his body. She put her arms around him and held him, stroking his dusty hair and holding her own grief in check until he was quiet again.

Quiet, but changed. There was no trace of the little boy in him now. He got up and walked away from her, and she felt the small space between them widening into a chasm. A void without a bridge to cross it.

"I'm sorry," she said.

He stared at the door. "I killed my son."

"Dainn, listen to me," she said. "I don't believe he's really gone."

"Then where is he?"

"I don't know. But what happened was not your fault. I know that Loki was there."

"Allow me to take responsibility for my own evil."

"It wasn't—" *yours*, she almost said, and then remembered what she had discovered inside his mind. But did *he* know it now? Had she freed the memories so thoroughly hidden in the most primitive corners of his brain?

She prayed he'd be spared that knowledge just a little longer.

"You will take responsibility for your own life," she said, "and the part you still have to play in this fight."

His eyes were dull when he looked at her. "What is that part now, Lady Mist?"

"You'll have to lie low until we can figure that out."

"The beast will return."

Mist thought about telling him that the beast was part of him, not the result of Odin's curse. But she couldn't bring herself to burden him with that knowledge now.

"Not while I have it," she said.

There was a beat of silence, and he blinked several times. "*You* have it?"

"Think, Dainn. You gave it to me. I bound it inside me, and it's not going to escape unless I let it go."

His pupils expanded, eclipsing the indigo blue of his irises. "It will destroy you."

"I don't think so. It doesn't have any power over me, Dainn."

"You do not understand what you have done," he said quietly.

"I understand that it's crippled you, and I can hold it as long as it takes for you to move forward without the constant fear of what the beast will do."

He turned away, his eyes gone dull again, and to Mist he seemed more than merely detached, more than grieving and hopeless. He felt empty.

But Mist felt . . . hope. She didn't know where it had come from, or how it could gain any kind of foothold after what had happened today. Yet she could imagine Danny taking her hand, smiling up at her, and telling her that everything was going to be all right. It was if he was right there with her.

She grabbed Dainn by the shoulders and forced him to look at her again. The Eitr, a live cable of energy, jumped the chasm between them.

The contact was electric, painful, and ecstatic at once, as intimate as any sharing of thoughts could be. Dainn's muscles stiffened and then relaxed, his expression coming alive again. Her body became

his, his hers. Desire and desperation intermingled and became insep-
arable.

She kissed him. A fierce joy took her, battering down the resistance in Dainn's mind, and he answered in kind.

The moment of union lasted the eternity of a heartbeat, and then
Dainn broke free. The cable snapped back as if it had been severed by
a well-honed blade, and Mist was in her own head again, alone in her
body, bereft.

Dainn backed away, his face wiped of all expression.

"I will do what must be done," he said.

Mist struggled to find her voice. Her lips throbbed. "You stay
here," she stammered. "I'll find a better place to hide you."

Touching his mouth as if it belonged to someone else, Dainn
didn't answer.

28

The camp was a madhouse when Mist went looking for Ryan. Odin's Einherjar seemed to be everywhere—giving orders, speaking to large groups of mortal fighters, and generally dominating the space that had once belonged to Mist's recruits. Multiple forges had been set up, every one producing mail and weapons suitable for Odin's warriors. She didn't see a single elf.

She stopped the first Einherji she ran across. He was at least a full six inches taller than she was, with the same perfect Viking build Loki had assumed when he'd posed as her lover so long ago.

"In a hurry, warrior?" she asked.

He shot her a distracted glance. "Odin has said—" He did a double take. "Lady Mist."

"What's going on here?"

"Odin has given orders that we reorganize this camp and train the mortals to become a more efficient fighting force."

"The camp was already organized, and our people are already good fighters."

"Some, perhaps. But even they are not good enough to serve the All-father."

"So you've taken over without mentioning it to me?"

He cocked an eye at her. "This is the will of the All-father. I am sure he has orders for you, as well."

Mist's worry for Dainn and her grief over Danny and the mortal victims of Odin's glorious debut had shortened her temper to the length of a burnt match stub. She thought about a certain spell that could turn the parking lot under the warrior's feet to the temperature of a very hot frying pan.

"I'm sure he does," she said with a heavy dose of sarcasm. "But last time I checked, he hadn't relieved me of command here."

He flashed teeth as big as a horse's. "I remember you now, Lady," he said. "I believe you once served me a cup of mead in Valhalla."

He was actually smirking at her, reminding her of a time when Valkyrie were as much servants in Odin's hall as they were battlefield riders who chose the honored dead to join Odin in Valhalla.

"It's far more likely that I dragged your body out of the blood and muck and gave you to Odin," she said, "though gods know why I'd have chosen *you*."

The warrior's jaw thrust out in a menacing frown. "Freya's daughter," he spat. "I do not even know why the All-father permitted you to live."

"Maybe it's *because* I'm Freya's daughter," she said, lowering her voice to a husky growl. "I have certain skills." She crooked a finger, inviting him to listen. "Have you ever lain with a Valkyrie?"

His gaze fell to her mouth. "Many times."

"No complaints?"

"I would be"—he thrust his groin at her—"honored to show you."

"I'm sure you would." She turned on the glamour, contempt for him burning away all the other unpleasant emotions. "But you wouldn't survive a night with me."

He stared. He licked his lips. His pupils shrank to pinpoints.

"Maybe if you beg," she said, "I'll let you go without removing the pitiful organ you seem so proud of."

It amused her to see him grovel with his tongue hanging out, desperate just to kiss her hand. He was almost on his knees when she realized what she was doing.

The dark side. The Freya side. The side that wanted the power to control people and steal their wills.

And maybe even a little of the beast she'd collared with a few strands of her hair. Gods help her.

"That's enough," she snapped, severing the spell. "If I see any of you shouting at my people or treating them as inferiors, I won't wait to take it up with Odin."

He scrambled to his feet and hurried off without a backward glance.

Furious at giving in to her vengeful impulses, Mist passed other Einherjar without looking at them and went on to the infirmary. Ryan wasn't there, and he wasn't in his usual place in the bunkhouse.

Mist blamed herself for not finding a way to let him know what had happened with Gabi. The girl hadn't returned to camp, and Mist could only hope that one of the regular patrols caught a glimpse of her. But she wasn't holding her breath.

Once she'd confirmed that no one else had seen Ryan for the past few hours, she bit the bullet and went on to Odin's hall. The All-father was sitting on his throne, chin on fist, watching a TV someone had put up on the wall. News tickers skated across the bottom of the screen, updates on the investigation into the slaughter of fifteen people on Columbus Avenue, surrounded by piles of ash. The newscaster's voice was high-pitched, conveying horror he was obviously fighting to hide. Images of the dead, faces blurred, filled the remainder of the screen, and reporters on the site, barred from the area by police tape and dozens of police cars and emergency vehicles, interviewed dazed witnesses.

"There were all these . . . men with swords and stuff," one man was saying, the reporter's mike shoved in his pale face. "And a guy with an eye patch riding on a . . . Look, it sounds crazy, but I saw it. A big guy on a horse with—" He broke off and stared into the camera. "I can't talk no more." He shoved the mike away and rushed off.

There were many others like him, clearly in a state of shock. Most of them covered their faces and refused to speak to the reporter. Others could barely form coherent sentences.

"End it," Odin said, leaning back with a faint smile.

Anna pointed the remote at the TV and turned it off. She was dressed in a way Mist had never seen before: black leather pants; tall black boots; and a black, gray, and white urban camouflage shirt. A sword hung from her belt, and her dark hair had been pulled back into a short braid.

"Mist," Odin said, his smile vanishing. "Where is the child-slaying traitor?"

It wasn't quite the greeting Mist had expected, and it made clear just how little Odin was willing to give her the benefit of the doubt.

But you did betray him, she thought, *more than once.* And she felt no guilt whatsoever. At the moment, she saw not a wise god on his throne but a ruthless warrior on his eight-legged warhorse, striking with his spear as mortals fell all around him.

But he had seen Loki with Dainn and Danny. She could ask him about what had really happened in the stable, the part that somehow hadn't gotten out to the rest of the camp.

Instinct told her to hold her peace.

"Dainn?" she asked, frowning. "I thought he would have been executed by now."

"You never asked to see him," Odin said. "Have you no interest in his fate, or that of the child?"

He was testing her, and he wasn't being subtle about it. She could only pray that the Alfr guards had kept their word to tell the story she'd arranged for them.

"Why should I doubt the judgment of the All-father?" she asked, holding his gaze.

"Indeed. Yet have you not defended the traitor on many occasions?"

"I would not call it 'defending,' All-father. And that was before he killed his son."

"As a mindless beast." Odin sipped from a large metal mug and extended it for Anna to fill from a bottle of Nogne Imperial Stout. "You know that he suffered my curse in Asgard with good reason."

"Yes."

"He has continued his evil works in Midgard. He prepared you for Freya's return. He turned to Loki when he believed she had abandoned him. He betrayed you, and yet you permitted him to live even after you captured him."

"I thought he could provide us with—"

"You knew that the boy had greater power than even I had guessed, yet you did not warn me."

"Where is his body, All-father?"

"Indeed," Odin said. "Where is it? Is the boy dead at all?"

Mist started. "You saw his body. Why would you think he might still be alive?"

"*I* told him," Ryan said, emerging from behind Odin's throne.

Mist looked the young man over carefully. He seemed completely recovered from the trauma of his near-death; his expression was calm, even remote.

But why in sweet Baldr's name had he come to Odin, a god who hadn't even acknowledged his presence when he'd nearly died at Loki's hands?

Of course he'd "met" Orn months ago at the loft, and Odin's physical presence might have sparked a whole new raft of visions. But, like everyone else in camp, Ryan had to have heard that Dainn had been condemned to die. Even if Dainn hadn't just saved Ryan's life, the young man would never believe that Dainn was anything but innocent.

Had he thought that if he volunteered his services to Odin and claimed that Danny was still alive in some inconceivable way, he'd be able to get the All-father to commute Dainn's sentence?

"*You have to be together,*" he'd said in the drug lab. "Many as one." But what in Hel did that *mean*?

"I've been worried about you, Ryan," she said, trying to give herself time to think. "Are you all right?"

Ryan touched his healed throat. "Fine," he said, just an edge of roughness to his voice.

"Why are you here?"

"The boy is a *spamadr*," Odin said, "as you well knew when he was Loki's hostage, and failed to tell me."

"Has he predicted that you'll win this war?" Mist asked, still watching Ryan's face.

The All-father was oblivious to her sarcasm. "That is a foregone conclusion. But he has already been useful to me. He predicted the trouble with Hel and informed me of it, and so I arrived in time to defeat her and win our first significant victory."

Victory? Mist thought. Ryan would have hoped to save lives by telling Odin what he'd "seen." He couldn't have realized how many mortals would die at the hands of the All-father and his allies.

"I saw his paradise," Ryan said, almost dreamily. "Grass and trees will grow where cities now stand."

Mist shivered, remembering Loki's warnings.

"I told you that you did well in the battle," Odin said, dismissing Ryan with a wave of his hand. "But you behaved with great foolishness in facing Hel alone. Of course you could never have beaten her."

Mist sensed that she was treading on very thin ice. "No, All-father."

"I will not permit you to put yourself in such danger again."

He made the command seem like an act of generosity, even of affection. But he'd started out the interview with an accusation, and he'd robbed her of any authority she had in camp. He was no longer treating her like a trusted servant and confidante.

There had to be a reason for his change of heart, and it wasn't only suspicion over her "dealings" with Dainn. As carefully as she'd tried to conceal it, maybe he sensed her horror at what he had done in North Beach.

Whatever his reason, she had to find a way to get back on his good side. She had to try to temper his nonchalant attitude toward "collateral" damage, or the next fight with Loki and his minions would be a massacre.

"If I have displeased you," Mist said, bowing deeply, "I beg your forgiveness. Grant me the honor of continuing to fight at your side."

"I *will* keep you at my side," Odin said, ". . . here, when I return from battle. You will not be alone. The *spamadr* and Horja will bear you company."

Horja. Mist looked up at Anna. Her once-expressive face could have been carved from ice. There were subtle changes in her jaw and cheekbones, even in the color of her eyes.

She'd shared the late Valkyrie's memories for a very long time. Now, it seemed, those memories had become reality.

If so, Anna might as well be dead. But had she wanted this, or had Odin forced it on her? How in Hel could she be saved, either way?

"What of my other Sisters?" Mist asked with a calm she didn't feel.

"Rota and Hild will continue to supervise the mortals," Odin said. "Olrun, Hrist, Skuld, and Regin will ride with me."

Because they were the ones he trusted, Mist thought. They were completely under his sway. "And the Einherjar?" she asked. "I was told that they are to assume the work of training the mortal fighters."

"So I have ordered."

"But my officers . . . Lord Konur, Captain Taylor . . ."

"They can join the other warriors." Odin took a deep swallow of his beer and wiped the drops from his mustache and beard with the back of his hand. "I will set you one task. The Alfar have seemed less than enthusiastic about serving me, though they have always been favored guests in Valhalla. Since you apparently have some influence with them, you will remind them that their purpose here has not changed. I will reward them with what Freya offered, and more."

By now, Mist thought, Odin must know that Konur was her father . . . though it was just as likely that he'd known all along and kept that knowledge from her. He might have good reason to distrust Freya's former lover. But if he doubted the elves as he had come to doubt *her* . . .

"Do you heed me, Valkyrie?" Odin said.

Mist straightened. "Yes, All-father. I will speak to the Alfar."

"Be certain to make clear to them that I will not tolerate another failure such as the one that permitted the traitor to escape."

Mist exhaled very, very quietly. "The Alfar let him escape?" she asked.

"He broke his chains and overpowered them, or so I am told."

"The Alfar hate him. They can't be too happy with themselves right now."

"In my experience, the elves never allow disadvantageous circumstances to temper their arrogance."

Look in the mirror, Mist thought. But Odin was smiling now, and she remembered how benevolent he could be to those he favored.

She decided to risk a direct question. "Now that you have Sleipnir's power," she said, "can we expect the other Aesir to arrive soon?"

"Very soon." Odin drained his cup and held it out for Anna-Horja to refill. "Have you learned anything more of the Gjallarhorn?"

"My people have been working on it night and day. Do you want me to continue supervising them, or will you put the Einherjar in charge?"

This time he didn't miss the barb. "You may continue," he said with a scowl, "but we must have the Horn before the final battle begins." He stared into her eyes. "And now it is time for you to return the Cloak."

At first Mist didn't know what he was talking about. Then she remembered the slight weight hanging from her neck, and covered the little pouch with her hand.

"Can you resurrect Bryn now, All-father?" she asked.

"After Loki is destroyed." He looked away as if he had become bored with the conversation. "Give the pouch to Horja."

Her heart heavy with misgivings, Mist pulled the cord over her head. Anna-Horja descended from the dais and took it from her, barely meeting her gaze before she resumed her position.

"You may go until I summon you again," Odin said with a flick of his fingers.

Mist hesitated. Her instincts still insisted that it would be a mistake to confront Odin about Loki's presence in the stable. If he was determined to blame Dainn, he wasn't likely to change his mind, and his trust in her would be further eroded. And if she couldn't keep his trust, she wouldn't be able to influence his behavior.

She had to find the answers some other way. If she had to hunt Loki down and hold Kettlingr to his throat, by Mimir's head she'd—

The door swung open, and an Einherji strode into the hall, his hand on the hilt of his sword. He spoke to Anna and quickly left. Anna bent to whisper in Odin's ear. Odin raised his head and beckoned to Mist.

"I do have one more task for you," he said. "We have found the elf.

Apparently he was seen wandering about in the camp, and gave himself up without a struggle." Odin shook his head. "Perhaps there is still some faint spark of honor left in him. It seems only right that you, my most loyal Valkyrie, should end his life."

∞

Loki let the frenzy claim him again. He smashed every glass in his liquor cabinet. He ranted at his absent daughter. He cursed Odin with the foulest curses that had ever been pronounced among gods or men, drawing Merkstaves on the wall with the blood draining out of the scar on his hand.

He had warned Dainn. He had warned Mist. But Dainn had trusted her, and she had trusted Odin.

And now Danny was dead.

They had been afraid to tell him, afraid he would kill the messenger. In fact, he had. But no thousands of deaths, Jotunar or mortal, could ever make up for the life taken from him.

He fell onto the couch, breathless, permitting himself a short rest before he began again. They had said that the child had been slaughtered by a beast. Dainn's beast.

Loki believed it. Not that Dainn had done it with any awareness of his actions; when Loki had captured Dainn and the young seer Ryan, he had seen that Dainn had regained the means to mute the beast's power without the use of the herb, just as he had gained the power to heal.

No. Odin had cursed Dainn with the beast in Asgard; he had witnessed Danny's power, and rekindled the curse to rid himself of father and son. Dainn, too, would die, the murderer of a child he had loved.

Jumping up from the couch, Loki destroyed every stick of furniture in the room. Then he retired to the meeting room and remained very still until his heartbeat had resumed its usual rhythm and his breathing was almost normal.

Someone knocked on the door, and Loki straightened in his chair. "Come in," he said.

Vali thumped into the room, took one look at Loki's face, and stopped.

"You wanted to see me?" he asked.

"I have all three of Thor's Treasures," Loki said, feeling a brief moment of satisfaction. "Soon you will have the power I promised you."

"I will use it wisely."

"I'm quite certain of that." Loki leaned back and closed his eyes. "It will take me some time to prepare the spell. If I am not careful, Thor's weapons may destroy you."

And that would not be such a bad thing, Loki thought, after Vali had served his purpose.

"I'm not afraid," Vali said, standing at parade rest with his hands tucked behind his back.

"Bravo." Loki straightened again and opened his eyes. "Listen well," he said. "I want you to learn exactly how my son died. I want to know what part Odin played in it. Do you understand?"

"Yes," Vali said. "But if it was the beast—"

"I'm not interested in your speculation. Go."

Vali went. Loki called the kitchen and ordered a bottle of Bowmore Islay. When he won this war, he would make the All-father suffer as no god had suffered before. There were places even more terrible than Niflheim, dimensions where the torment was endless, far worse than the Christian Hell.

And Dainn . . .

He would make it quick. Even now, he couldn't bear the idea of the elf dying in fear and pain. No, Loki would put him out of his misery gently, if Dainn had not already taken care of it himself.

Mist's death would lie somewhere in between. But he would most certainly take pleasure in it.

"How are you going to help Dainn?" Rick asked.

Mist's council—or what had *been* her council, before Odin had made clear that she didn't need it anymore—waited in silence for her answer. They were meeting in secret, though Mist didn't think the Einherjar were observant enough to notice a few mortals, Valkyrie, and Alfar wandering around the corner to Third Street and finding their way to the almost deserted coffee shop.

"They wouldn't let me see him," she said. "And they aren't going to let any Alfar near him again."

A flicker of anger passed across Konur's refined face. "Odin assigned elven guards to watch Dainn for a reason," he said. "In spite of Dainn's alienation from my people, Odin anticipated their collusion in his escape."

"Because Odin knew I would ask them to help me," Mist said bitterly. "It was all a test, and now he's got me right where he wants me."

"But you said they found Dainn wandering around the camp."

Mist pressed her lips together. From all she had learned, that part had been true. Dainn had deliberately abandoned the cover she'd created for him and let himself be caught.

"It doesn't matter," she said. "The final test will be the same. I will be expected to kill Dainn."

Everyone around the table fell silent. "Look," Rick said, "we know Dainn made things right with you somehow, I mean about Loki. How can you be so sure that he didn't kill—" He broke off and stared down at the table, flushed and angry.

"I'm not convinced that Danny is dead," Mist said.

"What?" Vixen said amid a wave of murmurs.

"Supposedly, the body disappeared," Mist said.

"What does that prove?" Rick asked, lifting his head. "How did it 'disappear'?"

"I don't know," Mist said. "It may not be easy to find out. Odin has reduced my authority over the allies just as he's reduced yours in running the camp. I was never supposed to remain a leader after the Aesir showed up. I didn't want to."

"Bullshit," Rick said. "I don't believe that for a second, and I don't think you believe it, either. This guy just expects you to kill someone who . . . someone who means something to you, after all you've done to make things ready for him?"

Mist swallowed several times. "In his mind, he has to execute a murderer, or he can't keep order."

"He's scared he's gonna lose it, with all these punk Einherjar hanging around?"

"He must stand firm," Mist said, "or admit that Loki was in the stable with him."

All the council members began talking at once. Mist held up her hand. "No one knows about this but Dainn, me, and Odin, and Odin doesn't know *I* know. I might think Loki was responsible, except that I don't believe he'd harm Danny, either."

"Whatever occurred," Konur said, "it is obvious that Odin fears Dainn too much to let him live."

Mist glanced at Konur, remembering every word of their conversation about Dainn and his abilities. "Why he wants Dainn dead doesn't matter," she said. "I'm not going to do as Odin commands."

Captain Taylor leaned over the table. "You're speaking of what Odin will regard as treason."

"Yes," Mist said, "though I hope he won't figure it out right away."

"Forgive me, but why follow him at all when he so clearly doesn't deserve your loyalty?"

Mist met Taylor's gaze. "I've served Odin all my life, and—"

"Did he slaughter innocents in Asgard?"

"I didn't finish, Taylor. I had few direct dealings with Odin in Asgard. He was a legend, even to those of us who served him." She lifted her chin. "Now I have seen what he's capable of in his quest to rule Midgard. I don't think he'll let anything stop him, not even if he has to rid the world of half its population to achieve the paradise he envisions."

For a full minute there was no sound at the table except quiet breathing and uneasy shiftings of position.

"What are you suggesting, Mist?" Rota asked.

"Rebellion," Hild said darkly.

The word echoed through the diner just a little too loudly. Mist waited until she was certain that the few mortal patrons weren't listening. "When it comes down to it," Taylor said, "you have the loyalty of all the recruits, the seasoned fighters and the Alfar."

"As you have ours," Hild said, nodding to Rota.

"And he's only got his Einherjar," Taylor said. "And four Valkyrie," Mist said, "and his own considerable magic. Apart from the fact that I'm not willing to risk your lives in a revolution, nothing would please Loki more than to see a deadly conflict break out among the allies. And Odin is still the only one who can defeat him."

"Are you so sure?" Taylor asked. "What you did to Hel's followers—"

"I'm not proud of what happened during that battle," Mist said, looking away.

Taylor shook his head. "It's not just about what happened with Hel. What are you really denying, Chief?"

"That she defeated Freya when the goddess tried to kill her," Konur said, "because she is far more powerful than she will ever admit."

There was another explosion of voices, quickly muted as Konur quietly and efficiently told the others a truncated and much-modified story of Freya's jealousy over her daughter and her mad attempt to claim Mist's body and soul for her own. When he was finished, everyone stared at Mist as if they'd never seen her before.

"Shit," Rick said. "I'm . . . we're all really sorry."

Murmurs of agreement circled the table, offers of sympathy and regret. "Now we know why you were acting so strange after you said Freya went away," Vixen said. "I wish you'd told us, so we could have—"

"The subject is closed," Mist said. She stared at Konur. "Whatever my abilities, new or old, I'm still no goddess, and never will be. There's still a chance that Odin can be persuaded that mortal lives can't be thrown away like trash."

"And if you don't succeed in convincing him?" Konur asked. "How will Odin rule beings he regards as expendable?"

Mist was gathering a reply when the pain took her. She doubled over, gasping for breath as the muscles in her belly contracted and the bile rose in her throat, threatening to choke her.

She had never been with child, but she had known thousands of pregnant women in her life, and what she felt now was like the kick of a fetus in the womb, reminding her that she was not alone in her own body.

The beast, she thought. But the pain stopped, and what came after was a question, a plea, and a soothing warmth that erased even the memory of pain.

When she had taken the beast from Dainn, she had taken something else . . . something he had saved without realizing what he did.

Now it was time to give it back.

"Mist?" Vixen said, kneeling beside her. "Are you all right?"

Mist looked up. "Yes," she said. "Now I know what I have to do."

29

Odin had always had a flair for the dramatic.

The execution was to occur at dawn. Newly armored Einherjar stood guard, as solemn as the handful of mortals who watched from behind them. Ryan, shivering in a thin jacket, observed from among Odin's immediate attendants, including Anna. Not a single elf was present except for Lord Konur, who looked on with a ferocity in his eyes rare in any of the Alfar.

Mist stood over Dainn, the blade in her hands. Many times Dainn had felt her try to reach him with her thoughts since she had walked inside his mind. He had blocked her at every turn, knowing that she would suffer even more deeply if they came together again.

He had surrendered himself to the Einherjar, but he had never anticipated that Odin would force Mist to carry out the execution. Now she had to complete it, because to refuse would turn Odin against her. If she lost her influence with the All-father, no magic in the universe, not even the Eitr, would prevent Loki and Odin from tearing the world apart.

Closing his eyes, he listened for the sound of the waves slapping against distant piers, the call of a bird in the nearby park, the ceaseless wind. The sky had grown so thick with clouds that no trace of light could penetrate it. He could smell the ozone and feel the crackling of electricity on his skin.

A thunderstorm was coming. The hair rose on the back of Dainn's neck, and he knew that it was not a natural one. Odin had the power to summon such a storm. . . .

But so did Mist.

No, he thought. *This is what I wish.*

He felt rather than saw her start at the touch of his mind. She tried to answer, but again he prevented her.

"Commence the execution," Odin said.

Dainn glanced at the All-father from the side of his eye, noting with faint amusement that the god had already warded himself against the weather. So ruthless in some ways, so cowardly in others.

Soon he would no longer be obliged to look upon that arrogant face again. He felt the parting of air as Mist raised Kettlingr to strike, and permitted himself to think of Danny, wondering if it was possible they might meet again in some other plane, beyond Hel or any mortal afterlife. If he had but one more chance . . .

He isn't dead.

Dainn started. The rain broke overhead, each drop like a Jotunn icicle.

Part of him is still alive, Dainn. Inside me.

Her thoughts made no sense to him. But still the blade did not swing, and Dainn felt suspended in time, caught in the very instant between life and death.

Papa?

Danny's voice, so faint that it hardly seemed to exist at all.

Because it did *not* exist. Mist imagined it, and *he*—

A deafening crack of thunder shook the asphalt under his knees.

Take him! Mist said.

No conscious thought guided Dainn then, only some impulse born of gut and instinct and faith. He opened himself. Agony roared through him, as if Mist's blade had plunged into his belly and twisted up into his heart, inch by inch, disemboweling him with excruciating and deliberate calculation.

When the lightning struck, it knocked the Einherjar from their feet. Dainn howled, blinded by the spear of light striking the tip of Mist's blade.

When he returned to consciousness, he was in the street in front of Loki's headquarters. Mortal pedestrians, still going about their business in spite of the horrors that had afflicted their city, escaped the onslaught of the storm by rushing under recessed doorways and dashing into buildings. Traffic had ground to a halt.

Disoriented by the teleportation, Dainn made his way to the sidewalk. He sat in the rain for several long minutes as understanding came to him, and he knew that Mist had been telling the truth.

She had saved his life, and given his son back to him.

Danny was *inside* him. And now Dainn was where he had never expected to be again, carried here by the hidden power within. Knowing what had to be done.

You have to be together.

Scrambling to his feet, Dainn made his way to Loki's door. The Jotunn guards stared at him in astonishment.

"You're alive," one of them said.

"I would speak to Loki," Dainn said.

"*Speak* to him?" the Jotunar said with an ugly laugh. "I think he'll want to do more than talk."

Dainn lifted his hand. He hardly had to envision the Runes, let alone sing them. The Jotunn gulped once and was silent.

"I will meet Laufeyson in his office," Dainn said.

Two of the Jotunar scrambled to open the door. The silenced one and his companion only stared. The second finally dared to speak.

"What are you?" he whispered.

◑◐

St. Elmo's fire raced up and down Mist's blade as her hand and arm became a conduit for the storm's unleashed fury. Her tattoo burned, but she hardly noticed the pain. Lightning struck again and again, forcing the Einherjar, the mortals, and even Odin himself to take cover.

Mist swung the sword down with all her strength. The concrete cracked open at the point of impact. Light exploded with the intensity of a nuclear blast, and the shockwave knocked the remaining guards off their feet.

Dainn vanished. She dropped Kettlingr and held the storm in the palm of her hand, her skin shivering with unspent electricity. Ecstasy swept over her, and she directed the lightning at Odin's "hall," destroying his throne in a single strike.

It wasn't nearly enough to satisfy her. The clouds grew so heavy that the city was plunged into the dark of a moonless, starless night, and wind beat against the nylon tents that sheltered the recruits displaced from their bunks in the warehouses.

Mist laughed. She glanced at the Einherji who lay gasping and drenched on the ground, and aimed the lightning at them.

The dark Eitr. She pulled it back just in time, and the lightning retreated behind the clouds. The rain fell to a steady downpour. She remembered where she was.

All that remained of Dainn was a pile of ash. Just as she had intended.

Odin strode up to her, eerily calm, and stared down at the blackened concrete. "The traitor is dead?" he asked.

She crouched to grab Kettlingr, rose, and pushed at the ash with the tip of her sword. "There is nothing left of him, All-father."

"The storm was of your making," Odin said. There was more than anger in his voice. She heard what she could have sworn was spite . . . and jealousy. "How dare you turn your abilities against me?"

Dangerous ground, Mist thought. She still hadn't told him about her use of the Eitr, and now . . .

"I didn't intend to," she said carefully. "You never asked me how I defeated Freya, but you knew I had—"

"Silence," he said, cutting her off. She became aware that an audience had gathered around them, and Odin clearly didn't want his warriors to hear his Valkyrie questioning him.

Insecure in his power, she thought.

Afraid. Of me.

But why? Did he recognize the Eitr within her, as Dainn had that day in his cell? And even if he did, could he believe that she would turn it against *him?*

Wouldn't you?

"We will speak of this later," he said, jerking his arm in a gesture of dismissal.

And how much would she tell him? Mist thought as she crossed the street to the loft. There had been so many omissions now, so many lies in such a short time. She wondered if it was possible that he doubted Dainn's death.

If he did, Mist was reasonably sure he'd have killed her on the spot.

She lay on her bed, numb and exhausted, and rested her hands on her empty belly. If Odin was worried about how she might use her abilities—if he had the notion that she might turn them against him—what would he do? Keep her locked up and under powerful binding spells until he needed her? Hector her until she had no choice but to tell him about her use of the ancient magic?

She couldn't let that happen. She'd made a decision without really realizing what she'd done, and she wasn't going back on it.

Sheer exhaustion finally got the better of her, and she drifted off into a fitful sleep. She had her knife at Ryan's throat before she was fully aware that he was in the room.

"It's me," he said in a strangled whisper.

She withdrew the knife and laid it on the bedside table. "I could have killed you," she said.

"Yeah, I know." Ryan rubbed his throat. "I didn't like it much the first time."

Mist winced, remembering the drug lab. "I'm sorry," she said, swinging her legs over the side of the bed. She met his gaze, and he looked away quickly, retreating to stand by the door.

Gods. Of course he thought she'd killed Dainn. And she couldn't tell him that Dainn was alive, not when he'd joined Odin's team.

How he must hate her. And himself, for serving the god who had ordered the execution of someone he loved.

"It's all right," he said, as if he were answering her thoughts. "I would have told you that I was going to Odin, but you were gone, and I saw the ghosts killing people. I couldn't just let it happen."

"Of course you couldn't," Mist said.

"But people died anyway," he said, his lips stretching in a bitter grimace.

"You couldn't help that."

"I know there's always a risk when I share my visions," he said. "I learned that Odin was responsible for innocent people getting killed. Then I found out about Danny, and what Odin planned to do to Dainn." He pressed his lips together. "I didn't believe what they said about him."

"Ryan—" Mist began.

"But once I proved that first vision was right," Ryan went on, "Odin believed the next one."

Mist stiffened. "And what was it, Ryan?"

"That Dainn would die."

"Ryan," Mist said, "you have to believe . . . I never wanted to—"

"I *knew* it was a lie."

Exhaling sharply, Mist got to her feet and locked her hands behind her back. "You lied about a vision?"

"I knew you had to have some kind of plan to save him. I just didn't see how it would happen." He almost smiled. "That was fantastic."

"Odin didn't think so," she said. "But you're right. Dainn is alive." She squeezed her fingers together so tightly that they ached. "He really doesn't know?"

Ryan shook his head. "I'm sure Odin was fooled. But he believes you're dangerous."

"He told you that?"

"It's obvious. I don't know why. You're powerful, but so is he. Why he'd be so scared . . ."

"Did you tell him anything else?"

"That you had to be with him if he was going to win." He squeezed his eyes shut. "Please don't ask me if that was a lie, too."

She didn't. "What did he say?" she asked.

"He at least pretended to believe me," Ryan said. "But I think he's going to watch you carefully during the next attack, and try to kill you if he doesn't like what he sees." He looked away. "I'm sorry, Mist."

"I wish I could say I'm shocked," Mist said, her body going numb, "but I'm not."

"I think the fight'll be a pretty big one," Ryan said, "since he keeps trying to find out if I can tell him anything specific. I just go blank and pretend I'm in some kind of trance."

"Do you remember saying something about trees and grass growing where cities now stand?"

"No," Ryan said, blinking. "Did I say that?"

"I don't want you to get hurt," Mist said. "Be very careful. If Odin ever finds out that you've deceived him . . ."

"He doesn't scare me," Ryan said, jerking up his chin. "I'll stay with him as long as I think I might be able to do some good."

"Promise me that you'll get away from Odin if you feel any danger at all," she said.

"I will."

She took his face between her hands and kissed his forehead. He flushed to the roots of his hair.

"I'd better go, before Odin notices I'm gone." He hesitated. "I haven't found any sign of Gabi. She was never the same after Eir died. Do you know what happened to her, Mist?"

"I know she can take care of herself," Mist said, hoping she wasn't lying to him. "You're still her best friend, and she wouldn't do anything to hurt you. She'll come back when she's ready."

Cupping his hand over the back of his neck, Ryan nodded slowly. "There's just one more thing," he said. "You need to believe that what Dainn is doing is right."

He slipped out before she could ask for clarification. She sat on the bed and touched her stomach again, remembering the pain. And the joy.

"*What Dainn is doing,*" Ryan had said. Present tense. She didn't know where Dainn had gone, or what he had planned to do. She only hoped he'd lay low, protect himself and the burden he carried.

But if Ryan had to *warn* her . . .

No, Dainn, she thought. *Don't do it.*

She knew it was already too late.

๑๑

"You're alive," Loki said. "How can you still be alive when our son is dead?"

The Jotunar burst into the room on Dainn's heels, and Loki tossed them back with a blast of ice-wind. He spun to face Dainn, a killing spell already on his lips.

"Calm yourself," Dainn said. He stood in the center of the well-furnished office, unmoving and unmoved, as if he had nothing of which to be ashamed, nothing to regret, nothing to grieve. "Danny is not dead."

Carefully containing his emotions, Loki felt his way to the nearest armchair and fell into it, quickly pouring himself a glass of whatever alcoholic beverage stood on the side table. Dainn didn't sit. His eyes were cold in a way Loki had never seen before.

"You drink too much," Dainn said. The old, almost comforting words, but dangerously flat. Loki decided that provoking Dainn now might be a very bad idea. He put the glass down.

"You say Danny is alive," he said. "*They* said you killed him."

"They?" Dainn asked. "Your spies? Vali, perhaps?"

Loki bounced out of his seat. "Do not push me too far, my Dainn."

Dainn inclined his head, all elvish dignity. Of the beast there was no sign. "I thought I killed him," he said. "It was what Odin wished."

"Odin," Loki breathed. Exactly as he'd suspected.

But Dainn had admitted his own guilt.

"Where is he?" Loki demanded. "Where is my son?"

"Odin intended to make it appear as if you had some part in his death."

The strength went out of Loki's legs, and he fell back into the chair. "How?"

"I was with Danny and Sleipnir in his stable, convincing Sleipnir to surrender to Odin. Odin made very clear what he would do if I failed. But then a second Danny appeared, speaking with your voice, and the real Danny fell unconscious. I had just urged you to take Danny away when Odin appeared and cursed me again."

"But *I* was never—"

"I did not realize then that Odin himself had posed as you in Danny's form, while maintaining an independent simulacrum of his own shape."

Loki banged his fist on the chair arm. "Odin hadn't used that trick in Asgard for years before the Last Battle, but he posed as a parrot and raven for decades in Midgard. I shouldn't be surprised that he'd use that magic again."

"He depended upon the ignorance of his followers. No one else witnessed what occurred. I—" Dainn's voice caught. "When his simulacrum cursed me, the beast . . . I attacked what I believed to be you. I tried to kill you."

"I am amazed," Loki said faintly, envisioning the scene with growing outrage.

"I thought you were dead until your body vanished, and I found Danny alone." He turned his face away. "I attacked the simulacrum, and he disappeared. He had intended for me to kill Danny once Sleipnir was released to him. I believed I had succeeded."

"Without injuring him?"

"I thought . . ." Dainn jerked up his head. "I thought my magic had killed him. But the situation was not what I believed."

"Your magic?" Loki stalked toward him. "*Where is Danny?*"

Dainn met Loki's gaze, his face neither cold nor warm, cruel nor gentle, but something precisely balanced between the two extremes.

"Danny is here," Dainn said, touching his own chest. "He sojourned with Mist for a short while, but she returned him to me, and he showed me the truth."

"He sojourned with—" Loki's heart was not subject to what mortals referred to as a myocardial infarction, but it might as well have been. "He is *inside* you?"

"Only his body is gone."

"And he . . . speaks to you?"

"He is a part of me."

Loki collapsed. Dainn caught him and eased him into the chair. Loki shook him off and scraped at his cheeks.

"Is he fully aware?" he asked at last.

"Yes. He shares my mind." Dainn closed his eyes. "When it seemed that the beast was in control, and that I had killed Danny with my magic, I had actually done something very different. I had unconsciously taken his soul, his . . . being into myself to save him from Odin. He was lost in my mind, but Mist found him again, and kept him until I understood what I must do."

"And the beast?"

"It is in Mist's keeping."

"How is that possible?"

"After the . . . incident, Odin had me bound and condemned. I was in a state of shock, unaware that Danny's spirit had joined with mine. Mist refused to accept that I would kill my son, even as the beast. She released me and entered my mind, taking Danny and the beast from me, but I did not understand. I let Odin's men catch me."

"And she helped you escape again."

"She was ordered to execute me at dawn this morning. She showed me that Danny still lived, and they . . . they arranged to set me free."

"Mist and Danny?" Loki said with a short laugh. "Her loyalty is to the All-father."

"Her loyalty is torn," Dainn said, sadness in his voice. "She defied Odin for my sake, but she was careful not to let him see what she did. She does not yet know the part Odin played in Danny's supposed death."

"I warned her," Loki said. "But would she listen to me?" He folded his arms across his chest. "How did she manage to get you away without exposing herself?"

"The storm," Dainn said.

"You mean the freakish weather that cut the power to over half the city?"

"Mist was responsible."

At least, Loki thought, he had grown beyond the tendency to experience unpleasant shocks where Mist's abilities were concerned. "Odd," he said, "how things turned out precisely the opposite of what you predicted would happen if I warned Mist of Freya's intentions."

"Even *I* underestimated her," Dainn said, "but if Odin still does, it will not be for much longer. I do not know what proof Mist left of my death, but Odin is not entirely a fool."

"And what did *he* think of the storm?"

"Eventually, he will guess it was her doing. Even now, I do not believe that he is fully aware of her capabilities."

"Her hero has feet of clay. Whatever he expected to find in Mist, it is not what he discovered when he came to Midgard. Will you wait until he comes to fear her so much that he takes direct action against her?"

"A great deal has changed since he and the Einherjar arrived, and she was relieved of much of her authority among the allies. I was confined when she fought Hel at Odin's side, but she experienced many shocks during the battle that troubled her greatly." His gaze hardened. "How many did you send your daughter to kill, simply to provoke the All-father?"

"I didn't . . ." Loki lowered his head and stared at Dainn from under his eyelashes. "*I* didn't send her. She decided to freelance."

"Then you cannot control your own children."

"It won't happen again." Loki shook off his anger. "How did you get here?"

"We teleported."

"Then if you can borrow Danny's magic whenever you need it, you should be able to find a way to get Mist a message without putting Danny at risk. A manifestation, perhaps . . ."

"Danny holds his own spirit alive inside me," Dainn said. "If he is too often distracted by such efforts, I do not know how long he can maintain his separate existence."

"You mean he'll just . . . disappear?"

"I know only what he fears. We must find another body, one that can contain his magic and has no soul of its own, and find a way to transfer his mind and spirit."

"No such child exists!" Loki exclaimed.

"Perhaps. But neither I nor Danny will permit him to return by means of destroying another living being, as Freya would have done with Mist."

"Why didn't the boy seer tell you what Freya planned?"

Dainn's hand snaked out and grabbed Loki by the neck. His grip was perfectly calculated to hurt but not damage, and Loki knew the slightest change in pressure would snap his spine.

As fast and deadly as the beast, Loki thought, but *not* the beast. This was something colder. And far more ancient.

"Why did you try to kill Ryan after we found Sleipnir?" Dainn asked.

Gripping Dainn's wrists, Loki tried unsuccessfully to free himself. "It was a test," he squeaked.

"Of what?"

There was little point, Loki thought, of keeping the secret now. "To see . . . if *you* had the Eitr. If you could heal him when he was at the very edge of death."

Dainn's grip eased. Loki gasped.

"If you had been wrong," Dainn said, "Ryan would have died."

"But I was . . . not wrong." Loki gagged. "When did you . . . know you could access it?"

"I wondered when Danny first manifested it in this house," Dainn said, "but I was not certain until Odin insisted upon acquiring it from me."

"He . . . knew you had it."

"And he knows that Danny has it as well. But you—" He tightened his grip again. "How long have you suspected?"

"Since"—he coughed—"Danny revealed his ability to wield it. I knew that ability had to come . . . from one of us."

"Why do I think you are lying?" Dainn asked.

"There was another time, when you helped defeat Danny's manifestation of Jormungandr. Do you remember how you made yourself a part of him and attacked him from within? Could you have done that with ordinary elven magic?"

"Why *then*? How could I not have known?"

"You were too busy fighting the beast."

Abruptly Dainn let Loki go, and Loki fell against the chair. He braced his arms behind him, watching Dainn's inscrutable face, ready to run. But Dainn was no longer looking at him.

"Odin told me," Dainn said, "that when I came to Asgard, I burned with the light of the Eitr. I have no memory of it, but I would think he destroyed any such ability when he released the beast."

"It was not destroyed," Loki whispered. "And you *did* shine. As Danny did, before—" The thought that came to Loki then erased all the pain in his throat. "You said we would need a body to restore Danny to full life," he said. "I think there may be another way."

30

Dainn's gaze swung back to Loki. "Explain," he said.

Loki took a deep breath and opened his right hand, revealing a swollen palm leaking watery blood. "It has not healed. Has yours?"

Slowly Dainn opened his hand to reveal the identical wound. "No," he said.

"I told you that it would always bind us. It is *your* Eitr that imbues these wounds, though I did not realize at the time why they would not close." He met Dainn's gaze. "You possess knowledge of the ancient Runes?"

"Why?" Dainn asked coldly. "Do you know how to break this bond?"

"It isn't for us," Loki said. "It's for our son."

"How?"

"You and I created Danny, whether or not you wish to acknowledge it," Loki said. "Your connection to the Eitr lives in Danny, as it lives in these wounds."

"Speak plainly," Dainn said.

"Perhaps . . . we can restore Danny, body and all. Together."

Dainn stared into Loki's eyes. His fists clenched. "You still hold some Eitr within you," he said.

"I had it before Danny was conceived," Loki said, "because Freya and I obtained it from you at a time when you were completely unaware of the magic you possessed."

A tense silence fell as Dainn digested what Loki had told him. "Obtained," Dainn said. "*Stole.* I had no knowledge of this."

"Because you lacked the memory and understanding to see yourself as you really were." *And still do,* Loki thought.

"Is that how you opened the first bridge to Midgard?" Dainn asked.

"And how Freya controlled the Aesir in the Asgard Shadow-Realm," Loki said, warily keeping his distance. "Obviously we made a very small dent in your supply. If Danny was the creation of your Eitr, he was also partly of mine. I believe that the mingling of our blood, aided by certain spells . . ."

"No."

At first Loki wasn't certain that he'd heard Dainn correctly. "No? Do you crave his power for yourself?"

His head snapped back as Dainn struck him. Loki moved to strike back, but his hand froze in midair as if caught in an invisible grip.

"Never suggest such a thing to me again," Dainn said, his eyes utterly black. He gestured, and Loki found his hand free.

Rubbing his jaw, Loki laughed. "Was that you, or Danny?"

"*He* would not hurt you. Not in that way."

"Even if you asked him to?"

Dainn's eyes unfocused. "No," he said, in a completely different voice. "I want to."

Danny, Loki thought. "What do you want?" he asked softly.

"I want to stay with Papa."

"Danny," Loki said. "If you don't leave Dainn now, you could be hurt. You could be—"

"He will not do it," Dainn said, his voice his own again.

"Ymir's bones," Loki swore. "Why not?"

"He will not tell me," Dainn said, blinking slowly. "He will reject any spell we attempt."

"Then what do you want of me?" Loki shouted.

Dainn told him. Loki sat down again.

"You want to . . . ally with me?"

"For the sole purpose of defeating Odin."

"You consider Odin worse than me?"

"Only your methods differ. I detest everything you are. But Odin is prepared to sacrifice any number of mortal lives to defeat you, and you are obviously prepared to do the same. Neither one of you can win without destroying the very world you wish to rule. Despite your evil acts, I know that is not your ultimate intention."

"It isn't Odin's, either."

Dainn sighed. "In the crack house, Ryan spoke of a vision. 'You have to be together,' he said, and he included me, Mist, and you in his prophecy. I know he fears the consequences of transmitting such information, and I do not think he would have risked it if he did not firmly believe that such an alliance is necessary."

"Or maybe *you* think I'll be easier to control when Odin is defeated?"

"I am not so foolish as to believe that you will give up your own quest for power. But we will deal with that when the battle is over."

"And Mist knows nothing of this . . . proposed alliance?"

"She will soon recognize the necessity."

Dainn met Loki's eyes. "When Mist realizes what must be done, I will be ready to support her." He leaned over the chair. "I know you will try to betray us. It is in your nature, as it is the nature of a cockroach to shun the light. But if you care for Danny, you will help us defeat Odin."

"Gladly, as long as you do not insist that I treat the All-father with mercy when he falls into my hands."

"I expect no mercy from you, and I want Odin dead."

Loki almost shivered. "I believe you," he said.

"Then we are agreed," Dainn asked. "You will keep complete control of Hel and Fenrir, but there will be no disregard of mortal lives. Mist will have final command until Odin is defeated."

Loki offered his hand. His scar was swollen and seeping blood. Dainn raised an equally gory hand. Blood mingled with blood as it had done at the making of the oath. Loki felt the shock of the Eitr pass into him and vanish.

"A kiss to seal the bargain," Loki said. Dainn turned his face aside, and Loki's lips brushed his cheek.

For now, it was enough.

"I have one suggestion," Loki said when Dainn stepped quickly out of reach. "If you and Danny feel up to it."

"What is this suggestion?" Dainn asked, deliberately wiping his cheek.

"Find the missing Treasure. Find the Gjallarhorn. With it, we may be able to control when the great battle begins."

◑◐

Traffic had come to a stop, dozens of mortals climbing out of their vehicles to point and stare. Late-afternoon pedestrians had dropped shopping bags, purses, and suitcases, forgetting everything but the astonishing sight of the man on the eight-legged horse and the army that marched behind him.

Mist walked just behind Sleipnir, trying not to see the onlookers the same way mortal pedestrians pretended they didn't notice the vagrants begging for money on the sidewalk.

"You will stand with me," Odin had said—not in anger, as she had expected, but with the calm confidence she had always expected of him . . . before. "You will not leave my side, and when I require it, you will summon a storm as you did before."

She'd known it wouldn't do any good to ask him why he didn't use his powerful Galdr to summon a storm himself, let alone try to explain that her magic could all too easily get out of hand.

Odin wouldn't care. Today he would make his first daylight strike at his enemy, without regard to Loki's defenses or the incredulous mortals around them. He had no patience for the games Freya had played, and during the past two weeks he had made very clear that he wasn't going to continue with skirmishes and raids and back-alley fights. Nor would he bother with the political machines Loki had built.

No, Mist thought grimly. He was going to make an *impression*. He knew he couldn't destroy Loki with a simple, open assault on his place of residence, but that mattered less to him than the declaration of intent. Loki's subtlety would be of no help to him now.

Once, it was what Mist had craved herself: plain, honest combat, without subterfuge or trickery. She'd hated the administrative duties that came with organizing mortals into a fighting force, despised the glamour she'd had to use to acquire those mortals. Give her a sword and a Jotunn to fight, and she was in her element.

Even when she'd known that kind of fight was no longer possible, she'd clung to the ideal. But reality didn't match what she'd thought she wanted. Odin had ignored her experts—the men and women who had worked so hard to research Loki's allies, the weak points in his strategies to control the city, the logistics of raids on his illegal facilities. All Odin's focus had been on training every mortal in the camp to fight, even if they didn't have the talent for it and wouldn't be ready for weeks.

And though he continued to warn of delays in bringing the other Aesir to Midgard, he managed to open bridges that delivered ever more Einherjar, warriors who nearly burst the camp at the seams, eating the food and confiscating bedrolls, working themselves into an ever-increasing frenzy of battle lust.

Now about a quarter of the Einherjar were strolling along behind Odin, singing and laughing as if they were going to a feast. With them were Anna and Odin's Valkyrie: Olrun, Hrist, Regin, and Skuld, all armored like Odin and the Einherjar in mail and leather. A good hundred mortal fighters marched behind them, and it was obvious that many of those mortals were unprepared to face Jotunn warriors, let alone to die for a god they'd barely seen. Odin hadn't even tried to win their personal loyalty or remind them of what they fought for; he had simply used his implacable authority to command them.

She'd dragged them into this, Mist thought, gripping Kettlingr's hilt until her knuckles ached. Their deaths would be on her shoulders. As would those of her friends who had insisted on coming: Captain Taylor, walking between the Valkyrie and his fighters; Rick, Vixen, Roadkill, and the other bikers; Konur and a band of ninety Alfar. She'd lost sight of Rota, who was also among the mortals, and Hild, whom she hadn't seen since they'd left camp.

At least Ryan was safe; as far as she knew, he hadn't been with

Odin lately, and she hoped that he'd put himself somewhere out of the All-father's reach. As much as she might like to protect him, he, like Gabi, was old enough to make his own decisions. He'd be better off staying out of the way.

A van bearing the logo of a local TV station pulled up on a curb just ahead of the column, drawing Mist's attention. The reporter and cameramen jumped out and set up without wasting a second. The reporter began a running patter, her eyes wide not only for effect but with genuine astonishment. Sirens approached from every direction, and more media vehicles arrived to cover the bizarre spectacle. The flash of cameras and light reflected from cell phone screens pierced the gloom like falling stars, there and gone in an instant.

By the time Odin was approaching Loki's headquarters, a bewildered crowd had fallen into step alongside the column. A few mortals laughed or chattered nervously, but most of them were silent.

They knew something was about to happen. Many might be remembering reports of the mysterious and horrible deaths in North Beach. Since no actual photos or videos of the incident had ever emerged, and no police or emergency vehicles had been able to get into the area until after the killings, reports of dead men and women fighting an armored man on an eight-legged horse had been put down to some kind of mass hysteria.

But that didn't keep the news services from reporting on the "delusions" of the witnesses. And a few of these onlookers might actually realize that this was no unexpected parade or protest march or one of the "special entertainment events" the mayor was so fond of providing.

Odin ignored them all until a dozen police cruisers and emergency vehicles blocked the street in front of him and twice as many cops took up defensive positions, guns aimed and ready to fire.

Not Loki's cops, Mist thought. Loki could still have arranged to send them, but he'd expect them to be no more than a momentary distraction, sacrificed to give him a little more time to prepare for the attack.

The All-father raised his hand, and the column gradually came to a stop. Twenty Einherjar moved forward to join Odin's personal bodyguard. Half were armed with spears, the rest with swords and axes.

"Put your weapons down," a woman's voice called through a megaphone. "On the ground. Sir, please dismount."

"You have one chance," Odin's herald called out to the cops. "Stand aside and remove yourselves, or be prepared to suffer the consequences."

Mist grabbed Odin's stirrup. "No, All-father," she said. "If you expect mortals to fight for you . . ."

He looked down at her without anger or reproach. "I will only show them what it means to defy their god," he said.

Their god. He had never used those words before.

"*Weapons on the ground!*" the woman's voice shouted.

"If you hurt them," Mist said, "you'll turn the whole city against you."

"Fear will teach them a lesson they will not soon forget."

"Please, All-father." She gripped his boot. "Permit me to try."

"Very well."

She hadn't expected him to give permission. She didn't want to do it. But the alternative was exactly the kind of chaos Loki would want.

And Odin seemed blind to how he might be playing right into Laufeyson's hands.

Striding forward to stand among the bodyguards, Mist closed her eyes. She smelled ozone, felt the latent electricity catch in her hair and raise goose flesh all over her arms. The clouds were already pregnant with moisture, waiting to be let loose.

Rain, she thought. Rain would be enough.

No spell was necessary. The elements came at her call, and suddenly hail burst from the clouds, striking uncovered flesh, pinging off metal, sending mortal spectators scurrying away from the street. The cops tried to hold their positions, but the downpour stung their eyes and beat on their hands with such force that they could no longer hold their weapons.

Odin gestured for his men to continue. A shot was fired, striking a warrior in the vanguard. He began to fall, and one of the man's comrades threw his spear into the center of the cluster of police vehicles.

Mist heard the cry as a mortal fell. She heard angry shouts, the woman's voice rising again, hoarse with the threat of violence.

Grabbing handfuls of the lowest clouds, Mist dragged them down to cover the ground. Visibility was reduced to less than three feet. Odin shouted at her.

Then the first Jotunn attacked, bursting from the fog as if he'd been hurled from a catapult. He impaled the nearest Einherji with an ice-spear, and frost spread in snowflake patterns across the asphalt as more and more giants materialized.

Mist let go of the fog, and suddenly the fight was all around her. She drew Kettlingr and went for the first Jotunn she saw, forcing him away from the man he had been about to kill.

The giants were going straight for Odin's weakest point, his mortal soldiers. And neither Odin nor the Einherjar were doing anything to stop them. Instead, the eternal warriors were attacking the Jotunar as the frost giants killed the mortals, while Odin spun Sleipnir around in circles, brandishing Gungnir and bellowing commands. Anna was fighting as if she'd been born with a sword in her hand, but Rick was trying to defend himself against a Jotunn almost twice his size. As Mist moved toward him, one of Konur's Alfar struck the giant down.

Moving into the very eye of the storm, Mist called on the elements once more. Thunder rattled the windows of every nearby building, and she snatched bolts of lightning out of the clouds, shaped them, bent them, diffused their energy so that they would stun but not kill. She flung the attenuated lightning at Einherjar and Jotunar alike.

"Mist!" Odin shouted. "Kill the Jotunar!"

She looked at him across the battlefield. He was smiling. There was no fear in his eyes, no concern that her magic might threaten him. Only supreme confidence that now, in the heat of battle, she would obey without question.

The battle would end and the mortals would be safe if she stopped the frost giants. *They* were the enemy, not the Einherjar.

When she next gathered the lightning, she flung each bolt with its full complement of lethal energy. One by one she felled the Jotunar, the rush of battle-fever claiming her again.

Then something changed. She remembered a voice, or a thought, or an image, and the lightning spun closer, clinging to her body like silver armor.

Odin killed Danny. The memory was wrong, but the feeling, the emotion, was more real than the broken weapons and Jotunn bodies on every side. She summoned another bolt and turned toward the All-father. Her tattoo blazed with living fire.

Strong arms grabbed her from either side, and a blade nicked her throat. She turned her own body into a live wire, electrocuting the Einherji who held her. Others reached for her, fearless in their loyalty to Odin, and she sent them flying.

But there was someone else with her, looking into her face with incomprehension and horror. Rota.

Her Sister. Her friend.

She let the energy drain from her body. The tattoo winked out. More hands caught at her, held her, forced her to kneel. Odin rode up to her, hand on his hip, while sirens and mortals screamed.

"I knew," he said. "You helped Dainn escape. You did not kill him. You always intended to turn against me."

"No," Mist whispered as a dagger nicked her throat. "Not always. I would have been—"

"Loyal, like my Anna?" He shook his head. "You are too much your mother's daughter, with all a woman's weakness and no man's will to hold your power."

"I wanted to . . . protect—"

"Your mortals? What are they to the Aesir, except servants, suppli-cants, and worshippers?"

"Worship?" she croaked. "Is that what you . . . demand?"

"I demand only what was ours, and to reclaim what is mine by right."

"Odin All-father . . . of the Northlands. *This* was never yours."

"No?" Odin raised Gungnir, leveled it, and swept it in a wide arc over the heads of mortals and Einherjar. Wherever it pointed, mor-tals fell—men, women, and children alike.

They died. And rose again—walking dead, but not like Hel's warriors. These, too, were Einherjar of a kind: free will destroyed, all gazing at Odin with sickening adoration. Prepared to serve him for eternity.

"Loki . . . was right," Mist whispered.

Odin ignored her. "Enter Loki's headquarters," he ordered the Einherjar. "Slaughter all within except any who can be questioned."

Releasing her muscles, Mist sagged to the ground. Before the Einherjar could drag her to her knees again, she laid both palms on the asphalt.

The earth shuddered. Cracks radiated out from the place where her hands touched, opening under Sleipnir's feet. The horse reared, nearly spilling Odin from the saddle. He lost his grip on Gungnir, which went flying. Horja—Anna—scooped it up and ran back to her master.

By then the earthquake had taken hold, so localized that not even the few mortals who still watched from the sidewalks were affected. Her guards toppled. Einherjar fell in dozens like wheat under a scythe. So did the mortal recruits, but Mist glimpsed Captain Taylor, Konur, and Vixen directing the others to retreat.

Concentrating until she was sure the quake would continue for the necessary few minutes, Mist scrambled up and ran toward Loki's building. The doors stood wide open. She could hear someone banging around inside, and so was ready when a pair of Einherjar emerged half-carrying a young woman between them. The red marks on her face told Mist that she'd been struck more than once, and her blouse was ripped.

Without hesitation, Mist shaped forge-Runes into iron staves that enclosed her fist like a boxing glove and struck both Einherjar in their midsections. They doubled over, releasing the woman, who fell to her knees.

"My God," the woman whispered. "My God, my God. He just left me here."

"Loki?" Mist asked, helping the young woman to her feet.

"Nicholas and all the techs got away. I was—"

"It's all right," Mist said. "Loki is gone?"

"And all the giants, and . . . everyone but me."

Mist glanced back at the doorway. This young woman must be one of the servants Odin had wanted to hold for questioning.

"They aren't going to hurt you again," Mist said. She led the mortal into the nearest room, a large office with handsome, traditional furniture. "What's your name?"

"Scarlet," she said. "Are you Mist?"

"How do you know that?"

"I can tell, just by—" She gasped, and Mist followed her stare. Incomprehensible Runes, painted in blood, covered the wall just inside the door. A message, left for someone who had the knowledge to read them.

"Sit down," Mist said. She laid her palms against the writing, and slowly the alien and yet beautiful markings resolved into ordinary Rune-staves.

"What does it say?" Scarlet asked with remarkable composure.

"It says where Loki has gone," Mist said, sounding out the words in her mind. "It says I'm to join him there."

"You? But he's your—"

"Dainn," Mist said, pressing her palm to the final word. "He was here."

Just as she had feared. But he hadn't killed Loki for any part he might have had in Danny's death. This was *his* blood, written in his hand.

They had called a truce, elf and godling. They had both predicted what Odin would become.

"*You have to be together,*" Ryan had said. But to make common cause with the Slanderer—Dainn's abuser, corrupter of mortals, slaughterer of innocents—

Like Odin? Mist thought.

"Are you going to kill Loki?" Scarlet whispered.

"Do you want me to?" Mist immediately regretted the harsh question, but Scarlet was already shaking her head.

"He can be a real son of a bitch," she said. "But he's . . ." She shrugged, but Mist could see that the young woman had fallen deeply under Loki's spell.

"I won't harm him unless he tries to hurt me or anyone I'm protecting," Mist said.

And since she was trying to protect almost everyone, Loki was bound to screw up. Dainn couldn't believe this would really work. *Dainn,* of all people . . .

"I can't stay with you," Mist said, "but I'll keep anyone else from getting in here. Is there a back way you can use?"

Scarlet nodded. "Where do I go?"

"Right now, just find somewhere safe to wait."

"I'd rather go to him."

"Not under these circumstances, you wouldn't." She glanced toward the door again. "I can make you do what I tell you. But I really don't want to."

The woman got up. "Please," she said. "No magic. I'll be quiet."

Mist had no choice but to take Scarlet at her word. She checked on the Einherjar as she left; both were out cold and were going to be in a lot of pain when they finally woke up. They'd gotten off lucky.

Outside, the quake had ended; so had the rain, but the sun might as well have gone out permanently. Red, blue, and white lights reflected off every surface as emergency personnel and cops scrambled back and forth across the street. Odin and the Einherjar were gone, along with the mortal troops. There was no sign of the humans Odin had murdered and resurrected, nor of the mortal and Einherjar warriors the Jotunar had killed.

The bodies of the giants were still there. EMTs, cops, and a CSI unit were busy examining the corpses. Pretty soon the authorities would know that they weren't dealing with *Homo sapiens.* And the panic would spread.

Wrapping herself in a cloak of invisibility, Mist ran east until she was well away from the chaos. She found a sheltered alley and leaned against the dirty yellow wall. Her whole body was shaking.

Dainn's Rune message had said that "her" mortals were safe. But what in Hel did that mean? Odin had cleared out fast, but had he somehow transported everyone back to camp? And what then?

She had to go back and see for herself. She had to get every mortal out of there, and the Alfar as well, if Konur hadn't already—

Idiot, she thought. *You go back there, Odin catches you, and punishes you by killing as many mortals as he can get his hands on. That is, until he kills you and makes it impossible for you to help anyone ever again.*

They'd be safer keeping their heads down, "worshipping" Odin and obeying him until they could find some way to escape. Captain Taylor was no fool; unless he'd been killed, he'd act accordingly to keep Odin pacified. At this point, Mist felt confident that Rota would share her judgment of Odin and stay away from him. She would be a solid ally. Rick and Vixen would do everything they could, and Konur would help them, regardless of the Alfar's current circumstances.

Unless Mist wanted to make things worse for them, she'd have to do as the Runes instructed. That, or draw on the Eitr so deeply that she'd forget whom she was supposed to be fighting. And even who she was.

She knew in the very core of her being that if she ever reached the furthest frontiers of her magic, she might never return.

Searching for a bike she could "borrow" to get to Golden Gate Park, she felt the sound before her ears registered it: an earth-shattering blast that rattled windows, set off every car alarm on the block, and sent her crashing to her knees. For a few moments she was too deaf even to think, and then she realized what she had just heard.

The Gjallarhorn. The herald of Ragnarok, the Last Battle, the end of the world. Someone had found it. And someone had decided that it was time for that final battle to begin.

31

It would end where it had all begun.

The circling storm made it impossible to guess the time, but Dainn knew by the angle of the barely visible sun that it was close to five in the evening. The Jotunar had cleared the area of any mortals who might have braved the park in spite of the inclement weather. The Polo Fields and surrounding area was cordoned off as efficiently and thoroughly as if by a high wall manned by experienced soldiers.

But the only soldiers here now were Loki's Jotunar and Hel with her dead. When the Gjallarhorn had blown across the city, arising from someplace not even Dainn could determine, he had known that there would be no turning back. The challenge had been laid down, and it only remained to see if Odin would accept.

And if Mist would be fighting at Dainn's side.

"Dainn," Loki said.

He followed Loki's gaze. Mist was striding onto the field, hair loose and glowing as if from within, shadows under her eyes and high cheekbones. Jotunar blood streaked her clothing, and Dainn's her sleeves.

She had read his message, as he had known she would. As he had known she would see Odin for what he was, and survive to fight against him.

"Mist," Loki said, acknowledging her arrival.

But she didn't seem to notice him. Her gray eyes were focused on Dainn's. She came to him, squeezing his ribs until he was unable to draw breath. He held her lightly, his cheek against hers, breathing in her earthy scent, perspiration and blood and woman. His body stirred, and he felt the power of her emotion: relief, confusion, grief, and more intimate feelings he could not afford to acknowledge.

He pulled away gently. "You saved my life," he said.

"I did what I could," she said. "But Danny was responsible. If he hadn't been—"

"We are both safe now." He paused to satisfy himself that none of the blood on her clothing was hers. "Are you well?"

"There's been a battle. But you know that. I'm not hurt."

"The beast?"

"Still quiet. I told you it can't harm me, Dainn." She scanned the area around them, her gaze resting briefly on the Jotunar ranked behind Loki. "When did you find the Gjallarhorn?"

"We didn't," Loki said. "It wasn't Odin?"

"No," Mist said.

They all stared at each other in consternation.

"The park is empty?" Mist asked.

"Of mortals, yes," Dainn said.

"And what of Odin?" Loki asked.

The light in her eyes dimmed. "I no longer follow him."

"Did he turn on you?" Dainn asked, mastering his rage.

"No," Mist said. "I turned on him first."

"Did he realize that you did not intend to kill me?"

"He was angry that I defended you in the past. But he also knows that I destroyed Freya. Now he fears me. He fears everything and everyone that might threaten his victory. He can't be allowed to rule this world."

"Fancy that," Loki muttered.

"If he suspects that the Eitr is the source of your magic," Dainn said, "he would hate and fear you for possessing what he covets."

"He already believes I turned it against him," Mist said.

"He wanted me to teach him how to access it again," Dainn said, "and he would surely have demanded the same of you if he had not determined that you were a threat to him."

"He killed people—children—swatted them down like flies just to make a point, and then resurrected them like Einherjar. I . . . re-acted."

"Was that what all the noise was about?" Loki asked.

"I am sorry," Dainn said, not knowing how to comfort her. "I knew this would come, but I could not answer your questions for you."

"Including the question of whether or not Loki is going to betray us as soon as our backs are turned?"

"I—" Loki began.

"We can't trust him, Dainn," Mist said. "Your message said he didn't have anything to do with hurting Danny, but . . . but he's proven his evil again and again."

"We have no choice," Dainn said, stripping all inflection from his voice. "There are now three sides in this conflict—Odin's, Loki's, and yours. You represent the mortal inhabitants of Midgard as Odin and Loki do not, but you cannot prevail against either one alone—"

"No, indeed," Loki said.

"—nor can you stand by while they destroy whatever lies between them and victory."

"Loki's piss—" Mist began.

"I beg your pardon?" Loki said.

"—you expect me to decide the fate of the whole world, here and now?"

"There is no more time. However it came about, the Gjallarhorn has been blown." He pulled Mist aside. "Ryan insisted that we must work together. If you make no alliance with him, Loki will use his forces to wreak havoc as you and Odin fight each other, and he will have the ultimate victory. I have already undertaken the decision on your behalf, but if you still believe Odin is Midgard's best hope and choose to make peace with him—"

"He will destroy you and everything you care for if he wins Mid-gard," Loki snapped. "But if we defeat him, the contest will come back to you and me, with no interference from other Asgardians. Which odds to you prefer, Mist?"

"Don't push it, Laufeyson," Mist growled. "You were right about Odin, but—" She hissed through her teeth. "Danny said, 'he will make everything bad.' I didn't know what he meant then, but I knew he wasn't talking about you."

"He spoke of Odin," Loki said. "Now you can be certain."

"Maybe you're both right, but after the things you've done to Dainn and—"

"Mist," Dainn said quietly, "I ask you to trust me."

"Do you think I didn't feel what it was like for you when Loki—" Mist blanched. "I'm sorry. I didn't mean—"

"I was ashamed when you took me from the garage," Dainn said. "I knew myself to be tainted and unworthy of you or the cause you fought for. Such feelings cannot weaken me now."

"But it's not because they're gone, is it?" Mist asked, searching his eyes. "No. It's because you've detached yourself from them. Nothing can touch you."

"That isn't quite true," Loki said. "I—"

She swung around and kicked him hard in the groin. He yelped and bent over, clutching himself as he scrambled out of Mist's reach.

"Mist," Dainn said, touching her cheek with the backs of his fingers. "I can no longer be certain of what I feel, as I cannot be sure of what I know. Danny and I are . . . very close now. His part in this is essential, though I do not understand what it will be. I cannot risk any lapse in judgment because of misplaced emotion."

"You're right," she said with a crooked smile. "I know what it's like not to be sure what you feel. But if we're wrong about Loki . . ."

"Odin tried to kill Danny," Dainn said.

He saw from Mist's expression that she had already known, or guessed. But the shock was still there, as if hearing the words spoken aloud had shaken her deeply.

Dainn told her the details, simply and without any interjection of emotion. "Even I did not realize what was happening at the time," he said, "as I did not know then how I had taken Danny into myself. He has no body of his own."

"Like Bryn," she said slowly. "Odin has her now, in the pouch that holds the Falcon Cloak."

"But he hasn't told you the rest," Loki said, circling Mist like a jackal stalking a lion. "He has his Eitr and Danny's at his fingertips, but he must take great care in using it. If too much is asked of Danny, he could cease to exist."

"I can still use the elf-magic," Dainn said, "as long as I do not push beyond its boundaries. And there is yet another way I can fight." Dainn met Mist's eyes. "Give the beast back to me."

"No!" Loki said. "It will see Danny as a rival for mastery of your soul, and—"

"Danny can help me control it," Dainn said.

"It's too great a risk," Mist said. "It could destroy you this time. We could lose everything."

"But you have already lost," Odin called.

❦

Mist turned. Odin sat astride Sleipnir, ranks of Einherjar behind him framed by the dull, listless sunset. Four Valkyrie stood with him, along with Anna Stangeland, who was no longer Anna at all.

Dainn took several long, deep breaths, maintaining his state of detachment. Odin didn't spare him as much as a glance.

"So," the All-father said. "Is this all you have brought with you, Loki Lie-smith?"

Following Odin's gaze, Mist seemed to notice Loki's army for the first time, the ranks of Jotunar and the dead.

"Oh, Hel," she whispered. "You brought *her*?"

"We fight Odin," Loki said, glancing back at his daughter. "We need—"

"She took mortal lives just to prove she could get away with it," Mist said. "If you think I'll fight beside *her* . . ."

One of the dead stepped in front of Hel, a man with a thin, raw-boned face and dressed in ragged shirt and trousers.

"Geir?" Mist said.

The man smiled, though much of his face remained in shadow. Dainn had neither seen him before nor heard his name, but it was clear that Mist spoke with more than mere recognition, or even surprise.

She had *known* him.

"I don't understand," Mist said, taking a step toward the phantom. "I thought—"

"Did you think he and his resistance would succeed?" Hel asked with a show of rotten teeth. "No rebellion against me has ever prospered, for the dead know their place, and there is nowhere they can go but into complete oblivion."

Geir met Mist's gaze. "I am sorry," he said. "But we were not among those who killed innocents for Hel's idle pleasure."

"My pleasures are never idle," Hel said. "And my father is most ungrateful, as are the rebels I have chosen to spare. Still, Lady Mist, I will permit you to hear this one speak."

"Mist," Geir said hoarsely, "you can't win without Hel. Only the dead can truly kill the Einherjar, so they cannot rise again. But that doesn't mean you have to become—"

He broke off with a choking sound and stumbled backward. "No!" Mist cried. She tried to follow, but Dainn gripped one arm and Loki the other, holding her until Geir faded and vanished among the dead.

"Believe me," Loki said, "you don't want to go there."

Mist swung around, and Loki let go, hastily covering his genitals.

"He is right," Dainn said, wondering what this Geir had been to Mist that she would so willingly walk into the mouth of Hel for him. "Nothing can be done for this man."

"Surrender now," Odin called to Mist, "and I may spare you that mortal's fate for the sake of the services you have done me in the past."

"He lies," Dainn said quietly. "He will obliterate you before he sends you to Hel."

"Odin Child-slayer," Mist said, sweeping her arm across her face, "you are not fit to rule Midgard."

"Then you will die, along with every mortal or Alfr who dares to follow you."

"Where *are* your people, Mist?" Loki asked in a low voice.

Mist looked at Dainn. "You said they were safe."

"Danny and I teleported them back to camp," Dainn said.

"Did that include the Alfar?"

"Yes," Dainn said, "but they will surely come."

"They know better," Odin said, shifting in his ornate saddle. "They gain nothing by giving their lives for the people of this world."

"They will have to decide how they plan to live in it," Mist said. She bent her head to Dainn. "I'm afraid for the mortals. I should never have gotten them involved."

Dainn touched her arm lightly. "Remember that most of them chose to serve you and fight for their world."

She smiled, as if his touch had restored some lost conviction. "For now, I guess it's just the three of us, Hel, and the Jotunar," she said.

"Remember that you possess the power of the Eitr," Dainn said.

"If I can use it without making things worse."

"You will." He summoned all his courage. "Return the beast to me now."

"Dainn—"

"You must trust me."

She gazed into his eyes, trying without success to find what they had shared when she had entered his thoughts and taken the beast. "You won't let me in," she said.

Inhaling deeply, Dainn tested the strength of the protective barrier he had built around Danny's soul and opened his mind. When she released the beast to him, he felt claws and teeth shredding his gut and lungs and liver and heart, scraping at anything that stood between it and Danny. He fell to his knees, unable to breathe, beginning to die.

"Dainn!" A touch like cool water alleviated the worst of the pain, and a healing force welled up from the very center of his being. The Eitr of light was there, the stuff of creation and growth, tempering the destructive power of the beast.

Within a few labored heartbeats, the struggle ceased. The beast was silent, and Danny . . .

Danny was still there, safe and whole.

"Dainn!" Mist lifted his head between her hands. "Is it all right?"

"Yes," he said. He let her help him to his feet. "Yes. You must—"

He never had a chance to complete his warning. "I hope you've finished dawdling," Loki said. "Here he comes."

Odin shook Gungnir, bellowing curses and battle cries. The Einherjar echoed him, one great roar of male voices, and Odin's Valkyrie joined with their higher-pitched yells.

Lifting Gungnir over his head, Odin attacked.

❧

Mist was already gathering the forge-magic as she rushed to meet the Einherjar vanguard. Dainn ran at her side, and she could feel the elf-magic awakening inside him. The Jotunar loped behind them, clubs and axes ready to swing.

Loki and Hel hung back, engaged in some kind of insanely ill-timed argument. Mist didn't have time to find out what it was about. She struck the first Einherjar with the full weight of her body . . . only half that of his, but she was the one who knocked him down. He raised his ax to defend himself, and Mist hesitated, remembering a thousand other battlefields when she had saved warriors just like him.

The ax swung at her legs, and she brought Kettlingr down, severing his arm from his body. Then she was facing the next Einherji, and the next, and Dainn was awakening dormant insects and worms from beneath the grass to swarm over the warriors, slowing but not stopping them. Jotunar beat their way through the crush of Einherjar, striking wildly and randomly at whatever they could reach.

Still Hel remained behind, and there was no sign of Loki. Mist was hardly surprised that he'd turned coward. As she felled two more Einherjar, three others she'd killed sprang to their feet.

That was Odin's great advantage, apart from his own magic. His army revived itself. There was no guarantee that any of the Einherjar would stay down without Hel and the dead to make sure of it.

But there might be another way to delay their resurrections.

"Dainn!" she shouted.

He broke off what he was doing—binding five Einherjar in writh-ing tree roots—and ran to join her.

"Keep them away," Mist said, indicating the next wave of Einher-jar with a jerk of her chin.

Dainn didn't ask her what she planned to do. He pulled sandy soil from the ground beneath his feet, sang an elven Rune-spell, and flung a wall of dirt at the warriors, who coughed and stumbled as they scrubbed at their eyes.

Mist called on the forge-magic, shaping Rune-staves of iron, steel, and fire into a net of fine but immensely heavy metal filaments, each one burning red and black. As one dead Einherji began to rise, she flung it over him, and he was trapped before the transformation was complete.

As Dainn continued to cover for her, she moved forward, creating more nets and flinging them wide wherever Odin's fallen warriors were returning to life. They began to go down in twos and threes, and the Jotunar continued to club and hack at the living Einherjar.

Realizing that she'd left Dainn behind, she spared a moment to look back. An Einherji had cut a deep laceration into his left arm, and he was losing blood quickly.

But the wound didn't slow him. He spoke, and she felt rather than heard the incomprehensible spells he sang. Edging her way closer to him, Mist saw that Dainn's arm was already healing.

He shouted to her, and she turned in time to deflect the blade of one of her Sisters: Olrun, who had once guarded the god Freyr's Sword—the weapon that needed no hand to wield it.

But Olrun was definitely wielding it, and with great expertise. Mist backed away.

"Olrun," she said. "You know who I am!"

"I know," Olrun said, her teeth flashing. "Traitor to our lord All-father."

"A lord who would slay women and children and common men without mercy!"

"He is our god," Olrun said, and attacked again. When Mist got in a blow to her shoulder, Olrun stepped back and let the Sword fight for her.

Mist parried and thrust, finding it difficult to predict the Sword's next movement without a body controlling it. There was nothing of Odin's soul left in the blade, but when she slipped in her defense and it cut the skin of her arm, she felt in her blood the hollow place left behind when Odin had drained the Sword of that part of himself.

An empty place she could fill. She attacked, swinging wildly to drive Freyr's Sword back toward Olrun, who hastily retreated.

Wasting no time, Mist sketched Rune-staves on Kettlingr's blade, letting some of her blood seep into the etching that spelled out the Sword's name. When Freyr's Sword came at her again, its fury redoubled, Mist made sure to parry with the part of her blade painted with blood.

The magic Sword groaned and snapped in two.

"Go, Olrun," Mist said, kicking the halves of the blade aside, "or I will have to kill you."

The Valkyrie looked from Mist to the broken weapon and ran. As Mist caught her breath, she looked for Dainn. He was dealing with several Einherjar, but it was obvious that he was having trouble. He had resorted to using a slim elven dagger, moving with a swift efficiency that outranked any knife work she'd ever seen.

Danny, she thought. *Dainn's afraid to take the magic too far.*

She spun around at the sound of eight hooves beating against the earth. Sleipnir was almost on top of her, but Odin didn't seem to see her. He was using an enormous ax to behead Jotunar, one after another, his beard and mail flecked and splashed with blue blood.

At the same time, the dead rushed forward from the back of the field, leaving the ash of straw-colored grass behind them as they came. Hel herself skimmed over the ground as if she rode on the wind of their passing, and the Wolf, Fenrir, loped in her wake—twice the size of any true wolf, intent on the one he had been destined to kill at the Ragnarok that never was.

Now, Mist thought, she had her chance. She reached inward for the Eitr, seeking the elements that would give her some hope of taking him down and leaving him at Hel's and Fenrir's mercy.

Her tattoo burned. The earth shuddered. Sleipnir reared, and the field fell silent.

Then the assault began: not of warriors or beings of the Homeworlds, but of the very elements Mist had hoped to deploy against the enemy.

But she hadn't done *this*. Eitr or not, Odin still had great power. The dull light that leaked through the heavy clouds disappeared, as if a giant hand had closed a shutter over the city. Hail shot down like bullets, carving divots out of the ground and slicing flesh without discrimination. Lightning slashed against the clouds, never quite touching the earth. Then the snow began to fall, heavily enough to cover the field, and everything on it, within a few minutes.

Mist peered through the fog, searching for Odin, for Hel, for anything she recognized. Then she heard wailing cries, and she slashed Kettlingr from side to side in front of her face, clearing wide swathes out of the falling snow.

The dead, unable to contend with the challenge of the heavy weather, were being struck down by Einherjar who had fought in such conditions for much of their original lives. Odin's Spear flashed gold as it hissed through the heavy air, taking down three Jotunar with one cast. He plunged out of the snowy veil, snatched up the Spear, and smiled right at Mist.

Suddenly Loki was there . . . and so were three Mists. Odin hesitated in confusion. Mist reached for the Eitr, felt it strike hard against Odin's magic like two blades clashing in a single powerful blow.

That was when the mortals arrived: Rick, Captain Taylor, Vixen, the hundreds of recruits who were willing to risk their lives for Midgard. She searched for Dainn and couldn't find him. As she sprinted across the field to join her allies, Loki appeared beside her. His feet barely touched the ground.

"How did *they* get here?" Mist gasped between breaths.

"I don't know," Loki said, "but you can be sure that Odin will use them against us, unless you harden your heart as a warrior must."

"Where is Dainn?"

"If he is to protect Danny, he must—"

He broke off as they reached the mortal troops. Rick and Taylor faced Mist squarely, braced against the unrelenting weather.

"How in sweet Baldr's name did you get here?" she demanded.

"We went straight back to Loki's HQ after we were sent back to camp," Captain Taylor said, holding his sword firmly at his side. "A woman there told us where to go."

"We heard the Horn, too," Rick said. "Hell, everyone this side of the bay must have heard it."

"The whole city's smothered in snow and ice," Taylor said. "Nothing is moving. Every mortal in San Francisco is a sitting duck."

"But Odin can't attack everywhere at once," Mist began, "even to—"

"Where the fuck—sorry—*is* that rat bastard?" Rick asked.

"Don't worry," Mist said. "He'll find *us*. Taylor, fall back as far as you can. Don't move unless I give the signal."

She waited until the mortals faded behind the wall of snow. Muffled footsteps alerted her, and she found herself facing Horja.

And not Horja. This was the Anna she'd seen standing beside Odin's throne, but her gaze was blank. She opened her mouth.

"The . . . pendant," she said hoarsely. "Give it to me."

"Anna," Mist said. "Listen to me. Remember who you are. Leave Odin, and come back to us."

Extending her arm, Anna reached toward Mist's neck. The pendant jumped under Mist's shirt. Anna lunged forward to grab it. The moment her fingers touched it, she fell.

And vanished. Lying in her place was a child with a familiar face and an expression of mingled fear and defiance.

"Mist," Rebekka said in a very small voice. "Don't kill me."

32

Listening to her heart instead of her head, Mist took Rebekka's hand and pulled her to her feet.

"Will you listen to me now?" she asked.

"I'm scared," Rebekka whispered. "Where am I?"

Mist hiked Rebekka up on her hip and called out to Dainn in her mind as a new wave of Einherjar charged toward her. Dainn stepped through a screen of snow, his hair nearly white with it.

"Take her!" Mist said, pushing Rebekka into Dainn's arms. She turned to face the Einherjar. Loki charged up beside her, urging his Jotunar to meet the attack.

Even as she fought, Mist was aware that something was wrong with Dainn and Rebekka. She retreated, fighting all the way, until she had a clear view of elf and child.

Rebekka was trembling wildly in Dainn's arms, and Dainn himself was as pale as the snow, his jaw clenched against some tremendous pain. Abruptly Rebekka squirmed out of his hold and turned to stare at Mist with eyes that had never belonged to a refugee child in Norway.

They were Danny's eyes, as dark as Dainn's, as old and wise as the eldest god's.

"Danny?" Mist stammered.

"No!" Dainn shouted. He grabbed at Rebekka as she—Danny—burst into a run, dashed past Mist, and ran between the strolling giants and Einherjar with no sign of fear. He reached Odin, who was overseeing the mêlée, and touched Sleipnir's broad shoulder with the palm of Rebekka's hand.

The horse's eyes shone white, and he reared, cutting at the Einherjar within reach, his hooves severing veins and carving deep slashes in the warriors' flesh. Odin lost hold of the reins and snatched at Sleipnir's mane, but he couldn't stay on as Sleipnir bucked and crow-hopped and bounced the All-father out of the saddle.

In an instant Danny-Rebekka was astride the stallion, and they were galloping away, literally disappearing before Sleipnir could leave more than four sets of hoofprints behind him in the snow.

Mist ran to Dainn, who was curled in on himself as if he had lost a part of his body. Loki appeared and grabbed hold of Dainn's arm.

"Where is Danny?" he asked Mist, panic in his voice.

"Gone," Mist said, stunned by Danny's act of coercion. "Anna took on Rebekka's shape, and Danny stole it, along with Sleipnir."

"The beast . . . began to break free," Dainn gasped. "Danny fled in the . . . only way he could."

He doubled over, coughing blood into the churned snow. Mist looked around wildly, hearing but unable to see the battle.

"Where are the Jotunar?" she asked Loki, lifting Dainn by the shoulder.

Loki shouted. Mist heard the giants' heavy feet pelting toward them, but suddenly the fog cleared and she saw that Odin was up again, red-faced and ready to kill. She had no sooner begun a defensive spell than he grabbed Gungnir off the ground, passed it over the Jotunar within his reach and killed every one of them.

Flinging back her head, Mist grabbed for the Eitr with both hands. Power flowed into her—from the earth, from the sky, from stone and snow and the blood of the fallen. Her tattoo blazed with agony. There was no direction to the magic, no control. She hurled every element straight at Odin's vengeful face.

※

"Do you feel Danny now?"

Loki's voice beat on Dainn's eardrums like pile drivers, and his arm ached where some weapon had sliced through his sleeve. But it was the gaping wound in his chest that hurt most.

He began to rise, but Loki pushed him down.

"Concentrate," Loki said. His face was unusually pale, his expression stark and sober. "Is he safe?"

"The beast," Dainn whispered, closing his eyes against the snow that blinded him.

Loki gripped Dainn's injured arm, twisting the slashed sleeve. "How?" he demanded.

"Too much . . . power," Dainn said, grateful for the pain. "Find Danny. I . . ." He convulsed again as the other spirit began to fill the hole Danny had left.

Dainn fought it. But he knew his hold on the beast was broken, and the temporary balance he had found with Danny's presence was shattered.

The beast laughed. It expanded, consuming flesh, mind, and spirit, twice as strong as it had been before.

A shock ran through Dainn's body, bending his spine and making him shake and jerk uncontrollably. He tasted fresh blood on his tongue, and opened his eyes. The beast's eyes.

Distantly, faintly, he heard a voice call his name. He ripped upward with his claws, felt them tear flesh. His prey fled out of his reach, still shouting, running.

He heaved himself to his feet and shook out his coat. Swinging his head left and right, he sniffed the air for the smell of his enemy.

One of them had to die, because there was no room in the elf's soul for both of them. He knew that if the boy won, the beast would cease to exist.

He broke into a run, glorying in the rush of wind and snow over his thick coat, the grip of his paws on frozen ground, the scent of death in his nostrils.

He had just caught the scent when he heard the hoofbeats. He charged the horse and the child on its back—the girl that was not a girl at all. He leaped, raking his claws across the horse's chest. It squealed, lashing at him with its hooves, but he dodged them easily.

The child looked down at him with wide, fearful eyes. The beast bunched his muscles to leap again.

A thickly furred body struck him from the side . . . a beast almost as large as he was, as heavy and powerful, but without his claws. He knew the name: Fenrir. Fenrisulfr, son of Loki Scar-lip, who had kept him weak and helpless so long.

Rage kindled in his heart as the Wolf seized his foreleg in its jaws. He felt pain and the flow of blood, but his own coat had taken the brunt of the bite. He doubled back on himself and snapped at the Wolf's neck, puncturing flesh. The Wolf howled and broke free to pant and glare.

Kicking snow into the Wolf's face, he looked again for the horse and child. Dark shapes rose in his path, led by a female of two colors and a body that stank of carrion.

He knew her, too. Hel, daughter of Loki. He charged again, and the dead ones fell upon him, clutching at his coat, clawing at his eyes, snatching at his tongue and his tail.

Then Hel touched him, and a great weariness came over his body. He wanted to lie down and sleep for a very long time. But he understood what she was doing to him, and he shook off the dead as if they were fleas.

The boy, he thought. When the boy was gone, only *he* would remain.

Power.

That was what Mist loosed now: such unrestrained power that it could not be contained except by the most extraordinary effort. She had no body, no form, but the Eitr caught fire within her, burning outward through invisible bone and flesh. She screamed. More power poured into her, and when the bolt struck, she struck back. Everything around her exploded like a gigantic star in its death throes.

"Mist!"

Something touched her, and suddenly she felt her fingers, her hand, her arm, all rematerializing as Ryan gripped her wrist. She blinked snow from her eyes and looked up into the young man's anxious face, becoming aware that she was lying in a hollow of mingled snow, ice, and dirt, and that smoke was rising from her clothes.

"Odin!" she said, ready to spring to her feet. Dizziness caught her, and Captain Taylor helped her sit again.

"Are you okay?" he asked. "Odin attacked you with his magic, but you put up one hell of a fight."

Mist felt her aching head. "I'm all right," she said. "How long have I been out?"

"Maybe five minutes," Taylor said. "We were about to move you when Ryan said you were coming out of it."

Five minutes, Mist thought. She'd gone into the fugue state at the moment she'd met Odin's attack . . . or at least she couldn't remember anything of the attack except a brilliant flare of light.

An explosion of light, as if from a dying star.

"Where is Odin now?" she asked.

"You forced him to retreat," Taylor said with grim satisfaction. "You knocked over a couple dozen of his fighters, and put the fear of God into him. I think he'll be licking his wounds a little while longer."

Mist nodded and met Ryan's gaze. "Where did you come from?" she asked. "You should have stayed in camp."

"I had to be here," Ryan said, sitting back on his heels. "This is where it happens."

Of course. She'd been stupid to think that anything could keep the kid away from the denouement of his visions.

But she couldn't ask him *what* was going to happen. And she knew he wouldn't tell her.

"Have you seen Sleipnir?" she asked Taylor. "Dainn? Loki?"

"They've disappeared," Rick said, kneeling beside Taylor. He glanced at the captain. "Hel's retreated, and—"

"Why?" Mist asked.

"Some kind of internal trouble with her army of the dead. We're still outgunned."

"How many have we lost?" Mist asked Taylor.

"It's impossible to tell in this storm," the captain said.

Mist made another effort to get up. She made it to her knees. "Listen," she said. "We need to find Sleipnir. He got away from Odin, and a little girl is riding him. I need you to find that girl."

"A little girl?" Rick asked. "Who the hell is she?"

"We can talk about that later," Mist said. "Taylor, try to keep our fighters in a holding action until—"

"Is *that* the girl?" Rick asked.

Mist followed his stare. Sleipnir was galloping toward them, Rebekka's small figure dwarfed by the huge saddle. Mist knew immediately that Danny still had control of the body. He slid off the stallion's back and ran to Mist.

"It's coming!" he said.

"Stand behind me," Mist said. She drew Kettlingr.

"Don't hurt Papa," Danny-Rebekka begged. He reached for Mist's free hand and clutched it tightly. "He saved everyone."

Mist looked down at him. His eyes swallowed her up, and she saw the exploding light, flinging out thousands of sparks . . . souls, living beings, cast into Ginnungagap from the Eight Homeworlds.

But alive. Alive, when they would have been killed at Ragnarok, as prophecy foretold.

The Dispersal.

Her mind erupted with ancient Runes and memories, and she became Danny, cradled in Loki's womb, a creature born to magic and utterly innocent. Then she was Dainn, who had tried to prevent Ragnarok with diplomacy . . . Dainn, ravaged by the beast and swimming in dark Eitr, cursed by Odin to kill Loki Laufeyson. Rage, and a flare of lost memory, a time before Asgard and Aesir.

Knowledge, understanding, revived at the perfect balance between dark and light. Dainn unconsciously sensing that to kill Loki would be to kill the son he hadn't known he had. Finding the means to stop Ragnarok . . . with a final act of magic that would split him in two.

But the magic hadn't been lost.

"I understand," Mist murmured, squeezing Danny-Rebekka's hand. "I know how to reach him."

"Mist?" Taylor said.

"Go," Mist said, giving Danny a gentle push toward the captain. "Take her and Sleipnir. I have other work to do."

Taylor grabbed Danny-Rebekka's hand and shouted to the others. Mist was alone when the beast came—tongue lolling, confident, fearless.

There was nothing of Dainn in his eyes.

Mist remembered the ancient Runes she had heard Dainn use before, the ones she had seen in Danny's mind. She knew their structure now, their alphabet, the way they worked. She sang them silently, one by one, and let them simmer in the back of her thoughts like a potent witch's brew.

The beast sat back on its haunches and laughed.

Mist, it said into her mind. *Give the child to me.*

"I know why you want him," she said, tightening her grip on Kettlingr. "You think that only one of you can exist inside Dainn, joined with his Eitr. You're wrong." She crouched and laid down her sword. "You know that Odin didn't create you. You were always the dark half of Dainn's power. His mistake was to deny that you existed until it was too late. When Odin cursed Dainn, you were set free. But even freedom isn't without limits."

I will never go back into the shadows.

"Odin made you into a weapon to turn against Loki during the Last Battle, but Dainn didn't let you win. Now Odin has you again, and he doesn't even have to tell you what to do."

I am no man's tool.

Mist looked deeply into the beast's eyes. "Dainn, fight it. You've mastered it before, without Danny. You can do it again. I have faith in you."

The beast roared, scraping deep furrows in the snow with its claws. She could feel Dainn struggling to break free, but Odin's curse lingered, a final barrier he couldn't overcome.

She plunged into the beast's mind, into its darkness, and made herself one with it. The beast convulsed, but Dainn remained beyond her reach. She let the Eitr flow into her, felt it merge with Dainn's, bubbling and seething and seeking destruction.

Her mind grew clouded, filled with thoughts of triumph just beyond her reach. It had to be finished.

A tall elf tried to stand in her way as she set off to find Odin, and she drew a narrow bolt of lightning out of the clouds to strike him down. A dark-skinned mortal pursued her, calling her name, and she wrenched a stone from the ground with half a thought and hurled it back at him.

No one else dared disturb her as she strode across the field. Odin stood alone on a hillock, guarded by a dozen mortal hostages and three times as many Einherjar who flailed at her with their axes and swords. She twisted her fingers, and heavy branches snapped off the nearest trees. She shaped them as they flew, and they impaled the Einherjar. Some went wide of the mark and struck mortals instead. Mist hardly noticed.

"All-father!" she called.

He looked up, teeth bared behind his blood-spattered beard. "Mist," he said. He waved his hand, and a dozen new mortals, men and women who had never seen a battle in their lives, ran to him like well-trained dogs. Whipped dogs, cringing and afraid.

"Come," Odin said. "I am ready."

Mist laughed.

∞

Ryan vomited into the snow, got to his feet again, and ran after Mist, calling her name again and again.

She was too busy killing to hear him. His stomach heaved, and he raised his voice.

As if she had just noticed a fly buzzing around her head, Mist glanced over her shoulder.

"This is only a part of you!" Ryan yelled. "Remember who you are!"

"This *is* what she is, boy!" Odin shouted, kicking fallen mortals away from his boots. "It is what she has always been! Or didn't your visions prepare you?"

They hadn't, Ryan thought. Not like this. But he was responsible, because somewhere along the line he'd made the wrong decision: to tell or not to tell what he had seen of the future, to act or remain passive. He could blame only himself.

Before he could speak again, the beast loped up behind him, tongue lolling, eyes slitted. Mist half-turned to face him, and for a moment she seemed torn between Dainn and Odin.

"Perhaps you can still save him," Odin shouted.

"Maybe I don't want to!" she answered. "We both want you dead!"

"But only one of you can face me," Odin said, brandishing Gungnir.

Immediately the beast turned on Mist. They stared at each other, bound by the dark Eitr, ready to kill.

"No!" Ryan called. "You're tied together now. You'll both die! You have to—"

Not fight it, he thought. That would only make the darkness stronger.

"Dainn!" he yelled. "Look at me!"

The beast swung its head around, blinking in confusion.

"Remember the light!" Danny said. "You saved a million lives! Can you take Mist's now?"

Crouching low, the beast backed away from Mist, stumbling over bodies in his way. He shook his head as if casting off parasites, and began to whine deep in his throat.

"I know you hear me, Dainn," Ryan said. "Mist remembers what you hid from yourself. You can see it. You can feel what she means to you. You are together, and the only way to save her is to save yourself."

Mist thrust Kettlingr at the beast. "Will you fight, cur?" she demanded.

He growled and whined and retreated, shivering violently.

"You can't just conquer the beast, Dainn," Ryan said. "It's part of you. You have to *accept* it. Just like Mist has to accept—"

A heavy stone from the enemy ranks struck Ryan full in the chest. He hit the ground hard and bit into his tongue. Something felt wrong inside his ribs.

It hurt, but not as much as screwing up. He *had* to make them understand.

"You *have* to accept," he whispered. "Both of you. Everything that . . . you are, dark and light, or it's all going to end."

With a contemptuous glance at Dainn, Mist moved to stand over Ryan. "Everything I am is here," she said.

"No." He coughed. "Dark and light," he said. "Both . . . necessary. Don't let . . . either one . . ."

Without warning, a little girl ran up to them, waving her arms. Rebekka's arms, Ryan thought, but also Danny's. Loki was right behind him. He tried to grab Danny, but Rebekka's body fought like a demon and ran straight to Dainn.

Ryan felt the beast struggle to escape Dainn's control. He clawed at his own chest, howled, tore at his flesh with razor fangs.

Then Ryan *felt* something pass between Dainn and Danny. The beast froze, and the little girl's body collapsed like a doll thrown into the snow. Loki fell to his knees beside Danny with a short, sharp cry.

Dainn knelt where the beast had been, his face drained of color. And Mist . . . Ryan felt her shock and horror, saw the dark Eitr spin madly inside her as if it had no way to escape.

With dazed eyes, Ryan looked for Odin. He was watching the drama play out as if he had nothing to do with it, the corners of his heavy mustache curving up in a slight smile. If he'd wanted to attack them, he and his soldiers could have done it anytime. The fact that he hadn't even tried scared Ryan more than the pain in his chest.

"Mist!" Odin said.

Her head swung toward him slowly. Ryan had the sense that the world was closing in around the three of them, the storm clearing in a circle wide enough to encompass Valkyrie, god, and Ryan.

Everything else had ceased to exist.

"This is *your* doing," Mist said to Odin, her face a mask of hatred.

"I underestimated your foolish devotion to the creatures who inhabit this world," Odin said, leaning his weight on Gungnir's shaft as Einherjar began to rise from the bloody ground at his feet.

"You speak of the 'creatures' who once looked to you for wisdom instead of death," Mist snarled.

"But I was also their god of battles," Odin said.

"You incited the peaceful to strife. You were the patron of outlaws."

"And what are you, Mist? Nothing but a bringer of death."

"You killed the first living being in our universe."

"All creation must come from death," Odin said. "The Eitr of Ginnungagap was the substance from which Ymir sprang, and my brothers and I could not create without the Eitr. His death gave us that power, and with it we made Midgard and its inhabitants."

"So the legends say."

"Nothing is beyond the power of the Eitr. It was mine to wield as I chose. But my access to the Eitr was stolen from me, along with the spells I used to control it. I had no memory of how to retrieve that power. My Aesir blamed the Vanir, and the Vanir refused to accept responsibility. So came the war between us."

"Which the Aesir won," Mist said. "But it wasn't one of *them* who stole it, was it?"

A black cloud seemed to settle over Odin's eye. "No," he said. "But I know who did."

33

"Loki," Mist said.

"Oh, no," Odin said. "He was never so powerful. But a being reborn into Loki's son—the offspring of the elf who can also touch the Eitr . . ."

"Danny?" Mist asked, her voice rising in disbelief. "You think he's the reincarnation of whatever stole your Eitr?"

"The reincarnation, the embodiment . . . what difference?" Odin asked. "I did not know until I saw him with Sleipnir and felt his magic, but then I recognized our greatest enemy. And the one from whom I must regain my power."

"He's a little boy, and you tried to kill him!"

"I arranged for Dainn to kill him. It seems as if he may finally have succeeded."

"You're insane," Mist said.

"Am I? What better parents could such a creature choose than the greatest of Tricksters and the First Elf?"

"The First Elf?" Mist repeated. "*Dainn?*"

"You knew he was very old, did you not?" Odin asked. "That he came to Asgard a wanderer, with no memory of his past?"

"The First Elf is said to have been born in the time of your father, Bor. How could he have forgotten his true self if you haven't?"

"I do not know, nor do I care. But he, too, possessed the Eitr when he came to Asgard. He has said he had no knowledge of it, but I saw in him what no other did . . . not only the light, but the darkness he had hidden away. The noble elf without flaw had a terrible secret. When I learned that Dainn had fallen to Loki's blandishments in pursuit of his hope to stop Ragnarok, I simply woke that darkness and gave it shape."

"I know," Mist whispered. "You turned it into the beast."

"I sent it to kill Loki," Odin said. "Dainn failed me that night. He let Loki live and came to Midgard, where at last he became Freya's tool."

"He believed Freya's lies when she said she could cure him."

"Only death will end its hold on him, and death will come as a mercy. You could have given him that mercy."

Mist was silent for a long time after that, and Ryan knew she was remembering something important, something Odin might not know. The burst of light, the supernova Ryan had seen so many times . . .

He laughed, though it hurt and made him cough up blood. It was so clear now. Maybe Odin was insane when he said that Danny had stolen his Eitr before the kid had even been born. Maybe he was lying. But he didn't seem to know that *Dainn* had stopped Ragnarok with the help of the dark part of himself.

"You have lost Dainn," Odin said. "His son's death will have driven him mad. But Dainn is no longer of concern to me. You *are*."

"I will never serve you again."

"Your mother bred you for one purpose: to wield the Eitr as she no longer could." He showed his teeth. "Yes, I know about your many fathers, as I knew you could navigate the fourth circle of magic the first time I met you in this body."

"You *knew*?"

"Did you believe me when I told you that the tattoo was only meant to track the first three circles of magic? It always responded to the Eitr. The truth was within in it all along.

"You were meant not only to be Freya's champion, but my destroyer. I made certain that my seed was planted in her womb at precisely the right time. You are my daughter, and now you will give me what I always wanted from you."

※

"I always wondered which god had a part in siring me," Mist said coldly, feeling the dark Eitr dissolve with her shock. "I hoped it wasn't Thor, but I never guessed it could be you."

"But you realized that you would not still be alive if you were not kin to me, whatever your magical gifts," Odin said. "I see that you still doubt me. Know, then, that with the Eitr I can end this war swiftly, with minimal loss of mortal life. Only the wicked will die, and Loki will join his daughter in the afterworld, never to return."

And you, Mist thought, *will rule as tyrant, destroying any being who doesn't bow his head to you.*

"Mist," someone called weakly behind her.

She spun around. Ryan was lying in bloodstained snow, his arm stretched toward her. She had been utterly oblivious to his presence.

"Don't listen to him," Ryan whispered.

A blast of noise and light swirled in around them, and Odin vanished. Mist saw the bodies of mortals broken in the snow where Odin had been standing a moment before. Men and women she had been responsible for.

She was the killer, the assassin, the wielder of dark Eitr.

"Ryan!" she cried, running to kneel beside him. The blood on his lips told her that he was hurt somewhere inside, and she didn't dare move him.

"Dainn!" she shouted, looking about wildly. "Gods, Dainn . . ."

He appeared out of the snow, his clothes sodden and his eyes black wells of despair. Loki trudged behind him, Danny-Rebekka in his arms. The child wasn't moving.

Shutting off her emotions, Mist forced herself to think only of the living. She looked into Dainn's eyes.

He was *not* mad, whatever Odin had claimed. But she had no time for relief.

"Dainn," she said, "you healed Ryan before. I need you to do it again."

The elf stared down at Ryan, his hands working at his sides, tears freezing on his cheeks. He knelt slowly. Mist looked away from Dainn's sorrow and saw other shapes emerge from the white, several of her own fighters and a dozen women wrapped tightly in colorful shawls. Gabi was among them.

So was Konur. He ran up to Mist, condensation wreathing his head, and took in the situation with a quick, perceptive glance. His gaze fixed on Loki, who stood unmoving, his expression blank.

"I've brought the Alfar from camp," Konur said without preamble. "Do you need us?"

"Did you see Odin?" she asked. "He was here, and then just disappeared."

"The fighting is concentrated near the west end of the Polo Fields," Konur said. "Odin is not there, but the Einherjar are doing considerable damage to your mortals."

Mist swore. She should be with her warriors, not here. But she couldn't abandon Ryan, or leave Loki and Dainn alone.

Dainn rose stiffly. "I cannot help Ryan," he said in a choked voice. Gabi moved up beside him, followed by the beshawled women, and flung herself down beside her friend.

"*Madre de Dios,*" she whispered.

"Gabi," Ryan said faintly. "Where did you . . . go?"

"Shut up," she said. "I have to heal you now."

The women gathered around Gabi, Ryan, Dainn, and Mist, forming another circle that cut off the rest of the world. Mist searched the unfamiliar faces—brown faces, some old and careworn, others young, all imbued with a quiet wisdom that was a balm in the midst of chaos. Each of them wore a cross around her neck, and some began to chant or sing softly as Gabi laid her hands on Ryan's chest.

Ryan gasped several times, fresh blood trickling from his mouth. He shuddered, teeth chattering, and suddenly lay still.

"Gabi!" Mist said.

"He's . . ." Gabi lifted her swollen hands. "*¡Mis madres, mis hermanas, ayuadame!*"

The girls and women linked arms, and the two nearest Gabi touched her head and shoulder. She laid her hands on Ryan again. His eyelids fluttered. His chest rose and fell in a deep sigh.

Gabi lifted her hands. They were a little swollen, a little red, but she was smiling.

"He'll be okay," she said. She looked at Mist, and her smile turned into a fierce expression Mist recognized all too well. "If he wakes up, don't let him tell you anything! He could die if he speaks any visions."

"I won't let him," Mist said.

The women broke the circle and spoke in soft Spanish, words of comfort and approval. Mist glanced at Dainn, whose gaze was turned inward, and beyond him to Loki and Danny-Rebekka. The girl's face was slack and pale. Loki came back to life as if someone had turned on a switch, radiating an almost fiery heat. His eyes glowed with savagery.

"If you're healers," he snarled, "help my son!"

Slowly Gabi rose, glancing at Mist. "His son?"

"And Dainn's. Will you help him?" She saw the look on Gabi's face and said, "Loki won't hurt you. He cares about Danny too much."

And it was true, Mist thought. He might not care about anyone else in the world, but he loved his son. Maybe almost as much as Dainn did.

Hesitantly, Gabi moved toward Loki and Danny. Loki conjured a blanket, laid Danny down on it, and stepped back.

After a few quiet prayers and whispered references to El Diablo, the women followed Gabi, who gathered Danny-Rebekka into her arms with great tenderness. Once again the *curanderas* formed a tight circle around the healer and her patient.

Then one of them cried out. The circle broke open, and Mist saw Gabi lying beside Danny in the snow. Before Mist could act, the *curanderas* had carried Gabi a little distance away and were already praying over her, while Danny-Rebekka was sitting up with Loki's support.

"What's wrong with Gabi?" Mist demanded. "*¿Que pasa con Gabi?*"

One of the women made a shushing gesture and turned back to the teenager. A few moments later, Ryan—apparently healed but still weak—staggered up to the wall of human bodies and pushed his way through to Gabi.

The women drew apart, heads bent. Ryan knelt beside Gabi, cradling her head in his lap. He looked up at Mist through eyes blurred with tears, a crust of blood still painting his lips and chin.

"She's gone," he whispered. "It was too much, healing me and then trying to . . ." He bent his head, snow settling unheeded on his hair.

"Sweet Baldr," Mist said, closing her eyes.

"It should have been *me*," Ryan said. "I knew there would be a sacrifice. . . ."

"You, too?" Dainn said sadly. He put his hand on Ryan's shoulder. "It was not in vain, Ryan. Have courage. This is not over."

"*No*," Ryan said, jumping to his feet. "You have what *you* wanted." He turned to Loki, eyes wild. "Where is Hel?" he demanded.

"I don't know," Loki said, rubbing Danny-Rebekka's back. "She had one of her tantrums, and—"

"I have to find her," Ryan gasped. Like a wild thing, he leaped into the arms of the storm and disappeared.

Mist prepared to go after him, but Dainn held her back. His eyes were clear again.

"He is driven by his visions," he said softly. "You must let him follow where they lead."

"He's crazed with grief," Mist said, trembling in Dainn's grip. "What can he want with Hel?"

"You have to trust him, Mist," Dainn said. He pulled her into a crouch beside Danny-Rebekka, who gazed at her with a child's naïve stare.

"Is he all right?" she asked Loki, struggling to put Ryan out of her mind.

"Papa?" Danny said. Before Loki could stop him, he touched Dainn's arm. Suddenly Mist could sense Danny's thoughts, see powerful images of a past Dainn himself was only beginning to remember. And this time every detail was crystal-clear.

Freya and Loki had stolen Dainn's Eitr in Asgard, taking advantage of his trusting nature and his amnesia. Even so, they had barely scratched the surface of his power. The vast majority had remained within him, and with it Dainn had caused the Dispersal. Though he had retained his elven magic and had continued to use it, his most powerful magic remained beyond his reach for many centuries.

But it hadn't been lost. The greater part of it had been passed on to one being, one innocent child still in Loki's womb.

Consciously or not, Dainn had poured the Eitr that was so much a part of him—the best of what he was—into his unborn son. But much of the darkness—the "beast" that he had refused to acknowledge for untold years before his coming to Asgard—remained to torment him.

Over the long centuries Dainn had gradually taken control of the beast, only to lose it again. But Danny was still the heart of his ancient magic, the embodiment of everything Dainn had lost in the Dispersal.

Dainn grabbed Danny and held him in his arms, burying his face in Rebekka's dark hair. Loki made to snatch Danny away. Mist drew Kettlingr and stood over him.

"Back off," she warned. "This has nothing to do with you."

"If you interfere again," Loki said, jumping to his feet, "our alliance—"

He broke off as Konur's lieutenant, Hrolf, jogged up to them. Hrolf glanced from Loki to Mist and then to Dainn, wiping blood from his mouth with the back of his hand.

"Konur sent me," he said. "We are hard-pressed. Odin is using more human shields gathered from outside the park, and Hel is still absent. Without her dead to fight the Einherjar . . ."

"I'm coming," Mist said, getting to her feet. "Loki, you'd better find your daughter if you still want to win this war."

"I'm taking my son away from here," Loki said, lunging toward Dainn.

But Danny was no longer there. Dainn's arms were empty. He looked up, his eyes almost calm.

"Where is he?" Loki demanded, grabbing Dainn's collar.

"I don't know," Dainn said. "I believe he is safe."

Elf and godling stared at each other, but Dainn's impassiveness gave Loki nothing to fight. He cursed foully and got to his feet.

"I'll find Hel," he said, "but there will be a reckoning when this is over."

With a flash of teeth and a burst of flame that cleared the ground of snow within a six-foot radius, Loki transformed into a crow and hurled himself skyward into the blowing sleet.

"Why did Danny leave?" Mist asked, kneeling beside Dainn.

But she knew. Danny was afraid. He was afraid of what would become of him if he made the right choice.

Dainn only shook his head. "We should go," he said. With a brief nod to Mist, he set off toward the distant sounds of battle. Mist caught up to him, and they ran together like wolves on the hunt.

◑◐

Like an endless wave of soldier ants, the Einherjar crashed upon them.

Rick, Vixen, Roadkill, Tennessee, and the surviving bikers fought with almost suicidal courage; in Hild's absence, Rota sang like the very soul of the storm; the other mortal recruits surged forward again and again under the command of Captain Taylor and his lieutenants, partially protected by the Alfar, who used their nature magic to entangle enemy feet in tree roots and blind their eyes with dirt and twigs. Loki's Jotunar beheaded Einherjar with their axes and pounded them into sacks of shattered bone.

But the Einherjar continued to rise from death, and when Mist and Dainn arrived, the situation was critical. Loki appeared a few minutes later with assurances that Hel was on her way. Beside Loki was Fenrir, snapping and snarling at any two-legged being that came near. Dainn threw himself in among his Brother and Sister Alfar, using his dagger with deadly precision and showing precious little regard for his own life. Mist fought beside him. As if he felt compelled to prove his courage equal to theirs, Loki joined Mist and Dainn at the front lines.

Using his gift for illusion, he "increased" the ragged troop of Jotunar by half again, forcing the Einherjar to retreat. He took on the shape of the mighty fire-giant, Surtr, who had once been destined to burn up the Homeworlds in a holocaust of fire. His body turned black and red, a living flame that incinerated anything it touched.

"Do I look like my father?" Loki said to Mist in a voice like hot coals.

Mist parried the swing of an Einherji's ax and cut off the warrior's hand. "Surtr?" she grunted.

"Did you never wonder why I have such a gift with fire? Surtr took my mother, Laufey, against her will. She never recovered, even after she"—he cut down a screaming Einherji—"married Farbauti."

There was little place for compassion in Mist's heart, but she found that she could pity Laufey. She had given birth to an evil creature, but that creature had never asked to be born as the child of assault.

Before she could speak again, Loki had moved ahead of her. An ax-head bit into his arm, another into his side. He fell to his knees, and the false army of giants behind him dwindled to less than fifty. The remaining Jotunar closed ranks around him.

Then the battle simply stopped, as if someone had laid an apathy spell over all the combatants. Captain Taylor, fighting beside Mist, suddenly lowered his sword with a look of profound bewilderment, and the Einherji he had been fighting did the same.

Odin's doing, Mist thought, though it was far too difficult a spell to hold for long. She pressed forward against the magic, and when she found Dainn again, he was facing Odin across a wall of Valkyrie and twenty Einherjar. Dead Alfar, Jotunar, and soldiers lay scattered on every side. A curving line had been drawn on the icy ground, red as blood. More than a hundred captive mortals, paralyzed like caterpillars stung by assassin bugs, floated just behind and above it, each one guarded by a very mobile Einherji, ready to strike.

Mist stared up into Odin's good eye. "Coward!" she shouted. "Come out of there and fight!"

Odin waved his hand, and a figure rose up behind him, blond-haired and bearded, bearing Thor's weapons: the Belt of Power, Megingjord, encircled his thick waist, and he held the Hammer Mjollnir with a hand gloved in Jarngreipr, which had once been in Rota's charge.

With such weapons, Thor had been almost impossible to defeat.

"Vali," Mist said. Loki crept up behind her and Dainn, his hand pressed to the clotting wound in his side.

"The trick is on you, Slanderer," Odin called out, smirking behind his beard. "Vali was ever *my* agent, not yours."

Loki sighed. "I *am* disappointed," he admitted. "And to think I provided him with those Treasures. One can expect no gratitude from one's inferiors these days."

Mist stared at him. "You're kidding."

"I admit my judgment was flawed in this matter."

"In *this* matter?"

With a quick glance at Dainn, Loki shook his head. "Perhaps in more than one. But if we are about to die, it's of little consequences, is it?"

"Why die when you can run?" Mist asked, sarcasm heavy in her voice.

"If I can keep my son safe, perhaps my ultimate fate is unimportant."

"You have changed, Loki," Dainn said quietly.

"Kindly don't insult me," Loki said. He snapped his fingers, and flames sputtered from his fingertips. "Shall we?"

"You are too weak," Dainn said. He met Mist's gaze. "And you must not face Odin and Vali alone." He closed his eyes, and Mist "heard" him reaching out to the beast.

All at once Danny was there, sliding down from Sleipnir's back, Rebekka's dark hair curling over his shoulders.

"Papa?" he said.

"Come to me, Danny," Loki urged. But the boy only gazed at Dainn with that peculiar, innocent wisdom that no longer seemed quite so strange. He gave Sleipnir a brief pat on one huge foreleg and walked slowly toward his father.

Dainn knelt, took Danny's small face between his hands, and touched his forehead to his son's.

"You should have stayed away, my son," he said.

"No, Papa." Danny smiled sweetly and brushed a tear from Dainn's cheek. "I'm ready."

Before Dainn could answer, Odin's Valkyrie came—Olrun, Regin, Hrist, and Skuld—shouting battle cries and sprinting toward Danny with the mad commitment of *berserkir*. Mist swung Kettlingr toward the new threat.

She wasn't nearly fast enough. Hrist and Regin grabbed Danny by his arms and carried him off, leaping with the grace and speed of battle-steeds. Too late, Dainn jumped up to snatch him back.

Loki stumbled after them, cursing as his wounds spattered blood in an uneven trail behind him. Before Mist could take more than a few steps, the Valkyrie had vanished behind Odin's wall of Einherjar, and the clash of battle resumed all around her. She heard the pounding of booted feet as the surviving Jotunar fled.

The moment Loki's foot touched the blood line in the snow, one of the mortal hostages fell to the sword of his Einherji guard. Mist stopped. Loki continued, and another mortal died.

"I know you care nothing for their lives, Laufeyson," Odin said, "but once you have walked over their bodies, Vali will crush your head with Mjollnir."

"Stop!" Mist shouted. "Loki, you can't help Danny this way!"

I can.

Mist turned. The beast was there, rising on its hind legs, eyes burning with savage intelligence. Dainn's intelligence, fully aware and in control.

With a wordless scream of rage, Loki hurled himself among the Einherji. As another hostage fell, Dainn leaped after Loki, seized him by his collar, and flung him back over the line.

After that, there was only a blur of black motion as the beast moved among the Einherjar, striking them down with ruthless efficiency before they could murder their hostages. Mist concentrated on getting the mortals across the line to the relative safety of the battle behind her. To her astonishment, Loki had deliberately attracted Vali's attention and was goading him into clumsy attacks on his former "master."

But Mist knew that distraction couldn't last. Odin bellowed a command, and Vali swung toward her and Dainn.

You know what you must do, Dainn said as he paused to catch his breath, his tongue lolling between red-stained teeth.

Mist knew. She had to call on the Eitr again.

I am with you, Dainn said.

Swallowing her fear, Mist opened herself to the Eitr. It came to her in wisps of cloud, more gray than white, veiling her face like netting. The root of the World Tree crept up through the soles of her feet.

Easy, she told herself. She reached for a little more, and the netting became more solid, circling outward to curl around the beast's face and those of the Einherjar and their remaining captives. Weaving the strands of Eitr, she sent them flying out like handfuls of ribbon, each strand working its way around the feet of an Einherji. The warriors tripped and stumbled as other strands snatched their axes and swords out of their hands and hurled them hundreds of feet away.

Odin shouted in rage, turning the storm into a fury of the elements. Jagged hail rained down on Mist's head, and Dainn stood over her, shielding her with the beast's immense, muscular body. As the Einherjar found their feet again, Mist pressed her palm to the earth, awakening the rock beneath, and the ground shuddered as thousands of small stones and pebbles worked their way to the surface. The warriors slipped and slid as they tried to retrieve their weapons. Dainn made certain they didn't.

"Mist!" Loki shouted. She spun to see Vali hovering over Laufeyson, the Hammer descending in a slow arc to smash the life out of him.

Without thinking, she grabbed a handful of storm and flung it at Vali. The full force of wind and snow, laced with stinging pebbles and sharp stones, struck Vali with the force of a wrecking ball. He fell back, the Hammer swinging wide. Loki scrambled well out of his way.

But Odin had not been idle while her attention was distracted. More mortal hostages emerged from his warriors' ranks . . . and among them was Rick Jensen. The big biker hung from Odin's grip like a puppy by the scruff of its neck, but his face was hard with defiance. Dainn's beast ran up to stand beside Mist and snarled.

"He is only the first!" Odin shouted. "I will pluck your friends from among your pitiful troops one by one, and they will suffer before they die."

The cloud of Eitr floating around Mist grew heavier and darker, and the branches of the World Tree growing inside her began to wither. "Let them go, Odin," she said.

"I could destroy this entire park, and everyone in it . . . including you."

The Eitr filled the air with an acrid tang of chemicals, mingled with the sickeningly sweet scent of decaying flowers. What had been a filmy veil became a thick, ropy tangle of black substance like swollen intestines spilling their rotted contents.

Mist breathed in the poison and coughed violently. The hotter her anger grew, the greater the risk that she would tear those grotesque organs apart and let the contamination spread. And there would be more where that came from . . . endless supplies of toxins and evil magic from the flip-side of creation.

"Don't, Mist," Rick croaked. "He wants you to fight him that way. He—"

Odin ran Rick through with Gungnir's sleek steel blade, and the biker slumped over the shaft. Odin jerked the Spear free and dropped Rick's body to the ground.

"Do not think of it as losing a friend," Odin said, "but of gaining another fighter for Hel."

34

With a scream of rage, Mist called up all her memories of battle, of every fallen companion and friend, of the joy of seeing an enemy fall. The storm screamed with her, and Dainn howled. Her hair crackled with electricity. Kettlingr hummed in her hand. She advanced, knocking the newly risen Einherjar to the ground with blasts of ice flechettes that pierced their armor and tore their flesh in a thousand places.

"Dainn, get the hostages out of here!" she shouted. Swift as a sheepdog, Dainn's beast rounded them up and drove them away. Then there was nothing between Mist and Odin. But Vali loomed behind his father, Mjollnir above his head, the leather and metal glove like some alien monster devouring his hand.

He came at her without hesitation, swinging Mjollnir to crush her bones. Kettlingr was already there to meet the Hammer. The sword cracked and shattered. Mist dropped it and, as Vali raised Mjollnir again, toppled a dozen moaning, leafless trees from the surrounding groves. The heavy shafts flew to her and stood around her like wooden guardians, linking branches like loving arms intertwining.

The first trees took the brunt of Vali's blow and split down to their torn and quivering roots. Mist placed spears of lightning into branches that served as arms and hands. Some trees stabbed at Vali, while the branches of others, turned to steel, wrapped around his wrist and dragged his arm and Mjollnir down to his side. He toppled like one of the trees, bound and helpless.

All around Mist the pockets of dark Eitr expanded, forming

coruscating bubbles that floated up into the evening sky. When she pushed her hand into one, her fingers emerged a mottled gray and something oily and malignant sizzled on her skin.

She flexed her fingers, spraying drops of poison that boiled away the snow and blackened the ground where they landed. She could catch one of those orbs and simply cast it at Vali. It would burn him alive, strip the flesh from cheeks and jaws and forehead, boil his brains inside his skull.

Let it go. Wasn't that what Freya had told her? Rick would be avenged. They would *all* be avenged.

Mist! a voice called. A beloved voice. She turned to look for Dainn, but it was Danny she saw, Danny, running out from behind Odin, his arms reaching for one who could protect him. The beast reared up beside Mist, dropped to all fours, and rushed toward the boy. Odin strode after Danny, laughing, fingers curled to seize and grasp. Danny wailed, and a mass of energy burst from him, striking Odin full in the chest. He rose off the ground, arms flung wide, his face blue and black like an ugly bruise.

Before Mist could get Danny to safety, Loki appeared to snatch up his son. As Loki fled into the storm, Mist heard the sounds of the main battle drawing closer, metal striking metal, the cries of pain and shouts of anger and fear from behind and to either side. The sickly orbs and the thick clouds of Eitr began to converge on Odin like hounds responding to their master's whistle.

He was *controlling* them. He had regained mastery of the Eitr, and that knowledge could only have come from Danny. Mist could do nothing to stop her former lord.

But she wasn't alone. The beast charged Odin, teeth bared, kicking mud-blackened snow behind him.

Catching one of the orbs between his hands, Odin cast it directly in Dainn's path.

The orb exploded against the beast, spitting liquid fire that slicked his heavy coat and set it aflame. The sharp odor of singed fur mingled with the smell of rot. He snarled and yelped and rolled wildly on the ground, but the fire would not be extinguished.

Discarding the dark Eitr, Mist skidded to the ground beside Dainn and drew all the moisture out of the air around them. She shaped it into a blanket and wrapped the beast tightly, smothering the flames.

Even when his fur had stopped smoldering, the foul essence of dark Eitr clung to him like the stench of carrion. Overhead, the sky began to darken again, the stars blotted out by the never-ending storm and the Eitr that leaked from the orbs and began to fill the spaces between. Odin floated to the ground, his boots scorching the earth where they landed.

Mist got to her feet, her fingers buried deep in the beast's mane, and faced Odin. "Do you know what you're doing?" she shouted. "You're bringing the Void to Earth! The Eitr is building. If you release it—"

"Everything will die," Odin finished, shaking the blood from Gungnir's blade. "Do you think I am such a fool, Daughter? I once wielded this magic as if it were a toy." He flicked his wrist, and a pockmarked, distorted sphere of Eitr floated sluggishly toward the battle raging behind Mist. "I shall build an entire new world, as was meant to be after Ragnarok. I will create new forests and fields and beasts, and shape a new mortal Ask and Embla to be the first man and woman. They will grow to love me as their sole ruler."

"And the other Aesir?" Mist asked. "You never intended to bring them here at all, did you?"

"Why should I? They would only meddle, ruin what I will build—"

"You have lost your way, Odin All-father," Dainn said. He stood in his elven shape again, his fair skin scorched and lashed with the stripes of burns, but his eyes were nearly black. "The Eitr of creation has gone beyond your reach."

"I took back what belonged to me," Odin said. "The boy has nothing left."

"You are wrong, Odin," Dainn said. "And I was the one who stole your Eitr from you after you completed your acts of creation, because with it you would have created monsters."

"So now you remember your past," Odin said. "You know who you were when you came to Asgard."

"And why I blocked my memory of the Eitr and the magic that controlled it," Dainn said. "Some part of me knew you could not be permitted to wield it again. Even now, all you bring is death."

"And all you ever wished for was peace?" Odin laughed. "All those mortals you killed after I gave life to the darkness you refused to acknowledge . . . so much blood on your claws."

"Yes," Dainn said. "And there will be more, because I will do my best to destroy you."

"We *will* stop you, All-father," Konur said, arriving behind Mist with a troop of Alfar.

"You're damned right," Vixen said, the tracks of tears evident across her mud-streaked face. A pitiful few mortal warriors joined her, but they, too, were not alone. Rota was still alive, and Hel had returned at last, her warrior dead drifting around her, semitransparent shapes bearing ghostly weapons.

"You have far fewer Einherjar than you did fifteen minutes ago," Captain Taylor said, wiping a big hand across his blood-smeared jaw. "I don't think Hel will be running again."

The goddess of death looked considerably worse for wear than she had the last time Mist had seen her, the black-and-white hair disheveled and dirty, her gown torn and her face stark with anger.

"Send your warriors to me, by all means," Hel said to Odin. "I shall be glad to have them."

The All-father didn't answer. Each misshapen orb around him seemed filled with wriggling rods and spirals like oversized bacteria. He lifted his hands with a discordant Rune-song, and the Eitr began to spread, bursting free of the orbs to form inky streaks across the sky. Vixen, Taylor, and the other mortals began to cough and gag.

Mist took Dainn's hand. "We can't let them die for us," she said. "I'm going back to the dark Eitr."

"No," Dainn said, his lip curling like an angry dog's. "I can take him down."

"Even if you give yourself over to the beast completely," Mist said, "you will never defeat him. I won't let you do it."

He looked into her eyes. "And if *you* lose yourself?"

"You once made me promise to kill you if you lost control of the beast," she said. "Can you do the same for me?"

He tipped up her chin and kissed her on the lips. Vali stomped through the allied troops, swinging Mjollnir left and right as regularly and precisely as a machine.

The screams woke Mist from her brief respite. She jumped back and summoned one of the Eitr spheres. With a wild cry, she brought lightning down from the sky and pierced the sphere in a dozen places, mingling the electricity with the poison of the dark Eitr. As Dainn leaped at Vali's legs, tearing with jaws more powerful than those of the biggest jaguar, Mist redirected the toxic lightning at Vali's chest.

The Hammer swung erratically as Vali staggered under the assault, his clothing sizzling with oily burns. Blood coursed down his legs to pool at the tops of his boots, but still he didn't fall. He cursed and turned Mjollnir against Dainn, catching the beast in the ribs. Mist heard the crack of breaking bones and screamed as she raised and slammed a half-buried boulder into Vali's body.

Vali crashed to the ground. When the smoking fumes cleared, he lay on his back, sightless eyes staring at the sky, Mjollnir's handle still in his slack hand.

Mist felt no pity, no regret for the friendship they had shared in another life. He had made his choice; she had made hers. She knelt beside Dainn, who lay panting on his side.

"Can you hear me, Dainn?" she asked. She buried her hands in his heavy coat. "Don't leave me now."

His breath hitched, and his animal's eyes were filled with sorrow.

Mist jumped to her feet. She called Hel to her side and plowed through the Einherjar standing between her and Odin, flinging their bodies directly into the waiting hands of Hel's dead.

It wasn't enough. Odin was still beyond her reach. She transformed the Eitr into boiling acid that she cast into the faces of their enemies, indifferent to their cries of agony as they clawed at melting flesh.

"No," Konur said. He slipped up beside her, laying his hand on her arm.

"No," Captain Taylor said, gripping her other arm.

The Einherjar fled beyond her reach. She stared into Konur's eyes.

"Release me," she snarled. "I *will* kill you."

"Freya did not create only an assassin, bound to fall into darkness," Konur said.

"We know you," Taylor said. "We know what you can be. I couldn't be prouder of you if you were my own daughter. And you almost are."

"Taylor's ancient ancestor was one of your sires," Konur said gently. "He was a hero of his day, a noble man. Svardkell was a Jotunn who strove for peace among our peoples. The dwarf Freya chose was no less a hero and leader of his people."

Laughing with contempt, Mist knocked Konur aside, snatched up an abandoned sword, and lifted it to kill Taylor. A small hand came to rest on her leg, and she looked down.

"You have to choose," Danny said. He glanced behind him, where the beast lay watching. Waiting. "Don't be afraid."

"Afraid," Loki said, appearing behind his son. His voice was rough and thick with something like grief. "You don't understand, do you? Odin has already stolen some of the Eitr from Danny, and now he will lose the rest." His voice broke. "He is returning it to its rightful owner. Dainn will never need fear the beast again."

"And the boy?" Mist asked with distant curiosity.

"He may cease to exist. But he knows what he is. Do you?"

"I know what I—"

She never finished. Danny patted her leg and turned toward the beast. Dainn rose shakily to four legs and tried to retreat, moving stiffly and in obvious pain. But Danny didn't stop. Ignoring Dainn's snarl of warning, he flung his arms around the beast's neck. When they came together, there was blinding light that cut through the dark Eitr like an archangel's sword.

Danny was gone. Dainn stood at the center of the light as it faded away, his eyes closed and his hands spread palm-up as if he were accepting a gift from the gods. He opened his eyes and looked directly at Mist.

"Come back, Mist," he said. "This is not who you were meant to be."

"Get out of my way!" she shouted. "Where is Odin?"

"Hiding behind his men," Konur said softly, struggling to his feet. "When you face him again, he will expect to meet his equal in darkness. Will you give him what he desires?"

Stabbing at the sky with stiffened fingers, Mist drew the Eitr down around her. Konur and Taylor sank to their knees. The allies began to wheeze, choking on air that had turned thick as tar.

"Odin will fall," she said. "And when *I* rule—"

"Mist," Dainn said, wrapping his hands around hers and working the sword's grip from her fingers. He let the weapon fall. "You told me to kill you if you lost yourself. Do not force me to destroy another thing I love."

"You cannot . . ." She trailed off, looking into his eyes. They were mesmerizing, changed almost out of all recognition: still indigo, but layered with emotions and thoughts she couldn't begin to interpret, a deep wisdom countered by a very mortal need.

"Danny has returned all the power I had lost," he said, his voice heavy with sorrow. He took her hand. "Let me take your anger, your hatred, your darkness. I can defeat it now." He kissed her left cheek and then her right. "I love you, Mist."

A great shudder took Mist, shaking her from the soles of her boots to the top of her head. Words were not enough. Words could never be enough. But Dainn rested his forehead against hers, and she felt the madness begin to dissolve, the lust for power drain out of her heart.

Dainn fell to his knees. Immediately Konur was beside him, and Gabi came running out from among the women who had appeared among the allies.

"Gabi?" Mist stammered, remembering her last sight of the girl lying still in Ryan's arms.

The teenager dropped down beside Dainn and touched his chest. His breathing was ragged, his skin nearly transparent.

"You have the cure, Mist," she whispered. "If you want to keep him alive, give him what he gave you."

Give him? Mist thought in confusion. She had nothing to give him. He was an ancient one, born at the time of creation.

"Tell him," Gabi insisted. "Tell him, *idiota!*"

So she spoke the words. And a great space opened up in her heart, big enough to take back the anger and hatred and hunger for power, take it back and swallow it up. Dainn sat up slowly. Loki stood behind him, his red hair sparking, his face taut with rage.

But not at Dainn, or Mist.

"I let you have what you wanted," he said. "Now give me Odin."

"Konur," Dainn said, taking Mist's hand. "Get everyone away."

As Konur and Taylor moved to obey, Dainn touched his chest and smiled at Mist. "We will do this. Together."

◑◐

Many as one.

Odin hid among his Einherjar—those not taken by Hel and her dead—who huddled close about him, still bold and courageous but well aware that they would be throwing their lives away by attacking now.

Many as one. Odin cursed himself, though it was as foolish an act as the Christian God swearing upon his own name. The second prophecy had seemed so clear. There would be no true Ragnarok. He who was also many would bring about a new world, destroy all that would stand in his way, and assume absolute rule of a pristine paradise.

He had always assumed that "one" was him. He had not simply waited for the prophecy to be fulfilled. He had placed his soul into twelve Treasures, knowing they would one day be reassembled. Many as one.

But now he knew he had been blind to the obvious. Perhaps it was because he had never taken the Gjallarhorn, leaving that smallest piece of his soul unclaimed. Whatever the cause, he had not seen what should have been so clear: Mist, the product of five fathers—including Odin All-father—was also many as one. Dainn Rune-bringer, with his beast and the child, were three as one . . . and there had been no number set to the "many."

If *they* were to fulfill the prophecy, then he would be the one brought low. He would never rule.

But he had one more test for Mist. He stepped out from among his personal guard and met her with a grin.

"Do you think you've won?" Odin asked. "What do you feel, Daughter? Triumph? Satisfaction? Do you think you will finally have everything your own way?" He looked over his shoulder. "Anna!"

She walked out from behind him, whole once more, a Valkyrie clad in armor and bearing a sword inscribed with Rune-staves that spelled out the word Odinsnautr, "Odin's Gift."

"As you can see," Odin said, "your prodigal child released Anna's body back to me. I will be most curious to see how you fare against her."

Mist looked past Odin at Anna. "Don't do this, Anna," she said.

"You should not fear for *her*," Odin said. "She holds the spirits of four Valkyrie, and my favor. She is your match."

"Four Valkyrie?" Mist asked in horror.

"Hrist, Regin, Skuld, and Olrun. Those that already belonged to me."

"What did you do to them?"

"They were of no further use to me."

"Mist," Dainn said. "You have no need to fight her. There are other ways."

Mist laughed. "I don't think I'll have much—"

"Kill her," Odin said, pointing Gungnir toward Mist.

Raising her sword, Anna charged Mist, fearless, nimble, ferocious. A strange hesitation seemed to take hold of Mist, and Anna struck the first blow, sinking her blade into Mist's arm.

Then Mist was fighting for her life. Hissing between her teeth, Mist wrenched free and struck out. Her sword sank into the mail covering Anna's thigh, and the mortal woman hopped backward.

She didn't stay away for long. Anna fought bravely, with all the skill imparted by Mist's slain Sisters. She felt no pain. And she was ruthless. Again and again she nicked Mist's flesh and forced her to retreat.

Odin felt new stirrings of triumph. Mist was too proud. She would never believe this girl could defeat her, and she wouldn't stoop to the Eitr now.

But she was not yet finished. Gaining herself a little distance, Mist grabbed the raven pendant from under her shirt and pulled it out for Anna to see.

"You wanted his before," she said, retreating with every swing of Anna's sword. "Do you remember what it meant when I gave it to Rebekka seventy years ago? How Geir took care of her? How she passed it down as a precious gift without knowing what it was?"

Anna paused, and Odin screamed for her to fight. Still the mortal remained frozen.

"Do you remember when Orn was just a parrot, your best friend?" Mist asked. "What happened to that friend, Anna?"

With a cry of rage, Anna attacked. She beat Mist to the ground, and the sword flew from Mist's hand.

But she wasn't alone. Dainn appeared between Anna and Mist, and when Anna struck, her blade passed through Dainn as if he didn't exist. Mist scrambled to her feet, grabbed the nearest abandoned sword, and caught Anna's blade with her own, twisting it to yank the weapon out of Anna's hand. Anna fell on her back like an overturned beetle, helpless and exposed. Bryn's pouch, which Mist had given her earlier at Odin's command, lay clearly visible upon her chest. Mist rested the point of her blade against Anna's exposed throat and sliced the cord around her neck, quickly tucking the pouch in her jacket pocket.

"What . . ." Anna stammered, staring up at Mist with wide eyes. "Where am I?"

Mist released her and stepped back. "Are you satisfied, All-father?" she shouted.

Odin's skin grew hot with rage. But he still understood one thing Mist did not. She had cast out the dark Eitr with Dainn's help, but it was not gone.

And Dainn . . . he believed he had gained complete control over the beast, silenced the darkness within himself, become the powerful being he had been long ago. But Odin knew that neither Mist nor Dainn had accepted that the darkness would always be there, a part of them. It would rise again, and the more they fought it the more entrenched and powerful it would become.

"Mist False-daughter!" Odin cried. "Dainn Son-slayer! Loki Lie-smith! Will you face me now, when nothing stands between us and all your allies have fled?"

Mist stepped forward, her chin high. "It's our charge to bring you down," she said. "You must pay for the lives you have taken and the evil of your hubris."

"And Laufeyson?" Odin asked. "How will he pay for what he has done to this city?"

Loki spat. "I have paid with my son," he said. "And I will make *you* suffer for it."

"It is Dainn you should cause to suffer, is it not?" Odin said, smiling at the elf. "Has he not robbed you of everything you loved?"

"No," Mist said. "We all have a greater enemy to fight now."

"With what?" Odin asked. He lifted his arms, and the clouds of toxic Eitr began to spin with the storm, whipping with heady violence around the field, dislodging trees with even the deepest roots, flinging shrubs in every direction. "All I need do is release the Eitr, and you will have no world to claim."

Mist began to sing in a rough, carrying voice, drawing ice from the air, raising stones from the ground, chanting spells of iron and steel. Ice and stone and steel formed densely woven cages, and one by one they encircled the distorted spheres of dark Eitr like ravenous cells in a body riddled with disease. Dainn summoned tree roots from under the ground to tangle about Odin's boots, and fading leaves from the trees to blind his eye. Loki bombarded Odin with missiles of fire.

And none of it touched on the dark Eitr. Mist would not risk it, nor would Dainn use his beast again. They were still afraid.

Laughing in the face of the storm, his single eye watering from the constant assault of debris and his mouth filled with grit, Odin sang the dark Eitr. One by one the globules of Void began to split open. Those encased by Mist's magic leaked only a little; those she had missed began to disgorge their contents in a steady stream, the mi-asma drifting upward to join the greasy haze that already floated over the park.

"You must work more quickly, Mist," Odin taunted. "The wind from the ocean is refreshing, is it not? How long will it take to carry the poison over the entire city?"

Clenching her fists, Mist raised her voice. She conjured more cages, but she could not keep pace with Odin's work, and the raw materials she had used became scarce. Dainn touched her arm. Her face screwed up in defiance, but the tone of her song changed, and suddenly the oozing drifts of Eitr turned against the force of the wind and curved back toward Odin.

Now Mist was using the dark Eitr, but she was not losing herself. Dainn was beside her, chanting spells not even Odin understood. They steadied Mist, and Odin witnessed the precise moment when she understood, when she accepted all she had become and could be. It was in the calmness of her expression, the way she held her body, the glance she gave Dainn as he rested his hand on her shoulder.

There was a force here that Odin had discounted, an emotion he had abandoned long ago and had no means to fight. As the Eitr drew nearer, he knew he would not be able to hinder Mist's determination or cripple her power with his own.

But as she threw all her concentration into guiding the Eitr pre-cisely where she wished it to go, she was vulnerable. He shifted his grip on Gungnir, preparing to throw.

Another hand seized it from his grip, and a ragged voice whispered close to his ear.

"She is mine," Vidarr said. And with a move as swift as it was deadly, Odin's son hurled Gungnir directly at Mist's heart.

35

Mist's legs gave way as the Spear's head pierced her chest and emerged from her back, just missing her heart.

But it was close enough. Dainn caught her and eased her down, his hands coated in blood, his breath seizing in his lungs.

"Mist!" he choked, holding her just off the ground. "Loki, get the others!"

But Loki had vanished, and so had Vidarr, Odin, and his followers. Mist's breath frothed on her lips. She tried to smile.

"Vidarr," she whispered. "Who would have thought—"

"Hush," he said, as much for himself as for her. His heart seethed with panic, but his mind still functioned.

Cradling her body in one arm, he curled his hand around the shaft of the Spear with the other. The healing Eitr was already within him; he sang the ancient magic, his voice grinding with fear, and visualized the metal and wood of the weapon dissolving inside her, the blood vessels mending, the bleeding stopped.

Mist gasped and arched upward. Gouts of fresh blood, bubbling with lost air, welled up around the shaft.

Dainn knew he was failing. Mist was only alive now because of her own will.

"Don't worry, Dainn," she said, blood gurgling in her throat. She touched his face. "If I . . . wind up with Hel, I'll . . . lead the rebellion my—"

Her eyes closed. Dainn raised his voice in a howl that shook the trees, and the others came: Rota, Konur and half the Alfar, Taylor and the surviving mortals, Gabi and her *curanderas*.

"Gabriella," Dainn rasped. "Help me."

The girl knelt beside him, her brown skin pale with shock, and laid her hand on Mist's chest. Opening his mind, Dainn tried to reach Gabi with the Eitr, to let her feel it and draw it into herself. She blinked rapidly, but Dainn knew that his attempt was failing.

"The wound's too bad for me," Gabi said, turning her head to wipe her face on her sleeve. She called to the *curanderas*, and they gathered close, chanting their prayers to the White Christ and their God.

But the life was leaving Mist, her heartbeat slowing, her breaths shallow and rattling. With a sudden twist of her body, Gabi pressed her palm to Dainn's chest.

"You're still not whole," she murmured. "You are still fighting it."

Hel drifted up behind her, casting a deeper shadow in the poisonous twilight. Two other shapes emerged from the gloom she wore like a cloak. One of them was Ryan, and he was dead.

"Ry!" Gabi cried.

He ignored her, fixing his blank stare on Dainn. "Accept," he said in a ghost's wasted voice. "You grieve for Danny, but he was never meant to live apart from you. The beast was always there, but you refused to . . ." He rolled his eyes at Hel. "There can be no life without death. Set the beast free."

Fury built in Dainn's chest, a feral rage he knew all too well. He reached deep into his soul to pull it out, held the beast at arm's length as it snapped and snarled and laughed at his weakness.

You will always fight me, it growled. *You will never admit that there is darkness in the first and the wisest. Give in. Let me—*

Dainn pulled the beast close. Its teeth sank into his neck as its claws raked at his belly, disemboweling him, shredding his organs and piercing his heart. Eating him alive.

But suddenly Danny was there, within him. He opened his arms, and the beast fell into him, both boy and beast dissolving into Dainn's blood and bone.

Whole for the first time in centuries, Dainn took Gungnir's shaft in both hands and sang the healing again. The wood began to disintegrate, the honed steel to crumble. Blood rushed from the gaping wound in Mist's chest, and just as suddenly stopped. He continued to sing until he was hoarse, mending each blood vessel, the torn lung, every severed muscle and tendon.

With a fit of violent coughing, Mist sat up. Dainn continued to hold her until her breathing was steady again. She felt her chest.

"Did I dream it," she asked, "or did someone just impale me?"

Dainn tried to laugh, without success. Gabi sobbed. There were other sounds, but Dainn could make no sense of them. He knew that Danny was gone, and that he was no longer afraid of the beast. He knew that somehow Ryan was dead, that Odin was still free, and that the dark Eitr continued to leak its poison into the air above the city.

But Mist was *alive*.

"Gabi?" Mist said, pushing herself up on her elbows. "You're all right?"

Dainn met the girl's gaze, and she looked away. He sensed that she knew what had happened to Ryan, but Mist clearly didn't realize that the young mortal was in Hel's possession, and Dainn wouldn't let her take on that burden now.

There was still hope. More than Dainn had felt in a very long time.

"Where's Odin?" Mist said, struggling and failing to stand until Dainn lifted her and held her up.

Something hard, white, and cold landed with a thump at her feet. Dainn recognized it as Vidarr's severed head, frozen through and close to shattering.

Loki arrived just afterward.

"Odin's taken off," he said, "literally." He kicked Vidarr's head, and a sizeable chunk of his jaw broke off. "He found Sleipnir and forced him to fly."

Mist met Loki's gaze. "The Einherjar?"

"Scattered. But we have a bigger problem. When that fog of Eitr descends onto the city . . ." Loki shrugged. "There will certainly be chaos, but not of my making. I would prefer to start over than let Odin steal my thunder."

"Then you start thinking up a way for us to follow him." She leaned heavily on Dainn and looked at Gabi again. "I've never been properly introduced to your healer friends. Are they prepared to deal with our casualties?"

"They've been helping people all along," Gabi said, her lower lip trembling. "Anything we can do, we will."

"*Gracias*," Mist said, inclining her head to the women. "Taylor, send people to find any survivors and make sure the *curanderas* get to them."

Taylor hesitated, as if he were reluctant to leave Mist again. Konur consulted with his elves.

"Would you have us join the hunt for Odin, or seek the remaining Einherjar?" he asked.

"Bring the bastards back, by any means necessary, and use whatever spells you have to keep them immobile." Mist glanced from Dainn to Loki. "Odin is *our* problem."

"Tell me," Loki said, "have you ever used the Eitr to fly?"

"I have the means to teleport," Dainn said softly, "but that is of no use to us if we do not know our destination."

"Mimir's eyeteeth," Mist said, "we can't do this from the ground." She sucked in a breath. "Can you smell it? The Eitr's getting thicker. Am I going to have to forge wings, or—"

A boom shook the park, as if a jet had just broken the sound barrier. Spurting gaseous ooze from its nostrils, a very large silver dragon landed a few yards away and uncoiled its serpentine body. Mist recognized it as one of Japan's supposedly mythical beasts, made to swim in rivers and oceans.

Or, on occasion, to fly.

"Jesus," Taylor whispered.

"Koji," Mist said.

"Koji?" Dainn repeated. He prepared a defensive spell in his mind as the long, almost canine head swung toward them, revealing a flickering tongue and serrated teeth.

I am going to regret this, the dragon said.

ᘓᘖ

Once they were aloft, Mist realized that Odin would have to wait. The Eitr had spread to cover the entire city, scattered by the storm, hanging above the streets and buildings like a shroud and dimming the lights of every building to fading embers. Wherever they flew, mortals sprawled on the streets and sidewalks, gasping and retching; cars had stalled in tangles of rubber and steel, and corrosion had already begun to eat away metal and plastic and concrete alike.

The dark Eitr was unmaking the city, and there was little time to stop it.

Mist knew what she had to do. She wasn't afraid anymore; Dainn was at her back, his arms around her waist, while Loki gave a Japanese dragon the illusory shape of a low-flying plane.

Again, she called up her own dark Eitr—as much a part of her now as her blond hair and gray eyes—inhaled deeply, and accepted the poison into herself, sucking it up as Koji flew, coiling and uncoiling, over the city. There was no limit to what she could absorb, and with every breath she set the Eitr to devouring itself, eating away at its own substance.

There was pain. That was inevitable. But Dainn held her steady against his chest as he healed her burns, and when the sky began to clear, showing the stars again, her relief smothered the pain completely. People began to move again as sirens wailed on the streets below, and the storm faded to a light snowfall.

They found Odin alive on Ocean Beach, his face blackened and his body wasted by his own poisons. Sleipnir stood with all eight legs in the surf, snorting and trembling, but when Dainn went to him he calmed and rubbed his head against Dainn's hair.

They returned to the park by the most direct route, Dainn on

Sleipnir with Odin's unconscious body and Mist with Loki on the dragon's back. When they set down in the park, all was quiet. Torn tree trunks and branches lay scattered like twigs over the Polo Fields and dead leaves and pine duff covered almost every surface, but the ice had melted and the earth, with the help of the Alfar, had begun to absorb the blood into itself.

The scars would remain, Mist thought as she dismounted. But a little more work would clear the worst of it, and in the end the mortals of San Francisco would remember a horror they could not explain. A horror that would never return.

"Remind me never to ride a dragon again," Loki griped as he slid off Koji's back. With great eloquence, Koji snorted into Loki's face and swung his head toward Mist.

Now I must face the wrath of my elders, he said with a familiar sparkle in his eye.

"Wait," Dainn said. "Why did you pose as a lawyer to seek Ryan last winter? Why did you help him find Mother Skye? What is your connection to her?"

There are alliances you know nothing of, Koji said. *Such alliances will always be necessary whenever this world is in danger.* He tipped his head toward Mist. *I go.*

Thank you, Koji, she said, resting her hand on the bewhiskered muzzle. "Good-bye."

He dipped his head, crouched, and hurled himself skyward. In a matter of moments he was only a flicker of silver lit by the moon. And then he was gone.

"Remarkable," Dainn said. "Did you never guess, in all the time he was your lover?"

"Dainn, that was only a—"

"I tease you," Dainn said. His eyes were quiet . . . a little sad, but no longer dark with horror and self-contempt. "I could have brought you no comfort then. I am grateful to him."

Sleipnir butted his head against Dainn's chest, and Dainn rubbed the horse's cheek. "The others are coming," he said.

Taylor and Konur, Rota and Hrolf, Vixen and Roadkill and the rest gathered around Mist, staring up at the sky or down at Odin's comatose body. "Orders?" Taylor asked.

"Gather the Treasures," she said. "Take Thor's weapons and Gungnir. The rest should still be at the camp."

"I'll retrieve Thor's," Loki said.

"And bring them right back here," Mist said, in a voice even Laufeyson couldn't ignore.

"What will you do?" Dainn asked Mist when Loki was gone.

"Capture Odin's soul with this," she said, pulling the raven pendant from beneath her torn shirt, "and divide it among the Treasures. He'll be back where he started, and we're not going to let him out again."

"Loki will not be pleased to lose his revenge."

"I'm not in the business of pleasing Loki, no matter how cooperative he's been." She touched Dainn's cheek. "Not after what he did to this city, and to you."

"What he did to me will be forgotten," Dainn said, taking her hand in his.

Will be, Mist thought. Eventually. "All I can say is that we'd better get those Treasures," she said. "If we don't act quickly—"

"You will need this." A dark-haired woman approached Mist, a curved horn in her hands.

"The Gjallarhorn," Dainn said, peering into the woman's face. "You are Kara. The one Valkyrie we could not find."

"Yes," the woman said. "It was difficult to evade all of you so long. But I could not allow any to possess the Horn before its time."

"But you blew it, didn't you?" Mist said, feeling cross. "Who gave *you* the right to choose the time?" She peered into the Valkyrie's face. "You don't look like the Kara I used to know."

"No," Dainn said. "She has another name."

The slender young woman began to change, to broaden, her hair turning gray and her garments transforming from Kara's jeans and jacket to a full, layered skirt hung with ribbons, bric-a-brac, pouches, and other things Mist couldn't begin to identify.

"My name is Mother Skye," she said, her voice deeper and rough with age. "I was once the Norn called Skuld, and the Valkyrie who carried this Horn once carried my name, though not my burden." She smiled sadly. "Skuld or Kara, she was my daughter. She died, and I could not save her, for I have long since lost the gift of altering Fate."

"But when you blew the Horn—" Mist began.

"A last hurrah, you might say."

"Ryan," Dainn said. "Mist, Ryan is—"

"Dead?" Mother Skye said. "I know. When his young friend was near death, he offered his own life to Hel in her place."

"Gods," Mist breathed. "I wondered why Gabi was still alive."

"He sacrificed himself," Mother Skye said with deep sadness. "But it was his choice. As it was yours, Dainn, to acknowledge your most potent magic, good and bad. And yours, Mist, to accept your power in all its forms."

"I won't accept Ryan's death," Mist said. "If Hel thinks she can hold him . . ."

"A challenge?" Hel said, floating up behind her. She was herself again, coldly beautiful and bitterly ugly. "Would you speak to my new acquisition?"

She gestured, and Ryan came forward, hollow-eyed but not yet transparent. "Mother Skye," he whispered.

The old woman smiled. "I did not know if we would meet again. You have done well."

"Is this what you call 'well'?" Mist snapped. "All his visions, coming to this?"

"Perhaps I sent him back too soon," Mother Skye said. "But I had no choice. I was the last of the Norns, and I had lost my power. Ryan came to me at the right time to take that duty from me."

"You were wrong," Ryan said. "*Everything* was wrong."

"But Fate has been reset," Mother Skye said. "The Second Prophecy, the one I gave Freya and Odin so long ago, has been fulfilled. Many as one have saved this last Homeworld. Mortal and elf, Jotunn and the child of gods. The battle is over."

"Not quite," Mist said. She turned on Hel. "I want you to give him back."

"And what," Hel asked, "shall I receive in return?"

"Some small place to make your own new Niflheim," Mist said, "somewhere no one is going to stumble across you . . . after you've freed every mortal you took since this fight began."

Hel's dark half turned almost as pale as the light side. "You dare—"

"They aren't ancient Northmen, so you never had any right to them in the first place." Mist leaned companionably against Dainn, relishing the steady beat of his heart and the warmth of his hands on her shoulders. "And you're not to take any more of the dying unless they follow the Northmen's faith. The rest can have their own afterworlds without your interference."

"I'd take the deal, if I were you," Loki said. He strolled up to them, Fenrir panting at his heels. "I'm not having you and your skulking minions lodging with me. This one is enough." He tossed Thor's Treasures at Mist's feet. "Can she keep the dead Einherjar?"

"Be my guest," Mist said.

An abominable sound came out of Hel's throat, and she stamped her rotting feet. "It isn't fair, Father," she said.

"Kindly remember that you almost lost everything to these rebellious dead of yours," Loki said. "I got you out of it. If you fight Mist over this, you're on your own."

"I would not advise it," Dainn said dryly.

"Take him, then." Hel shoved Ryan, and he stepped out of the gloom into the breaking moonlight. He breathed deeply, and the color came back into his face.

"Thank you," he said to Mist, his eyes bright with tears. He turned to Mother Skye. "You're going?" he asked.

She reached out to stroke his hair. "You know I must. But as nothing lasts forever, neither is anything lost forever." She kissed his forehead. "You are free. Farewell."

Her round form faded and winked out. Ryan scraped his face with his palm.

"Shit," he said. "Does it ever get any—"

A girl's voice shrieked somewhere behind him, and his face lit with a grin. He turned and ran toward Gabi, his arms outstretched.

"I have seen enough," Hel said sourly. "I shall be waiting for my new home."

"Wait," Mist said. "You haven't let the others go."

With a sharp sigh, Hel opened her robes. Men and women began to emerge, still in their torn and dirty clothes . . . mortal and Alfar fighters who had lost their lives to the Einherjar and fallen to Hel's grasping hands. They staggered and stumbled as they found their bodies again, laughed and cried and embraced. Rick stepped out of the shadows and felt his chest, grinning broadly.

One man came last.

"Geir," Mist said, pulling away from Dainn.

He gave her a faded grin. "We tried," he said. "We almost took her out this time, too."

Grabbing him by his frayed collar, Hel reeled him back in. "You will suffer, rebel," she said. "There are torments even you—"

"Geir!"

Anna crept into their strange circle, still draped in half-ruined armor, her eyes haunted with memories she couldn't erase. "Papa," she said in a little girl's voice. "Don't leave me."

Mist searched for a sword, but Dainn caught her wrist. "She was in Odin's thrall," he said, "but she is no more. Look at her."

Mist looked more carefully. She saw nothing of Horja's strong-boned face, no fanatical warrior willing to protect and serve her lord at any cost.

What Mist "saw" was a little girl and a young woman, still intertwined. But Rebekka, whose body Danny had so briefly borrowed, was fading.

"She was ours, once," Geir said to Mist. "I loved her, as I loved you. But now it is time to let go."

"*Oldefar*," Anna whispered. "Grandfather."

"Enough!" Hel said.

But Geir fought her pull with all the strength Mist remembered from the war. "You are free, *lille*," he said to Anna. "Let Rebekka return to the past. This is your world. Take it, and live."

Anna smiled through her tears. "I will, *Oldefar*."

"Let him go," Mist said, facing Hel again.

The goddess laughed. "Never."

"He was a brave soldier. If he had been taken to Valhalla, I know he would never have fought for Odin."

"No," Geir said, "but there are other battles." He winked at Hel. "Perhaps one endless day I can convince our mistress to improve conditions in our barracks." He reached out as if to stroke Mist's cheek. "*Farvel*, Mist."

With a last glance at Anna, Geir began to fade. He was still smiling when he vanished.

"Admit it, Daughter," Loki said, reminding everyone that he was still there. "Life in Niflheim is deadly dull. You like a little conflict now and then."

"Father . . ." Hel twitched her robes around her legs, stuck her tongue out at Loki, and slowly sank into the earth. Anna began to shed her armor, and when she met Mist's gaze there was only a single young woman in her eyes.

"You have won again," Dainn said softly, turning Mist in his arms.

"It doesn't feel like a victory," Mist said, tracing his lips with her fingertips.

"There is always sacrifice," Dainn said. "Let us be sure that none of them were made in vain."

36

Mist pulled his head down and kissed his forehead, his eyelids, and his lips. "I'm so sorry, Dainn. For so long, I didn't really understand what Danny really was, that he and your ancient powers couldn't be separated."

"It is fortunate that we now have healers among us," Konur said, coming to join them. "We will need much of their skill, for body and soul."

"This city will need a lot of healing," Mist said, shaking off her sadness. "And explanations. The whole infrastructure Loki built is about to implode."

"You do me far too little credit," Loki said. "It runs like a well-oiled machine. A few adjustments here and there . . ."

"Not by you," Mist said, grabbing at her belt for the sword that wasn't there. "You're going to find somewhere to put all your Jotunar, as far away from any mortal habitation as possible. I don't care if it's the Sahara Desert or the Antarctic, but I want them gone. Then you're going to let us in on all your little secrets, including who's in charge of what and which leaders we need to topple."

"You've stacked your plate rather high, haven't you?" Loki asked. "Why should I help you at all?"

"I have the Eitr," Mist said. "Dainn has the Eitr. Do you really want to find out?"

Loki raised his hands. "This subject obviously requires further discussion."

Mist turned her back on him. "Thank you, Konur," she said. "You and Taylor both, for reminding me who I am."

"We did very little," Konur said, "and too late." He bowed. "The victory was all yours. And Dainn's."

Shaking her head, Mist watched Gabi and Ryan talking animatedly to each other, gesticulating and laughing. The recently dead were sitting quietly, absorbing their return to life, while the Alfar gathered the wounded for the *curanderas*.

"We're going to have to get all these people back to their homes and jobs," she murmured. "They might find it difficult to return to their normal lives, and they'll never be able to tell anyone what they did here tonight."

"*Homo sapiens* has proven to be a remarkably adaptable species," Dainn said. "What of the Einherjar?"

"There are a lot less of them now than there were when this battle began," Mist said, "thanks to Hel. But we can't just let the rest of them run loose in human society. They may have no purpose without Odin, but they're still by and large an arrogant bunch of pricks."

"Then we must consider their fate most carefully," Dainn said. "Perhaps the safest bet is to open a bridge and return them to the Shadow-Realms, where they can do no harm. That is well within your capability now."

He fell into a brooding silence, and Mist punched his shoulder gently.

"What is it?" she asked.

"I think of the Alfar who must also adapt to this world," he said. "They must have quiet, untouched places with forests and rivers in order to thrive."

"They'll look to you for guidance."

"No. I left them long ago. I am no longer one of them."

"Someday you'll have to tell me what it means to be the First Elf and a Rune-bringer."

"Even *I* do not remember. I think it was a deliberate choice to forget, as was my refusal to face the darkness that lies in all of us. I could not tolerate the idea of being less than wise and good, so I created a being to hold that darkness apart from me."

"Psychiatrists would have a field day with that one."

"I do not think the mortal medical establishment is ready to psychoanalyze an elf." He glanced at the sky. "How long can it be before mortalkind realizes that they are not alone in this universe?"

"Not very long, I'm afraid. Especially with other gods flying around. I have a feeling this war has stirred up more deities than Koji's *kami* and Eir's desert spirits."

"Indeed. And what of the Aesir? You will have no difficulty in opening the bridges now. Will you let them cross?"

"Loki's—" She glanced in Laufeyson's direction and grimaced. "Sweet Baldr, I don't know."

"Eventually, they will require the Apples of Idunn if they are to survive."

Mist chewed on her lower lip. "That could be a problem. But if any of them have ambitions like Odin's . . ."

"Indeed. Thor comes to mind."

"This is my world now. I intend to protect it."

"No one could have done better."

She touched his chest. "You're wrong, Dainn."

His smile was melancholy. "It is good to be arguing again." He looked down at her hand and took it in his. "Your wrist," he said.

Mist knew what she would see before she followed his gaze. The tattoo was lifeless, a pale gray pattern of numbness that would never burn again.

"The thing was always about keeping tabs on my Eitr," Mist said. "But I haven't lost anything."

"*He* has," Dainn said. "His bond to you is broken."

"So now I can go back to having one father, and part of another, if you consider that Taylor is really only the descendent of—"

Jerking up his head, Dainn looked to the west. Sleipnir was trotting toward them, Hild beside him . . . and a dozen or so very fine-looking horses ambling along in her wake.

Hild waved. "What did I miss?" she asked, her usually phlegmatic demeanor unexpectedly cheerful.

"Where did *they* come from?" Mist said, gesturing at the horses as Dainn made his way toward them.

"Oh, they're Sleipnir's get." She glanced at Dainn, who was murmuring to the horses in what sounded suspiciously like baby talk. "I intended to get here a lot earlier and have them ready for the war."

"I think the Alfar will be glad to have them now," Mist said. "In fact, it would be a good idea to have a few elves take these horses out of the city as soon as possible."

"How many did you lose?" Hild asked softly.

"Too many."

Sleipnir tossed his head. Hild laid her hand on the side of his neck. "There's someone he's missing pretty badly," she said.

"Danny's gone," Mist said, glancing away.

"I'm sorry," Hild said. "He was the one who showed me how to open the portal to the steppes again, before he died in the stable."

Mist considered explaining that Danny had never "died" at all . . . until he had finally given his whole being to Dainn.

"Hild—" she began.

"I won't trouble you further now," Hild said. "I'll find a place to put the horses until the Alfar are ready to take them."

Leaving Sleipnir behind, she led the horses away. Sleipnir rubbed his chin against Dainn's shoulder as if seeking comfort, and Dainn kissed the broad nose.

Mist swallowed, thinking of Danny. It was going to be very hard to go on without him. He'd been very real to her, even if he had turned out to be a kind of manifestation of Dainn's connection to the Eitr. If he'd been allowed to grow up as a normal child . . .

"Curse it," she said, catching sight of moving figures out of the corner of her eye. "Just what we need."

Sleipnir wheeled around with a challenging snort. Dainn's nostril's flared.

"*Berserkir,*" he said. His voice dropped low. "Edvard."

Behind Edvard padded a few dozen men and animals—bears, wolves, and boars. Edvard most resembled a sheep, at least going by his expression. He approached Dainn and Mist at a shambling walk and stopped, lowering his shaggy head.

Dainn stared at him. "You should not be here," he said sternly.

"We, uh . . ." Edvard shuffled his feet. "I'm sorry about everything that happened. I actually thought we could get here sooner and help you fight."

"Funny how that happens," Mist said flatly.

"Uh, yeah." He risked a glance at Dainn. "But I need to tell you . . . You see . . ." He cleared his throat. "The herb . . . it was our cure for a disease among the *berserkir*. The disease was making us into things we couldn't control, like your beast did to you. But we have this legend . . . The herb was a kind of test . . ."

"Not again," Mist groaned.

"Uh, we had this legend about a kind of *berserkr* different from all the others, the first of our kind. He would find our cure for us, and bring us out into the light. When I met Bryn, I knew we'd find him if he existed anywhere on Earth. And we knew he'd be the one if he could use the herb to control his beast." He shot Dainn a nervous look. "It didn't look like you fit the bill."

"And so you went to Loki," Mist said.

He cleared his throat again. "It seemed like the right thing to do at the time. I thought he could help my people if he won. But when I saw what happened in the garage, I was pretty sure we'd found the first *berserkr* after all."

"I think you got a lot more than you bargained for," Mist said. "And you put Dainn through Hel because of it."

"Not entirely," Dainn said. "I learned a great deal from the experience."

His voice was too flat to convey anything but disapproval, and Edvard dropped his gaze.

"Do you still think you can help us?" he said in a very unbearlike voice.

"You can hunt any Jotunar who have escaped our nets," Dainn said, "and hold them until we are ready for them. But I would suggest you remain in your human forms."

"Yes. Of course." Edvard backed away as if he had just been to an audience with a king.

"Isn't it nice to be wanted?" Mist asked.

Dainn only shook his head. "Edvard mentioned Bryn," he said. "Do you still . . ."

Mist showed him the feathered pouch. "I don't know how to restore her," she said.

"Nor I," he said as he stepped back. "But we still do not know the limits of your power. And do not forget that she, too, made her choice, to serve Freya even if it meant surrendering her body."

"Maybe someday she'll get a chance to tell us why."

"I'm certain she will," Loki said, reappearing in front of them. "Now, if we may resume our discussion . . ."

"Oh, yes," Mist said. "The question about what the Hel to do with you."

Loki smiled. "Since we have been allies, it obviously goes without saying that we should divide this city between us."

"Only *this* city?" Mist asked sweetly. "That hardly seems fair to you, after all the work you've done."

"True, but I am willing to compromise."

"Your idea of compromise," Dainn said, "is complete chaos."

The two men stared at each other, and for a moment Mist thought that Dainn was going to slug Loki. But Dainn unclenched his fist and let his hand fall to his side.

"*My* idea of compromise," Mist said, "is that you go straight back to the Shadow-Realms and stay there."

Loki sighed. "I really am fond of San Francisco."

"Get unfond of it, fast," Mist said. "Maybe I'll let you join your Jotunar in Antarctica, where you can contemplate your sins."

"Some sins, unfortunately, cannot so easily be forgotten. But restitution might be made." He opened his palm to reveal the unhealed scar of the blood-oath he'd made with Dainn nearly a year ago. "Will he permit it now, Dainn?"

"Who?" Mist asked. "Permit what?"

Dainn's face turned to stone. "I will kill you for that, Loki."

"Do you think I'm mocking you?" Loki said, both brows rising. "Can you truly not feel him?"

"Let me have Loki first," Mist said to Dainn.

"I . . . felt him before, when I set the beast free again," Dainn said.

"He is still there," Loki said, stepping back. "Look inside, Dainn."

Blank-eyed, Dainn turned inward. Mist held her breath.

"Ymir's blood," Dainn whispered. "I *do* feel him."

"Sweet Baldr," Mist said.

"He can be restored," Loki said, "the way I suggested before. If Danny will agree."

"I . . . cannot reach him," Dainn said, every muscle in his body tense with anxiety.

"Then we must simply try, and hope it works," Loki said.

"Try what?" Mist demanded.

Without looking away from Loki, Dainn told her what he and Loki had discussed before the battle.

"I know that Loki and Freya stole your Eitr in Asgard," she said.

"*How* do you know?" Loki asked.

"Danny told me," Mist said.

"They took far less of it than they believed. Loki still possesses a fraction of it," Dainn said. He displayed his own slashed palm. "He believes that this bond may be the key."

"Yes," Loki said. "But as with all great magic, there is danger involved. Creation and destruction are finely balanced, and one cannot take place without the other. As Dainn now holds all but a little of the Eitr, it is his life most at risk."

"Forget it," Mist said. "Dainn, you know Loki can't be trusted. Whatever he's got in mind—"

"It could work," Dainn said, real hope in his eyes. "With the proper spells, the precise Runes . . ."

"I won't lose you, too."

"Mist." Dainn cupped her face in his uninjured hand. "Would you rob me of my chance to have my son again?"

"At the cost of your life?"

"Perhaps at the cost of my access to the Eitr. That is a price I am willing to pay. I will never again be what I was when I first came to Asgard, no matter what ancient power I hold." He smoothed back her hair. "Will you wish me luck?"

"Only if I can stay right here beside you."

"You can prevent anything from disturbing the ritual," he said. "Will that be acceptable?"

In the end, Mist knew she had no choice but to agree. After Loki and Dainn had discussed the procedure—as coolly and clinically as two doctors reviewing a difficult pregnancy—they found a small, undamaged grove of trees and sat in a rough triangle. Dainn removed his shirt. He held his wounded hand out to Loki, watching Laufeyson's face.

Squeezing his hand into a fist, Loki dripped his own blood into Dainn's palm. Dainn winced. Mist began to move, but Dainn shook his head. He closed his fist until his blood was well mingled with Loki's and then painted his own chest with his fingertip, writing the ancient, incomprehensible Rune-language in even lines from one side of his torso to the other.

Mist closed her eyes and opened them again. She couldn't read what he'd spelled out. But then Dainn began to sing—ethereal music, flowing like water, floating like cirrus clouds in spring.

Her heart filled with joy, wrapped in the love of her fathers and Dainn and Ryan and all the others. Suddenly she found herself singing with Dainn, though she still didn't understand the words. She could *feel* Danny, and as her sense of his presence grew, Loki began to sing in a surprisingly clear tenor.

She drifted, floating on the spell and the music. When she opened her eyes, Danny was there. He was as naked as the day he was born, but his skin was clear, his cheeks rosy, and his grin as big as Sleipnir's.

"Papa!" he said, and flung himself into Dainn's arms.

∞

As it turned out, freeing Danny hadn't done anything to Dainn's magic, ancient or otherwise. Danny, however, seemed to have no magic at all. He ran back and forth between Dainn and Mist, laughing, dressed in Dainn's shirt carefully tucked up so it wouldn't drag on the ground. He seemed younger than his apparent age, but Dainn wasn't concerned.

"He still has much to learn," he'd said, pride and love so vivid in his eyes that Mist could actually feel it, the way she could still hear his thoughts when she concentrated.

"I should be on my way."

She snapped her head up. Loki had been leaning against a tree, watching with an inscrutable expression and making no attempt to attract Danny's attention or join in. His hand, like Dainn's, no longer bore so much as a faint mark.

"You haven't forgotten that you're going to Antarctica," Mist said, rising to face Loki.

"You think that you can confine me to a single, deserted continent?"

"She has the means to enforce her commands," Dainn said, his voice very low and calm. "And I will help her."

"No visiting rights?" Loki asked with a sideways glance at Danny. "He is still my son."

Mist snorted. "Maybe in a few centuries. And believe me, I'll know if you return to civilization before we're ready to let you out."

Loki sighed. Dainn opened his arms to Danny, and the boy fell into them, laughing. He didn't notice Loki at all. Just for a moment, Mist was distracted.

Loki vanished.

A stream of curses burst from Mist's mouth. Raising Danny to his shoulder, Dainn stood beside her.

"Idiot," Mist spat. "I should have bound him the minute you had Danny back. I almost forgot what he is."

"That is part of his skill," Dainn said, his voice muffled in Danny's red hair. "Both you and I have fallen for his duplicity more than once."

"You aren't angry?"

"With his Jotunar gone, he will have no resources, and no means of obtaining help from Asgard. He is not so foolish as to doubt that you will be watching for signs of his interference in the mortal world. He will have to lie low."

"But is that enough, Dainn? After all he's done?"

"You cannot spend your life searching for him. He will make a mistake, and when he does, we will be ready for him."

◑◐

It was only a matter of ten minutes for Dainn and Mist to devise and perform the spell that sent slightly over one hundred Jotunar to the Antarctic and bound them there indefinitely. "You are being merciful," Dainn commented as the Jotunar disappeared. "At least they will not be troubled by the weather there."

Returning Odin to the Treasures was slightly more complicated. Odin was just beginning to wake when the process began. Feeling considerably less than merciful, Mist muted his voice with a flick of her fingers and set to work, Dainn burning bright with the Eitr beside her. Konur, Rota, Anna, Rick, and a few others gathered to watch at a respectful distance while Mist pressed the raven pendant to Odin's chest. His eye widened, he thrashed and struggled in his bonds . . . and still Mist felt no pity.

One by one Mist gave Odin's soul back to the Treasures, piece by piece, until Odin's body became nearly transparent. With the last Treasure he vanished entirely, and a parrot stood in his place, its eyes lively, intelligent, and utterly without a single divine spark.

"You can carry him safely now," Mist said to Anna. But she shook her head and walked away, no longer able to bear the sight of the creature that, not so long ago, had been a beloved pet.

"We'll have to keep him ourselves," Mist said with a sigh.

"Will it not be a constant reminder of Odin's treachery?" Dainn asked.

"At least I can keep an eye on it," Mist said. "As long as it stays just a parrot, it'll have a decent home. In a large, reasonably pleasant cage."

"And Eir?" Dainn asked solemnly. "Her body still lies in the vault."

"Hel never got the chance to grab her," Mist said, glancing at the torn and muddy ground. "We'll take her back to New Mexico, to lie among her desert spirits."

"She will like that," Dainn said.

Their work accomplished, Mist and Dainn took Danny from Hild, who had been looking after him, and remained in the park to maintain the outer wards until all the Jotunn and Einherji bodies had been removed. The hostages who had died, released back to life by Hel, were clandestinely left near the emergency vehicles surrounding the park. Alfar and human warriors who had died and come back to life, as well as those unhurt in the battle, helped the injured warriors return to camp, where they would receive care from the Alfar and *curandera* healers. Mist sent Rick to inform the servants at Loki's mansion and headquarters that they were free and no longer had anything to fear from their master.

When no trace of the battle remained save uprooted trees, snapped branches, and scattered stones, Mist and Dainn started for home, walking because no traffic was moving and emergency vehicles blocked every major street near the park. The storm had damaged many parts of the city—the dark Eitr hadn't done it any good, either—but the weather had cleared for the first time in the better part of a year. The sun was shining, and it was actually warm. That alone might give the mortal citizens of San Francisco real hope. Hope of a change for the better.

And though some of the real story would probably get out, Mist thought, no one outside this city would believe the reports.

Unless it happened to *them*. There was still the matter of those other pantheons, and—

Something made her look up. A thread of silver ribbon coiled and swam in the blue sky.

We will be watching, Koji said.

Dainn lifted his hand in acknowledgment, and Koji plunged down toward the bay. As if by magic, an empty taxi pulled up to the curb. Danny waved at the driver, who grinned back as if all was right with the world.

They climbed into the backseat, Danny ensconced on Mist's lap. When they got to the loft, the camp was unnaturally quiet.

"What's all this?" the cabbie asked, pushing back his baseball cap.

Mist started. The ward was still in place, blocking the camp from mortal sight. This man shouldn't be able to see anything but abandoned factories and a vast expanse of battered parking lots.

"It's a long story," Mist said, peering into the cabbie's eyes. She searched her torn back pocket. "Curse it," she muttered. "My wallet—"

The cabbie shook his head. "This one's on the house. After all, you've earned it."

Dainn and Mist and Danny stared after the cab long after it had turned the corner.

"I don't think I want to know," Mist said.

The loft was quiet. Dainn set Danny down on one of the kitchen chairs, and Mist put a glass of milk in front of him. He drank with surprising neatness and grinned at Mist through a very large milk mustache.

"You know what we'll have to do very soon?" Mist asked.

"What would that be?" Dainn asked, leaning his chin on his hand, his eyes drifting shut.

"Make sure the bedroom is still in working order."

He opened his eyes. "Indeed."

They put Danny to bed in Dainn's old room once they were certain that he wasn't afraid of being left alone. He dropped off to sleep instantly, his blanket tucked up around his chin.

Dainn kissed his forehead, and he and Mist left together. They checked to make certain that the bedroom was, indeed, in good working order. Dainn was a little hesitant at first, still haunted by his time with Loki, but Mist was careful. They both had plenty of things to forget.

After they were done, they went outside to admire the stars in a clear night sky. Mist looked for the dragon, but she knew he wasn't coming back. At least she hoped he wasn't.

We will be watching.

They went back inside, hand in hand. Dainn sniffed the air and stopped just inside the kitchen door.

"What is it?" Mist asked. "Did I leave the stove on?"

He looked at the kitchen table. A folded note lay on it, her old, ridiculous Thor bobble-head holding it pinned in place. It was sealed with the image of a coiled serpent.

"He wouldn't dare," Mist said.

Dainn picked up the paper and mouthed the words. Mist grabbed it out of his hand.

See you soon, my darlings.
—L.L.

The paper caught fire in her hand and burned to ash.